DUDLEY PUBLIC LIBRARIES

The loan of this book may be renewed if not required by other readers, by contacting the library from which it was borrowed.

Billionaire Boss

Billionaire Boss: Falling for the Billionaire

CAROLE MORTIMER

NINA MILNE

CATHERINE MANN

MILLS & BOON

First Published in Great Britain 2020
By Mills & Boon, an imprint of HarperCollins*Publishers*
1 London Bridge Street, London, SE1 9GF

BILLIONAIRE BOSS: FALLING FOR THE BILLIONAIRE
© 2020 Harlequin Books S.A.

Rumours on the Red Carpet © 2013 Carole Mortimer
Claimed by the Wealthy Magnate © 2017 Nina Milne
Playing for Keeps © 2013 Catherine Mann

ISBN: 978-0-263-29827-7

MIX
Paper from
responsible sources
FSC™ C007454

This book is produced from independently certified FSC™ paper to ensure responsible forest management.

For more information visit: www.harpercollins.co.uk/green

Printed and bound in Spain
by CPI, Barcelona

RUMOURS ON THE RED CARPET

CAROLE MORTIMER

CHAPTER ONE

'ENJOYING THE VIEW...?'

Thia tensed, a shiver of awareness quivering down the length of her spine at the sound of that deep voice coming out of the darkness behind her, before turning quickly to search those shadows for the man who had just spoken to her.

She was able to make out a tall figure in the moonlight just feet away from where she stood, alone on the balcony that surrounded the whole of this luxurious penthouse apartment on the fortieth floor of one of the impressive buildings lighting up the New York skyline. Only dim light spilled from the open French doors of the apartment further down the balcony—along with the sound of tinkling laughter and the chatter of the fifty or so party guests still inside—making it impossible for Thia to see any more than that the man was very tall, dark and broad-shouldered. Imposingly so.

Dangerously so...?

The wariness still humming through her body just at the sound of the deep and seductive timbre of his voice said a definite *yes!*

Thia's fingers tightened about the breast-high balustrade in front of her. 'I was, yes...' she answered pointedly.

'You're a Brit,' he observed deeply.

'From London,' Thia confirmed shortly, really hoping that he would take note of that terseness and leave her to her solitude.

The New York night skyline, amazing as it was, hadn't been Thia's main reason for coming outside into the balmy evening air fifteen minutes ago, when the other guests had all been preoccupied with their excitement at the late arrival of Lucien Steele, American zillionaire business-man, and the party's guest of honour. That so many high-profile actors, actresses and politicians had turned out for the event was indicative of the amount of power the man wielded.

After all Jonathan's hype about him Thia had to admit that she hadn't found him so prepossessing—a man of middle age and average height, slightly stocky and bald-ing. But maybe all that money and power made him more attractive? In any event, Thia had just been grateful that he had arrived at last—if only because it had allowed her to slip outside and *be* alone—instead of just *feeling* alone.

Thia certainly hadn't intended to find herself alone on the balcony with a man who exuded such an intensity of power and sexual attraction she could almost taste it…

'A Brit, from London, who's avoiding the party in-side…?' that deep voice guessed with dry amusement.

Having been to three other parties just like this one in the four days since her arrival in New York, Thia had to admit to having become slightly bored—jaded?—by them. The first one had been fun—exciting, even—meeting people she had only ever seen on the big or little screen before, world-famous actors and actresses and high-profile politicians. But the artificiality of it was all becom-ing a bit samey now. The conversations were repetitive and too loud, the laughter even more so, with everyone seem-ingly out to impress or better everyone else, their exces-sive wealth literally worn on their sleeves.

This constant round of parties also meant that she'd had very little opportunity for any time or private con-versation with Jonathan, the man she had come to New York to visit...

Jonathan Miller, the English star of *Network,* a new American thriller television series set in New York, di-rected by this evening's host, Felix Carew, and co-starring his young and sexy wife Simone as the love-interest.

The show had been an instant hit, and Jonathan was currently the darling of New York's beautiful people—and, as Thia had discovered these past four days, there were a *lot* of beautiful people in New York!

And not a single one of them had felt any qualms about ignoring the woman who had been seen at Jonathan's side on those evenings once they'd learnt that Thia was of no social or political value to them whatsoever.

Not that Thia minded being ignored. She had very quickly discovered she had no more in common with New York's elite than they had with her.

She was pleased for Jonathan's success, of course. The two of them had known each other for a couple of years now, after meeting at the London restaurant where Thia always worked the late shift, leaving her free to attend her university course in the day.

She and Jonathan had met quite by chance, when he had been appearing in a play at the theatre across the street from the restaurant and had started calling in late in the evening a couple of times a week for something to eat, once the theatre had closed for the night.

They had chatted on those evenings, then dated casually for a few weeks. But there had been no spark between them and the relationship had quickly fallen into the 'just friends' category. Then, four months ago, Jonathan had landed the lead role in the television series over here, and Thia had accepted that even that friendship would be over once Jonathan moved to New York.

He had telephoned a couple of times in the months that followed, just light and friendly conversations, when they had caught up on each other's lives, and then a month ago Jonathan had flown back to England for the weekend, insisting he had missed her and wanted to spend all his time back home with her. And it had been fun. Thia had arranged to have the weekend off so that they could have dinner together in the evening, visits to museums and walks in the parks during the day, before Jonathan had to fly back to New York to start filming again on the Monday.

But no one had been more surprised than Thia when a first-class plane ticket for a week-long stay in New York had been delivered to her by messenger just two days later!

She had telephoned Jonathan immediately, of course, to tell him she couldn't possibly accept such generosity from him. But he had insisted, saying he could well afford it and, more to the point, he wanted to see her again. He wanted to show her New York, and for New York to see her.

Thia's pride had told her she should continue to refuse, but Jonathan had been very persuasive, and as she hadn't been able to afford a holiday for years the temptation had just been too much. So she had accepted, with the proviso that he cancelled the first class ticket and changed it to a standard fare. Spending that amount of money on an airfare seemed obscene to her, in view of her own financial difficulties.

Jonathan had assured her that she would have her own bedroom in his apartment, and that he just wanted her to come and enjoy New York with him. She had even gone out and spent some of her hard-earned savings on buying some new clothes for the trip!

Except Jonathan's idea of her enjoying New York with him was vastly different from Thia's own. They had attended parties like this one every night, and Jonathan would sleep off the effects the following morning. Meanwhile his late afternoons and early evenings were usually spent secluded somewhere with Simone Carew, going over the script together.

Seeing so little of Jonathan during the day, and attending parties in the evenings, Thia had started to wonder why he had bothered to invite her here at all.

And she now found herself irritated that, once again, Jonathan had disappeared with Simone shortly after they had arrived at this party he had claimed was so important to him on account of the presence of Lucien Steele, the American billionaire owner of the television station responsible for *Network*. That desertion had left Thia being considered fair game by men like the one standing in the shadows behind her...

Well...perhaps not *exactly* like this man. The way he seemed to possess even the air about him told her that she had never met a man quite like this one before...

'Beautiful...' the man murmured huskily as he stepped forward to stand at the railing beside her.

Thia's heart skipped a beat, her nerve-endings going on high alert as her senses were instantly filled with the light smell of lemons—his cologne?—accompanied by an insidious maleness that she guessed was all him.

She turned to look at him, tilting her head back as she realised how much taller he was than her, even in her four-inch-heeled take-me-to-bed shoes. Taller, and so broad across the shoulders, with dark hair that rested low on the collar of his white shirt and black evening jacket. His face appeared to be all hard angles in the moonlight: strong jaw, chiselled lips, long aquiline nose, high cheekbones. And those pale and glittering eyes—

Piercing eyes, that she now realised were looking at *her* in admiration rather than at the New York skyline!

Thia repressed another quiver of awareness at having this man look at her so intently, realising that she was completely alone out here with a man she didn't know from—well, from Adam.

'Have they all stopped licking Lucien Steele's highly polished handmade Italian leather shoes yet, do you think?' she prompted in her nervousness, only to give a pained grimace at her uncharacteristic sharpness. 'I'm sorry—that was incredibly rude of me.' She winced, knowing how important Lucien Steele's goodwill was to Jonathan's success in the US. He had certainly emphasised it often enough on the drive over here!

'But true?' the man drawled dryly.

'Perhaps.' She nodded. 'But I'm sure that Mr Steele has more than earned the adoration being showered upon him so effusively.'

Teeth gleamed whitely in the darkness as the man gave a hard and humourless smile. 'Or maybe he's just so rich and powerful no one has ever dared to tell him otherwise?'

'Maybe,' she conceded ruefully. 'Cynthia Hammond.'

She thrust out her hand in an effort to bring some normality to this conversation. 'But everyone calls me Thia.'

He took possession of her hand—there was no other way to describe the way the paleness of her hand just disappeared inside the long bronzed strength of his. And Thia could not ignore the jolt of electricity zinging along her fingers and arm at contact with the warmth of his skin...

'I've never been particularly fond of being a part of what everyone else does,' he murmured throatily. 'So I think I'll call you Cyn...'

Just the way he said that word, in that deliciously deep and sexy voice, was enough to send yet more shivers of awareness down Thia's spine. Her breasts tingled with that awareness, the nipples puckering to tight and sensitive berries as they pressed against the sheer material of the clinging blue ankle-length gown she wore.

And it was a totally inappropriate reaction to a complete stranger!

Jonathan might have done yet another disappearing act with Simone forty minutes ago, but that certainly didn't mean Thia was going to stand here and allow herself to be seduced by some dark-haired hunk, who looked sinfully delicious in his obviously expensive evening suit but so far hadn't even been polite enough to introduce himself!

'And you are...?'

Those teeth gleamed even whiter in the darkness as he gave a wolfish smile. 'Lucien Steele.'

Thia gave a snort. 'I don't think so!' she scoffed.

'No?' He sounded amused by her scepticism.

'No,' she repeated decisively.

He raised one dark brow. 'Why not?'

She breathed her impatience. 'Well, for one thing you aren't nearly old enough to be the self-made zillionaire

Lucien Steele.' She estimated this man was aged somewhere in his early to mid-thirties, ten or twelve years older
than her own twenty-three, and she knew from the things
Jonathan had told her about this evening's guest of honour that Lucien Steele had not only been the richest man
in New York for the last ten years, but was also the most
powerful.

He gave an unconcerned shrug of those impossibly
wide shoulders. 'What can I say? My parents were wealthy
to begin with, and I'd made my own first million by the
time I was twenty-one.'

'Also,' Thia continued, determined, 'I saw Mr Steele
when he arrived.'

It had been impossible to miss the awed reaction of the
other guests. Those incredibly rich and beautiful people
had all, without exception, fallen absolutely silent the moment Lucien Steele had appeared in the doorway. And
Felix Carew, a powerful man in his own right, had become
almost unctuous as he moved swiftly across the room to
greet his guest.

Thia gave a rueful shake of her head. 'Lucien Steele
is in his early forties, several inches shorter than you are,
and stocky, with a shaved head.' In fact on first glance she
had thought the man more resembled a thug rather than
the richest and most powerful man in New York!

'That would be Dex.'

'Dex…?' she echoed doubtfully.

'Mmm.' The man beside her nodded unconcernedly.
'He takes his duties as my bodyguard very seriously—to
the point that he always insists upon entering a room before I do. I'm not sure why,' he mused. 'Perhaps he expects
there to be an assassin on the other side of every door…'

Thia felt a sinking sensation in the pit of her stomach as

she heard the amused dismissal in this man's—in Lucien Steele's?—voice. Moistening her lips with the tip of tongue before speaking, she said, 'And where is Dex now…?'

'Probably standing guard on the other side of those French doors.' He nodded down the balcony to the same doorway Thia had escaped through minutes ago.

And was Dex making sure that no one came outside, or was he ensuring that Thia couldn't return inside until this man wished her to…?

She gave another frown as she looked up searchingly at the man now standing so near to her she could feel the heat emanating from his body on the bareness of her shoulders and arms. Once again she took note of that inborn air of power, arrogance, she had sensed in him from the first.

For all the world as if he was *used* to people licking his highly polished handmade Italian leather shoes…

Lucien continued to hold Cyn's now trembling hand and waited in silence for her to gather her breath as she looked up at him between long and silky lashes with eyes a dark and mysterious cobalt blue.

Those eyes became shadowed with apprehension as she gave another nervous flick of her little pink tongue over the moist fullness of her perfectly shaped lips. 'The same Lucien Steele who owns Steele Technology, Steele Media, Steele Atlantic Airline *and* Steele Industries, as well as all those other Steele Something-or-Others?' she murmured faintly.

He shrugged. 'It seemed like a good idea to diversify.'

She determinedly pulled her hand from his grasp before tightly gripping the top of the balustrade. 'The same Lucien Steele who's a zillionaire?'

'I believe you said that already…' Lucien nodded.

She drew in a deep breath, obviously completely un-aware of how it tightened the material of her dress across her breasts and succeeded in outlining the fullness of those—aroused?—nipples. Nipples that were a delicate pink or a succulent rose? Whatever their colour, he was sure they would taste delicious. Sweet and juicy, and oh so ripe and responsive as he licked and suckled them.

He had noticed the woman he now knew to be Cynthia Hammond the moment he'd entered Felix and Simone Carew's penthouse apartment a short time ago. It had been impossible not to as she'd stood alone at the back of the opulent room, her hair a sleek and glossy unadorned black as it fell silkily to just below her shoulders, her eyes that deep cobalt blue in the beautiful pale delicacy of her face.

She wore a strapless ankle-length gown of that same deep blue, leaving the tops of her breasts, shoulders and arms completely bare. The smoothness of her skin was a beautiful pearly white unlike any other Lucien had ever seen: a pale ivory tinted lightly pink, luminescent. Smoothly delicate and pearly skin his fingers itched to touch and caress.

The simple style of that silky blue gown allowed it to cling to every curvaceous inch of her full breasts, slender waist and gently flaring hips, so much so that Lucien had questioned whether or not she wore anything beneath it.

He still questioned it...

But what had really made him take notice of her, even more than her natural beauty or the pearly perfection of her skin, was the fact that instead of moving towards him, as every other person in the room had done, this pale and delicately beautiful woman had instead taken advantage of his arrival to slip quietly from the room and go outside onto the balcony.

Nor had she returned by the time Lucien had finally managed to extract himself from the—what had she called it a few moments ago? The licking of his 'highly polished handmade Italian leather shoes'. His curiosity piqued—and very little piqued his jaded palate nowadays!—Lucien hadn't been able to resist coming out onto the balcony to look for her the moment he had managed to escape all that cloying attention.

She drew in another deep breath now before speaking, causing the fullness of her breasts to once again swell deliciously over the bodice of that clinging blue gown.

'I really do apologise for my rudeness, Mr Steele. It's no excuse, but I'm really not having a good evening—and my rudeness to you means that it has just got so much worse!' she conceded with another pained wince. 'But that is really no reason for me to have been rude about you—or to you.'

He quirked one dark brow. 'I don't think you know me well enough *as yet* to speak with any authority on whether or not I *deserve* for you to be rude to me or about me,' he drawled mockingly.

'Well…no…' She was obviously slightly unnerved by his emphasis on the words 'as yet'… 'But—' She gave a shake of her head, causing that silky and completely straight black hair to glide across the bareness of her shoulders and caress tantalisingly across the tops of her breasts. 'I still shouldn't have been so outspoken about someone I only know about from the media.'

'Especially when we all know how inaccurate the media can be?' he drawled wryly.

'Exactly!' She nodded enthusiastically before just as quickly pausing to eye him uncertainly. 'Don't you own something like ninety per cent of the worldwide media?'

'That would be contrary to monopoly regulations,' he drawled dismissively.

'Do zillionaires bother with little things like regulations?' she teased.

He chuckled huskily. 'They do if they don't want their zillionaire butts to end up in court!'

Thia felt what was becoming a familiar quiver down the length of her spine at the sound of this man's throaty laughter. As she also acknowledged that, for all this man unnerved her, she was actually enjoying herself—possibly for the first time since arriving in New York.

'Are you cold?'

Thia had no chance to confirm or deny that she was before Lucien Steele removed his evening jacket and placed it about the bareness of her shoulders. It reached almost down to her knees and smelt of the freshness of those lemons as his warmth surrounded her, and of the more insidious and earthy smell of the man himself.

'No, really—'

'Leave it.' Both his hands came down onto the shoulders of the jacket as she would have reached up and removed it.

Thia shivered anew as she felt the warmth of those long and elegant hands even through the material of his jacket. A shiver entirely due to the presence of this overwhelming man—also the reason for her earlier shiver—rather than any chill in the warm evening air...

His hands left her shoulders reluctantly as he moved to stand beside her once again, that pale gaze—silver?—once again intent on her face. The snug fit of his evening shirt revealed that his shoulders really were that wide, his chest muscled, his waist slender above lean hips and long legs; obviously Lucien Steele didn't spend *all* of his days sitting in boardrooms and adding to his billions.

'Why aren't you having a good evening?' he prompted softly.

Why? Because this visit to New York hadn't turned out to be anything like Thia had imagined it would be. Because she had once again been brought to a party and then quickly abandoned by—well, Jonathan certainly wasn't her boyfriend, but she had certainly thought of him as a friend. A friend who had disappeared with their hostess within minutes of their arrival, leaving her to the untender mercies of New York's finest.

Latterly she wasn't having a good evening because she was far too aware of the man standing beside her—of the way the warmth and seductive smell of Lucien Steele's tailored jacket made her feel as if she was surrounded by the man himself.

And lastly because Thia had no idea how to deal with the unprecedented arousal now coursing through her body!

She gave a shrug. 'I don't enjoy parties like this one.'

'Why not?'

She grimaced, taking care not to insult this man for a second time this evening. 'It's just a personal choice.'

He nodded. 'And where do you fit in with this crowd? Are you an actress?'

'Heavens, no!'

'A wannabe?'

'I beg your pardon…?'

He shrugged those impossibly wide shoulders. 'Do you wannabe an actress?'

'Oh, I see.' Thia gave a rueful smile. 'No, I have no interest in becoming an actress, either.'

'A model?'

She snorted. 'Hardly, when I'm only five feet two inches in my bare feet!'

'You aren't being very helpful, Cyn.' There was an underlying impatience in that amused tone. Thia had seen far too much of the reaction of New York's elite these past four days not to know they had absolutely no interest in cultivating the company of a student and a waitress. Lucien Steele would have no further interest in her, either, once he knew. Which might not be a bad thing...

Her chin rose determinedly. 'I'm just a nobody on a visit to New York.'

Lucien totally disagreed with at least part of that statement. Cynthia Hammond was certainly somebody. Somebody—a woman—whose beauty and conversation he found just as intriguing as he had hoped he might...

She quirked dark brows. 'I believe that's your cue to politely excuse yourself?'

His eyes narrowed. 'And why would I wish to do that?'

She shrugged her shoulders beneath his jacket. 'It's what everyone else I've met in New York has done once they realise I'm of use to them.'

Yes, Lucien could imagine, knowing New York society as well as he did, that its members would have felt no hesitation whatsoever in making their lack of interest known. 'I believe I've already stated that I prefer not to be like everyone else.'

'Ain't that the truth? I mean—' A delicious blush now coloured those pale ivory cheeks as she briefly closed her eyes before looking up at him apologetically. 'I apologise once again. I'm really *not* having a good evening!' She sighed.

He nodded. 'Would you like to leave? We could go somewhere quiet and have a drink together?'

Cyn blinked those long lashes. 'I beg your pardon…?'

Lucien gave a hard, humourless smile. 'I hate parties like this one too.'

'But you're the guest of honour!'

He grimaced. 'I especially hate parties where I'm the guest of honour.'

Thia looked up at him searchingly, not sure whether or not Lucien Steele was playing with her. Not sure why he was bothering, if that should be the case!

The steady regard of those pale eyes and the grimness of his expression told her that this was a man who rarely, if ever, played.

He was seriously asking her to leave the Carews' party with him…

CHAPTER TWO

THIA GAVE A rueful shake of her head as she smiled. 'That really wouldn't be a good idea.'

'Why not?'

'Are you always this persistent?' She frowned.

He seemed to give the idea some thought before answering. 'When I want something badly enough, yes,' he finally murmured, without apology.

The intensity in that silver gaze as he looked down at Thia told her all too clearly that right now Lucien Steele wanted *her*.

Badly.

Wickedly!

She repressed another shiver of awareness just at the thought of how those chiselled lips and strong hands might feel as they sought out all the secret dips and hollows of her body.

'I really think it's time I went back inside.' She was slightly flustered as she slipped his jacket from about her shoulders and held it out to him. 'Please take it,' she urged when he made no effort to do so.

He looked down at her searchingly for several seconds before slowly taking the jacket and placing it dismissively over the balustrade in front of him—as if it *hadn't* cost as much as Thia might earn in a year as a waitress including tips!

'Cyn...'

He wasn't even touching her, and yet he managed to hold her mesmerised just by the way he murmured his own unique name for her in that deeply seductive voice, sending more rivulets of awareness down Thia's spine and causing a return of that tingling sensation in her breasts, accompanied by an unaccustomed warmth between her thighs.

'Yes...?' she answered breathlessly.

'I *really* want you to leave with me.'

'I can't.' She groaned in protest at the compulsion in the huskiness of his voice, sure that this man—a man who was not only sinfully handsome but rich as Creosus—rarely, if ever, asked for anything from anyone. He just took.

'Why not?'

'I just— What colour are your eyes, exactly...?' Whatever colour they were, they held Thia captive by their sheer intensity!

He blinked at the unexpectedness of the question. 'My eyes...?'

'Yes.'

His mouth twisted in a rueful smile. 'I believe it says grey on my passport.'

Thia gave a shake of her head. 'They're silver,' she corrected, barely able to breathe now, even knowing this was madness—that she was so totally aware of Lucien Steele, her skin so sensitised by the intensity of that glittering silver gaze fixed on her so intently, that she could feel the brush of each individual strand of her hair as it caressed lightly, silkily, across her shoulders and the tops of her breasts.

A totally unexpected and unprecedented reaction.

To any man. Goodness knew Jonathan was handsome enough, with his overlong blond hair, laughing blue eyes and lean masculinity, but for some reason she had just never found him attractive in *that* way. Just looking at Lucien Steele, knowing she was aware of everything about him, of all that underlying and leashed power, she knew that she never would be attracted to Jonathan—that Lucien Steele was so overpowering he ruined a woman's appreciation for any other man.

'Grey…silver…they can be whatever the hell colour you want them to be if you'll only leave with me now,' Lucien Steele urged again, with that same intensity.

She was tempted—Lord, was Thia tempted!—but it wouldn't do. No matter how distracted and inattentive Jonathan might choose to be, she couldn't arrive at a party with him and then leave with another man. Especially a man she found as disturbing as she did Lucien Steele!

A man who was over six feet of lean and compelling muscle. A man who was too handsome for his own good. A man who was just too…too intense—too much of everything—and whom she had discovered she found so mouthwateringly tempting.

Thia straightened her spine determinedly. 'I came here with someone.'

Those silver eyes narrowed with displeasure. 'A male someone?'

'Yes.'

His gaze moved to her left hand. 'You aren't wearing any rings.'

Thia gave a shake of her head. 'He isn't that sort of friend.'

'Then who is he?'

'I don't think that's any of your business—'

'And if I choose to make it so?'

'He's just a friend,' she dismissed impatiently, not sure even that was true any longer. Jonathan had made it obvious he inhabited a different world from her now—a world she had no inclination or desire ever to become a part of.

Lucien Steele's expression was grim as he shook his head. 'He can't be that much of a friend if he brought you here and then just left you to your own devices.'

This was the same conclusion Thia had come to over the past four days! 'I'm an adult and perfectly capable of looking after myself, thank you very much,' she assured him tartly.

Lucien Steele raised dark brows. 'So much so that you came out here alone rather than remain at the party?'

She felt stung by the mockery in his tone. 'Maybe I just wanted to get away from all that boot-licking?' she challenged.

'Handmade Italian leather shoes,' he corrected dryly.

'Whatever,' Thia dismissed impatiently. 'I'm sure you didn't come here alone tonight, either...' She vaguely recalled Jonathan mentioning something about Lucien Steele currently being involved with the supermodel Lyndsay Turner. A woman who, six feet tall and blond, couldn't be any more Thia's opposite!

Lucien's mouth thinned as he recalled the scene that had taken place with Lyndsay a week ago. A scene in which the supermodel had seriously overestimated his feelings for her and that had resulted in the end of their month-long relationship. Hell, he didn't *do* promises—let alone engagement and wedding rings.

He grimaced. 'As it happens, I did. And I want to leave with *you*,' he added determinedly, knowing it had been a long time since he had wanted anything as much as he now wanted to spend time alone with Cynthia Hammond.

'You don't know the first thing about me,' she dismissed exasperatedly.

'Which is precisely the reason I want the two of us to go somewhere quiet and talk—so that I can get to know you better,' he pushed insistently. The more this woman resisted him the more determined he became to leave the party with her this evening. At which time he intended to find out exactly which of Felix Carew's male guests was the friend Cyn had mentioned…

She attempted to tease. 'Has no one ever told you that it isn't possible to have *everything* you want?'

'No.' A nerve pulsed in Lucien's tightly clenched jaw.

'Because you're so rich and powerful no one would ever dare to tell you otherwise?' she asked softly, reminding him of his earlier comment.

'No doubt.' Again he answered unapologetically.

Thia gave an exasperated laugh at this man's unrelenting arrogance; she really had never met a man quite like him before! 'Then I shall have the distinction of being the first to do so! It's been…*interesting* meeting you, Mr Steele, but I really should go back inside and— What are you doing…?' She gasped softly as his gaze continued to hold hers captive even as his head slowly descended towards her, the warmth of his breath as light as a caress against her cheeks and lips.

'I want—I'd *like* to kiss you,' he corrected huskily, his lips just centimetres away from her own. 'Are you going to let me?'

'No…' Thia was aware her protest sounded half-hearted and she found herself unable to look away from those mesmerising silver eyes.

'Say yes, Cyn.' He moved slightly, his lips a hot and brief caress against the heat of her cheek before he raised his head and looked at her once again, not touching her with anything but the intensity of that glittering gaze.

She couldn't breathe, couldn't move so much as a muscle, as she continued to be held captive by the intensity of those eyes. Much like a deer caught in the headlights of an oncoming car. Or a freight train. Either of which was capable of flattening whatever stood in their way. As Lucien Steele's brand of seduction was capable of crushing both Thia and her resistance...

She drew in a shaky breath before stepping back and away from him. 'Thank you for the invitation, Mr Steele, but no.'

'Lucien.'

She shook her head. 'I believe I would prefer to continue calling you Mr Steele. Not that we'll ever meet again after this evening. But even so—'

'Why not?'

Thia gave a lightly dismissive laugh at the sharpness of his tone. 'Because you inhabit this world and I—I inhabit another one.'

'And yet here you are...?'

'Yes, here I am.' And she wouldn't be coming back again if she could help it! 'I really do have to go back inside now—'

'And look for your *friend*?' he prompted harshly.

'Yes.' Thia grimaced, very much afraid that she and that 'friend' were going to have words before the evening was over. Certainly she had no intention of letting Jonathan get away with bringing her to another party like this one and then leaving her to go off somewhere with the beautiful Simone. Jonathan's habit of just forgetting Thia's

existence the moment they arrived at one of these parties
was becoming tedious as well as a complete waste of her
time, when she really didn't enjoy being here.

'Who is he?'

'It's really none of your business,' Thia snapped in irritation at Lucien Steele's persistence.

Those silver eyes narrowed, his jaw tightening. 'At least
tell me where you're staying in New York.'

She gave an exasperated grimace. 'That's even less your
business! Now, if you'll excuse me…' Thia didn't wait for
him to reply before turning on her four-inch-heeled shoes
and walking away, her head held determinedly high as she
forced herself not to hurry, not to reveal how desperately
she needed to get away from Lucien Steele's disturbingly
compelling presence.

Even if she *was* completely aware of that silver gaze
as a sensual caress across the bareness of her shoulders
and down the length of her spine and the slender curve
of her hips!

Lucien Steele was without doubt the most disturbingly
sexual man she had ever—

'Where the *hell* have you been?' Jonathan demanded
the moment she stepped back into the Carews' huge sitting
room. The expression on his boyishly handsome face was
accusing as he took a rough hold of her arm.

An entirely unfair accusation, in Thia's estimation, considering *he* was the one who had gone missing with their
hostess for almost an hour, leaving her to be approached
by Lucien Steele!

'Can we talk about this somewhere less…public, Jonathan?' She glared at him, very aware of the silent—listening?—presence of Lucien Steele's bodyguard, Dex, just

feet away from the two of them. 'Preferably in the privacy of your car, once we've *left*,' she added pointedly.

Jonathan looked less than pleased by her last comment. 'You know damned well I can't leave yet,' he dismissed impatiently, even as he physically dragged her over to a quieter corner of the room.

'Could that possibly be because you haven't yet had a chance to say hello to Lucien Steele?' Thia felt stung into taunting him as she rubbed the top of her arm where Jonathan's fingers had dug so painfully into her flesh that she would probably have bruises to show for it tomorrow. 'I noticed you and our beautiful hostess were noticeably absent when he arrived.'

'What does *that* mean?' he glowered darkly. 'And what the hell's got into you, talking to me like that?'

'Nothing's got into me.' She gave a weary sigh, knowing that not all of her frustration with this evening was Jonathan's fault. Her nerves were still rattled from that encounter with Lucien Steele on the balcony—to a degree that she could still feel the seductive brush of those chiselled lips against her cheek and the warmth of his breath brushing against her skin… 'I just want to leave, that's all.' She grimaced.

'I've told you that I can't go just yet.' Jonathan scowled down at her.

'Then I'll just have to go downstairs and get a taxi—'

'It's a cab,' he corrected impatiently. 'And you aren't going anywhere until I say you can,' he added determinedly.

Thia looked at him searchingly, noting the reckless brightness of his eyes and the unaccustomed flush to his cheeks. 'Have you been drinking…?'

'It's a party. Of course I've been drinking!' Jonathan eyed her impatiently.

'In that case I'm definitely taking a cab back to your apartment,' Thia stated firmly.

'I said you'll leave when I *say* you can!' His eyes glittered.

Thia's cheeks warmed as she stared at him incredulously. 'Who do you think you are to talk to me like that?' she gasped.

Jonathan's expression darkened. 'I think I'm the man who paid for you to come to New York!'

Her eyes widened incredulously. 'And you believe that gives you the right to tell me what I can and can't do?'

'I think it gives me the right to do with you whatever the hell I feel like doing!' he sneered.

Thia felt the colour drain from her cheeks at the unmistakable threat in his voice. 'I don't know what's got into you, Jonathan.' Her voice shook as she tried to hold back tears of hurt. 'But I do know I don't like you like this. You're obviously drunk. Or something.' She wasn't a hundred per cent certain that reckless brightness in his eyes and the flush to his cheeks had been caused by alcohol alone...

Jonathan certainly wasn't behaving this evening— hadn't been for the past four days, if she was completely honest—like the charming and uncomplicated friend she had known in England...

She drew in a deep breath. 'I think it's best if I leave now, Jonathan. We can talk later. Or tomorrow—'

'You're staying put, damn it.' He reached out and grasped the top of her arm once again, the fingers of his other hand like a vice about her wrist as he twisted painfully.

Thia gave a gasp at the pain he was deliberately—
viciously—inflicting on both her arm and her wrist.
'You're hurting me, Jonathan,' she breathed, very much
aware of the other guests in the room and the curious sideways glances that were now being sent their way.

'Then stop being so damned difficult! I've said you
aren't going anywhere and that's an end to it—' Jonathan
broke off abruptly, his gaze moving past Thia and over
her left shoulder and his eyes widening before he abruptly
released her arm and wrist and forced a charmingly boy-
ish smile to his lips.

Thia's spine stiffened as she guessed from the sudden
pause in the conversation around them, the expectant stillness in the air and the way her skin tingled in awareness,
exactly who was standing behind her.

Only one man had the power to cause such awe in
New York's elite and the ability to possess the very air
about him...

The same man who exuded such sexual attraction that
it caused every nerve-ending in Thia's body to react and
strain towards the pull of that raw sensuality!

Lucien Steele...

Lucien had remained out on the balcony for several more
minutes after Cynthia Hammond had walked away from
him, giving the hardness of his arousal time to subside
even as he pondered the unexpected fierceness of his physical reaction to her.

Her skin—that pearly, luminescent skin—had been as
soft and perfect to the light caress of his lips against her
cheek as he had imagined it would be, and he could still
smell her perfume...something lightly floral along with
underlying warmly desirable woman. The same warmth

that had surrounded him, enveloped him, as he'd shrugged back into his evening jacket ready for returning to the Carews' party as if the woman herself were wrapped around him.

Lucien couldn't remember the last time he'd had such a visceral reaction to a woman that he wanted to take her right here and right now. If he ever had...

All the more surprising because Cynthia Hammond, at little over five feet tall, ebony-haired and probably only twenty or so, wasn't the type of woman he usually found himself attracted to. He had always preferred tall, leggy blondes, and women nearer to his own age of thirty-five. Women who knew and accepted that his interest in them was purely physical, and that it would be fleeting.

Cynthia Hammond looked too young, too inexperienced to accept the intensity of passion Lucien would demand from her even for the brief time that his interest lasted. And it would be brief—a week or two, a month at the most—before Lucien once again found himself feeling restless, bored with having the same woman in his bed.

No, better by far, he had decided, that he stay well away from the too-young and too-inexperienced Cynthia Hammond.

And he would have done so if, when he had finally stepped back into the Carews' apartment, Dex hadn't felt it necessary to take him to one side and inform him of the way Jonathan Miller had verbally berated Cynthia Hammond the moment she'd returned to the party, before physically dragging her away.

Did that mean that Jonathan Miller, the star of one of the television series currently airing on Lucien's own network, was the friend Cyn had come to the party with?

Watching the couple as they'd stood together on the opposite side of the room, talking softly but obviously heatedly, Lucien had been unable to stop the narrowing of his eyes when he saw the way Cyn suddenly paled. His fists had clenched at his sides as he'd realised that Miller had a painful grip on her arm and his other hand was twisting her wrist, despite Cyn's obvious efforts to free herself. The thought of a single bruise marring the pearly perfection of her skin had been enough to send Lucien striding forcefully across the room.

Jonathan Miller was one of the reasons Lucien was back in New York at the moment. The actor's behaviour this past few months had become a definite cause for concern and required that Lucien intervene personally after receiving information that the verbal warning he had given Miller six weeks ago, about his drug habit and the affair he was having with his married co-star—the wife of the show's director—had made little difference to the other man's behaviour.

Another private meeting with Jonathan Miller would have to wait until tomorrow. At the moment Lucien was more concerned with the aggressive way the younger man was currently behaving towards Cyn. No matter how intense or demanding Lucien's own physical needs might be, he would never deliberately hurt a woman—he much preferred to give pleasure rather than pain—and he wouldn't tolerate another man behaving in that way in his presence, either.

His gaze settled on Cyn as she stood with her bared shoulders turned towards him. 'Are you ready to leave now...?' he prompted huskily.

Thia's heart leapt into her throat as Lucien Steele reiterated his invitation to leave the party with him, as he offered to take her away from this nightmare. Away from Jonathan. A Jonathan who was becoming unrecognisable as the charming man she had met two years ago—a man she had thought was her friend.

But friends didn't deliberately hurt each other, and the top of her arm still ached from where Jonathan's fingers had dug so painfully into her flesh just seconds ago, and her wrist was sore from where he had twisted it so viciously. Not only had he hurt her, but he had frightened her too when he had spoken to her so threateningly. And it shamed her, embarrassed her, to think that Lucien Steele might have witnessed that physical and verbal attack.

'Cyn…?'

She could see the confusion in Jonathan's eyes and he was the one to answer the other man lightly. 'I think you've made a mistake, Mr Steele. This is Thia Hammond, my—'

'Cyn…?'

Long, elegant fingers slipped possessively, gently beneath her elbow and Lucien Steele continued to ignore the other man as he came to stand beside her. Thia felt that now familiar shiver down the length of her spine just at the touch of those possessive fingers against her skin, accompanied by the compulsion in Lucien Steele's husky voice. She could actually *feel* that compulsion as that voice willed her to look up at him.

She turned slowly, much like a marionette whose strings were being pulled, her lids widening, pupils expanding, and all the air suddenly sucked from her lungs as she took her first clear look at Lucien Steele in the glare of light from the chandeliers above them.

Oh. My. God.

She had thought him mesmerising, compelling, as they

had stood outside together in the moonlight, but that was as nothing compared to the intensity of the magnetism he exuded in the brightly lit sitting room of the Carews' apartment. So much so that even this huge room, the size of a tennis court, seemed too small to hold all that raw and savage power.

His hair was so deep a black it appeared almost blue beneath the lights of the chandelier, and his bronzed face was beautifully sculptured. His high, intelligent brow, the sharp blade of a nose between high cheekbones, and his mouth—oh, God, his mouth!—were sinfully, decadently chiseled. His top lip was slightly fuller than the bottom—an indication of the sensuality he had exuded when they were outside together on the balcony?—and his jaw was square and determined, darkened by the shadow of a dark stubble.

It was the face of a warrior, a marauder, a man who took what he wanted and to hell with whoever or whatever stood in his way.

As if that savagely beautiful face wasn't enough, his perfectly tailored evening suit—had Thia *really* had that gorgeous jacket wrapped about her just minutes ago?—and white silk shirt showed the perfection of his widely muscled shoulders and chest, his tapered waist, powerful thighs and long, lean legs encased in matching black trousers above those soft Italian leather shoes she had referred to so scathingly such a short time ago.

All the trappings of urbanity, in fact—an urbanity that was dispelled the moment she looked at that handsomely savage face!

A face that was dominated by those amazing and compelling silver eyes surrounded by long and silky dark lashes.

Those same compelling silver eyes now held Thia's own gaze captive, hostage, and refused to release her until she acquiesced, surrendered to that raw and demanding power…

CHAPTER THREE

'Cyn...?' Lucien questioned for the third and last time—and that was twice more than he would have allowed any other woman.

If Cyn Hammond ignored him for a third time then he would take it that she was a willing participant in Miller's abusive treatment. It wasn't to Lucien's personal taste, but that was Cyn's business—not his. No matter how much he might desire her himself...

'Thia?' Jonathan Miller looked totally confused by this whole encounter.

Lucien's eyes moved past Cyn to the other man, hardening to steel as he pinned Miller with his razor-sharp gaze. Bruises were already forming on Cyn's arm where Miller had held her too tightly just minutes ago, and her wrist looked red and sore. An unforgivable assault, as far as Lucien was concerned, on the perfection of that pearly unblemished skin.

'You hurt her, Miller,' he rasped harshly, his own fingers curling reassuringly about Cyn's elbow as he felt the way she still trembled. An indication that she really *wasn't* happy about Miller's rough treatment of her...

The other man's face flushed with anger—an emotion he quickly masked behind the boyishly charming smile that was currently holding American television audiences so enrapt, but succeeded only in leaving Lucien cold.

'Thia and I have had a slight misunderstanding, that's all—'

'It was *your* misunderstanding, Jonathan, not mine.' Cyn was the one to answer coldly and Lucien felt her straighten determinedly. 'Mr Steele has very kindly offered to drive me home, and I've decided to accept his offer.'

There were two things wrong with that statement as far as Lucien was concerned. One, he knew he was far from kind. Two, he had offered to take Cyn for a drink somewhere quieter than the Carews' apartment—not to drive her home. Especially if that 'home' should also happen to be Miller's apartment…

But the details could be sorted out later. For the moment Lucien just wanted to get Cyn away from here. He could still feel the slight trembling of her slender but curvaceous body. Those cobalt blue eyes were dark, there was an enticing flush to her cheeks, her pouting lips were moist and parted, and those deliciously full breasts were once again swelling temptingly against the bodice of her gown as she breathed.

And Lucien could think of a much better use for all that pent up emotion than anger…

'How do the two of you even know each other?' Jonathan Miller scowled darkly.

'If you'll excuse us, Miller?' Lucien didn't spare the other man so much as a glance, let alone answer him, as he turned to give Dex a slight nod of his head. He held Cyn to his side by a light but firm grasp of her elbow as he walked away, the other guests immediately clearing a pathway for them to cross the room to the Carews' private elevator in the hallway.

'What the hell is going on—?'

Lucien gave a cold smile of satisfaction as he heard Miller's protest cut short, knowing that Dex would have responded to his silent instruction and, in his own inimitable and deadly style, prevented the actor from attempting to follow the two of them. Lucien's smile hardened, his eyes chilling to ice as he thought of the conversation he was going to have with Jonathan Miller tomorrow. A conversation that would now include a discussion on the other man's treatment of the delicately lovely woman at his side…

Thia had no idea what she was doing, agreeing to leave the Carews' party with the dangerously compelling Lucien Steele, of all people. Especially when he had made his physical interest in her so obvious during the time the two of them had been outside on the balcony together!

She just wanted to get away from here. From a Jonathan she no longer recognised. And from the curious glances of all the other guests as they observed the tension between the three of them—some surreptitiously, some blatantly.

But was leaving with the dangerously attractive Lucien Steele, a man who was so arrogant she wasn't sure she even liked him, really the answer…?

'Shouldn't we say goodbye to the Carews before we leave?' she prompted hesitantly as Lucien Steele pressed a button and the lift doors opened.

'Dex will deal with it,' he dismissed unconcernedly.

'I—then shouldn't we at least wait for him…?' Thia made no move to enter the lift, her nervousness increasing the longer she spent in this man's compelling company.

'He'll make his own way down.' Lucien Steele released her elbow as he indicated she should enter the lift ahead of him.

Thia still hesitated. She wanted to get away from Jonathan, yes, but she now realised she felt no safer with Lucien Steele—if for a totally different reason!

'Changed your mind…?' he drawled mockingly.

Her chin rose at the taunt. 'No.' She stepped determinedly into the lift, her gaze averted as Lucien Steele stepped in beside her and pressed the button for the mirror-walled lift to descend.

Thia shot him several nervous glances from beneath her lashes as he stood broodingly on the other side of the lift, feeling that now familiar quiver trembling down her spine as she found herself surrounded by numerous mirrored images of him. This man was impressive under any circumstances, but she stood no chance of remaining immune to him in the confines of a lift.

Lucien Steele was sin incarnate, right from the top of his glossy hair—so much blacker than Thia's own, like shiny blue-black silk, the sort of tousled, overlong hair that made Thia's fingers itch to thread their way through it—to the soles of those Italian leather shoes.

He was a man so totally out of Thia's league that she had no business being there with him at all, let alone imagining threading her fingers through that delicious blue-black hair.

'Ask.'

Thia's startled gaze moved from that silky dark hair to the sculptured perfection of his face. Once again she felt that jolt of physical awareness as she found herself ensnared by the piercing intensity of those silver eyes. 'Um—sorry?'

He shrugged. 'You have a question you want to ask me.'
'I do…?'

His mouth twisted ruefully. 'You do.'

She chewed briefly on her bottom lip. 'Your hair—it's beautiful. I—I've never seen hair quite that blue-black colour before…?'

He raised a brow equally as dark. 'Are you sure you want *that* to be your one question?'

Thia blinked. 'My one question?'

He gave an abrupt inclination of his head. 'Yes.'

She frowned slightly. Surely he wasn't serious…? 'I've just never seen hair that colour before…' she repeated nervously. 'It's the colour of a starless night sky.'

His mouth twisted derisively. 'That was a statement, not a question.'

Yes, it was. But this man unnerved Thia to such a degree she couldn't think straight.

Lucien Steele sighed. 'Somewhere way back in my ancestry—a couple of hundred years or so ago—my great-great-grandfather is reputed to have been an Apache Indian who carried off a rancher's wife before impregnating her,' he dismissed derisively. 'The black hair has appeared in several generations since.'

Dear Lord, this man really was a warrior! Not an axe-wielding, fur-covered Viking, or a kilt-wearing, claymore-brandishing Celt, but a clout-covered, bow-and-arrow-carrying, bareback horse-riding Native American Indian!

It was far too easy for Thia to picture him as such—with that inky-black hair a long waterfall down his back, his muscled and gleaming chest and shoulders bare, just that clout-cloth between him and the horse he rode, the bareness of his long muscled legs gripping—

'Surely I haven't shocked you into silence?' he taunted.

Thia knew by his mocking expression that he wanted her to be shocked, that Lucien Steele was deliberately trying to unnerve her with tales of Apache warriors carrying off innocent women for the sole purpose of ravishing them.

In the same way he was doing the modern equivalent of carrying her off? Also for ravishment...?

Her chin rose. 'Not in the least.'

Those silver eyes continued to mock her. 'My father is a native New Yorker, but my mother is French—hence I was given the name Lucien. My turn now,' he added softly.

She gave a wary start. 'Your turn to do what...?' she prompted huskily.

Those chiselled lips curled into a derisive smile as he obviously heard the tremble in her voice. 'Ask you a question.'

She moistened dry lips. 'Which is...?'

'Cyn, if you don't stop looking at me like that then I'm going to have to stop the elevator and take you right now.'

As if to back up his statement he pressed a button and halted the lift's descent, before crossing the floor with all the grace of the predator he undoubtedly was and standing just inches in front of her.

Thia's eyes had widened, both at his actions and at the raw desire she could hear beneath the harshness of his tone. 'I—you can't just stop the lift like that...!'

'I believe I already did,' he dismissed arrogantly.

Thia found herself totally unable to look away from the intensity of that glittering silver gaze as Lucien looked down at her from between narrowed lids, her cheeks flushed, her heart beating wildly—apprehensively?—in her chest. 'I—that wasn't a question, either.'

'No.'

She winced. 'How was I looking at you...?'

'As if you'd like to rip my clothes from my body before wrapping your legs about my waist as I push you up against the wall and take you!' His voice was a low and urgent rasp.

Thia's breath caught in her throat as she imagined herself doing any or all of those things, her cheeks flushing, burning. 'I don't think—'

'It's probably better if you don't.'

Lucien Steele's gaze continued to hold hers captive.

She stepped away instinctively, only to feel her back pressing up against the mirrored wall. Lucien Steele dogged her steps until he again stood mere inches away from her and slowly raised his hands to place them on the mirror either side of her head. Lowering his head, he stared down at her with those compelling silver eyes, causing Thia to once again moisten her lips with the tip of her tongue.

'I advise you not to do that again unless you're willing to take the consequences!' he rasped harshly.

Thia's tongue froze on her parted lips as she was once again beset by the feeling of being trapped in the headlights of a car—or, more accurately, the glittering compulsion of Lucien Steele's gaze.

Her throat moved as she swallowed before speaking. 'Consequences?'

He nodded abruptly. 'I'd be more than willing to participate in your fantasy.' His jaw was tight, and desire gleamed in his eyes.

It was a depth of desire Thia had never encountered before, and one that caused her breath to hitch in her throat and her skin to flush with heat: a single-minded depth of desire that made her feel like running for the hills!

'What's Miller to you?' Lucien Steele prompted abruptly.

She blinked long dark lashes. 'Is that your question?'

He bared his teeth in a parody of a smile as he nodded. 'Contrary to my Apache ancestor, I make it a rule never to take another man's woman.'

'"Take another man's"—!' She frowned. 'You really *are* something of a barbarian, aren't you?'

Rather than feeling insulted at the accusation, as she had intended, Lucien Steele instead bared his teeth in a wolfish smile. 'You have no idea.'

Oh, yes, Thia definitely had an idea. More than an idea. And her response to this man's raw sexuality terrified the life out of her. Almost as much as it aroused her...

'Cyn?' Lucien pressed forcefully.

She shrugged bare shoulders, those ivory breasts swelling invitingly against her gown. 'I already told you—Jonathan is just a friend—'

'A friend who had no hesitation in hurting you?' Lucien glared his displeasure as he looked down to where dark smudges were already appearing on the smooth paleness of her arm. Her wrist was still slightly red too. 'Who left his mark on you?' he added harshly as he gave in to the temptation to brush his fingertips gently over those darkening smudges.

'Yes...' Her bottom lip trembled, as if she were on the verge of crying. 'I've never seen him behave like that before. He was out of control...' She gave a dazed shake of her head. 'He's never behaved aggressively with me before,' she insisted dully.

'That's something, I suppose.' Lucien nodded abruptly.

'I—would you please restart the lift now...?' Those

tears were trembling on the tips of her long dark lashes, threatening to overflow.

He was *scaring* her, damn it!

Because this—his coming on to her so strongly—was too much, too soon after Miller's earlier aggression.

Or just maybe, despite what she might claim to the contrary, her relationship with Miller wasn't as innocent as she claimed it to be…?

In Lucien's experience no woman was as ingenuous as Cyn Hammond appeared to be. Her ingenuousness had encouraged him to reveal more about himself and his family in the last five minutes than he had told anyone for a very long time. Not that Lucien was ashamed of his heritage—it was what it was. It was his private life in general that he preferred to keep exactly that—private.

He straightened abruptly before stepping back. 'A word of advice, Cyn—you should stay well away from Miller in future. He's bad news.'

Her expression sharpened. 'What do you mean?'

'I believe you've more than used up your quota of questions for one evening.' His expression was grim.

'But you seem to know something I don't—'

'I'm sure I know a lot of things you don't, Cyn,' he rasped with finality, before turning to press the button to restart the elevator.

'Thank you,' Cyn breathed softly as it resumed its soundless descent.

'I didn't do it for you.' Lucien gave a hard, dismissive smile. 'The elevator has been stopped between floors for so long now Dex is probably imagining you've assassinated me.'

Thia frowned. 'Is it a defence mechanism, or are you really this arrogant and rude?'

His gaze was hooded as he answered her. 'Quite a bit of the latter and a whole lot of the former.'

'That's what I thought.' She nodded, able to breathe a little easier now that he wasn't standing quite so close to her. Well…perhaps not easier. Lucien Steele's presence was still so overpowering that Thia challenged anyone, man or woman, to be completely relaxed in his company.

He put his hand beneath her elbow again as the lift came to a stop, the doors opening and allowing the two of them to step out into the marble foyer of the luxurious Manhattan apartment building.

Thia's eyes widened as she saw Dex was already there, waiting for them. 'How did you…?'

'Service elevator,' the man supplied tersely, dismissively, his censorious glance fixed on his employer.

'Stop looking so disapproving, Dex,' Lucien Steele drawled. 'I checked before getting in the elevator: there's absolutely nowhere that Miss Hammond could hide a knife or a gun beneath that figure-hugging gown.'

Thia felt the colour warm her cheeks. 'Definitely a *lot* of the latter,' she muttered, in reference to their previous conversation and heard Lucien Steele chuckle huskily beside her even as she turned to give the still frowning Dex a smile. 'Mr Steele does like to have his little joke.'

There was no answering smile from the bodyguard as he opened the door for them to leave. 'I've had the car brought round to the front entrance.'

'Good,' Lucien Steele bit out shortly, his hand still beneath Thia's elbow as he strode towards the black limousine parked beside the pavement, its engine purring softly into life even as Dex moved forward to open the back door for them to get inside.

'I can get a taxi—a cab—from here,' Thia assured

Lucien Steele quickly. His behaviour in the lift wasn't conducive to her wanting to get into the back of a limousine with him.

'Get in.'

That compelling expression was back on Lucien Steele's face as he raised one black brow, standing to one side as he waited for her to get into the back of the limousine ahead of him.

Thia gave a pained frown. 'I appreciate your help earlier, but I'd really rather just get a cab from here...'

He didn't speak again, just continued to look down at her compellingly. Because he was so used to everyone doing exactly as he wished them to, whenever he wished it, he had no doubt Thia was going to get into the limousine.

'I could always just pick you up and put you inside...?' Lucien Steele raised dark brows.

'And I could always scream if you tried to do that.'

'You could, yes.' He smiled confidently.

'Or not,' Thia muttered as she saw the inflexibility in his challenging gaze.

Sighing, she finally climbed awkwardly into the back of the limousine. She barely had enough time to slide across the other side of the seat before Lucien Steele got in beside her. Dex closed the door behind them before getting into the front of the car beside the driver and the car moved off smoothly into the steady flow of evening traffic.

'I don't like being ordered about,' Thia informed Lucien tightly.

'No?'

'No!' She glared her irritation across the dim interior of the car. The windows were of smoked glass, as was the partition between the front and back of the car. 'Any more than I suspect you do.' Once again he was intimidating in the close confines of the car, so big and dark, and she could smell his lemon scent again, the insidious musk of the man himself, all mixed together with the expensive smell of the leather interior of the car.

'That would depend on the circumstances and on what I was being ordered to do,' he drawled.

Her irritation deepened along with the blush in her cheeks. 'Do you think you could get your mind out of the bedroom for two minutes?'

He turned, his thigh pressing against hers as he draped his arm along the back of the seat behind her. 'There's no need for a bedroom when this part of the car is completely private and soundproofed.'

'How convenient for you.'

'For *us*,' he corrected huskily.

Thia's throat moved as she swallowed nervously. 'Unless it's escaped your notice, I'm really not in the mood to play sexual cat-and-mouse games.' She moved her thigh from the warmth of his and edged further along the seat towards the door. 'You offered to drive me home—not seduce me in the back of your car.'

'I believe my original offer was to take you for a quiet drink somewhere,' he reminded her softly.

She gave a shake of her head. 'I'm not in the mood for a drink, either,' she added determinedly.

He smiled slightly in the darkness. 'Then what *are* you in the mood for?'

Thia ignored the innuendo in his voice and instead thought of Jonathan's brutish and insulting behaviour this evening—that reckless glitter in his eyes—all of which told her that it wouldn't be a good idea for her to go back to his apartment tonight. In fact after tonight she believed it would better for both of them if she moved out of Jonathan's apartment altogether and into a hotel, until she flew back to London in a couple of days' time.

Not that she could really afford to do that, but the thought of being any more beholden to Jonathan was no longer an option after the way he had spoken to her earlier. She was also going to repay the cost of the airfare to him as soon as she was able. She was definitely going to have bruises on the top of her arm from where he had gripped her so tightly. It was—

'Cyn?'

She turned sharply to look at Lucien Steele, flicking her tongue out to moisten the dryness of her lips—only to freeze in the action as that glittering silver gaze followed the movement, reminding her all too forcefully of his earlier threat. 'I—could you drop me off at a hotel? An inexpensive one,' she added, very aware of the small amount of money left in her bank account.

This situation would have been funny if Thia hadn't felt quite so much like crying. Here she was, seated in the back of a chauffeur-driven limousine, with reputedly the richest and most powerful man in New York, and she barely had enough money in her bank account to cover next month's rent on her bedsit, let alone an 'inexpensive' hotel!

Lucien Steele pressed the intercom button on the door beside him. 'Steele Heights, please, Paul,' he instructed the driver.

'Will do, Mr Steele,' the disembodied voice came back immediately.

'I totally forgot about the worldwide Steele Hotels earlier in my list of Steele Something-or-Others...' Thia frowned. 'But I'm guessing that none of your hotels are inexpensive...?'

The man beside her gave a tight smile. 'You'll be staying as my guest, obviously.'

'*No!* No...' she repeated, more calmly. 'Thank you. I always make a point of paying my own way.'

Her cheeks paled as she recalled that the one time she hadn't it had been thrown back in her face. She certainly had no intention of being beholden to a man as dangerous as Lucien Steele.

Unfortunately she was barely keeping her head above water now on the money she earned working evening shifts at the restaurant. That would change, she hoped, once she had finished her dissertation in a few months' time and hopefully acquired her Masters degree a couple of months after that. She could then at last go out and get a full-time job relevant to her qualifications. But for the moment she had to watch every penny in order to be able to pay her tuition fees and bills, let alone eat.

A concept she realised the man at her side, with all his millions, couldn't even begin to comprehend...

'Why the smile...?' Lucien prompted curiously.

Cyn gave a shake of her head, that silky dark hair cascading over her shoulders. 'You wouldn't understand.'

'Try me,' he invited harshly, having guessed from her request to go to a hotel that she had indeed been staying at Miller's apartment with him. Lucien had meant it when he'd said he didn't poach another man's woman. *Ever.*

His own parents' marriage had been ripped apart under just those circumstances, with his mother having been seduced away from her husband and son by a much older and even wealthier man than his father. They were divorced now, and had been for almost twenty years, but the acrimony of their separation had taken its toll on Lucien. To a degree that he had complete contempt for any man or woman who intruded on an existing relationship.

The fact that Cyn Hammond claimed she and Jonathan Miller were only friends didn't change the fact that she was obviously staying at the other man's apartment with him. Or at least had been until his aggression this evening...

She gave a grimace as she answered his question. 'I'm a student working as a waitress to support myself through uni. *Now* do you believe you inhabit a different world from me? One where you would think nothing of staying at a prestigious hotel like Steele Heights. I've seen the Steele Hotel in London, and I don't think I could afford to pay the rent on a broom cupboard!'

'I've already stated you will be staying as my guest.'

'And I've refused the offer! Sorry.' She grimaced at her sharpness. 'It's very kind of you, Lucien, but no. Thank you,' she added less caustically. 'As I said, I pay my own way.'

He looked at her through narrowed lids. 'How old are you?'

'Why do you want to know?' She looked puzzled by the question.

'Humour me.'

She shrugged. 'I'm twenty-three—nearly twenty-four.'

'And your parents aren't helping you through university?'

'I'm sure they would have if they were still alive.' She smiled sadly. 'They were both killed in a car crash when I was seventeen, almost eighteen,' she explained at his questioning look. 'I've been on my own ever since,' she dismissed lightly.

The lightness didn't fool Lucien for a single moment; his own parents had divorced when he was sixteen, so he

knew exactly how it felt, how gut-wrenching it was to have
the foundations of your life ripped apart at such a sensitive
age. And Cyn's loss had been so much more severe than
his own. At least his parents were both still alive, even if
they were now married to other people.

The things Cyn had told him went a long way to explaining the reason for her earlier smile, though; Lucien
had more money than he knew what to do with and Cyn
obviously had none at all.

'I can relate to that,' he murmured huskily.

'Sorry?'

'My own parents parted and divorced when I was sixteen. Obviously it isn't quite the same, but the result was
just as devastating,' he bit out harshly.

'Is that why you're so driven?'

'Maybe.' Lucien scowled; he really had talked far too
much about his personal life to this woman.

'It was tough for me, after the accident, but I've managed okay,' she added brightly. 'Obviously not as okay as
you, but even so… I worked for a couple of years to get
my basic tuition fees together, so now I just work to pay
the bills.'

He frowned. 'There was no money after your parents
died?'

Cyn smiled as she shook her head. 'Not a lot, no. We
lived in rented accommodation that was far too big for me
once I was on my own,' she dismissed without rancour.
'I've almost finished my course now, anyway,' she added
briskly. 'And then I can get myself a real job.'

It all sounded like another world to Lucien. 'As what?'

She shrugged her bare shoulders. 'My degree will be
in English Literature, so maybe something in teaching or
publishing.'

He frowned. 'It so happens that one of those other Steele Something-or-Others is Steele Publishing, with offices in New York, London and Sydney.'

She smiled ruefully. 'I haven't finished my degree yet. Nor would I aim so high as a job at Steele Publishing once I have,' she added with a frown.

Lucien found himself questioning the sincerity of her refusal. It wouldn't be the first time a woman had downplayed the importance of his wealth in order to try and trap him into a relationship.

Thia had no idea why she had confided in Lucien Steele, of all people, about her parents' death and her financial struggles since then. Maybe as a response to his admission of his own parents' divorce?

She *did* know as she watched the expressions flitting across his for once readable face, noting impatience quickly followed by wariness, that he had obviously drawn his own conclusions—completely wrong ones!—about her reason for having done so!

She turned to look out of the window beside her, stung in spite of herself. 'Just ask your driver to drop me off anywhere here,' she instructed stiffly. 'There are a couple of cheap hotels nearby.'

'I have no intention of dropping you off anywhere!' Lucien Steele rasped. 'This is New York, Cyn,' he added as she turned to protest. 'You can't just walk about the streets at night alone. Especially dressed like that.'

Thia felt the blush in her cheeks as she looked down at her revealing evening gown, acknowledging he was right. She would be leaving herself open to all sorts of trouble if she got out of the car looking like this. 'Then *you* suggest somewhere,' she prompted awkwardly.

'We'll be at Steele Heights in a couple of minutes, at which time I *suggest* you put aside any idea of false pride—'

'There's nothing false about my pride!' Thia turned on him indignantly. 'It's been hard-won, I can assure you.'

'It *is* false pride when you're endangering yourself because of it,' he insisted harshly. 'Now, stop being so damned stubborn and just accept the help being offered to you.'

'No.'

'Don't make me force you, Cyn.'

'I'd like to see you try!' She could feel the heat of her anger in her cheeks.

'Would you?' he challenged softly. 'Is that what all this is about, Cyn? Do you enjoy it…get off on it…when a man bends you to his will, as Miller did earlier?'

'How dare you—?'

'Cyn—'

'My name is *Thia,* damn it!' Her eyes glittered hotly even as she grappled with the door handle beside her, only to find it was locked.

'Tell Paul to stop the car and unlock this damned door. *Now,*' she instructed through gritted teeth.

'There's no need for—'

'Now, Lucien!' Thia breathed deeply in her fury, not sure she had ever been this angry in her life before.

He sighed deeply. 'Aren't you being a little melodramatic?'

'I'm being a *lot* melodramatic,' she correctly hotly. 'But then you were a lot insulting. I don't— Ah, Paul.' She had at last managed to find what she sincerely hoped was the button for the intercom.

'Miss Hammond…?' the driver answered uncertainly.

'I would like you to stop the car right now, Paul, and unlock the back doors, please,' she requested tightly.

There was a brief pause before he responded. 'Mr Steele…?'

Thia looked across at Lucien challengingly, daring him to contradict her request. She was so furious with him and his insulting arrogance she was likely to resort to hitting him if he even attempted to do so.

He looked at her for several more minutes before answering his driver. 'Stop the car as soon as it's convenient, Paul. Miss Hammond has decided to leave us here,' he added, and he turned to look out of the window beside him uninterestedly.

As if she were a petulant child, Thia acknowledged. As if he hadn't just insulted her, accused her of—of— She didn't even want to think about what he had accused her of!

She kept her face turned away from him for the short time it took Paul to find a place to safely park the limousine, her anger turning into heated tears. Tears she had no intention of allowing the cynical and insulting Lucien Steele the satisfaction of seeing fall.

'Thank you,' she muttered stiffly, once the car was parked and Paul had got out to open the door beside her. She kept her face averted as she stepped out onto the pavement before walking away, head held high, without so much as a backward glance.

'Mr Steele…?' Dex prompted beside him uncertainly.

Lucien had uncurled himself from the back of the car to stand on the pavement, his expression grim as he watched Cynthia Hammond stride determinedly along the crowded street in her revealing evening gown, seemingly unaware—or simply uncaring?—of the leering looks being directed at her by the majority of the men and the disapproving ones by the women.

'Go,' Lucien instructed the other man tightly; if Cyn—Thia—had so little concern for her own safety then someone else would have to have it for her.

CHAPTER FOUR

A REALLY UNPLEASANT thing about waking up in a strange hotel room was the initial feeling of panic caused by not knowing exactly where you were. Even more unpleasant was noticing that the less-than-salubrious room still smelt of the previous occupant's body odour and cigarette smoke.

But the worst thing—the *very* worst thing—was returning to that disgusting-smelling hotel bedroom after taking a lukewarm shower in the adjoining uncleaned bathroom and realising that you had no clothes to leave in other than the ankle-length blue evening gown you had worn the night before, along with a pair of minuscule blue panties and four-inch-heeled take-me-to-bed shoes.

All of which became all too apparent to Thia within minutes of her waking up in that awful hotel bedroom and taking that shower!

She had been too angry and upset the evening before—too furious with the arrogantly insulting Lucien Steele—to notice how faded and worn the furniture and décor in this hotel room was, how threadbare and discoloured the towel wrapped about her naked body, let alone the view outside the grimy window of a rusted fire escape and a brick wall.

Thia had been sensible enough the night before, after

the lone night porter on duty had openly leered at her when she'd booked in, to at least lock and secure the chain on the flimsy door, plus push a chair under and against the door handle, before crawling between the cold sheets and thin blankets on the bed.

Not that it had helped her to fall asleep—she'd still been too angry at the things Lucien Steele had said to be able to relax enough to sleep.

She dropped down heavily onto the bed now and surveyed what that anger had brought her to. A seedy hotel and a horrible-smelling room that was probably usually let by the hour rather than all night. God, no wonder the night porter had leered at her; he had probably thought she was a hooker, waiting for her next paying customer to arrive.

At the moment she *felt* like a hooker waiting for her next paying customer to arrive!

How was she even going to get out of this awful hotel when she didn't even have any suitable clothes to wear?

Thia tensed sharply as a knock sounded on the flimsy door, turning to eye it warily. 'Yes...?'

'Miss Hammond?'

She rose slowly, cautiously, to her feet. 'Dex, is that you...?' she prompted disbelievingly.

'Yes, Miss Hammond.'

How on earth had Lucien Steele's bodyguard even known where to find her...? More to the point, *why* had he bothered to find her?

At that moment Thia didn't care how or why Dex was here. She was just relieved to know he was standing outside in the hallway. She hurried across the room to remove the chair from under the door handle, slide the safety chain across, before unlocking the door itself and flinging it open.

'Oh, thank God, Dex!' She launched herself into his arms as she allowed the tears to fall hotly down her cheeks.

'Er—Miss Hammond…?' he prompted several minutes later, when her tears showed no signs of stopping. His discomfort was obvious in his hesitant tone and the stiffness of his body as he patted her back awkwardly.

Well, of *course* Dex was uncomfortable, Thia acknowledged as she drew herself up straight before backing off self-consciously. What man wouldn't be uncomfortable when a deranged woman launched herself into his arms and started crying? Moreover a deranged woman wearing only a threadbare bathtowel that was barely wide enough to cover her naked breasts and backside!

'I'm so sorry for crying all over you, Dex,' she choked, on the edge of hysterical laughter now, as she started to see the humour of the situation rather than only the embarrassment. 'I was just so relieved to see a familiar face!'

'You—do you think we might go into your room for a moment?' Dex shifted uncomfortably as a man emerged from a room further down the hallway, eyeing Thia's nakedness suggestively as he lingered over locking his door.

'Of course.' Thia felt the blush in her cheeks as she stepped back into the room. 'I—is that my suitcase…?' She looked down at the lime-green suitcase Dex had brought in with him; it was so distinctive in its ugliness that she was sure it must be the same one she had picked up for next to nothing in a sale before coming to New York. The same suitcase that she had intended collecting, along with her clothes, from Jonathan's apartment later this morning… 'How did you get it?' She looked at Dex suspiciously.

He returned that gaze unblinkingly. 'Mr Steele obtained it from Mr Miller's apartment this morning.'

'Mr Steele did…?' Thia repeated stupidly. 'Earlier this morning? But it's only eight-thirty now…'

Dex nodded abruptly. 'It was an early appointment.'

She doubted that Jonathan would have appreciated that, considering he hadn't emerged from his bedroom before twelve o'clock on a single morning since her arrival in New York. 'And Lu—Mr Steele just asked him for my things and Jonathan handed them over?'

Dex's mouth thinned. 'Yes.'

Thia looked at him closely. 'It wasn't quite as simple as that, was it?' she guessed heavily.

He shrugged broad shoulders. 'I believe there may have been a…a certain reluctance on Mr Miller's part to co-operate.'

Thia would just bet there had. Jonathan had been so angry with her yesterday evening that she had been expecting him to refuse to hand over her things when she went to his apartment for them later. An unpleasant confrontation that Lucien Steele had circumvented for her by making that visit himself. She could almost feel sorry for Jonathan as she imagined how that particular meeting would have panned out. Almost. She was still too disgusted with Jonathan's unpleasant behaviour the previous evening to be able to rouse too much sympathy for him.

But she was surprised at Lucien Steele having bothered himself to go to Jonathan's apartment himself to collect her things; Lucien had let her leave easily enough last night, and he didn't give the impression he was a man who would inconvenience himself by chasing after a woman who had walked away from him as Thia had.

She drew a shaky breath. 'No one was hurt, I hope?'

'I wasn't there, so I wouldn't know,' Dex dismissed evenly.

'I had the impression you accompanied Mr Steele everywhere?' Thia frowned her puzzlement.

'Normally I do.' His mouth flattened. 'I spent last night standing guard in the hallway outside this room, Miss Hammond.' He answered her question before she had even asked it.

Thia took a step back in surprise, only to have to clutch at the front of the meagre towel in order to stop it from falling off completely. Her cheeks blushed a furious red as she tried to hold on to her modesty as well as her dignity. 'I—I had no idea you were out there...' Maybe if she had she wouldn't have spent half the night terrified that someone—that dodgy night porter, for one!—might try to force the flimsy lock on the door and break in.

A suitable punishment, Lucien Steele would no doubt believe, for the way in which she had walked away from him last night! Because there was no way that Dex had spent the night guarding the door to her hotel room without the full knowledge, and instruction of his arrogant employer...

'I doubt you would have been too happy about it if you had.' Dex bared his teeth in a knowing smile before reaching into the breast pocket of his jacket and pulling out an expensive-looking cream vellum envelope with her name scrawled boldly across the front of it. 'Mr Steele had Paul deliver your suitcase here a short time ago, along with this.'

Thia stared at the envelope as if it were a snake about to bite her, knowing that it had to be Lucien Steele's own bold handwriting on the front of it and dreading reading what he had written inside.

At the same time she felt a warmth, a feeling of being

protected, just knowing that Lucien had cared enough to ensure her safety last night in spite of herself...

'A Miss Hammond is downstairs in Reception, asking to see you, Mr Steele. She doesn't have an appointment, of course,' Ben, his PA, continued lightly, 'but she seems quite determined. I wasn't quite sure what I should do about her.'

Lucien looked up to scowl his displeasure at Ben as he stood enquiringly on the other side of the glass-topped desk that dominated this spacious thirtieth-floor office. Lucien wasn't sure himself what to do about Cynthia Hammond.

She was so damned stubborn, as well as ridiculously proud, that Lucien hadn't even been able to guess what her reaction might be to his having had her things delivered to her at that disgustingly downbeat hotel in which she had chosen to stay the night rather than accept his offer of a room at Steele Heights. He certainly hadn't expected that she would actually pay him a visit at his office in Steele Tower.

And he should have done—Cynthia Hammond was nothing if not predictably unpredictable. 'How determined is she, Ben?' He sighed wearily, already far too familiar with Cyn's stubbornness.

'Very.' His PA's mouth twitched, as if he were holding back a smile.

The wisest thing to do—the *safest* thing to do for Lucien's own peace of mind, which would be best served by never seeing the beautiful Cynthia Hammond again—would be to instruct Security to show her the door...as if she didn't already know exactly where it was! But if Cyn was determined enough to see him, then Lucien didn't doubt that she'd just sit there and wait until it was time for him to leave at the end of the day.

He pulled back the cuff on his shirt and glanced at the plain gold watch on his wrist. 'I don't leave for my next appointment for ten minutes, right?'

'Correct, Mr Steele.'

He nodded abruptly. 'Have Security show her up.'

Lucien leant back in his high-backed white leather chair as Ben left the office, knowing this was probably a mistake. He already knew, on just their few minutes' acquaintance the evening before, that Cynthia Hammond was trouble.

Enough to have caused him a night full of dreams of caressing that pearly skin, of making love to her in every position possible—so much so that he had woken this morning with an arousal that had refused to go down until he'd stood under the spray of an ice-cold shower!

He had even had Paul drive by the hotel where he knew she had spent the night on his way to visit Jonathan Miller's apartment this morning. The neighbourhood was bad enough—full of drug addicts and hookers—but the hotel itself was beyond description, and fully explained Dex's concern when he had telephoned Lucien the night before to tell him exactly which hotel Cyn had checked into and to ask what he should do about it. What the hell had possessed her to stay in such a disreputable hovel?

Money. Lucien answered his own question. He knew from his conversation earlier that morning with Jonathan Miller that Cyn really was exactly what she had said she was: a student working as a waitress to put herself through university, and just over here for a week's visit.

Her finances were not Lucien's problem, of course, but he had been infuriated all over again just looking at the outside of that disgusting hotel earlier, imagining that vulnerable loveliness protected only by the flimsy door Dex had described to him. Dex had been so worried about the situation Lucien believed the other man would have decided to stand guard over her for the night whether Lucien had instructed him to do so or not!

Just another example of the trouble Cynthia Hammond caused with her—

'*Wow!* This is a beautiful building, Lucien! And this office is just incredible!'

Lucien also gave a *wow,* but inwardly, as he glanced across the room to where Cynthia Hammond had just breezily entered his office. A Cynthia Hammond whose black hair was once again a straight curtain swaying silkily to just below her shoulders. The beautiful delicacy of her face appeared free of make-up apart from a coral-coloured lipgloss and the glow of those electric blue eyes. She was dressed in a violent pink cropped sleeveless top that left her shoulders and arms bare and revealed at least six inches of her bare and slender midriff—as well as the fact that she wore no bra beneath it. And below that bare midriff was the tightest pair of skinny low-rider blue denims Lucien had ever seen in his life. So tight that he wondered whether Cyn wore any underwear beneath...

And that was just the front view. Ben's admiring glance, as he lingered in the doorway long enough to watch Cyn stroll across the spacious office, was evidence that the back view was just as sexily enticing!

Cyn did casual elegance well—so much so that Lucien felt decidedly overdressed in his perfectly tailored black suit, navy blue silk shirt and black silk tie. 'Don't you have some work to do, Ben?' he prompted harshly as he stood up—and then sat down again as he realised his arousal had sprung back to instant and eager attention. The benefits of his icy cold shower earlier this morning obviously had no effect when once again faced with the enticing Cynthia Hammond.

Trouble with a capital T!

'Thanks, Ben.' Thia turned to smile at the PA before he closed the door on his way out, then returned her gaze to the impressive office rather than the man seated behind the desk, putting off the moment when she would have to face the disturbing Lucien Steele. Just a brief glance in his direction as she had entered the cavernous office had been enough for her to feel as if all the air had been sucked from her lungs, and her nerve-endings were all tingling on high alert.

This black and chrome office was not only beautiful, it was *huge*. Carpeted completely in black, it had an area set aside for two white leather sofas and a bar serving coffee as well as alcohol, and another area with a glass and marble conference table, as well as Lucien Steele's own huge desk, bookshelves lining the wall behind him, and an outer wall completely in glass, giving a panoramic view of the New York skyline.

It really was the biggest office Thia had ever seen, but even so her gaze was drawn as if by a magnet inevitably back to the man seated behind the chrome and black marble desk. The office was easily big enough to accommodate half a dozen executive offices, and yet somehow—by sheer force of will, Thia suspected—Lucien Steele still managed to dominate, to *possess*, all the space around him.

As he did Thia?

Maybe she should have power-dressed for this meeting rather than deciding to go casual? She did have one slim black skirt and a white blouse with her—they would certainly have blended in with the stark black, white and chrome décor of his office. Much more so than her shockingly pink cropped top.

Oh, well, it was too late to worry about that now. She would have to work with what she had.

'Say what you have to say, Cyn, and then go,' Lucien Steele bit out coldly. 'I have to leave for another appointment in five minutes.'

Her breath caught in her throat as she looked at Lucien. A Lucien who was just as knee-tremblingly gorgeous this morning as the previous night. Thia had convinced herself during her restless night of half-sleep that no one could possibly be that magnetically handsome, that she must have drunk too much of the Carews' champagne and imagined all that leashed sexual power.

She had been wrong. Lucien Steele was even more overpoweringly attractive in the clear light of day, with the sun shining in through the floor-to-ceiling windows turning his hair that amazing blue-black, his bronzed face dominated by those silver eyes, and his features so hard and chiselled an artist would weep over his male beauty. And as for the width of those muscled shoulders—!

Time for her to stop drooling! 'Nice to see that you're still living up to my previous description of you as being arrogant and rude,' she greeted with saccharine sweetness.

He continued to look at her coldly with those steel-grey eyes. 'I doubt you want to hear my opinion of *you* after the stunt you pulled last night.'

She felt the colour warm her cheeks and knew he had to be referring to the hotel in which she had spent the night, which Dex would no doubt have described to his employer in graphic detail. 'I didn't have the funds to stay anywhere else.'

'You wouldn't have needed any funds if you had just accepted the room I offered you at Steele Towers,' Lucien reminded her harshly.

'Accepting the room you offered me at Steele Towers would have put me under obligation to you,' she came back, just as forcefully.

Lucien stilled, eyes narrowing to steely slits. 'Are you telling me,' he asked softly, 'that the reason you refused my offer last night was because you believed I would expect to share that bedroom with you for the night as payment?'

'Well, you can't blame me for thinking that after the way you came on to me outside on the balcony and then again in the lift!'

Lucien raised dark brows. 'I can't *blame* you for thinking that?'

'Well...no...' Cyn eyed him, obviously slightly nervous of his quiet tone and the calmness of his expression.

And she was wise to be! Because inwardly Lucien was seething, furious—more furious than he remembered being for a very long time, if ever. Even during the visit he had paid to Jonathan Miller's apartment earlier this morning he had remained totally in control—coldly and dangerously so. But just a few minutes spent in the infuriating Cynthia Hammond's company and Lucien was ready to put his hands about her throat and throttle her!

If it weren't for the fact that he knew he would much rather put his hands on another part of her anatomy, starting with that tantalisingly bare and silky midriff, and stroke her instead...

Thia took a step back as Lucien Steele stood up and moved round to the front of his desk. His proximity, and the flat canvas shoes she was wearing, meant she had to tilt her head back in order to be able to look him in the face. A face that made her wish she were an artist. What joy, what satisfaction, to commit those hard and mesmerising features to canvas. Especially if Lucien could be persuaded into posing in traditional Apache clout cloth, with oil rubbed into the bare bronzed skin of his chest and arms, emphasising all the dips and hollows of those sleek muscles—

'What are you thinking about, Cyn?'

She looked up guiltily as she realised her appreciative gaze had actually wandered down to that muscled chest as she imagined him bare from the waist up—. 'I—you—nice suit.' She gave him a falsely bright smile.

Lucien Steele's mouth tilted sceptically, as if he knew exactly what she had been thinking. 'Thanks,' he drawled derisively. 'But I believe we were discussing your reckless behaviour last night and your reasons for it?' His voice hardened and all humour left his expression. 'Do you have any idea what could have happened to you if Dex hadn't stayed outside your room all night?'

She had a pretty good idea, yes. 'It was stupid of me. I accept that.'

'Do you?' he bit out harshly.

She nodded. 'That's why I'm here, actually. I wanted to thank you.' She grimaced. 'For allowing Dex to stand guard last night. For having my things delivered to the hotel this morning. And for sending that keycard, in the envelope Dex gave me, for a suite at Steele Heights.'

For all her expectations of what Lucien Steele *might* have put in that vellum envelope Dex had handed her this morning, there had been nothing in it but a keycard for a suite at Steele Heights, which he had obviously booked for her.

Thia had wrestled with her pride over accepting, of course, along with that old adage about accepting sweets from strangers. This was a different sort of suite, of course, but she told herself it was still sensible to be wary. But pride and wariness weren't going to put a roof over her head tonight, and she couldn't possibly go back to Jonathan's.

Lucien leant back against his desk and seemed to guess some of her thoughts. 'I trust you've overcome your scruples and moved in there now?'

'Yes.' Thia grimaced. Just the thought of that luxurious suite—the sitting room, bedroom and equally beautiful adjoining bathroom—was enough for her to know she had done the right thing. It might take her a while, but she fully intended to reimburse Lucien for his generosity.

He quirked one dark brow. 'Does that mean you no longer mind feeling under obligation to me?'

Thia looked up at him sharply, unable to read anything from his mocking expression. 'I think the question should be do *you* believe I'm under any obligation to you?'

'Let me see...' He crossed his elegantly clad legs at the ankles as he studied her consideringly. 'I left a perfectly good party last night because I thought we were going on somewhere to have a drink together. A drink that never happened. You flounced off in a snit after I offered to drive you somewhere, which greatly inconvenienced me as Dex was then forced to stand guard over your room all night. And I was put to the trouble this morning of asking your ex-boyfriend to pack up your belongings in that hideous lime-green suitcase before having my driver deliver it to that seedy hotel.' He gave a glance at the slender gold watch on his wrist. 'Your unexpected visit here this morning means I am now already three minutes late leaving for my next appointment. So what do *you* think, Cyn? *Are* you obligated to me?'

Well, when he put it like that... 'Maybe,' Thia allowed with a pained wince.

'I would say there's no *maybe* about it.' He slowly straightened to his full height of several inches over six feet, that silver gaze fixed on her unblinkingly as he took a step forward.

Thia took a step back as she was once again over-whelmed by the unique lemon and musk scent of Lucien Steele. 'What are you doing?'

'What does it look as if I'm doing?'

He was standing so close now she could feel the warmth he exuded from his body against the bareness of her mid-riff and arms. His face—mouth—only was inches away from her own as he lowered his head slightly.

She moistened her lips with the tip of her tongue. 'It looks to me as if you're trying to intimidate me!'

He gave a slow and mocking smile as he regarded her through narrowed lids. 'Am I succeeding?'

'You must know that you intimidate everyone.'

'I'm not interested in everyone, Cyn, just you.'

Thia's heart was beating such a loud tattoo in her chest that she thought Lucien must be able to hear it. Or at least see the way her breasts were quickly rising and falling as she tried to drag air into her starved lungs. 'You're stand-ing far too close to me,' she protested weakly.

He tilted his head, bringing those chiselled lips even closer to hers. 'I like standing close to you.'

She realised she liked standing close to Lucien too. That she liked him. That she wanted to do so much more than stand close to him. She wanted Lucien to pull her into his arms and kiss her. To make love to her.

Which was strange when she had never felt the least inclination to make love with any man before now. But Lucien wasn't just any man. He was dark and dangerous and overpoweringly, mesmerisingly, sexually attractive— a combination Thia had never come across before now. She knew her breasts had swelled, the nipples hard nubs, pressing against her cropped top, and between her thighs she was damp, aching. For Lucien Steele's touch!

As if he was able to read that hunger in her face, Lucien's pupils dilated and his head slowly lowered, until those beautiful sculptured lips laid gentle but hungry siege to hers.

Thia felt as if she had been jolted with several thousand volts of electricity. And heat. Such burning heat coursing through her. She stepped in closer to that hard, unyielding body and her arms moved up and over Lucien's wide shoulders as if of their own volition. The warmth of his strong hands spanned the slenderness of her bare waist as her fingers became entangled in that silky black hair at his nape, her lips parting as she lost herself in the heat of his kiss.

Trouble...

Oh, yes, Cyn Hammond, with her black hair, electric-blue eyes, beautiful face and deliciously enticing body, was definitely Trouble with a capital T...

But at this moment, with the softness of her responsive lips parted beneath his, his hands caressing, enjoying the feel of the soft perfection of her bare midriff, Lucien didn't give a damn about that.

Nothing had changed since last night. If anything he wanted her more than he had then.

Again. Right here.

And right now!

Lucien deepened the kiss even as he moulded her slender curves against his own much harder ones, intoxicated, lost in Cyn's taste as he ran his tongue along the pouting softness of her bottom lip. Groaning low in his throat, he let his tongue caress past those addictive lips and into the heat beneath, plunging, possessing that heat as his hands moved restlessly, caressingly, down the length of her spine. Soon Lucien was able to cup that shapely bottom and pull her snugly into and against the pulsing length of his arousal.

The softness of her thighs felt so good against his, so hot and welcoming. He shifted, the hardness of his shaft now cupped and cushioned in that softness, and moved one of his hands to cup her breast through her T-shirt. It was a perfect fit into the palm of his hand, the nipple hard as an unripe berry as Lucien brushed the soft pad of his thumb across it and heard Cyn's gasp of pleasure, felt her back arching, pressing her breast harder into his cupping hand in a silent plea.

Her skin felt as smooth as silk beneath Lucien's fingertips as he slipped his hand beneath the bottom of her top to cup her bare breast—

Thia wrenched her mouth from Lucien's and pulled out of his arms before taking a stumbling step backwards—as if those few inches in any way nullified Lucien's sexual potency, or the devastation wrought upon her senses by that hungry kiss and those caressing hands!

'No...' she breathed shakily, her cheeks ablaze with embarrassed colour as she attempted to straighten her top over breasts that pulsed and ached for the pleasure she had just denied them.

Lucien's gaze was hooded. There was a flush across those high cheekbones, a nerve pulsing in his clenched jaw. 'No?'

'No,' Thia repeated more firmly. 'This is—I don't do this.'

'"This" being…?'

'Seduction in a zillionaire's office!'

He arched one dark brow. 'How many zillionaires do you know?'

Her cheeks warmed. 'Just the one.'

He nodded. 'That's what I thought.' He crossed his arms in front of his chest and he looked at her from between narrowed lids. 'Just what did you think was going to happen, Cyn, when you came to my office dressed—or rather undressed—like that?' That glittering silver gaze swept appreciatively over her breasts, naked beneath the crop top, her bare midriff and hip-hugging denims.

She hadn't allowed herself to think before coming here—had just acted on impulse, knowing she had to thank Lucien Steele for his help some time today and just wanting to get it over with. But, yes, now that he mentioned it she wasn't exactly dressed for repelling advances. Deliberately if subconsciously so? Lord, she hoped not!

'Stop calling me Cyn,' she snapped defensively.

'But that's what you are to me… Sin and all that word implies.' He all but purred. 'You have all the temptation of a candy bar in that shocking pink top. One that I want to lick all over.'

Thia felt heat in her already blushing cheeks at the provocative imagines that statement conjured in her mind. 'You—I don't—didn't—' She gave a shake of her head. 'Could we get back to our earlier conversation?' *Please,* she added silently, knowing she would have plenty of time later today to think about and to remember with embarrassment the touch of Lucien's lips and hands on her body. 'For one thing, Jonathan was only ever my friend,' she continued determinedly.

'Not any more he isn't.' Lucien nodded with grim satisfaction. 'He made it clear before I left his apartment earlier this morning that he was feeling decidedly less than charitable towards you,' he explained dryly.

Thia's eyes widened. 'What did you say to him?'

'About you?' He shrugged. 'As you have neither a father nor brother to protect you, I thought it necessary that someone should warn Miller against laying so much as a finger on you with the intention of hurting you ever again.'

She gasped. 'I can look after myself!'

'Is that why you spent the night at a less-than-reputable hotel? Why you have bruises on your arm?' Lucien's expression darkened with displeasure as his glittering silver gaze moved to the purple-black smudges at the top of her left arm. 'If I had known the extent of your bruising I would have inflicted a few of my own on him this morning, rather than just firing his ass!'

Thia gasped even as she looked up searchingly into that ruthlessly handsome face, totally unnerved by the dangerous glitter in Lucien's eyes as he continued to glower at the bruises on her arms. 'You fired Jonathan from *Network?*'

He looked up into her face as he gave a humourless smile of satisfaction. 'Oh, yes.'

Oh, good grief...

CHAPTER FIVE

LUCIEN'S HUMOURLESS SMILE became a grimace as he saw the expression of horror on Cyn's face. 'Don't worry. My decision to fire Miller wasn't because of anything he did or said to you. Although that was certainly a side issue in the amount of satisfaction I felt doing it.'

'Then why did you fire him?' She looked totally bewildered.

Lucien gave another impatient glance at his wristwatch. 'Look, can we continue this conversation later? Possibly over dinner? I really do have to leave for my appointment now.' He moved around his desk to pick up the file he needed for his meeting before putting it inside his black leather briefcase and snapping it shut. 'Cyn?' he prompted irritably as she stood as still as an Easter Island statue.

He was more than a little irritated with himself for having suggested the two of them have dinner together when he knew that the best thing for both of them was not be alone together again. His response to Cyn—as he had proved a short time ago!—was so different than to any other woman he had ever met. She was so different from those preening, self-centred, high-maintenance women he usually dated...

'Hmm?' She looked across at him blankly.

'Dinner? Tonight?' he repeated shortly.

'I—no.' She shook her head from side to side. 'You've been very kind to me, but—'

'You consider my almost making love to you just now as being *kind* to you…?' Lucien bit out derisively.

Her cheeks flushed a fiery red. 'No, of course not—'

'Dinner. Tonight,' he said impatiently. He couldn't remember the last time he had been late for a business appointment. Business always came first with him, pleasure second. And making love to Cyn just now had been pure pleasure. 'We can eat at the hotel if that would make you feel…*safer?*' he taunted.

Thia easily heard the mockery in Lucien's voice. A mockery she knew she deserved.

So Lucien had kissed her. More than kissed her. She wasn't a child, for goodness' sake, but a twenty-three-year-old woman, and just because this was the first time that anything like this had happened to her it was no reason for her to go off at the deep end as if she were some scandalised Victorian heroine!

Besides which, it was obvious Lucien wasn't going to tell her any more now about why he had fired Jonathan, and she desperately wanted to know.

Was it even possible for him to dismiss Jonathan so arbitrarily? Admittedly this was Lucien Steele she was talking about—a man who had already proved how much he liked having his own way—but surely Jonathan had a contract that would safeguard him from something like this happening. Besides which, *Network* was the most popular series being shown on US television at the moment; sacking its English star would be nothing short of suicide for both the series *and* Steele Media. And Lucien *was* Steele Media.

'Fine, we'll eat at Steele Heights,' she bit out abruptly. 'What time and which restaurant?' There were three of them, but obviously Cyn hadn't eaten at any.

Lucien moved briskly from behind his desk, briefcase in hand, and took hold of her elbow with the other hand. 'We can talk about that in the car before I drop you off at the hotel.'

'I'm not going back to the hotel just yet.' Thia dug her heels in at being managed again, even as she recognised that familiar tingling warmth where Lucien's fingers now lightly touched her arm. 'I'm going to the Empire State Building this afternoon.'

He raised dark brows. 'Why?'

'What do you mean, *why?*' She looked up at him irritably. 'It's a famous New York landmark, and I've been here five days already and not managed to go to the top of it yet.'

Lucien's mouth twisted derisively. 'I was born in New York, have lived here most of my thirty-five years, and I can honestly say I've never been even to the top of the Empire State Building.'

'You could always come with me—' Thia broke off as she realised the ridiculousness of her suggestion. Of course Lucien Steele, zillionaire entrepreneur, didn't want to do something as mundane as go with her to the top of the Empire State Building any more than Thia really wanted him to accompany her. Did she...? No, of course she didn't. She had succumbed to this man's sexual magnetism enough for one day—made a fool of herself enough for one day—thank you very much.

'Forget it,' she dismissed, with a lightness she was far

from feeling. She wasn't one hundred per cent sure *what* she was feeling at the moment, or thinking. She was too tremblingly aware of Lucien having kissed her just minutes ago to be able to put two coherent thoughts together. 'You said you had a meeting to get to?' she reminded him.

Yes, he did. But strangely, just for a few seconds, Lucien had actually been considering cancelling his business meeting and going with Cyn to visit the Empire State building instead. Unbelievable.

Zillionaires didn't get to be or stay zillionaires, by playing hooky from work to go off and play tourist with a visitor from England. Even if—*especially* if—that visitor was Cyn Hammond. A woman who apparently had the ability to make Lucien forget everything but his desire to be with her and make love to her.

Something that had definitely not happened to him before today.

But, damn it, Cyn really did look like a tempting stick of candy in that pink top... And it took no effort at all on Lucien's part to imagine the pleasure of licking his tongue over every inch of that soft and silky flesh...

He nodded abruptly. 'I can drop you off at the Empire State Building on my way.'

'It's such a lovely day I think I'd rather walk,' she refused lightly, lifting a hand in parting to Ben as they passed through his office and out into the hallway before stepping into the private elevator together.

Just the thought of Cyn wandering the streets of New York dressed in nothing more than that skimpy pink top and those body-hugging denims was enough to bring a dark scowl back to Lucien's brow. 'Do you have *any* sense of self-preservation at all?' he rasped harshly as he released her elbow to press the button for the elevator to take them down to the ground floor.

'It's the middle of the day, for goodness' sake!' She glanced at him with those cobalt blue eyes through lushly dark lashes.

Lucien eyed her impatiently. 'Remind me to tell you later tonight about the statistics for daytime muggings and shootings in New York.'

She chewed on her bottom lip. 'You still have to tell me what time I'm meeting you this evening, and at which restaurant in the hotel,' she said firmly.

'Eight o'clock.' He frowned. 'Go down to the ground floor. I'll have someone waiting to show you to the private elevator that will bring you directly up to the penthouse apartment.'

Her eyes widened. 'The penthouse? You live in an apartment at the top of the Steele Heights Hotel?' Thia was too surprised not to gape at him incredulously.

He gave a smile of satisfaction at her reaction. 'I occupy the whole of the fiftieth floor of Steele Heights when I'm in New York.'

'The whole floor?' she gasped. 'What do you have up there? A tennis court?'

'Not quite.' Lucien smiled tightly. 'There is a full-sized gym, though. A small pool and a sauna. And a games room. A small private cinema for twenty people.' He quirked a dark brow as Cyn gaped at him. 'Changed your mind about having dinner with me at the hotel this evening?' Those silver eyes mocked her.

It didn't take too much effort on Thia's part to realise Lucien was challenging her, daring her. He expected her to baulk at agreeing to have dinner with him now that she knew they would be completely alone in his penthouse apartment. And good sense told Thia that it would be a wise move on her part *not* to rise to this particular challenge, to just withdraw and concede Lucien as being the winner.

Unfortunately Thia had never backed down from a challenge in her life. She wouldn't have been able to survive the death of her parents or worked as a waitress for the past five years in order to support herself through uni if that was the case. And she had no intention of backing down now, either.

Even if she did suspect that Lucien wasn't just challenging her by inviting her to his apartment and that the main reason he wanted them to dine in the privacy of his apartment was because he didn't want to be seen out with her in public.

She knew enough about Lucien Steele to know he was a man the media loved to photograph, invariably entering some famous restaurant or club, and always with a beautiful model or actress on his arm. Being seen with a waitress student from London hardly fitted in with that image.

'Fine.' She nodded abruptly. 'Eight o'clock. Your apartment.'

'No need to dress formally,' Lucien told her dismissively. 'Although perhaps something a little less revealing than what you're currently wearing might be more appropriate,' he added dryly.

'It's a crop top, Lucien. All women are wearing them nowadays.'

'None of the women *I've* escorted have ever done so,' he assured her decisively.

'That's your loss!' Thia felt stung by Lucien's casual mention of those women he'd escorted. Which was ridiculous of her. The fact that they were eating dinner at his apartment told her that this wasn't a date, just a convenient way for the two of them to be able to finish their conversation in private. Well away from the public eye…

'Yes.' He bared his teeth in a wolfish smile as the two of them stepped out of the lift together, causing Thia to blush as he reached out to grasp one of her hands lightly in his before raising it to skim his lips across her knuckles. 'Until later, Cyn.'

Thia snatched her hand from within his grasp, aware of the stares being directed their way by the other people milling about in the lobby of Steele Tower even if he wasn't. 'I hope you're enjoying yourself,' she hissed, even as she did her best to ignore the tingling sensation now coursing the length of her arm. And beyond…

'It has its moments.' His eyes glittered with satisfied amusement as he looked down at her.

Thia glared right back at him. 'You could have told me your reason for firing Jonathan in the time we've been talking together.'

'I do things my own way in my own time, Cyn,' he bit out tersely. 'If you have a problem with that, then I suggest—'

'I didn't say I had a problem with it,' she snapped irritably. 'Only that—oh, never mind!' Lucien had the ability to rob her of her good sense, along with any possibility of withstanding his lethal attraction.

A lethal attraction that affected every other woman in his vicinity, if the adoring glances of the receptionists were any indication, as well as those of the power-dressed businesswomen going in and out of the building.

All of them, without exception, had swept a contemptuous gaze over the casually dressed Thia—no doubt wondering what a man like Lucien Steele was doing even wasting his time talking to someone like her—before returning that gaze longingly, invitingly, to the man at Thia's side. One poor woman had almost walked into a potted plant because she had been so preoccupied with eating Lucien up with her eyes!

It was a longing Thia knew she was also guilty of.

Challenge or no challenge, she really shouldn't have agreed to have dinner alone with him in his apartment this evening…

Thia looked in dismay at the chaos that was her bedroom in the suite on the tenth floor of the Steele Heights Hotel. Clothes were strewn all over the bed after she had hastily tried them on and then as quickly discarded them. Finding exactly the right casual outfit to wear to have dinner with the dangerously seductive Lucien Steele in—oh, hell—fifteen minutes' time was proving much more difficult than she had thought it would. And she hadn't dried her hair yet, or applied any make-up.

She had been late getting back to the hotel as the long queues at the Empire State Building had meant she'd had to wait in line for a long time before getting to the top. It had been worth the wait when she finally got there, of course, but by that time it had been starting to get late.

She'd also had the strangest feeling all afternoon that she was being followed…

Lucien's warnings earlier had made her paranoid. That was more than a possibility. Whatever the reason, Thia had felt so uncomfortable by the time she'd come down from the top of the Empire State Building and stepped back out into the street that she had decided to treat herself and take a taxi back to the hotel.

She had taken out her laptop and gone online for half

an hour once she was back in the hotel suite, determined to know at least a little more about the enigmatic Lucien Steele before they met again this evening.

Unfortunately the moment she'd come offline and lain back on the bed she had fallen asleep, tired from her outing, and also exhausted from the previous sleepless night she had spent at that awful hotel. No surprise, then, that she hadn't woken up again until almost seven-thirty!

Which now meant she was seriously in danger of being late—and she still hadn't found anything to wear that she thought suitable for having dinner with a man like Lucien Steele!

Oh, to hell with it. Black denims and a fitted blouse the same colour blue as her eyes would have to do; she simply didn't have any more time to waste angsting over what she should or shouldn't wear to have dinner with a zillionaire. And the blue blouse also had the benefit of having elbow-length sleeves, meaning those bruises Jonathan had inflicted on her arm the previous evening, which had so angered Lucien earlier, would be safely hidden from his piercing gaze.

Jonathan....

If she concentrated on the fact that it was only because she wanted to know exactly why Lucien had decided to fire Jonathan from *Network* that she had agreed to have dinner with Lucien—even if she no longer believed that!—then maybe she would be able to get through this evening.

The butterflies fluttering about in her stomach didn't seem to be listening to her assurances as she stood alone in the private lift minutes later, on her way up to the penthouse apartment. Her hair still wasn't completely dry and her face felt flushed. No doubt it looked it too, despite her application of a light foundation.

The manager of the hotel himself had been waiting on the ground floor to show her into the private coded lift. The sheer opulence of the lift in which she was now whizzing up fifty floors to the penthouse apartment—black carpet, plush bench seat along one mirrored wall, a couple of pot plants—and the thought of the overwhelmingly sexy man who would be waiting up there for her were so far beyond what was normal for Thia, was it any wonder she was so nervous she felt nauseous?

Or maybe it was just the thought of being alone with Lucien again that was making her feel that way... Her online snooping about him earlier had informed her that he was thirty-five years old—something Lucien had already told her—and the only child of New Yorker Howard Steele and Parisian Francine Maynard. Educated at private school and then Harvard, he had attained a law degree and in his spare time designed a new gaming console and graphics for many computer games, enabling him to make his first million—or possibly billion?—before he was twenty-one. That was something else Lucien had already told her. He had taken full advantage of this success by diversifying those millions into any number of other successful businesses.

There had also, depressingly, been dozens of photographs of him with dozens of the women he had escorted at some time or other during the past fifteen years: socialites, actresses, models. All of them, without exception, were extremely beautiful, as well as being tall and blond.

And this was the man that Thia, five-foot-two, raven-haired and merely pretty, had agreed to have dinner alone with this evening...

Knowing she simply wasn't his type should have made her feel less nervous about the evening ahead. Should have.

But it didn't. How could it when she only had to think of the way Lucien had kissed her so intensely this afternoon, of his caressing hands on her bare midriff—and higher!—to know that he had felt desire for her then, even if she *was* five-foot-two and raven-haired!

After all her apprehension, the man who had caused all those butterflies in her stomach was nowhere to be seen when Thia stepped out of the lift into the penthouse apartment seconds later. The apartment itself was everything she had thought it would be—white marble floors, original artwork displayed on ivory walls. She walked tentatively down the hallway to the sitting room in search of Lucien. It was a spaciously elegant room, with the same minimalist white, black and chrome décor of Lucien's office. Had the man never heard of any other colours but white, black and chrome?

The view from the floor-to-ceiling windows was even more spectacular than the one from the Carews' apartment—

'I'm sorry I wasn't here to greet you when you arrived, Cyn. My meeting ran much later than I had anticipated and I only got back a few minutes ago.'

Thia turned almost guiltily at the sound of Lucien's voice, very aware of the fact that she had just walked into his private apartment and made herself at home, only to stand and stare, her mouth falling open, blue eyes wide and unblinking, as she took in his rakishly disheveled and practically nude appearance.

Lucien had obviously just taken a shower. His black hair was still damp and tousled, a towel was draped about his shoulders, and he wore only a pair of faded blue denims sitting low down on the leanness of his hips, leaving that glistening bronzed chest and shoulders—the same ones

Thia had fantasised about earlier this afternoon!—openly on view. Revealing he was just as deliciously muscled as she had imagined he would be. His nipples were the size and colour of two dark bronze coins amongst the dusting of dark hair that dipped and then disappeared beneath the waistband of his denims.

If Lucien had wanted to lick her all over this afternoon then Thia now wanted to do the same to him... Dressed in those low-slung denims, with his bronzed shoulders and chest bare, overlong blue-black hair sexily dishevelled, his bare feet long and elegant, Lucien definitely looked good enough to eat!

'Cyn...?' Lucien eyed her questioningly as she made no response.

Or perhaps she did...

She was wearing another pair of those snug-fitting denims this evening—black this time—with a fitted blouse the same electric blue colour as her sooty-lashed eyes. The material of the blouse was so sheer it was possible for Lucien to see that she wore no bra beneath it. Her breasts were a pert shadow, nipples plump as berries as they pressed against the soft gauzy material. Hard and aroused berries...

'I—er—shouldn't you go and finish dressing...?'

Lucien dragged his gaze slowly, reluctantly away from admiring those plump, nipple-crested breasts to look up into Cyn's face, instantly noting the flush to her cheeks and the almost fevered glitter to her eyes as she shifted uncomfortably from one booted foot to the other. As if her breasts weren't the only part of her body that was swollen with arousal...

Instead of doing as she suggested Lucien stepped further into the sitting room. 'I'll get you a drink first.' He threw the damp towel down onto a chair as he strolled over to the bar in the corner of the room. 'Bottled water, white wine, red wine...something stronger...?' He arched a questioning brow.

Was Lucien strutting his bare, bronzed stuff deliberately? Thia wondered. As a way of disconcerting her? If he was then he was succeeding. She had never felt so uncomfortably aware of a man in her life as she was now by all his warm naked flesh. Or so aroused!

The man should have a public health warning stamped on his chest. Something along the lines of 'Danger to all women with a pulse' ought to do it. And Thia was the only woman with a pulse presently in Lucien Steele's disturbing vicinity! Her throat felt as if it had closed up completely, and her chest was so tight she could barely breathe, let alone speak.

She cleared her throat before even attempting it. 'Red wine would be lovely, thank you,' she finally managed to squeak, in a voice that sounded absolutely nothing like her own, only to draw a hissing breath into her starved lungs as Lucien turned away from her. The muscles shifted in his back beneath that smooth bronzed skin as he bent to take a bottle of wine from the rack beside the bar, and even more muscles flexed in his arms as he straightened to open it, the twin dips at the base of his spine clearly visible above the low-riding denims.

Twin dips Thia longed to stroke her tongue over, to taste, before working her way slowly up the length of that deliciously muscled back...!

'Here you go.' Lucien strolled unconcernedly across the room carrying two glasses of red wine—one obviously meant for Thia, the other for himself.

Evidence that he didn't have any intention of putting any more clothes on in the immediate future? And why should he? This was his home, after all!

His close proximity now meant that Thia was instantly overwhelmed by that smell of lemons and the musky male scent she now associated only with this man, and her hand was trembling slightly as she reached out to take one of the wine glasses from him—only to spill some of the wine over the top of the glass as a jolt of electricity shot up her arm the moment her fingers came into contact with his.

'Sorry,' she mumbled self-consciously, passing the glass quickly into her other hand with the intention of licking the spilt wine dripping from her fingers.

'Let me…' Lucien reached out to catch her hand in his before it reached her parted lips, his gaze easily holding hers as he carried her fingers to his own mouth before lapping up the wine with a slow and deliberate rasp of his tongue. 'Mmm, delicious.' He licked his lips. 'Perhaps I should consider always drinking wine this way…?' His shaft certainly thought it was a good idea as it rose up hard and demanding inside his denims!

'Lucien—'

'Hmm?' He continued to lick the slenderness of Cyn's silky fingers even after all the wine had gone, enjoying the way her hand was trembling in his and watching the slow rise and fall of those plumped breasts and aroused nipples, his erection now almost painful in its intensity.

She snatched her hand away from his to glare up at him. 'Are you doing this on purpose?'

'Doing what…?'

Her eyes narrowed. 'Would you please go and put some clothes on?'

Lucien straightened slowly to look at her from between

narrowed lids. 'You seem a little...tense this evening, Cyn. Didn't the Empire State live up to your expectations?'

'The Empire State was every bit as wonderful as I always imagined it would be. And I'm not in the least tense!' She moved away jerkily until she stood apart from him.

Far enough that she thought she had put a safe distance between them.

Lucien was so aroused right now he didn't think the other side of the world would be far enough away to keep Cyn safe from him...

His meeting that afternoon had not gone well. No, that wasn't accurate. It hadn't been the meeting that was responsible for his feelings of impatience and dissatisfaction all afternoon. That had been due to the intrusive thoughts he'd had of Cyn all through that lengthy meeting—not just the silkiness of her skin, her responsive breasts, the delicious taste of her mouth, but also the fact that he *liked* her...her sense of humour, the way she answered him back, everything about her, damn it! It had caused Lucien to finally call a halt to negotiations and reschedule the meeting for another day next week.

Needless to say he had not been best pleased that he had allowed the distraction of those thoughts of Cyn to infringe on his business meeting, but one look at her tonight, dressed in those snug-fitting black denims and the delicate blue blouse, with the silky darkness of her hair loose about her shoulders, and his earlier feeling of irritated dissatisfaction had instantly been replaced by desire.

'I thought that I had been invited up here for dinner,' she snapped now. 'Not to witness a male strip show!'

Lucien made no effort to hold back his grin of satisfaction at her obvious discomfort at seeing his bare chest. It seemed only fair when he had thought of her all afternoon.

When his shaft was now an uncomfortable, painful throb against his denims. 'I'm wearing more now than I would be on a beach,' he reasoned.

'Unless you haven't noticed, we don't happen to *be* on a beach.' She frowned. 'And I do not have any intention of providing your amusement for the evening.'

He eyed her mockingly. 'Oh, I haven't even begun to be amused yet, Cyn.'

'And as far as I'm concerned you aren't going to be, either!' She placed her glass down noisily on the coffee table before straightening and turning, with the obvious intention of walking out on him.

Lucien reached out and grasped her arm as she would have stormed past him—only to ease up on the pressure of that grasp as he saw the way she winced. 'Are your wrist and arm still hurting you?' he rasped.

'No. I—they're fine.' She gave a dismissive shake of her head, her eyes avoiding meeting his piercingly questioning gaze. 'You just caught me unawares, that's all.'

'I don't believe you.'

She sighed her impatience. 'I don't care whether or not— What are you doing?' she demanded as Lucien released her arm before moving his hands to the front of her blouse, his fingers unfastening the tiny blue buttons. 'Lucien? Stop it!' She slapped ineffectually at his hands.

'I don't trust your version of "fine", Cyn. I intend to see for myself,' Lucien muttered grimly as he continued unfastening those buttons.

'Stop it, I said!' She pulled sharply away from him—a move immediately followed by a delicate ripping sound as Lucien refused to release his hold. The gauzy blouse ripped completely away from the last remaining buttons, leaving Cyn's breasts completely bared to his heated gaze.

Full and beautifully sloping breasts…tipped by two perfect rosy-red nipples…those nipples were plumping and hardening in tempting arousal as Lucien continued to look down at them appreciatively.

CHAPTER SIX

'I CAN'T BELIEVE you just did that!' Thia was the first to re-
cover enough to speak, staring accusingly at Lucien even
as her shaking hands scrabbled desperately to pull the two
sides of her blouse together over her bared breasts, feeling mortified by her nakedness in front of a man she already found far too overpoweringly attractive for comfort.

Her knees had once again turned to the consistency of
jelly at the heat she saw in those silver eyes…!

'I believe, if you think about it, you'll find that *we* just
did that,' Lucien drawled hardly. 'You pulled away. I didn't
let go.' He shrugged.

Thia bristled indignantly, clutching on to anger as a
means of hiding her embarrassment—and arousal—at the
continued heat in Lucien's gaze. 'You shouldn't have been
unbuttoning my blouse in the first place!'

'I wanted to see your bruises. I still want to see them,'
he added determinedly.

'You saw a lot more than my bruises!' she snapped.
'And I believe we've already had one discussion about
my feelings concerning what you do or don't want. In this
instance what you wanted resulted in the ruination of a
blouse I was rather fond of and saved for weeks to buy.'

'I'll replace it for you tomorrow.'

'Oh, won't that be just wonderful?' She huffed her exasperation. 'I can hear your telephone conversation with the woman in the shop now—*Send a blue blouse round to Miss Hammond's suite at Steele Heights Hotel. I ripped the last one off her!*' She attempted to mimic his deep tones. 'Are you laughing at me, Lucien?' Thia eyed him suspiciously and she thought—was *sure*!—she saw his lips twitch.

He chuckled softly. 'Admiring the way you sounded so much like me.'

'Well, I certainly can't stay and have dinner with you *now*.'

'Why not?' All amusement fled and his expression darkened.

'Hello?' She gave him a pitying look. 'Ripped blouse and no bra?'

'I noticed that.' Lucien nodded, silver eyes once again gleaming with laughter even if his expression remained hard and unyielding. 'We've met three times now, and on none of those occasions have you been wearing a bra,' he added curiously.

Thia's cheeks blushed a fiery red as she thought of the revealing gown she had been wearing last night—no way could she have been wearing a bra beneath *that*. And the intimacy of Lucien's caresses in his office earlier today had shown him that she hadn't been wearing a bra under her pink crop top, either. As for ripping her blouse just now and baring her breasts…!

'I—the uniform I have to wear when I'm working at the restaurant is of some heavy material that makes me really hot, so I usually go without one and it's just become a habit,' she explained defensively.

'Don't get me wrong. I'm not complaining.'

'Why am I not surprised?' If she were honest, Thia's initial shock and anger were already fading and she now felt a little like laughing herself—slightly hysterically—at this farcical situation. Hearing her blouse rip, seeing the initial shock on Lucien's face, had been like something out of a sitcom. Except Thia didn't intend letting him off the hook quite that easily...

Oh, she had no doubt that ripping her blouse had been an accident, and that she was as much to blame for it as Lucien was. But if he hadn't been behaving quite so badly by insisting on having his own way—again!—he would never have been in a position to rip her blouse in the first place. Or to bare her breasts. And that really had been embarrassing rather than funny.

Besides, she really did find Lucien far too disturbing when he was only wearing a pair of faded denims and showing lots of bare, muscled flesh. Her ripped blouse was the perfect excuse for her to cry off having dinner with him this evening.

'We haven't talked about the Jonathan Miller situation yet.'

Lucien had just—deliberately?—said the one thing guaranteed to ensure Thia stayed exactly where she was!

Lucien had found himself scowling at the idea of Thia working in a public restaurant night after night, wearing no bra, with those delicious breasts jiggling beneath her uniform for all her male customers to see and ogle.

Just as it now displeased him that Cyn was so obviously rethinking her decision about not having dinner with him only because he had mentioned the Jonathan Miller situation.

The other man had physically hurt her, was responsible for her having had nowhere to sleep last night other than that disreputable hotel, and yet Miller hadn't given a damn what had happened to her when he'd thrown her belongings haphazardly into a suitcase this morning and handed them over to Lucien.

Worst of all, Lucien now knew, from his conversation with Miller, that the other man had been using Cyn for his own purposes. He had believed—wrongly, as it happened—that her presence in his apartment in New York would give the impression that his affair with Simone Carew, was over. Something Cyn was still totally unaware of...

'Well?' he rasped harshly.

She gave a pained frown. 'Perhaps you have a T-shirt I could wear? And maybe you could find one for yourself while you're at it?' she added hopefully.

How did this woman manage to deflate his temper, to make him want to smile, when just seconds ago he had been in a less than agreeable mood at how distracted he had been all afternoon? Because of this woman...

But smile he did as he crossed his arms in front of his chest. 'It really bothers you, doesn't it?'

'All that naked manly chest stuff? Yes, it does.' She nodded. 'And it isn't polite, either.'

'That was a rebuke worthy of my mother!' Lucien was no longer just smiling. He was chuckling softly.

'And?'

'And far be it from me to disobey any woman who can scold like my mother!'

'You're so funny.' She eyed him irritably.

He gave an unconcerned shrug. 'I'll get you one of my T-shirts.' No doubt Cyn would look sexy as hell in one of his over-large tops!

Her eyes narrowed suspiciously. 'You're being very obliging all of a sudden.'

Lucien quirked a dark brow. 'As opposed to…?'

'As opposed to your usual bossy and domineering self—' She broke off to eye Lucien warily as he dropped his arms back to his sides before stepping closer to her.

'You know, Cyn,' he murmured softly, 'it really isn't a good idea to insult your dinner host.'

'Would that be the same dinner host who almost ripped my blouse off me a few minutes ago?'

The very same dinner host who would enjoy nothing more than ripping the rest of that blouse from her body! The realisation made Lucien scowl again.

This woman—too young for him in years and experience, and far too outspoken for her own good—made him forget all his own rules about the women in his life— namely, only older, experienced women, who knew exactly what they were getting—or rather what they were not going to get from him, such as marriage and for ever— when they entered into a relationship with him.

He'd had little time even for the *idea* of marriage after his parents had separated and then divorced so acrimoniously, and making his own fortune before he was even twenty-one had quickly opened his eyes to the fact that most women saw only dollar signs when they looked at him, not the man behind those billions of dollars.

So far in their acquaintance Cyn Hammond had resisted all his offers of help, financial or otherwise, and that pride and independence just made him like her more.

'Good point.' He straightened abruptly. 'I'll be back in a few minutes.'

Thia admired Lucien's loose-limbed walk as he left the room, only able to breathe again once she knew she was alone. She knew from that determined glitter in Lucien's eyes just now that she had only barely—literally!—managed to avert a possibly physically explosive situation. Just as she knew she wasn't sure if she had the strength of will to resist another one...

The truth was her breasts tingled and she grew damp between her thighs every time she so much as dared a glance at all that fascinating naked and bronzed flesh!

Lucien was without doubt the most nerve-sizzling and gorgeous man Thia had ever seen. His whole body was muscled and toned but not too much so, in that muscle-bound and unattractive way some men were. And as for the strength and beauty of that perfectly chiselled face...!

All that wealth and power, and the man also had a face and body that would make poets of both sexes wax lyrical. Hell, *she* was writing a sonnet in her head about him!

And now she was completely alone with him, in his fiftieth floor apartment, with her tattered and ripped blouse pulled tightly across her bare breasts...

She should have kept to her earlier decision to leave. Should have made her escape as quickly and as—

'Here you go—what is it?' Lucien questioned sharply, having come back into the room and seen how pale Cyn's face had become in his absence. Her eyes were dark and troubled smudges between those sooty lashes. 'Cyn?' he prompted again concernedly as she only continued to look at him nervously, with eyes so dark they appeared navy blue.

Her creamy throat moved as she swallowed before speaking. 'I think it would be better if I left now, after all...'

Lucien frowned. 'What have you eaten today?'

She looked puzzled by the change of subject. 'No breakfast, but I bought a hot-dog from a street vendor on the way to the Empire State Building for lunch.'

'Then you need to eat. Put this T-shirt on and then we'll go into the kitchen and see what Dex has provided us with to cook for dinner.' He held out the white T-shirt he had brought back for her to wear, having pulled on a black short-sleeved polo shirt over his own naked chest. A naked chest that had seemed to bother her as much as she bothered him...

Her eyes widened. 'Does Dex do your food shopping for you, too?'

'When necessary, yes.'

'What else does he do for you...?'

'Many, many things,' Lucien drawled derisively.

'You probably wouldn't know how to go about buying your own groceries anyway,' she dismissed ruefully.

'Probably not,' he acknowledged easily. 'Does it bother you that we're eating here?'

Cyn shrugged. 'I just assumed you would be ordering hotel room service this evening.'

'Most of the time I do.' He nodded.

'But you decided tonight would be an exception?' she said knowingly.

'I just thought you would prefer to eat here. Don't tell me.' He grimaced. 'You don't know how to cook?'

'Of course I know how to—' She broke off, eyes narrowing suspiciously. 'You're challenging me to get your own way again, aren't you?'

He quirked a brow. 'Is it working?'

Some of the tension eased from her expression. 'Yes.'

He nodded. 'Then that's exactly what I'm doing.'

Cyn eyed him frustratedly. 'Why are you so determined to keep me here?'

Lucien had absolutely no idea! Especially when he had initially made the suggestion of dinner in his apartment just to see what Cyn's reaction would be. Boy, had *that* backfired on him! 'Why are you so determined to leave?' he came back challengingly.

'Yep, the face of an angel and the wiles of the devil...'

Lucien heard her mutter the words irritably. 'Sorry?' he said. He knew exactly what Cyn had said—he just wanted to see if he could get her to say it again. Especially the part where she said he had the face of an angel...

'Nothing.' Cyn refused to humour him and gave a rueful shake of her head. 'Okay, give me the T-shirt.' She took it out of his outstretched hand before holding it up defensively in front of her breasts. 'Why don't you just disappear off into the kitchen while I slip off my blouse and put this on?' she prompted as he made no effort to leave.

'And if I'd rather stay here and watch you slip off your blouse...'

He enjoyed the flush that instantly coloured her cheeks. Enjoyed teasing Cyn, full-stop. So much so that, despite her being so disruptive and stubborn, teasing her was fast becoming one of Lucien's favourite pastimes. Exclusively so.

'Life is just full of little disappointments!' she came back, with insincere sweetness.

'Oh, it wouldn't be a *little* disappointment, Cyn,' he assured her huskily. And it wouldn't be; Lucien could imagine nothing he would enjoy more than to see Cyn strip out of her blouse, allowing him to look his fill of those pert little breasts and plump, rose-coloured nipples.

'Go,' she instructed firmly.

'And you accuse *me* of being bossy...'

'You've made a fine art of it. I'm just doing it out of self-defence.'

Lucien gave a wicked 'wiles of the devil' grin. 'Do you need defending from me?'

She eyed him irritably. 'Now you're deliberately twisting my words.'

He shrugged. 'Maybe that's because you're trying to spoil my fun.'

She gasped. 'Because I won't let you stand there and gawp at me while I change my blouse?'

'I never *gawp,* Cyn,' he drawled derisively. 'If I stayed I would just stand here quietly and appreciate.'

Her face warmed. 'You aren't staying.'

Lucien gave another appreciative grin; she really was cute when she got her dander up.

Cute? He had never found a woman *cute* in his life!

Until now…

Because Cyn, all hot and bothered and clutching his T-shirt tightly to her as if it were her only defence, was most definitely cute.

'Okay, I'll leave you to change,' he murmured dryly. 'I'll take the bottle of wine and glasses through with me.'

'Fine.' She nodded distractedly.

Anything to get him out of the room while she changed her top, Lucien acknowledged ruefully as he collected up the bottle of wine and glasses before leaving. As if such a flimsy barrier—*any* barrier!—could have stopped him if he had decided he wanted her naked!

'Did you have Dex follow me today…?' Thia prompted huskily when she entered the kitchen.

Lucien turned from taking food out of the huge chrome refrigerator that took up half the space of one wall in what was a beautiful kitchen—white marble floors again, extensive kitchen units a pale grey, a black wooden work table in the middle of the vast room, silver cooking utensils hanging from a rack next to a grey and white cooker. No doubt there was a dishwasher built into one of those cabinets, too.

He hadn't answered her question yet...

'Lucien?' she said softly as she lifted her replenished glass from the table and took a sip of red wine.

'I got so distracted by how sexy you look in my T-shirt that I've forgotten what the question was,' he came back dryly.

No, he hadn't. This man didn't forget anything. *Ever.* And his prevarication was answer enough. He *had* instructed Dex to follow her this afternoon. And Thia wasn't sure how she felt about that. Annoyed that he had dared to have her followed at all, but also concerned as to why he continued to feel it necessary...

And sexy was the last thing she looked in Lucien's white T-shirt. The shoulder seams hung halfway down her arms, meaning that the short sleeves finished below her elbows, and it was so wide across the chest it hung on her like a sack, so long it reached almost to her knees. Well...it didn't hang *completely* like a sack, Thia realised as she glanced down. Colour once again warmed her cheeks as she saw the way the T-shirt skimmed across the tips of her breasts. Across the hard, aroused thrust of her nipples!

Even so, *ridiculous* was the word Thia would have used to describe her current appearance, not sexy.

'*Did* you have Dex follow me today?' she repeated determinedly.

'I did, yes.'

'Can I ask why?' she prompted warily.

'You can if you can make salad and ask at the same time.' Lucien seemed totally relaxed as he placed the makings of a salad down on the kitchen table before returning to the fridge for steaks.

Thia rolled her eyes. 'I'm a woman, Lucien. Multitasking is what we do best.' She took the salad vegetables out of the bags and put them in the sink to wash them.

'That sounds…interesting.' He turned to arch mocked brows.

She was utterly charmed by this man when he became temptingly playful. And she shouldn't allow herself to be.

It wasn't just those twelve years in age that separated them, it was what Lucien had done in those twelve years that set them so far apart—as evidenced by all those photographs of him online, taken with the multitude of women he had briefly shared his life with. Or, more accurately, his bed.

And at the grand age of twenty-three Thia was still a virgin. Not deliberately. Not even consciously as in 'saving herself' for the man she loved and wanted to marry.

She had just been too busy keeping her life together since her parents died to do more than accept the occasional date, and very rarely a second from the same man. Jonathan had been the exception, but even he had become just a friend rather than a boyfriend. Thia had never been even slightly tempted to deepen their relationship into something more.

And yet in the twenty-four hours she had known Lucien Steele she seemed to have thought of nothing else but how it would feel to go to bed with him. To make love with him.

Weird.

Dangerous!

Because Lucien might desire her, but he didn't do falling in love and long-term relationships. And why should he when he could have any woman—as many women as he wanted? Except...

'What are you thinking about so deeply that it's making you frown...?' he asked huskily.

Thia snapped herself out of imagining how it would feel to have Lucien Steele fall in love with her. A ridiculous thought when she so obviously wasn't his type.

And yet here she was, in this apartment, with a relaxed and charming Lucien, and the two of them intended to cook dinner together just like any other couple spending the evening at home together.

She took another sip of wine before answering him. 'Nothing of any importance,' she dismissed brightly as she put the wine glass down to drain the vegetables. 'Do you have any dressing to go with the salad or shall I make some?'

'Can you do that?'

Thia gave him a scathing glance as she crossed the room to open the vast refrigerator and look inside for ingredients for a dressing. 'I'm a waitress, remember?'

'You're a student, working as a waitress in your spare time,' he corrected lightly.

She straightened slowly. 'No, I'm actually a waitress who's working for a degree in my spare time,' she insisted firmly. 'And you still haven't answered my original question.'

'Which was...?'

'Why did you have Dex follow me today?' she repeated determinedly, knowing that Lucien was once again trying to avoid answering one of her questions.

He shrugged. 'Dex suggested it was necessary. I agreed with him.'

'What does that mean?'

'It means that he was obviously as concerned about your walking about New York on your own as I was. You might have been robbed or attacked. Speaking of which...' Lucien strolled across the kitchen, checking her wrist first, which was only slightly reddened from where Jonathan's fingers had twisted it, before gently peeling back the sleeve of the white T-shirt. He drew in a hissing breath as he saw the livid black and blue bruises on the top of her arm.

'They look worse than they feel.' Thia pulled out of his grasp before turning to take down a chopping board and starting to dice vegetables for the salad. 'Isn't it time you started cooking the steaks...?' she prompted dryly.

'Deflection is only a delaying tactic, Cyn. Sooner or later we're going to talk about those bruises,' he assured her grimly.

'Then let's make it later,' she dismissed. 'Steaks, Lucien?' she repeated pointedly when she turned to find him still watching her from between narrowed lids.

He gave a deep sigh. 'Okay, Cyn, we'll do this your way for now,' he conceded. 'We'll eat first and then we'll talk.'

'It really is true what they say—men don't multi-task!' She smiled teasingly.

'Maybe we just prefer to do one thing at a time and en- sure that we do it really, really well?' Lucien murmured huskily, suggestively, and made a determined effort to damp down the renewed anger he felt at seeing those bruises on Cyn's delicately lovely skin.

Colour washed over her cheeks. 'You're obviously wast- ing your talents as an entrepreneur, Lucien; you should have been a comedian.'

But what Lucien was actually doing was mirroring her own deflection…

Because he was once again so angry after seeing Cyn's bruises—bruises inflicted by Miller—that he didn't want to have to answer her question as to why he'd had Dex follow her on her outing this afternoon just yet.

Oh, he accepted that he would have to answer it some time—just not yet. Talking about the reason Dex had followed her to the Empire State Building earlier, and how his concern was directly linked to Jonathan Miller, was not conducive to the two of them being able to enjoy cooking and eating a meal together. And, despite Lucien's earlier irritation, he was totally enjoying Cyn's company.

'How do you like your steak?' he prompted as he moved to turn up the heat beneath the griddle, hoping he remembered how to cook steaks. Cyn's assumption earlier had been a correct one: it had been years since Lucien had cooked for himself or anyone else.

'Medium rare, please,' she answered distractedly as she put the salad into a wooden bowl. 'Are we eating in here or in the dining room?'

'Which would you prefer?'

Her brows rose. 'You're actually asking for my opinion about something now?'

Lucien turned to lean back against one of the kitchen cabinets. 'Smart-mouthed young ladies are likely to get their bottoms spanked!'

Her eyes widened. 'Dinner hosts who threaten their female guests are likely to get cayenne pepper sprinkled on their half of the salad dressing. What is it?' she questioned curiously as Lucien began to chuckle. 'You aren't used to being teased like this, are you?' she realised slowly.

'No, I'm not,' he conceded ruefully, unable to remember the last time anyone had dared to tease him, let alone argue with him in the way that Cyn so often did. 'My mother does it occasionally, just to keep it real, but only mom/son stuff.' He shrugged.

Cyn eyed him wistfully. 'Have you remained close to both your parents?'

He nodded. 'I don't see either of them as often as I could or should—but, yeah, I've stayed close to both of them.'

'That's nice.'

Lucien looked at her searchingly. 'Don't you have any family of your own?'

'None close, no.' She grimaced. 'Don't feel sorry for me, Lucien,' she added lightly as he still frowned. 'I had great parents. I lost them a little earlier than I would have wished or wanted, but I still count myself lucky to have had them to love and be loved by for seventeen years.'

The more Lucien came to know about Cynthia Hammond, the more he came to appreciate that she really was unlike any other woman he had ever known. So obviously beautiful—inside as well as out. And that outward beauty she could so easily have used to her advantage these past six years, if she had wanted to, by snaring herself a rich husband to support her. Instead she had chosen independence.

No feeling sorry for herself at the premature death of her parents. She was just grateful to have had them for as long as she had. And instead of bitching about the necessity to fend for herself after their deaths she had picked herself up and started working her way through university. And instead of bemoaning the fact that Jonathan Miller, a man she had believed to be her friend, had let her down royally since she'd come to New York she had done all she could to remain loyal to him.

It was fast becoming an irresistible combination to Lucien when coupled with the fact that she was so bright and bubbly she made him laugh, was mouthwateringly beautiful, and obviously intelligent.

She also, Lucien discovered a short time later—once the two of them were seated opposite each other at the small candlelit table in the window of the dining room, where they could look out over the city—ate with such passionate relish that he found himself enjoying watching her, devouring her with his eyes rather than eating his own food.

The expression of pleasure on her face as she took her first forkful of dessert—a New York cheesecake from a famous deli in the city—was almost orgasmic. Her eyes were closed, cheeks flushed, pouting lips slightly moist as she licked her tongue across them.

Lucien groaned inwardly as his erection, having remained painfully hard and throbbing inside his denims during the whole of dinner, rose even higher, seeming to take on a life of its own. To such a degree that he had to shift on his seat in order to make himself more comfortable!

Not that he was complaining. No, not at all. His thoughts had turned to the possibility of taking Cyn to his bed, of making love to her until he saw that same look on her face over and over again as he pleasured her to orgasm after orgasm.

'That was…indescribably good.' Thia sighed her pleasure as she placed her fork down on her empty dessert plate. 'Aren't you going to eat yours…?' She hadn't realised until now that Lucien was watching her rather than eating his own cheesecake.

Dinner with Lucien Steele had been far more enjoyable than she had thought it would be. The food had been good, and the conversation even more so as they'd discussed their eclectic tastes in books, films, television and art. Surprisingly, their opinions on a lot of those subjects had been the same, and the times when they hadn't been they had argued teasingly rather than forcefully. Thia liked this more relaxed Lucien. Too much so!

Lucien pushed his untouched dessert plate across the table towards her. 'You have it.'

'I couldn't eat another bite,' Thia refused, before chuckling huskily. 'I bet you're doubly glad now not to be seen out in public with me. I've realised since I've been here that it isn't really the done thing in New York for a woman to actually *enjoy* eating. We're supposed to just pick at the food on our plate before pushing it away uninterestedly. I've always enjoyed my food too much to be able to do that.' She gave a rueful shake of her head. 'Besides, it's rude not to eat when someone has taken you out for a meal or cooked for you. And I've enjoyed this much more than going out, anyway. Cooking dinner is probably the first normal thing I've done since coming to New York! Do you think…?' Her voice trailed off as she realised that Lucien had gone very quiet.

An unusual occurrence for him, when he seemed to have something to say on so many other subjects!

'Lucien…?' Thia eyed him warily as she saw the way his eyes glittered across at her with that intense silver light. His mouth had thinned, his jaw tensed—all signs, she recognised, of his displeasure.

What had she said to annoy him? Perhaps he hadn't

liked her comment on the expectations of New York society? After all, he was a member of that society.

Whatever she had said, Lucien obviously wasn't happy about it...

CHAPTER SEVEN

THERE WAS A cold weight of anger in Lucien's chest, making it difficult for him to breathe, let alone speak. Cyn actually thought—she believed that he—

Lucien stood up abruptly, noisily, from the table, thrusting his hands into his pockets as he turned to look sightlessly out of the window, breathing deeply through his nose in an effort to control that anger. If he said anything now he was only going to make the situation worse than it already was.

'Lucien?'

The uncertainty, hesitation in Cyn's voice succeeded in annoying him all over again. Just minutes ago they had been talking so comfortably together—occasionally arguing light-heartedly about a book, a film or a painting they had both read or seen, but for the most part finding they shared a lot of the same likes and dislikes.

That easy conversation, coupled with Cyn's obvious enjoyment of the food they had prepared, had resulted in Lucien feeling relaxed in her company in a way he never had with any other woman. Not completely relaxed. He was too aware of everything about her for that: her silky midnight hair, those beautiful glowing cobalt blue eyes, her flushed cheeks, the moist pout of her lips, the way his borrowed T-shirt hugged the delicious uptilting curve of her breasts whenever she moved her arms to emphasise a point in conversation… But Cyn's complete lack of awareness of Lucien's appreciation of those things had been another part of his enjoyment of the evening. There had been none of the overt flirting that he experienced with so many other women, or the flaunting of her sexuality in an effort to impress him. Cyn had just been her usual outspoken self. An outspoken self that he found totally enticing…

And now this!

He drew a deep breath into his starved lungs before turning back to face her, his own face slightly in shadow as he stood out of the full glow of the flickering candlelight. 'You believe I made a conscious decision not to take you out to a restaurant for dinner this evening because I didn't want to be seen publicly in your company?'

Ah. That was the comment that had annoyed him…

Thia gave a dismissive shrug. 'It's no big deal, Lucien. Believe me, I've seen photos of the women you usually escort, and I don't even come close—'

'Seen how?' he prompted suspiciously.

She gave a self-conscious grimace. 'I—er—checked you out online earlier this evening,' she admitted reluctantly, wishing Lucien wasn't standing in the shadows so that she could see the expression on his face.

'Why did you do that?'

'Because I wanted to know more about the man I had agreed to have dinner with, alone in his apartment,' she came back defensively. 'I was using that sense of self-preservation you seem to think I have so little of.'

He gave a terse inclination of his head. 'And after reading about me online, seeing photographs of the women I usually escort, you came to the conclusion I was deliberately keeping you hidden away in my apartment this evening because I didn't want to be seen out in public with you?'

'Oh, no. I decided that after you made the invitation earlier today,' Thia dismissed easily.

His brows rose. 'Can I ask why?'

She sighed heavily. 'When was the last time you cooked dinner for a woman in your apartment?'

'What does that—?'

'Just answer the question, please, Lucien,' she cajoled teasingly.

He shrugged. 'I think tonight is the first time I've cooked dinner in my apartment at all—let alone for or with a woman.'

'Exactly.' Thia had noticed earlier that none of the state-of-the-art equipment in the kitchen looked as if it had ever been used.

His mouth thinned. 'If you must know, I made the invitation initially because I suspected your having dinner alone with me here would throw you into something of a panic, and I wanted to see what you would do.'

'And I called your bluff and accepted.' She gave a rueful shake of her head.

'Yes, you did.' He nodded slowly.

'Probably best not to challenge me again, hmm?'

'I don't regret a single moment of this evening.'

Thia's cheeks bloomed with heated colour as she recalled the earlier part of the evening, when Lucien had ripped her blouse. 'You were also aware, because I told you so last night, that New York society has absolutely no interest in furthering its acquaintance with a waitress from

London. Just think how shocked they would have been to see Lucien Steele in a restaurant with *me!*'

He breathed his impatience. 'I don't give a damn what anyone else thinks.'

'I'm really not in the least offended by any of this, Lucien.' Thia smiled. 'I had a good time this evening. As for New York society…I don't enjoy their company either, so why should it bother me what any of them think of me?'

'Do you have so little interest in what *I* might think of you?' he prompted softly.

That was a difficult question to answer. Thia was so attracted to Lucien that of course it mattered to her whether or not he liked her—just as it mattered what he thought of her. But by the same token it also didn't. Because they wouldn't ever see each other again after tonight. Even the money for the suite, which Thia was so determined to pay back to him, no matter how long it took her to do so, could be sent to his office at Steele Tower when the time came. They had no reason to see each other again once she left here this evening. Which, although disappointing, was just a fact of life. Their totally different lives…

'I like to think I'm a realist, Lucien,' she answered lightly. 'Zillionaire Lucien Steele—' she pointed to him '—and Cynthia Hammond, waitress/student, living from payday to payday.' She pointed to her own chest. 'Not exactly a basis for friendship.'

'I have no interest in being your *friend!*' he rasped with harsh dismissal.

She flinched at the starkness of his statement. 'I believe I just said that—'

'I have no interest in being your friend because I want to be your lover. Touch me.' Lucien stepped forward to grasp her hand impatiently in his before lifting it to the bulge at the front of his denims.

Evidence of an arousal that Thia had been completely unaware of until that moment. She couldn't possibly remain unaware of it now—not when she could feel the long, hard length of Lucien's swollen shaft, the heat of it burning her fingertips as she stroked them tentatively against him. Her eyes widened as she felt the jolt, the throb, of that arousal in response to her slightest caress.

She moistened her lips with the tip of her tongue and looked up at Lucien. 'Does one preclude the other...?'

His mouth twisted derisively. 'In my experience, yes.'

In Thia's limited experience too...

She'd only dated maybe half a dozen times these past six years, and had always ended up being friends with those men rather than lovers. Including Jonathan. Although she suspected that their friendship had ceased after his behaviour yesterday, and yet again this morning, when he had packed her belongings into her suitcase and handed it over to Lucien seemingly without a second thought as to where or how she was.

'Stop thinking about Miller,' Lucien rasped.

She blinked. 'How did you know—?'

'I think I'm intelligent enough to know when the woman I'm with is thinking about another man,' he bit out harshly, having known from the way Cyn's gaze had become slightly unfocused that her attention was no longer completely here with him. Which, considering her hand was currently pressed against his pulsing erection, was less than flattering.

She gave a rueful smile. 'I sincerely doubt it's happened to you often enough for that to be true.'

'It's never happened to me before, as far as I'm aware,' he grated.

He lifted her hand away impatiently before pulling her to her feet, so that she now stood just inches in front of him. His other hand moved beneath her chin to raise her face, so that she had no choice but to look up at him. 'And, yes, I was challenging you earlier. I wanted to unnerve you a little by inviting you to my apartment. But I did *not* have dinner with you here as a way of hiding you away. I'm insulted that you should ever have thought that I did.' He was more than insulted—he actually felt hurt that Cyn could believe him capable of behaving in that way where she was concerned...

Thia could see that he was. His eyes glittered danger-ously, there was angry colour along those high cheekbones, his lips had thinned and his jaw thrust forward forcefully.

'I apologise if I was mistaken.'

'You were,' he bit out. 'You still are.'

She nodded; Lucien was too upset not to be telling her the truth.

'Have I succeeded in ruining the evening?' She looked up at him through long dark lashes.

Lucien eyed her impatiently. 'I have absolutely no idea.'

She drew in a shaky breath. 'How about we clear away in here while you decide?'

His eyes narrowed. 'Are you humouring me, Thia?'

The fact that Lucien had called her Thia for the first time was indicative of how upset he was. 'Is it working?' she deliberately used the same phrase he had to her ear-lier, when she had challenged him about always wanting his own way.

Some of the tension left his shoulders. 'Maybe a little,' he conceded dryly. 'And we can just blow out the candles in here and leave all this for housekeeping to clear away in the morning.' He indicated the dinner table beside them.

Thia's stomach did a somersault. 'Oh...'

He gave a rueful shake of his head. 'I have no idea how you do that...'

'Do what?' She looked up at him curiously.

'Make me want to laugh when just seconds ago I was so angry with you I wanted to kiss you senseless!' He gave a self-disgusted shake of his head as the last of his earlier tension eased from his expression.

'Senseless, hmm?' Thia eyed him teasingly. 'According to you, that wouldn't be too difficult!'

'See?' Lucien chuckled wryly, shaking his head.

The sudden hunger in Lucien's gaze told Thia this was the ideal time for her to suggest she return to her own suite in the hotel, to thank Lucien for dinner, and his company and conversation, and then leave, never to see or hear from him again.

It was the latter part of that plan that stopped her from doing any of those things... 'Does one preclude the other?' she repeated provocatively, daringly.

'You *want* me to kiss you senseless...?' he prompted gruffly.

She drew in a sharp breath, knowing this was a moment of truth. 'Even more than I enjoy watching you laugh,' she acknowledged shyly.

Lucien's piercing gaze narrowed on her searchingly. 'Be very sure about this, Thia,' he finally warned her. 'I want you so badly that once I have you in my bed I'm unlikely to let you out of it again until I've made love to you at least half a dozen times.'

Thia's heart leapt as he jumped from kissing her senseless to taking her to his bed. Her heart pounded loudly in her chest at the thought of all that currently leashed but promised passion. Of having this man—having *Lucien Steele!*—want to make love to her with such an intensity of feeling. It was an intensity of passion she didn't know, in her inexperience, that she could even begin to match...

But she would at least like to the opportunity to try!

'Can you do that? I thought that men needed to...to rest for a while...recuperate before...well, you know...'

He arched dark brows. 'Let's give it a try, shall we? Besides, I don't recall giving any time limit for making love to you those half a dozen times.'

No, he hadn't, had he? Thia acknowledged even as her cheeks burned. In embarrassment or excitement? She really wasn't sure! 'I only have one more full day left before I leave New York, and don't you have to go to work tomorrow?'

'Not if I have you in my bed, no,' Lucien assured her softly.

Thia's heart was now beating a wild tattoo in her chest and she breathed shallowly, feeling as if she were standing on the edge of a precipice: behind her was the safety of returning to her own hotel suite, in front of her the unknown of sharing Lucien's bed for the night.

She drew in a shaky breath. 'Well, then...'

Lucien's control was now so tightly stretched that he felt as if the slightest provocation from Cyn would make it snap. That *he* would snap, and simply rip that T-shirt off her in the same way he had her blouse earlier.

It was an uncomfortable feeling for a man who never lost control. Of any situation and especially of himself. But this woman—barely tall enough to reach his shoulders, so slender he felt as if he might crush her if he held her too tightly—had thrown him off balance from the moment he first saw her.

Just twenty-four admittedly eventful hours ago…!

'Well, then…what…?' he prompted slowly.

The slenderness of Cyn's throat moved as she swallowed before answering him. 'Let's go to bed.'

'No more arguments or questions? Just "Let's go to bed"?' He raised dark brows.

She moistened her lips with the tip of her tongue before replying huskily. 'I—if that's okay with you, yes.'

If it was okay with him?

If Cyn only knew how much he wanted to rip her clothes off right now, before laying her down on the carpet and just taking her, right here and right now, plunging into the warmth of her again and again, then she would be probably be shocked out of her mind. *He* was out of his mind—for this woman.

Which was the reason Lucien was going to do none of those things. He was balanced on the edge of his self-control right now, and needed to slow things down. For Cyn's sake rather than his own. Because he didn't want to frighten her with the intensity of the desire she aroused in him.

'It's more than okay with me, Cyn,' he assured her gruffly, blowing out the candles on the table and throwing the room into darkness before putting his arm about the slenderness of her waist as he guided her out of the dining room and down the hallway towards his bedroom.

Thia's nervousness deepened with each step she took down the hallway towards sharing Lucien's bed. To sharing Lucien Steele's bed!

Those other women—the ones she had seen online,

photographed with Lucien—had all looked sophisticated and confident, and they no doubt had the physical experience, the confidence in their sexuality, to go with those looks. Whereas she—

For goodness' sake, she was twenty-three years old and she was going to lose her virginity some time—so why not with Lucien, a man she found as physically exciting as she did knee-meltingly attractive. A man who made her feel safe and protected as well as desired.

Was that *all* she felt for Lucien?

Or was she already a little—more than a little!—in love with him?

And wouldn't that be the biggest mistake of her life—in love with a man whose relationships never seemed to last longer than a month?

'Cyn?'

She blinked as she realised that while she had been so lost in thought they had already entered what must be the master bedroom—Lucien's bedroom. A huge four-poster bed dominated the shadowed room, and those shadows made it impossible for her to tell whether the black, white and chrome décor Lucien seemed to prefer had spilt over into his bedroom. The carpet beneath her feet was certainly dark, as were the curtains and the satin cover and cushions piled on the bed, but the actual colours eluded her in the darkness...

'Say now if you're feeling...less than sure about this,' Lucien prompted gruffly, his hands resting lightly on her waist as he turned her so that she was looking up at him.

The one thing Thia was totally sure about was that she wanted Lucien. Her body ached with that longing; her breasts were swollen and tingling, nipples hard and aroused, and there was a heated dampness between her thighs. At the same time she *so* didn't want to be a disappointment to him!

It would have been better if he had just made love to her right there in the dining room. If he hadn't given her time to think, to become so nervous.

But this was Lucien Steele, a man of sophistication and control. He wasn't the type of man to be so desperate for a woman he would rip her clothes off—well, apart from Thia's blouse earlier. But that had been an accident rather than passion! Or the type of man to make wild and desperate love to her.

Thia chewed worriedly on her bottom lip as she looked up into his hard and shadowed face, at those pale eyes glittering down at her intently in the darkness. 'I am a little nervous,' she admitted softly. 'I'm not as experienced as you are, and there have been all those other women for you—' She broke off as he placed silencing fingertips against her lips.

'I'm clean medically, if that's what's bothering you.'

'It isn't,' she assured him hastily, her cheeks blushing a fiery-red. 'And I—I'm—er—clean too.' How could she be anything else when she had never been to bed with anyone?

He nodded abruptly. 'And that's the last time I want to talk about other people for either of us.'

'But—'

'Cyn, neither of us is experienced when it comes to each other.' He moved his hand to gently cup her cheek. 'Half the fun will be in learning which caress or touch pleases the other,' he added huskily.

Fun? Going to bed with a man, making love with him, was *fun?* Thia had never thought of it in quite that light before, but she had no reason to doubt what Lucien said. He had always been totally, bluntly honest when he spoke to her.

'You're right.' She shook off her feelings of nervousness and straightened determinedly. 'Is it okay if I just use the bathroom?'

'Of course.' Lucien released her before stepping back. 'Don't be long,' he added huskily as he opened the door to the adjoining bathroom and switched on the light for her.

Thia leant back weakly against the door the moment it closed behind her and she was alone in the bathroom, her legs shaking so badly she could no longer stand without that support at her back.

Lucien stared at that closed bathroom door for several seconds after Cyn had closed it so firmly behind her, a frown darkening his brow as he considered her behaviour just now. She was more than just nervous. She seemed almost afraid. Just of him? Or of any man?

Why? Had something happened to her in the past? Maybe even with Miller? Something to make her nervous about going to bed with another man? It seemed highly possible, when she'd admitted she *had* been thinking of the other man when he'd called her on it a few minutes ago. It made Lucien wish now that he had given in to the impulse he'd had this morning to punch the other man in the face as Miller threw Cyn's belongings into her suitcase without so much as a thought or a question as to what was going to happen to her.

Whatever the reason for Cyn's nervousness, Lucien didn't intend adding to it. He was glad now that he had shown such restraint a few minutes ago. He wanted to make slow and leisurely love to her, no matter the cost to his own self-control. Wanted to touch and pleasure Cyn until she could think of nothing else, no one else, but him and their lovemaking—

Lovemaking? Was he actually falling in love with Cyn?

It was an emotion he had always avoided in the past, and his choice of women—experienced and self-absorbed—was probably a reflection of that decision. Until now. Cyn was like no other woman he had ever known. And, yes, she was slipping—already *had* slipped?—beneath his defences.

None of which he wanted to explore too deeply right now.

Lucien crossed the bedroom to turn on the bedside lamp before turning back the bedcovers and quickly removing his clothes. His shaft bobbed achingly now that it was free of the confines of his denims.

He lingered beside the bed, looking down at the black silk bedsheets as he imagined how right Cyn would look lying there, with that beautiful, pale, luminescent body spread out before him like a feast he wanted to gorge himself on. Just the thought of it was enough to cause his aching erection to throb eagerly, releasing pre-cum onto the bulbous tip before it spilt over and dripped slowly down his length.

Sweet heaven!

Lucien grasped his length before smoothing that liquid over it with the soft pad of his thumb, knowing he had never been this aroused before, this needy of any woman. Not in the way he now needed—desired—Cyn...

Thia studied herself critically in the mirror over the bathroom sink once she had taken her clothes off. Her face was pale, eyes fever-bright, her hair a silky black curtain across her bared shoulders. Her skin was smooth and un-

blemished, breasts firm and uptilting, tipped by engorged
rosy-red nipples. Her waist was slender, hips flaring gently around the dark thatch of curls between her thighs,
her legs long and slender.

She was as ready as she was ever going to be to walk
out of here and go to bed with Lucien!

That courage didn't include walking out stark naked,
though, and quickly she pulled on the black silk robe she
had found hanging behind the bathroom door, tying the
belt of what was obviously Lucien's own bathrobe tightly
about the slenderness of her waist before taking a deep
breath and opening the bathroom door, switching off the
light…

Only to come to an abrupt halt in that doorway as she
realised that Lucien had turned on a single lamp on the
bedside table, allowing her to see that the bedroom was
indeed decorated in those black, white and chrome colours Lucien favoured. Lucien himself was already lying
in the bed, that bronzed chest bare, only a black silk sheet
draped over him and concealing his lower body.

She had thought they would make love in the darkness—had imagined slipping almost anonymously beneath
the bedcovers and then—

'Take off the robe, Cyn.'

She raised a startled gaze to Lucien and saw he was
leaning up on his elbow, causing the muscles to bulge in
his arm, as he looked across at her with those glittering
silver eyes. The darkness of his overlong hair was now
tousled and falling rakishly over his forehead, probably
after he had removed his T-shirt.

He was utterly beautiful in the same way that a deadly
predator was beautiful—with all the power in that sleek
and muscled body just waiting to be unleashed.

'I want to look at you,' he encouraged gruffly.

Thia's throat had gone so dry she could barely speak. 'Doesn't that work both ways?'

'Sure.' The intensity of his gaze never left hers as he slowly kicked down the black silk sheet.

Thia's breath caught in her throat and she could only stand and stare. At the width of his shoulders. At his muscled chest covered in that misting of dark hair. She could now see that it trailed down over his navel and grew thicker at the base of his arousal.

Oh. Good. Grief.

That was never going to fit inside her!

Lucien was a tall man, several inches over six feet and his bronze-skinned body was deeply muscled, so it was no surprise that his aroused shaft was in perfect proportion to the rest of him—at least nine, possibly ten inches long, and so thick and wide Thia doubted her fingers would meet if she were to clasp them around it as she so longed, ached to do. Just as she longed to caress, to touch and become familiar with every perfect inch of him!

Even so, her wide gaze moved back unerringly to the heavy thrust of his arousal.

Maybe it was like those 'one size fits all' pairs of socks or gloves you could buy? Hadn't she read somewhere, in one of those sophisticated women's magazines often left lying around in a dentist's waiting room, that if a woman was prepared properly, with lots of foreplay, she was capable of stretching *down there,* accommodating any length or thickness—

'Cyn?'

Her startled gaze moved back up to Lucien's face and, her cheeks flamed with colour as she met the heat in his eyes. He looked across at her expectantly, his hand held out to her invitingly, obviously waiting for her to unfasten the robe and remove it completely before joining him in the bed...

CHAPTER EIGHT

LUCIEN TAMPED DOWN the urgency he felt to get out of bed and go to Cyn and instead waited patiently, allowing Cyn to take her time, to adjust. Allowing her to be the one to come *to* him.

They had all night—hours and hours for him to pleasure her into coming *for* him!

Right now her face was so pale that her ivory skin appeared almost translucent. Blue veins showed at the delicacy of her temples and her cobalt-blue eyes were dark and shadowed as she continued to look across at him, cheeks pale, her lips slightly parted, as if she were having trouble breathing.

'I'm starting to get a complex, Cyn,' he murmured ruefully.

Her startled gaze was quickly raised to his. 'You are…? But you're beautiful, Lucien,' she murmured huskily.

'So are you.' Lucien slowly lifted his arm to hold out his hand to her again, holding his breath as the nervousness in Cyn's gaze told him that she might turn tail and run if he made any sort of hasty move in her direction. Something he found surprisingly endearing rather than irritating.

Cyn was so different from the women he had been with in the past. Beautiful women, certainly, but it was usually a pampered and sometimes enhanced beauty, after hours spent at beauty salons and spas or beneath a plastic surgeon's knife. And all those women, without exception, had been confident of their perfectly toned bodies, of their sexual appeal.

Cyn, on the other hand, obviously had no time or money to spend at beauty salons or spas. The sleekness of her body was just as nature had intended it, as was her breathtaking beauty. A beauty that was all the more appealing because Cyn seemed so completely unaware of it, of its effect on him and every other man she came into contact with. The women in New York society might have no interest in furthering the acquaintance of student/waitress Cynthia Hammond from England, but Lucien very much doubted the men felt the same way!

And Lucien was the lucky man who had her all to himself—for tonight, at least…

Thia was frozen in place—couldn't move, couldn't speak, could only continue to stand in the bathroom doorway as she stared across at Lucien in mute appeal, inwardly cursing herself for her gauche behaviour but unable to do anything about it.

'Please, Cyn!' he said gruffly.

It was the aching need that deepened Lucien's voice to a growl which finally broke her out of that icy cage, causing Thia to take one step forward, and then another, until she finally stood beside the bed, allowing Lucien to reach out and enfold one of her trembling hands in his much warmer one.

He lifted it slowly to his lips, his gaze still holding hers as those lips grazed the back of her knuckles, tongue rasping, tasting. 'You are so very beautiful, Cyn.'

The warmth of his breath brushed lightly against her over-sensitised skin. She swallowed. 'I believe you'll find the saying is *Beautiful as sin...*'

'Nothing could be as beautiful as you.' He gave a slow shake of his head.

At this moment in time, Thia finished ruefully inside her head. Right here and right now she had Lucien's complete attention. But tomorrow it would be different—

Oh, to hell with tomorrow!

For once in her carefully constructed life she was going to take not what was safe, or what she could afford, but what she *wanted*.

And tonight she so very much wanted to be here with Lucien.

She lowered her lashes and pulled her hand gently from his grasp, before moving to unfasten the belt of the robe, shrugging the black silk from her shoulders and hearing Lucien's breath catching in his throat as she allowed the robe to slide down her arms to fall onto the carpet at her feet. She was completely naked in front of him as she finally raised her lashes to look at him.

'You're exquisite,' Lucien groaned, taking the time to admire each and every curve and dip and hollow of her naked body before moving smoothly up onto his knees at the edge of the bed, nullifying the difference in their heights, putting his face on a level with hers as his arms moved about the slenderness of her waist.

Her hands moved up to clasp onto his shoulders as he pulled her in closer to him. Her skin felt so soft and she was so slender Lucien felt as if he could wrap his arms about her twice. His palms spread, fingers splayed across her shapely bottom, as he settled those slender curves into his much harder ones before touching his mouth lightly against hers.

Lucien moved his lips across her creamy soft cheek to the softness beneath her ear, along the column of her throat. The rasp of his tongue tasted the shady hollows at the base of her throat as one of his hands curled about the gentle thrust of her breast, the soft pad of his thumb unerringly finding, stroking the aroused nipple.

'Look at the two of us, Cyn,' he groaned throatily. 'See how beautiful we are together,' he encouraged as she looked down to where his hand cupped her breast. He looked at that contrast himself. Ivory and bronze...

Her skin looked so white against the natural bronze tone of Lucien's. Ice and fire. And fire invariably melted ice, didn't it?

Thia's inhibitions were melting, and her earlier apprehension along with it, as she twined her arms over those strong, muscled shoulders, her fingers becoming entangled in silky dark hair as she initiated a kiss between them this time—gentle at first, and then deeper, hungrier, as their passion flared out of control.

Lucien continued to kiss her even as Thia felt his arms move beneath her knees and about her shoulders. He lifted her easily up and onto the bed, lying her down almost reverently onto the black silk sheets before stretching his long length beside her, his gaze holding hers before his head lowered, lashes falling down against those hard cheekbones, and his lips parted. He drew her nipple into his mouth, gently suckling, licking that aroused nub, even as his hands caressed the ribcage beneath her breasts, the slender curve of her waist, before moving lower still.

Thia arched into his caresses as her nervousness faded completely and pleasure coursed through her—building,

building, until she moved restlessly against him, needing more, wanting more. She was groaning low in her throat as she felt Lucien's fingers against the silky curls between her thighs, seeking and finding the nubbin hidden there and moving lower still, to where the slickness of her juices had made her wet, so very wet, circling, moistening her swollen lips.

His thumb pressed delicately against the nubbin above and still she wanted more, needed more. She felt as if she were poised on the edge of a precipice, one that burned. Flames were licking up and through her body, sensitising her to every touch of Lucien's hands, to every sweep of his tongue across the swollen hardness of her nipples, as he divided his attentions between the two, first licking, then suckling. Each lick and suck seemed to increase the volcanic pleasure rising between her thighs.

'Please, Lucien!' Her fingers tightened in his hair and she pulled his head up, forced him to look at her with eyes that glittered pure silver. His lips were swollen and moist. 'Please…!' she groaned beseechingly. 'Lucien…'

He moved so swiftly, so urgently, that Thia barely had time to realise he now lay between her parted thighs.

'You are so beautiful *here,* Cyn,' he murmured. His breath was a warm caress as the soft pads of his thumbs slicked her juices over those plump folds and the sensitive knot of flesh above. 'Look at us, Cyn,' he encouraged gruffly. 'Move up onto your elbows and show me those pretty breasts.'

Thia would have done anything Lucien asked of her at that moment. Her cheeks were flushed, eyes fever-bright, as she looked down at him, at his hair midnight-black against the paleness of her skin, bronzed back long and muscled, buttocks taut.

His gaze held hers as he cupped his hands beneath her bottom and held her up and open to him. 'I'm going to eat you up, Cyn,' he promised, and his head lowered and his tongue swept, rasped against her slick folds.

Over and over again he lapped her gently, and then harder, until Thia was no longer able to hold herself up on her elbows as the pleasure grew and grew inside her. Lucien's fingers were digging almost painfully into the globes of her bottom as he thrust a tongue deep inside her slick channel, sending her over that volcanic edge as the pleasure surged and swelled, surged and swelled again and again, taking Thia into the magic of her first ever climax.

It was the first of many. Lucien continued to pleasure her, taking her up to that plateau again and again, each time ensuring that he took her over the edge and into the maelstrom of pleasure on the other side, until Thia's throat felt ragged and sore from the sobbing cries of each climax. Her body was becoming completely boneless as those releases came swifter and fiercer each time, and Lucien's arms were looped beneath her thighs now, holding her wider to allow for the ministrations of his lips and tongue, increasing her pleasure each and every time she came.

'No more, Lucien!' Thia finally gasped, her fingers digging into his muscled shoulders. Blackness had begun to creep into the edges of her vision and she knew she couldn't take any more. There was foreplay and then there was hurtling over the edge into unconsciousness. Which was exactly what was going to happen if her body was racked by one more incredible climax! 'Please, Lucien. I just can't…' She looked at him pleadingly as he raised his head to look at her, his cheeks flushed, lips swollen and moist.

'I'm sorry—I got carried away. Are you okay?' He gave a shake of his head.

'Yes...'

'You just taste so delicious...' He groaned achingly as he moved up beside her, his hands shaking slightly as he cupped the heat of her cheek. 'Like the finest, rarest brandy. I just couldn't stop drinking your sweet essence. Taste yourself, Cyn,' he encouraged huskily, and brushed his lips lightly against hers.

The taste was sweet and slightly salty, with an underlying musk. Thia's cheeks blazed with colour at the knowledge that Lucien now knew her body inside and out, more intimately than she did. That he—

She tensed to stillness as the telephone began to ring on the bedside table. Lucien scowled his displeasure and didn't even glance at the telephone. 'Ignore it,' he rasped.

'But—'

'Nothing and no one is going to intrude on the two of us being together tonight. I won't allow it,' he stated determinedly.

'But it could be important—'

'Obviously not,' he murmured in satisfaction as the telephone fell quiet after the sixth ring, allowing him to reach out and remove the receiver to prevent it from ringing and disturbing them again.

He rolled onto his back, hands firm on Cyn's hips, and lifted her up and over him. Her thighs now straddled his, and the dampness of her folds pressed against the hardness of his shaft as she sat upright, the swell of her breasts, tipped by strawberry-ripe nipples, peeping through the dark swathe of her hair.

'Do you have birth control, Cyn?'

'I didn't think...' she groaned. 'I—no, I don't.' Her cheeks were fiery red. 'Do you?'

Lucien would have preferred there to be nothing between him and Cyn the first time he entered her, but at the same time he liked that her lack of protection indicated she wasn't involved sexually with any other man right now.

He reached out and opened a drawer on the side table before taking out a silver foil packet and opening it. 'Would you...?' he invited huskily.

'Me?' Her eyes were wide.

'Perhaps not.' Lucien chuckled softly before quickly dealing with it himself. 'I want to be inside you now, Cyn...' he said huskily. 'In fact if I don't get inside you soon I think I'm going to spontaneously combust.' He settled her above him. 'I promise I'll go slower next time, but for the moment I just need—'

'Next time...?' Cyn squeaked.

'You said earlier that you would stay with me until I had made love to you half a dozen times, remember?' Lucien gave a hard, satisfied smile.

She gasped. 'But I—I already—I've lost count of how many times I've already—'

'Foreplay doesn't count,' he dismissed. 'When I'm inside you and we climax together—something I'm greatly looking forward to, by the way—that's when it counts. And I want you so badly this time I'm not going to last,' he acknowledged.

He knew it was true. His liking for Cyn, his enjoyment of her company as well as her body, had enhanced their lovemaking to a pitch he had never known before...

Thia gasped. All those incredible, mind-blowing climaxes didn't *count*? He couldn't truly think that she was going to be able to repeat this past hour—or however long it had been since Lucien had started making love to her. She had completely lost track of time! If they did she wouldn't just lose consciousness, she would surely die. And wouldn't that look great on her headstone—*Here lies Cynthia Hammond, dead from too much pleasure!*

But what a wonderful way to go…

Emotion—love…?—swelled in Thia's chest as she looked down at the man sprawled beneath her on the bed. Lucien really was the most gorgeous, sexy man she had ever met—breathtakingly handsome, elegantly muscled and loose-limbed. And he was all hers.

For the moment, that taunting little voice whispered again inside her head.

This moment was all that mattered. Because it was all there was for her and Lucien. They had no tomorrow. No future. Just here and now.

And she wanted it. Wanted Lucien.

She held that silver gaze with her own and eased up on her knees before reaching down between them, fingers light, as she guided his sheathed length to the slickness of her channel—only to freeze in place as she suddenly heard the unexpected sound of Mozart's *Requiem* playing!

'It's my mobile,' Lucien explained impatiently when he saw Cyn's dazed expression. 'Damn, it!' His hands slapped down forcefully onto the mattress beside him. He should have turned the damn thing off before making love with Cyn. Should have—

'You need to answer it, Lucien.' A frown marred Cyn's brow. 'It must be something important for someone to call again so quickly—and on your mobile this time.'

Nothing was more important at this moment than his need to make love with Cyn. *Nothing!*

'Lucien...?' she prompted huskily as his damned mobile just kept on playing Mozart's *Requiem*.

Which, in the circumstances, was very apt...

Talk about killing the moment! One interruption was bad enough. Lucien had managed to save the situation the first time, but he doubted he would be able to do so a second time.

A sentiment Cyn obviously echoed as she slid off and away from him, over to the side of the bed, before bending down to pick up the black silk robe from the floor. Her back was long and slender, ivory skin gleaming pale and oh-so-beautiful in the glow of the lamp, before she slipped her arms into the robe, pulling it about herself and then standing up to fasten the belt. She turned to face him.

'You have to answer the call, Lucien.' Her gaze remained firmly fixed on his face rather than lower, where he was still hard and wanting.

Oh, yes, there was no doubting he had to answer the call—and whoever was on the other end of it was going to feel the full force of his displeasure!

He slid to the side of the bed before reaching for his denims and taking his mobile out of the pocket to take the call. 'Steele,' he rasped harshly.

Thia winced at the coldness of Lucien's voice, feeling sorry for whoever was on the other end of that line. At the same time she couldn't help but admire the play of muscles across the broad width of Lucien's shoulders and back beneath that bronzed skin as he sat on the other side of the bed, his black hair rakishly tousled from her fingers earlier.

Earlier...

Her cheeks warmed as she thought of those earlier intimacies. Lucien's hands, lips and tongue caressing her, touching her everywhere. Giving pleasure wherever they touched. Taking her to climax again and again.

Her legs trembled just at remembering that pleasure—

'I'll be down in five minutes,' Lucien grated harshly, before abruptly ending the call and standing up decisively to cross the room and collect up the clothes he had taken off earlier, his eyes cold, his expression grimly discouraging.

Thia looked at him dazedly. He seemed almost unaware of her presence. 'Lucien…?'

He was scowling darkly as he turned to look at her. 'That was Dex,' he bit out economically. 'It appears that your ex-boyfriend is downstairs in Reception and he's been making a damned exhibition of himself!'

She gasped. 'Jonathan?'

Lucien nodded sharply. 'Unless you have any other ex-boyfriends in New York?'

She gave a pained wince at the harsh anger she heard in his tone. Misdirected anger, in her opinion. 'I told you—Jonathan was never my boyfriend. And isn't it more likely he's making an exhibition of himself in *your* hotel because you fired him from *Network* this morning?'

It was a valid, reasoned argument, Lucien acknowledged impatiently—but at the same time he knew he was just too tense at the moment to be reasoned with. Even by Cyn.

He had enjoyed this evening with her more than he had enjoyed being with a woman for a very long time—if ever. Not just making love to her, but cooking dinner with her, talking freely about everything and nothing, when usually he was careful of how much he revealed about himself to the women he was involved with—a self-defence reflex that simply hadn't existed with Cyn from the beginning.

And now *this*.

His mouth thinned with his displeasure. 'I apologise for being grouchy. I just—' He ran his hand through the dark thickness of his hair. 'I'll get dressed and go down and sort this situation out. I shouldn't be long. What are you doing...?' He frowned as Cyn turned towards the bathroom.

'Getting dressed so that I can come with you.'

'You aren't coming downstairs with me.'

'Oh, but I am,' she assured him.

'No—'

'Yes,' she bit out firmly, her hands resting on her hips as she raised challenging brows.

Lucien's nostrils flared. 'My hotel. My problem.'

'Your hotel, certainly. But we don't know yet whose problem it is,' she insisted stubbornly.

His jaw clenched. 'Look, Cyn, there are some things about Miller I don't believe you're aware of—'

'What sort of things?' She looked at him sharply.

'Things,' Lucien bit out tersely. This evening had already gone to hell in a handbasket. Cyn did not need to know about all of Jonathan Miller's behaviour, or the reason the other man had been using her, which was sure to come out if Miller was as belligerent as Dex had said he was. 'In the circumstances, the best thing you can do is—'

'Please don't tell me that the best thing I can do is to stay up here and make coffee, like a good little woman, and wait until the Mighty Hunter returns!' Her eyes glowed deeply cobalt.

Apart from the good little woman and Mighty Hunter crack, that was exactly what Lucien had been about to say. 'Well...maybe you could forget the coffee,' he said dryly.

'And maybe I can forget the whole scenario—because

it isn't going to happen!' She thrust her hands into the pockets of his silk robe.

Lucien noted that it was far too big for her; it was wrapped about her almost twice, with the sleeves turned up to the slenderness of her wrists, and the length reached down to her calves—altogether making her look like a little girl trying to play grown-up.

'Dex has managed to take Miller to a secure room for the moment, but it could get nasty, Cyn.'

'I've been a waitress for six years; believe me, I know how to deal with *nasty,*' she assured him dryly.

Lucien was starting to notice that Cyn seemed to use the waitress angle as a defence mechanism. As if in constant reminder to herself, and more probably Lucien, of who and what she was…

Who she was to Lucien was Cynthia Hammond—a beautiful and independent young woman whom he admired and desired.

What she was to Lucien was also Cynthia Hammond—a beautiful and independent young woman whom Lucien admired as well as desired.

The rest, he realised, had become totally unimportant to him—was just background noise and of no consequence.

Not true of Cyn, obviously…

He drew in a deep breath. 'I would really rather you didn't do this.'

'Your opinion is noted.' She nodded.

'But ignored?'

'But ignored.'

'Fine,' he bit out between clenched teeth, knowing he couldn't like Cyn's independence of spirit on the one hand and then expect her not to do exactly as she pleased on the other. 'I'll be leaving in about two minutes. If you aren't ready—'

'I'll be ready.'

She hurried into the bathroom and closed the door behind her.

Lucien drew in several controlling breaths as he glared at that closed bathroom door, knowing that the next few minutes' conversation with Miller would in all probability put an end to Lucien and Cyn spending the rest of the night together...

CHAPTER NINE

'MAKING AN EXHIBITION of himself how?' Thia prompted softly.

Lucien was scowling broodingly where he stood on the other side of the private lift as it descended to the ground floor.

He was once again dressed in those casual denims and black T-shirt, although the heavy darkness of his hair was still tousled—from Thia's own fingers earlier, and also Lucien's own now as he ran his hands through it in impatient frustration. Probably because of her stubbornness in insisting on accompanying him downstairs rather than Jonathan's behaviour, Thia acknowledged ruefully.

Silver eyes glittered through narrowed lids. 'He came in and demanded to see me. According to Dex, once both the receptionist and the manager had told him I wasn't available this evening, Miller then decided to start shouting and hurling the potted plants about. When that failed to get him what he wanted he resorted to smashing up the furniture, which was when Security arrived and took charge of the situation.'

'How…?'

'Two of them lifted him up and carried him away to a secure room before calling Dex,' Lucien explained grimly.

Thia winced as she pictured the scene. 'I can imagine Jonathan might be upset after what happened this morning, but surely this isn't normal behaviour?'

Lucien gave her an irritated frowning glance. 'Cyn, have you *really* not noticed anything different about him since you came to New York?'

Well...she *had* noticed that Jonathan was more self-absorbed than he'd used to be. That he slept the mornings away and barely spoke when he did emerge, sleepy-eyed and unkempt, from his bedroom. And he had insisted on the two of them attending those awful parties together every night, at which he usually abandoned her shortly after they had arrived. And he had been extremely aggressive at the Carews' party last night—she had the sore wrist and the bruises on her arms to prove that!

She chewed on her bottom lip. 'Maybe he's a little more...into himself than he used to be.'

'That's one way of describing it, I suppose.' Lucien nodded grimly, standing back as the lift came to a halt and allowing her to step out into the marbled hallway first.

Thia eyed him guardedly as she walked along the hallway beside him; Lucien obviously knew which room Jonathan had been secured in. 'How would *you* describe it?'

Lucien's mouth thinned. 'As the classic behaviour of an addict.'

She drew in a sharp breath as she came to an abrupt halt in the hallway. 'Are you saying that Jonathan is—that he's taking drugs?'

'Amongst other things.' Lucien scowled.

'He's drinking too?'

'Not that I know of, no.'

'Then what "other things" are you talking about...?' Thia felt dazed, disorientated, at Lucien's revelation about

Jonathan. Admittedly Jonathan hadn't seemed quite himself since she arrived in New York, but she had put that down to reaction to his sudden stardom. It must be difficult coping with being so suddenly thrust into the limelight, finding himself so much in demand, as well as having so many beautiful women throwing themselves at him.

Lucien grimaced. 'This is not a good time for me to discuss this with you.'

'It's exactly the time you should discuss this with me,' Thia insisted impatiently. 'Maybe if someone had thought to discuss it with me earlier I might have been able to talk to him about it—perhaps persuaded him to seek help.' She gave a shake of her head. 'As things now stand he's not only messed up his career, but the rest of his life as well!'

Lucien frowned as he heard the underlying criticism in her tone. 'Damn it, Cyn, do *not* turn this around on me. Miller was given a warning about his behaviour weeks ago. In fact he's been given two warnings.'

'When, exactly?'

'The first was two months ago. And again about five weeks ago, when it became obvious he had taken no notice of the first warning. I have a strict no-drugs policy on all contracts,' he added grimly.

'What sort of warn—? Did you say *five weeks* ago...?' she prompted guardedly.

Lucien quirked dark brows. 'Mean something to you?'

'Jonathan visited me in London a month ago...' She chewed on her bottom lip. 'I hadn't seen him for almost three months, and he had only telephoned me a couple of times since he'd left for New York, and then he—he just turned up one weekend.'

Lucien nodded. 'And subsequently invited you to come and stay with him in New York?'

'How do you know that?'

He scowled. 'I just did the math, Cyn.'

'I don't understand...'

Lucien didn't see why he should be the one to explain Miller's behaviour, either. Cyn already considered him callous for firing Miller. He wasn't going to be the one to tell her that Miller had only invited her to New York as a cover for his affair with another—married!—woman!

The fact that Cyn was with him now would probably be enough for Miller to realise she must have been with Lucien in his apartment when Dex telephoned a short time ago. Add that to the fact that she was so obviously wearing a man's oversized T-shirt and Miller was sure to add two and two together and come up with the correct answer of four!

Which was precisely the reason Lucien hadn't wanted Cyn with him during this confrontation. Well, okay, it wasn't the whole reason. He really would have preferred it that Cyn stayed in his apartment, made coffee, like the good little woman, and waited for the Mighty Hunter to return. He wanted to protect her from herself, if necessary. As it was, he somehow doubted that Cyn would be returning to his apartment tonight at all...

'Could we get a move on, do you think?' Lucien snapped tersely, giving a pointed glance at his wristwatch. 'I told Dex I'd be there in five minutes and it's been over ten.'

Cyn blinked at his vehemence. 'Of course. Sorry.'

She grimaced as she once again fell into step beside him, leaving Lucien feeling as if he had just delivered a kick to an already abused and defenceless animal.

Not that he thought of Cyn as defenceless—she was too independent, too determined ever to be completely that.

But he had no doubt that Miller's real reason for inviting her to come to New York was going to upset her.

It was hard to believe, considering the tension between them now, that the two of them had been making love just minutes ago—that he now knew Cyn's body intimately, and exactly how to give her pleasure.

On the plus side, his erection had got the message that the night of pleasure was over and had deflated back to normal proportions. Not that it would take much to revive his desire…just a sultry look from cobalt blue eyes, the merest touch of Cyn's hand anywhere on his body. Which Lucien already knew wasn't going to happen in the immediate future. If ever again.

Another reason for Lucien to be displeased at Miller's increasingly erratic behaviour. If he needed another reason. Which he didn't. Forget the drugs and the affair with Simone Carew; the man was an out-and-out bastard for attempting to use Cyn as a shield for that affair. Not that the ruse had worked, but that didn't excuse Miller's callous behaviour towards a woman who had thought he was her friend. Or the fact that the other man had held Cyn so roughly the evening before he had succeeded in badly bruising her.

And Cyn was annoyed with *him*, because he had fired Miller for blatant and continuous breach of contract!

'Dex.' He greeted the other man grimly as they turned a corner and he saw his bodyguard standing outside a door to the right of the hallway. 'He's in there?' He nodded to the closed door.

Dex scowled. 'Yes.'

'And has he quietened down?'

'Some.' Dex nodded grimly before shooting Cyn a frowning glance. 'I don't think it's a good idea for Miss

Hammond to go in with you. Miller is violent, and he's also throwing out all sorts of accusations,' he warned with a pointed glance at Lucien.

'I'm going in,' Cyn informed them both stubbornly.

Lucien's mouth tightened. 'As you can see, Dex, Miss Hammond insists on accompanying me.'

'It's really not a good idea, Miss Hammond,' Dex warned her gently.

It was a gentleness Lucien hadn't even known the other man was capable of. No doubt Dex found Cyn's beauty and her air of fragility appealing—but the fragility was deceptive. There was a toughness beneath that fragile exterior that made Lucien think Cyn would be capable of stopping a Humber in its tracks if she chose to do so! Hopefully Dex was concerned in a fatherly sort of way, because Lucien knew he wouldn't be at all happy with his bodyguard having a crush on the woman he—

The woman he what…? Was falling in love with? Was already in love with?

Now was hardly the time for Lucien to think about what he might or might not be feeling for Cyn. Damn it, they had met precisely three times now, and shared one evening together. Admittedly it had been the most enjoyable—and arousing!—evening Lucien had ever spent with a woman…

The depth of his desire for Cyn was unprecedented—to the point that Lucien really had thought he was going to come just at the taste of her on his tongue.

And for the early part of the evening she had believed him to have deliberately hidden her away in his apartment because he didn't want to be seen in public with her. She may still believe that, for all he had denied it.

Damn it, he should have tanned her backside earlier rather than making love to her!

'I appreciate your concern, Dex.' Thia answered the older man softly. 'But Jonathan is my friend—'

'No. He really isn't,' Lucien rasped harshly.

'And I have every intention of speaking with him to-night,' she continued firmly, at the same time giving Lucien a reproving frown.

'I agree with Mr Steele,' Dex murmured regretfully. 'Mr Miller's behaviour earlier was…out of control,' he added.

Thia had come to like and trust this man over the past couple of days—how could she *not* like and trust a man who had stood guard all night outside her bedroom in that awful hotel in order to ensure she came to no harm from any of the staff or other guests staying there? In fact she felt slightly guilty now, for thinking Dex looked like a thug the first time she had seen him. He might look tough, but she didn't doubt there was a heart of gold under that hard exterior.

And she valued his advice now—as she did Lucien's. Although his scowling expression indicated he thought otherwise! She just didn't feel she could abandon Jona-than when he so obviously needed all the friends he could get. She had no doubt that all those shallow people who had been all over Jonathan at those celebrity parties would drift away the moment they knew he had been dropped as the star of *Network*.

'I appreciate your concern, Dex.' She smiled her grati-tude as she placed a hand lightly on his muscled forearm. 'I really do.'

'But she's going to ignore it,' Lucien said knowingly.

Her smile faded as she turned to face him, knowing

how displeased he was with her by the coldness in his eyes as he looked down the length of his nose at her, but unable to do anything about it.

She accepted, despite that interruption to their lovemaking, that Lucien had become her lover this evening—was closer to her and now knew her more intimately than any other man ever had. But by the same token she had been friends with Jonathan for two years now, and she didn't desert her friends. Especially when one of those friends was so obviously in trouble.

She drew in a deep, steadying breath. 'Yes, I'm afraid I am.'

Lucien had known she would. She had to be the most irritatingly stubborn woman he had ever known!

As well as being the most beautiful—inside as well as out. And the funniest. Her comments were sometimes totally outrageous. She was also the sexiest woman Lucien had ever known. And definitely the most responsive!

That in itself was such a turn-on—an aphrodisiac. Lucien was an accomplished lover, and had certainly never had any complaints about his sexual technique, his ability to bring a woman to climax, or in finding his own release. But with Cyn there had been no need for that measured and deliberate technique—just pure pleasure as, after her initial shyness, she had held absolutely nothing back and responded to his lightest touch, at the same time heightening his own pleasure and arousal.

To such an extent that Lucien knew Cyn was fast becoming his own addiction...

And yet here they were at loggerheads again, just minutes later—and over Jonathan Miller, of all people. A man

Lucien didn't consider as being good enough to lick Cyn's boots, let alone to deserve her loyalty and friendship.

'Fine,' he bit out harshly before turning away. 'You had better unlock the door and let us in, then, Dex. The sooner we get this over and done with the better for all of us,' he added grimly.

'Lucien…?' Cyn prompted almost pleadingly.

'You've made your decision, Cyn.' He rounded on her angrily, hands clenching at his sides. 'I only hope you don't live to regret it. No, damn it, I *know* you're going to regret it!' He glared down at her.

Thia had a sinking feeling she would too… Both Dex and Lucien seemed convinced of it, and she had no reason to distrust the opinion of either man.

Yes, Jonathan had been less than a polite host since she'd arrived in New York—to the point where his behaviour the previous evening meant she'd had no choice but to move out of his apartment. She just couldn't quite bring herself to turn her back on him if he needed a friend.

Lucien followed Dex into the room, the two of them blocking her view of Jonathan until they moved aside and Thia finally saw him where he stood silhouetted against the darkness of the window. He looked a mess: his denims were covered in soil—from the pot plants he had thrown about the hotel reception?—his T-shirt was ragged and torn, but it was the bruises on his face and the cut over one eye that dismayed her the most.

His lips curled back into a sneer as he saw the shocked expression on her face. 'You should see the other guy!'

'The "other guy" is at the hospital, having stitches put in the gash to the head he received when you smashed a lamp over him,' Lucien rasped harshly.

Jonathan turned that sneering expression onto the older man. 'He shouldn't have got in my way.'

'Watch your mouth, Miller. Unless you want him to press charges for assault,' Lucien warned grimly.

Thia paled at the knowledge that Jonathan had attacked another man with a lamp, necessitating that man needing to go to the hospital for stitches. 'You're just making the situation worse, Jonathan—'

'Exactly what are *you* doing here, Thia?' Jonathan turned on her, eyeing her speculatively as he took in the whole of her appearance in one sweeping glance. 'You look as if you just fell out of bed. Oh. My. God.' He gave a harsh laugh as he turned that speculative gaze on Lucien and then back to Thia. 'You just fell out of *his* bed! How priceless is that—'

She winced. 'Jonathan, don't.'

'Shut up, Miller,' Lucien bit out coldly at the same time.

'The prudish Thia Hammond and the almighty Lucien Steele!' Jonathan ignored them both as he laughed all the harder at a joke obviously only he appreciated.

Thia felt numb. Lucien was obviously icily furious. Dex remained stoically silent.

Jonathan's humour was so derisive and scathing Thia felt about two inches high—as he no doubt intended her to do. 'You aren't helping, Jonathan.'

'I have nothing left to lose,' he assured her scornfully as he gave a shake of his head. 'You stupid little fool—don't you know that he's just using you to get back at me?' He looked at Thia pityingly.

'You're the one who used her, Miller,' Lucien scorned icily.

Jonathan glared. 'I tried to convince you that Thia and I were involved, yes. In the futile hope of getting you off my back. But what you've done tonight—seducing Thia—is ten times worse than anything I did!' He gave a disgusted shake of his head before turning to Thia with accusing eyes. 'Damn it, Thia, we actually dated for a while two years ago—until you made it obvious you weren't interested in me in that way. And yet you only met Steele yesterday and already you've been to bed with him! Unbloody-believable!' He eyed her incredulously.

When he put it like that it *was* pretty incredible, Thia acknowledged with an inner wince. Not that she and Lucien had completely consummated their lovemaking, but that was pure semantics. After the number of times Lucien had brought her to sobbing orgasm he was definitely her lover. A man, as Jonathan had just pointed out, she had only known for twenty-four hours…

Lucien had heard enough—seen enough. Cyn's face was tinged slightly green and she was swaying slightly, as if she was about to pass out! 'I suggest we talk about this again tomorrow, Miller,' he snapped icily. 'When you've had a chance to…calm down.' He eyed the other man disgustedly, knowing by Miller's flushed cheeks and overbright eyes that he was high on something—something he needed to sleep off overnight. Preferably with Dex keeping a sharp eye on him to ensure he didn't take anything else.

'You would no doubt prefer it if Thia didn't hear all the sordid details?' the younger man taunted.

Lucien shrugged. 'They're your sordid details.'

'Not all of them,' Miller challenged. 'Something I'm pretty sure you won't have shared with Thia either.'

Lucien's mouth tightened. 'Not only do your empty threats carry no weight with me, but they could be decidedly dangerous. To your future career,' he added softly.

'You don't think Thia has a right to know that the *real*

reason you've been trying to break my contract the last couple of months—the reason for your being with her tonight—is because I've been having an affair with the woman I seduced out of *your* bed?'

'We both know that isn't true, Miller.' Lucien's teeth were clenched so tightly his jaw ached.

'Do we?'

'Yes!' he rasped. 'Something I will discuss with you in more detail tomorrow,' he added determinedly.

'And will you also fill me in on all the juicy details of how you succeeded in seducing and deflowering the Virgin Queen?' Miller came back tauntingly.

'What the hell...?' Lucien muttered.

'It's what I've always called Thia in my mind.' The other man grinned unrepentantly.

Lucien stilled as all thought of Miller's accusations fled his mind. Barely breathing, he felt his heart pounding loudly in his chest as he gave Cyn a brief disbelieving glance—just long enough to show him that she had somehow managed to go even paler. Her cheeks were now paper-white.

The Virgin Queen?

Was it possible that on this subject at least Miller might be telling the truth and Cyn had been a virgin? Correction: she was still technically a virgin—despite the intensity of their lovemaking earlier.

Had Lucien taken a virgin to his bed and not even known it? Would he only have realised it the moment he ripped through that delicate barrier?

Lucien was the one who now felt nauseous. Sick to his stomach, in fact, at how close he had come to taking Cyn's innocence without even realising until it was too late.

Perhaps he should have known.

He had noted that disingenuous air about her the first time they met. There had also been her shyness earlier, in regard to her own nudity as much as his. Her confusion when he had assured her he had a clean bill of health and her hesitant confirmation that she did too. And the glaringly obvious fact that Cyn wasn't on any birth control.

Because she was a virgin.

Even during the wildness of his youth Lucien had never taken a virgin to his bed—had stayed well away from any female who looked as if she might still be one. A woman's virginity was something to be valued—a gift—not something to be thrown away on a casual relationship, and Lucien had never felt enough for any of the women he had been involved with to want to take a relationship any further.

What had Cyn been thinking earlier?

Maybe she hadn't been thinking at all? Lucien knew he certainly hadn't. He had been too aroused, too caught up in the intensity of his desire for Cyn—of his growing addiction to her—to be able to connect up the dots of her behaviour and their conversation and realise exactly how innocent she was. As it was, he had been on the point of thrusting into her, of taking her innocence, when the ringtone of his mobile had interrupted them.

Sweet, merciful heaven…!

CHAPTER TEN

'LUCIEN—'

'Not now, Thia.'

She almost had to run to keep up with Lucien's much longer strides, and Jonathan's mocking laughter followed them as they walked down the deserted marble hallway towards where the main lifts were situated, in the reception area of the hotel. The lifts Thia would need to use if she was returning to her suite on the tenth floor. Which it seemed she was about to do...

'Is Dex going to stay with Jonathan tonight?' Thia hadn't been able to hear all the softly spoken conversation that had taken place between Lucien and Dex before Lucien had taken a firm hold of her arm and escorted her from the room, but she had gathered that Dex intended taking Jonathan out of the back entrance of the hotel and then driving him to his apartment.

Lucien nodded abruptly. 'If only to make sure he stays out of trouble for the rest of the night.'

She winced. 'Is the drug thing really that bad?'

'Yes,' he answered grimly.

Thia frowned. 'Lucien, what did Jonathan mean? He seemed to be implying that there was a woman involved in your decision to fire him from *Network*?'

Lucien turned to look down at her with icy silver eyes. 'I don't think that's the conversation we should be having right now, Thia.'

The fact that he kept calling her Thia in that icily clipped tone was far from reassuring... Not that she wasn't totally aware of the reason for Lucien's coldness. It was as if an arctic chill had taken over the room the moment Jonathan had so baldly announced her virginity. Lucien's shocked reaction to that statement had been unmistakable. As if she had a disease, or something equally as unpleasant! Good grief, he had been a virgin himself once upon a time—many years ago now, no doubt, but still...

'I don't understand why you're so annoyed.' She frowned. 'It's my virginity, and as such I can choose to lose it when I damn well please. It's no big deal.'

'I'm guessing that's why you've waited twenty-three years to even think about doing so?'

Thia smarted at his scathing tone. 'It isn't the first time I've considered it—and that's my bruised arm, Lucien!' she complained, when his fingers tightly grasped the top of her arm as he came to a halt in the deserted hallway before swinging her round to face him.

He released her as abruptly, glaring down at her, nostrils flaring as he breathed deeply. 'What the hell were you thinking, Thia? What were you doing going alone to a man's apartment at all?'

'Accepting an invitation to dinner in a man's apartment isn't saying *Here I am—take me to bed!*'

'It's been my experience that that depends on the woman and her reasons for accepting the invitation.'

She bristled. 'I don't think I like the accusation in your tone.'

'Well, that's just too bad,' he bit out harshly. 'Because

my tone isn't going to change until I know exactly why you went to bed with me earlier this evening!'

Her cheeks blazed with colour. 'I thought I was making love with a man whom I desired and who also desired me!'

His jaw tightened. 'Not good enough, Thia—'

'Well, it's the only explanation I have. And stop calling me that!' Tears stung her eyes.

'It's your name,' he dismissed curtly.

'But *you've* never called me by it.' She blinked back those heated tears. 'And I—I liked it that only you had ever called me Cyn,' she admitted huskily, realising it was the truth. She had found Lucien's unique name for her irritating at first, but had very quickly come to like that uniqueness.

His nostrils flared in his impatience. 'Answer the damned question, Thia!'

'Which one?' she came back just as angrily. He'd called her that name again. 'Why did I decide to have dinner alone with you in your apartment this evening? Or why did I choose you as the man to whom I wanted to lose my virginity? Or perhaps to you they're one and the same question?' she challenged scornfully. 'You obviously think that I had pre-planned going to bed with you this evening! That I was attempting to—to entrap you into—into *what,* exactly?' Thia looked at him sharply.

Lucien was still too stunned at the knowledge of Cyn's virginity—at the thought of her never having been with anyone else—to be able to reason this situation out with his usually controlled logic. As a consequence he was talking without thinking about what he was saying, uncharacteristically shooting straight from the hip. But, damn it, if his mobile had rung even a few seconds later—!

'Damned if I know,' he muttered exasperatedly.

'Oh, I think you *do* know, Lucien.' Cyn's voice shook with anger. 'I think you've decided—that you believe—I deliberately set out to seduce you this evening.'

'I believe *I* was the one who did the seducing—'

'Ah, but what if I'm clever enough to let you *think* you did the seducing?' she taunted, eyes glittering darkly.

He gave a rueful shake of his head. 'You aren't—'

'It's a pity you asked about birth control, really,' she continued without pause. 'Otherwise I might even have discovered I was pregnant in a few weeks' time. And wouldn't that have been wonderful? I can see the headlines in the newspapers now—*I had Lucien Steele's lovechild!* Except we aren't in love with each other, and there isn't ever going to be a child—'

'Stop it, Cyn!' he rasped sharply, reaching up to grasp her by the shoulders before shaking her. 'Just *stop* it!'

'Let me go, Lucien,' she choked. 'I don't like you very much at the moment.' Tears fell unchecked down the paleness of her cheeks, her eyes dark blue pools of misery.

Lucien didn't like himself very much at the moment either. And it was really no excuse that he was still in shock from Miller's 'Virgin Queen' comment. His knee-jerk angry comments had now made Cyn think—believe— that he was angry about her virginity. When in actual fact he felt like getting down on his knees and worshipping at her beautiful feet. A woman's virginity was a gift. A gift Cyn had been about to give to *him* this evening. The truth was he was in total awe at the measure of that gift.

And he had made her cry. That was just unacceptable.

He released her shoulders before pulling her into his arms—a move she instantly fought against as she tried to push him away, before beating her fists against his chest when she failed to release herself.

'I said, let me go, Lucien!' She glared up at him as he still held her tightly against his chest.

'Let me explain, Cyn—'

'I have questions I want answered too, Lucien. And so far you've refused to answer any of them. Including explaining about this woman Jonathan reputedly stole from you—'

'I don't consider Miller's fantasies as being relevant to our present conversation!' He scowled darkly.

'And I disagree with that opinion. Jonathan said that the two of us making love together this evening was deliberate on your part—that you seduced me to get back at him—'

'Does that *really* sound like something I would do?' he grated, jaw clenched.

'Any more than entrapment sounds like something I would do?' she came back tauntingly. 'I don't really know you, Lucien…'

'Oh, you know me, Cyn,' Lucien assured her softly. 'In just a few short days I've allowed you to know me better than anyone else ever has. And the conversation we need to have is about what happened between the two of us this evening.'

'I think we—you, certainly—have already said more than enough on that subject!' she assured him firmly.

'Because I was understandably stunned at learning of your—your innocence?'

'Was that you being stunned? It looked more like shock to me!'

'You're being unreasonable, Cyn—'

'Probably because I *feel* unreasonable!' Cyn gave another push against his chest with her bent elbows, those tears still dampening her cheeks. 'So much has happened this evening that I—Lucien, if you don't release me I'm going to start screaming, and I think the other guests staying at the hotel have already witnessed enough of a scene for one evening!'

'You're upset—'

'Of *course* I'm upset!' Cyn stilled to look up at him incredulously. 'I've just learnt that the friend I came to New York to visit has not only become involved in taking drugs, but has also been using me to hide his affair with another woman. Add to that the fact that the man I had dinner with and made love with earlier this evening also seems to have been involved with that woman—'

'I'm not involved with anyone but you.'

'I think that gives me the right to be upset, don't you?' she continued determinedly.

Lucien frowned his own frustration with the situation as he released her, before allowing his arms to drop slowly back to his sides, knowing he had handled this situation badly, that his first instinct—to kneel and worship at Cyn's feet—was the one he should have taken.

'I apologise. It— I— It isn't every day a man learns that the woman he has just made love with is a virgin.'

'No, I believe we're becoming something of an endangered species.' She nodded abruptly. 'Thank you for the fun of cooking dinner together this evening, Lucien. I enjoyed it. The sex too. The rest of the evening... Not quite so much.' She stepped back. 'I'll make sure I have your T-shirt laundered and returned to you before I leave on Saturday—'

'Do you think I give a damn about my T-shirt?' he bit out in his frustration with her determination to leave him.

'Probably not.' She grimaced. 'I'm sure you have dozens of others just like it. Or you could *buy* another dozen like it! I would just feel better if I had this one laundered and returned to you.'

So that she didn't even have *that* as a reminder of him once she had returned to her life in London, Lucien guessed heavily.

Lucien wouldn't need anything to remind him of Cyn once she had gone.

He had spoken the truth when he'd told her that he had been more open, more relaxed in her company, than he ever had with any other woman.

As for the sex…!

He'd had good sex in his life, pleasurable sex, and very occasionally mechanical sex, when mutual sexual release had been the only objective, but he'd never had such mind-blowing and compatible sex as he'd enjoyed tonight with Cyn, where the slightest touch, every caress, gave them both unimagined pleasure.

He had always believed that sort of sex had to be worked at, with the two people involved having a rapport that went beyond the physical to the emotional.

He and Cyn had something between them beyond the physical. Lucien had known Cyn a matter of days, and yet the two of them had instinctively found that rapport. In and out of bed. Only to have it all come crashing down about their heads the moment Dex rang to tell them of Miller's presence downstairs in the hotel reception area.

Not only that, but Cyn was a virgin, and now that Lucien knew that he realised that her shyness earlier was an indication that she was an inexperienced virgin. A *very* inexperienced virgin, who had climaxed half a dozen times in his arms. Which was surely unusual—and per-haps an indication that she felt more for him than just physical attraction?

Or was that just wishful thinking on his part…?

Lucien didn't know any more. Had somehow lost his perspective. On everything. A loss that necessitated in him needing time and space in which to consider exactly what he felt for Cyn. Time the mutinously angry expression on Cyn's face now told him he simply didn't have!

'Fine.' He tersely accepted her suggestion about returning the T-shirt. 'But I'll see you again before you leave—'

'I don't think that's a good idea.' She backed up another step, putting even more distance between the two of them.

Lucien scowled darkly across that distance. 'You're being unreasonable—'

'Outraged virgin unreasonable? Or just normal female unreasonable?' she taunted with insincere sweetness.

'Just unreasonable,' he grated between clenched teeth, not wanting to lose his temper and say something else he would have cause to regret. The fact that he was in danger of losing his temper at all was troubling. He *never* lost his control—let alone his temper. Tonight, with Cyn, he had certainly lost his control, and his temper was now seriously in danger of following it. 'You're putting words into my mouth now, Cyn,' he continued evenly. 'And we *will* see each other again before you leave. I'll make sure of it.'

She raised midnight brows. 'I'd be interested to know how.'

Lucien gave a humourless smile. 'I believe, ironically, that you're travelling back to London on Saturday on the Steele Atlantic Airline.'

'How on earth did you know that?' She stared at him incredulously.

'I checked.' He shrugged. 'I thought it would be a nice gesture to bump your seat up to First Class. Miller was a cheapskate for not booking you into First Class in the first place!'

'He did,' she snapped. 'I'm the one who insisted he change it to Economy.'

'No doubt because you have every intention of paying the money back to him.' Lucien sighed, only too well aware of Cyn's fierce independence. It was a knowledge that made his earlier comments—accusations!—even more ridiculous. And unforgivable.

'Of course.' She tilted her chin proudly.

Lucien nodded. 'Nevertheless, if you avoid seeing me again before you leave for the airport on Saturday, one telephone call from me and the flight gets delayed...or cancelled altogether.'

Cyn gasped. 'You wouldn't seriously do that?'

He raised a mocking brow. 'What do you think?'

'I think you're way way out of line on this—that is what I *think*!' she hissed forcefully.

He shrugged. 'Your choice.'

'You—you egomaniac!' Thia glared at him. Arrogant, manipulative, *impossible* ego-maniac!

Lucien gave a hard, humourless smile. 'As I said, it's up to you. We either talk again before you leave or you don't leave.'

'There are other airlines.'

He shrugged. 'I will ensure that none are available to you.'

She gasped. 'You can't do that—'

'Oh, but I can.'

Her eyes widened. 'You would really stop me from leaving New York until we've spoken again...?'

His mouth thinned. 'You aren't giving me any alternative.'

'We all have choices, Lucien.' She gave a shake of her

head. 'And your overbearing behaviour now is leaving *me* with no choice but to dislike you intensely.'

He sighed. 'Well, at least it's *intensely;* I would hate it to be anything so insipid as just mediocre dislike! Look, I'm not enjoying backing you into a corner, Cyn,' he reasoned grimly as she glared at him. 'All I'm asking for is that we both sleep on this situation and then have a conversation tomorrow. Is that too much to ask?'

Was it? Could Thia even bear to be alone with him again after all that had been said?

Oh, she accepted that Lucien had been shocked at the way Jonathan had just blurted out her physical innocence. But Lucien's response to that knowledge had been— damned painful. That was what it had been!

'Okay, we'll talk again tomorrow.' She spoke in measured tones. 'But in a public place. With the agreement that I can get up and leave any time I want to.'

His eyes narrowed. 'I'm not sure I like your implication...'

'And my answer to that is pretty much the same as the one you gave me a few minutes ago—that's just too bad!' She looked at him challengingly.

Lucien gave a slow shake of his head. 'How the hell did we get into this situation, Cyn? One minute I have my mouth and my hands all over you, and the next—'

'You don't,' she snapped, the finality of her tone implying he never would again.

Except...it was impossible for Lucien not to see the outline of her nipples pouting hard as berries against the soft material of his T-shirt. Or not to note the way an aroused flush now coloured her throat and up into her cheeks. Or see the feverish glitter in the deep blue of her eyes.

Cyn was angry with him right now—and justifiably so

after his own train-wreck of a conversation just now—but that hadn't stopped her from remembering the fierceness of the desire that had flared between them earlier, or prevented the reaction of her body to those memories.

'Tomorrow, Cyn?' he encouraged huskily. 'Let's both just take a night to calm down.'

She frowned. 'It's my last day and I'd planned on taking a boat ride to see the Statue of Liberty. Don't tell me!' She grimaced as she obviously saw his expression. 'You've never been there, either!'

He smiled slightly. 'You live in London—have *you* ever been to the Tower of London and Buckingham Palace?'

'The Palace, yes. The Tower, no.' She shrugged. 'Okay, point taken. But tomorrow really is my last chance to take that boat trip...'

'Then we'll arrange to meet up in the evening.' Lucien shrugged.

Cyn eyed him warily. 'You're being very obliging all of a sudden.'

He grimaced. 'Maybe I'm trying to score points in the hope of making up for behaving like such a jackass earlier?'

'And maybe you just like having your own way,' she said knowingly. 'Okay, Lucien, we'll meet again tomorrow evening. But I'll be out most of the day, so leave a message for me at the front desk as to where we're supposed to meet up.'

He grimaced. 'Not the most gracious acceptance of an invitation I've ever received, but considering the jackass circumstances I'll happily take it.'

'This isn't a date, Lucien.' Cyn snapped her impatience.

She was doing it again—making him want to laugh when the situation, the strain that now existed between the two of them, should have meant he didn't find any of this in the least amusing! Besides which, Lucien had no doubt that if he *did* dare to laugh Cyn would be the one throwing potted plants around the hotel's reception—in an attempt to hit him with one of them!

Just thinking of Miller's behaviour earlier tonight was enough to dampen Lucien's amusement. 'I want your word. I would *like* your word,' he amended impatiently, bearing in mind Cyn's scathing comment earlier about his always wanting to have his own way, 'that you will stay away from Miller's apartment tomorrow.'

'I thought I might just—'

'I would really rather you didn't,' Lucien said frustratedly. 'You saw what he was like this evening, Cyn. His behaviour is currently unpredictable at best, violent at worst. You could get hurt. Far worse than just those bruises on your arm,' he added grimly.

She looked pained as she shook her head. 'Jonathan's life is in such a mess right now—'

'And it's a self-inflicted mess. Damn it, Cyn.' He scowled. 'He's already admitted he was only using you as a shield for his affair with another woman when he invited you to stay with him in New York!'

'Even so, it doesn't seem right—my just leaving without seeing him again.' She gave a sad shake of her head. 'I would feel as if I were abandoning him... Not everyone is as capable of handling sudden fame and fortune as you were,' she defended, when Lucien looked unimpressed.

'Damn it, Cyn.' He rasped his impatience with her continued concern for a man who didn't deserve it. 'Okay, if I see what can be done about getting Miller to accept help, maybe even going to a rehab facility, will you give me your promise not to go to his apartment tomorrow?'

'And you'll reconsider firing him from *Network*?'

'Don't push your luck, Cyn,' Lucien warned softly.

To his surprise, she gave a rueful grin. 'Okay, but it was worth a try, don't you think, as you're in such an amenable mood?'

Some of the tension eased from Lucien's shoulders as he looked at her admiringly. 'You are one gutsy lady, Cynthia Hammond!'

Thia was feeling far from gutsy at the moment. In fact reaction seemed to be setting in and she suddenly felt very tired, her legs less than steady. A reaction no doubt due to that fierceness of passion between herself and Lucien earlier as much as Jonathan's erratic, and...yes, she admitted *dangerously* unbalanced behaviour.

She was willing to concede that Lucien was right about that, at least; she had hardly recognised Jonathan this evening as the man she had known for two years.

But there were still so many questions that remained unanswered. The most burning question of all, for Thia, being the name of the woman Jonathan claimed to have seduced out of Lucien's bed.

Mainly because Thia simply couldn't believe that any woman would be stupid enough ever to prefer Jonathan over Lucien...

CHAPTER ELEVEN

'YOU JUST NEVER listen, do you? Never heed advice when it's given, even when it's for your own safety!'

Lucien's expression was as dark as thunder as he strode past Thia and into her hotel suite early the following evening, impressively handsome in a perfectly tailored black evening suit with a snowy white shirt and red silk bow-tie—making it obvious he had obviously only called to see her on his way out somewhere.

'Do come in, Lucien,' she invited dryly, and she slowly closed the door behind him before following him through to her sitting room. Her hair was pulled back in a high ponytail and she was wearing a pale blue fitted T-shirt and low-rider denims. 'Make yourself at home,' she continued as he dropped a large box down onto the coffee table before sitting down in one of the armchairs. 'And do please help yourself to a drink,' she invited.

He bounced restlessly back onto his feet a second later to cross the room and open the mini-bar, taking out one of the miniature bottles of whisky and pouring it into a glass before throwing it to the back of his throat and downing the fiery contents in one long swallow.

'Feeling better?'

Lucien turned, silver eyes spearing her from across

the room. 'Not in the least,' he grated harshly, taking out another miniature bottle of whisky before opening it and pouring it into the empty glass.

'What's wrong, Lucien?' Thia frowned.

His eyes narrowed to glittering silver slits. 'You gave me your word last night that you wouldn't see Miller today—'

'I believe I said that I wouldn't go to his apartment,' she corrected with a self-conscious grimace, knowing exactly where this conversation was going now.

'So you invited him to come here instead?'

Thia sighed. 'I didn't *invite* him anywhere, Lucien. Jonathan turned up outside my door. You only just missed him, in fact...'

His jaw tightened. 'I'm well aware of that!'

She arched a brow. 'Dex?'

Lucien's eyes narrowed. 'It was totally irresponsible of you to be completely alone with Miller in your suite—'

'But I wasn't completely alone with him, was I?' Thia said knowingly. 'I'm pretty sure Dex followed me to the docks today, and that he was standing guard outside the door to this suite earlier. And no doubt he ratted me out by telephoning you and telling you Jonathan was here.'

Lucien's eyes glittered a warning. 'Dex worries about your safety almost as much as I do.'

'Who's watching your back while Dex is busy watching mine?'

'I can take care of myself.'

'So can I!'

Lucien gave a disgusted snort. 'I discovered the first grey hair at my temple when I looked in the mirror to shave earlier—I'm damned sure it's appeared since yesterday.'

'Very distinguished,' she mocked. 'But there is abso-

lutely no need for either you or Dex to worry about me,'
she dismissed lightly. 'Jonathan only came by to apologise
for the way he's behaved these past few weeks. He also
said that when the two of you spoke earlier today you offered to give him another chance on *Network* if he agrees
to go to rehab.'

'An offer I am seriously rethinking.'

She sighed. 'Don't be petty, Lucien.'

An angry flush darkened his cheeks. 'I made the offer
because you asked me to, Cyn. Not for Miller's sake.'

'And because you know it makes good business sense,'
she pointed out ruefully. 'It would be indescribably bad
business for you to sack the star of *Network* when the pro-
gramme—and Jonathan—are obviously both so popular.'

Lucien's mouth thinned. 'And you seriously think losing a few dollars actually *matters* to me?'

Thia slipped her hands into the back pockets of her denims so that Lucien wouldn't see that they were shaking
slightly—evidence that she wasn't feeling as blasé about
this conversation and Jonathan's visit earlier as she wished
to give the impression of being.

She had seen Lucien in a variety of moods these past
few days: the confident seducer on the evening they met,
the focused billionaire businessman at his office the following day, playful and then seductive in his apartment
yesterday evening, before he became cold and dismissive
towards Jonathan, and then a total enigma to her after Jonathan deliberately dropped the bombshell of her virginity
into the conversation.

But Lucien's mood this evening—a mixture of anger
and concern—was as unpredictable as the man himself.

Her chin rose. 'I thought we had agreed to meet in a
public place this evening?'

'I decided to come here after Dex called up to the penthouse and informed me of Miller's visit.'

'You could have just telephoned.'

'I could have *just* done a lot of things—and, believe me, my immediate response was to do what I've threatened to do several times before and put you over my knee for having behaved so damned irresponsibly,' he bit out harshly.

Thia frowned. 'Correct me if I'm wrong, but shouldn't *I* be the one who's feeling angry and upset?' she challenged.

Lucien's expression became wary. 'About what?'

'About *everything!*' she burst out.

He stilled. 'What else did Miller tell you earlier?' Lucien's expression was enigmatic as he picked up the whisky glass and moved to stand in the middle of the room—a move that instantly dominated the space.

'Nothing I hadn't already worked out for myself,' Thia answered heavily. She had realised last night, as she'd lain alone in her bed, unable to sleep, exactly who the woman involved in the triangle must be. There had been only one obvious answer—only one woman Jonathan had spent any amount of time alone with over the past few days. And it wasn't a triangle but a square. Because Simone Carew, Jonathan's co-star in *Network,* also had a husband...

And if, as Jonathan claimed, he had seduced Simone away from Lucien's bed several months ago, then Jonathan's assertion that Lucien, believing Thia was Jonathan's English lover, had seduced her as a way of getting back at Jonathan, it all made complete sense.

Painfully so.

Perhaps it was as well she would be leaving New York tomorrow, with no intentions of seeing Lucien or Jonathan ever again.

Not seeing Jonathan again didn't bother her in the

slightest—they had said all they had to say to each other earlier.

Not seeing Lucien again—that was something else entirely.

Because Thia had realised something else as she'd lain alone in her bed the previous night. Something so huge, so devastating, that she had no idea how she was going to survive it.

She was in love with Lucien Steele.

Thia had heard of love at first sight, of course. Of how the sound of a particular voice could send shivers of awareness down the spine. How the first sight of that person's face could affect you so badly that breathing became difficult. Of how their touch could turn your legs to jelly and their kisses make you forget everything else but being with them.

Yes, Thia had heard of things like that happening— and now she realised that was exactly what had happened to her!

The worst of it was that the man she was in love with was Lucien Steele—a man who might or might not have been deliberately using her but who certainly wasn't in love with her.

'Such as?' Lucien prompted harshly as he saw the pained look on Cyn's face. 'Damn it, Cyn, even the condemned man is given an opportunity to defend himself!' he said as she remained silent.

She looked up, focusing on him with effort. 'You're far from being a condemned man, Lucien.' She gave a rueful shake of her head. 'And I think it's for the best if we forget about all of this and just move on.'

'Move on to where?' he prompted huskily.

She gave a pained frown. 'Well, Jonathan to rehab,

hopefully. Me back to England. And you—well, you to whatever it is you usually do before moving on to another relationship. Not that we actually *had* a relationship,' she added hurriedly. 'I didn't mean to imply that—'

'You're waffling, Cyn.'

'What I'm doing is trying to allow both of us to walk away from this situation with a little dignity.' Her eyes flashed a deep dark blue.

'I don't remember saying I wanted to walk away.' He quirked one dark brow.

She gave a shake of her head. 'I know the truth now, Lucien. I worked out most of it for myself—Simone Carew. Jonathan filled in the bits I didn't know, so let's just stop pretending, shall we? The condensed version of what happened is that you gave Jonathan two separate verbal warnings, about Simone and the drugs, he invited me over here in an attempt to mislead you about his continuing relationship with Simone at least, and you—you flirted with me to get back at him for taking Simone from you. End of story.'

'That's only Miller's version of the story, Cyn...' Lucien murmured softly as he placed his whisky glass carefully, deliberately, down on the coffee table before straightening.

His deliberation obviously didn't fool Cyn for a moment, as she now looked across at him warily. 'I told you— some of it I worked out for myself and the rest... It really isn't that important, Lucien.' She gave a dismissive shake of her head.

'Maybe not to you,' he bit out harshly. 'I, on the other hand, have no intention of allowing you to continue believing I have ever been involved with a married woman. It goes against every code I've ever lived by.' He drew in a sharp breath. 'My parents' marriage ended because my mother left my father for someone else,' he stated flatly.

'I would never put another man through the pain my father went through after she left him.'

Cyn's eyes widened. 'I didn't realise... Did your relationship with Simone happen *before* she married Felix?'

Lucien gave an exasperated sigh. 'It never happened at all!'

She winced at his vehemence. 'Then why did Jonathan say that it did...?'

'I can only assume because that's what Simone told him—probably as a way of piquing his interest.'

'I— But— *Why?* No, strike that question.' Cyn gave an impatiently disgusted shake of her head. 'I've met Simone Carew a few times over the past few days and she's a very silly, very vain woman. So, yes, I can well believe she's capable of telling Jonathan something like that just for the kudos. It isn't enough that she's married to one of the most influential directors in television—she also had to claim to having had a relationship with the richest and most powerful man in New York!'

Lucien gave a humourless smile. 'I knew you would get there in the end!'

'This isn't the time for your sarcasm, Lucien.' Cyn glared. 'And if you knew she was going around telling such lies why didn't you stop her?'

'Because I didn't know about it until Miller blurted it out to me a few weeks ago.' He scowled. 'And once I did know it didn't seem particularly important—'

'Simone Carew was going around telling anyone who would listen that the two of you'd had an affair, and it didn't seem particularly important to you?' Cyn stared at him incredulously. 'What about her poor husband?'

Lucien gave a weary sigh. 'Felix is thirty years older than Simone and he knew exactly what he was getting into when he married her. As a result, he chooses to look the other way when she has one of her little extra-marital flings.'

'Big of him.'

'Not really.' Lucien grimaced. 'He happens to be in love with her. And there are always rumours circulating in New York about everyone—most of them untrue or exaggerations of the truth. So why would I have bothered denying the ones about Simone and me? Have you never heard people say the more you deny something the more likely people are to believe it's the truth?'

'I wouldn't have!'

'That's because *you* are nothing like anyone else I have ever met,' Lucien dismissed huskily.

Thia didn't know what to say in answer to that comment. Didn't know what to say, full-stop.

Oh, she believed Lucien when he said he hadn't ever had an affair with Simone—why wouldn't she believe him when he had no reason to bother lying to her? It was totally unimportant to Lucien what *she* believed!

It did, however, raise the question as to why Lucien had pursued *her* so determinedly...

'What's in the box, Lucien?' Thia deliberately changed the subject as she looked down at the box Lucien had dropped down onto the coffee table when he first entered the suite.

'End of subject?'

She avoided meeting his exasperated gaze. 'I can't see any point in talking about it further. It's—I apologise if I misjudged you.' She gave a shake of her head. 'Obviously I'm not equipped—I don't understand the behind-the-scenes machinations and silly games of your world.'

'None of that is *my* world, Cyn. It's an inevitable part of it, granted, but not something I have ever chosen to involve myself in,' he assured her softly. 'As for what's in the box…why don't you open it up and see?'

Thia eyed the box as if it were a bomb about to go off, having no idea what could possibly be inside.

'It's a replacement for the blouse that was ripped!' she realised with some relief, her cheeks warming as she recalled exactly how and when her blouse had been ripped. And what had followed.

She couldn't think about that now! *Wouldn't* think about that now. There would be time enough for thinking about making love with Lucien, of being in love with him, in all the months and years of her life yet to come…

'Open it up, Cyn,' Lucien encouraged gruffly as he moved to sit down on the sofa beside the coffee table.

'Before I forget—I had your T-shirt laundered today—'

'Will you stop delaying and open the damned box, Cyn?'

'I can do it later,' she dismissed. 'You're obviously on your way out somewhere.' She gave a pointed look at his evening clothes. 'I wouldn't want to delay you any more than I have already—'

'You aren't delaying me.'

'But—'

'What is so difficult about opening the box, Cyn?' He barked his impatience with her prevarication.

Thia worried her bottom lip between her teeth. 'I just—I'm sorry if I'm being less than gracious. I'm just a little out of practice at receiving gifts…'

Lucien's scowl deepened as he realised the reason for that: Cyn's parents had died six years ago and she'd admitted to having no other family. And her relationship with Miller obviously hadn't been of the gift-giving variety—he was a taker, not a giver!

'It isn't a gift, Cyn,' Lucien assured softly. 'I ruined your blouse. I'm simply replacing it.'

A delicate blush warmed the ivory of her cheeks, emphasising the dark shadows under those cobalt blue eyes. Because Cyn hadn't slept well the night before?

Neither had Lucien. His thoughts had chased round and round on themselves as he'd tried to make sense, to use his normal cold logic, to explain and dissect his feelings for Cyn. In the end he had been forced to acknowledge, to accept, that there was no sense or reason to any of it. It just was.

There was now a dull ache in his chest at the realisation he wanted to shower Cyn with gifts, to give her anything and everything she had ever wanted or desired. At the same as he knew that her fierce independence would no doubt compel her to throw his generosity back in his face!

Lucien was totally at a loss to know what to do about this intriguing woman. Was currently following a previously untrodden path—one that had no signs or indications to tell him where to go or what he should do next. Except he knew he wasn't going to allow her to just walk out of his life tomorrow.

He took heart from the blush that now coloured her cheeks at the mention of her blouse ripping the night before. 'I would like to know if you approve of the replacement blouse, Cyn,' he encouraged gruffly.

'I would love to have been a fly on your office wall during *that* telephone conversation!' she teased as she finally moved forward to loosen the lid of the box before removing it completely.

'I went to the store this morning and picked out the blouse myself, Cyn.'

She gave him a startled look. 'You did?'

'I did,' he confirmed gruffly.

'I— But— Why…?'

He shrugged. 'I didn't trust a store assistant to pick out a blouse that was an exact match in colour for your eyes.'

'Oh…'

'Yes…oh…' Lucien echoed softly as he looked into, held captive, those beautiful cobalt blue eyes. 'Do you like it?' he prompted huskily as she folded back the tissue paper and down looked at the blouse he had chosen for her.

Did Thia *like* it?

Even if she hadn't this blouse would have been special to her, because Lucien had picked it out for her personally. As it was, Thia had never seen or touched such a beautiful blouse before. The colour indeed a perfect match for her eyes, and the material softer, silkier, than anything else she had ever owned.

Tears stung her eyes as she looked up. 'It's beautiful, Lucien,' she breathed softly. 'Far too expensive, of course. But don't worry,' she added as a frown reappeared between his eyes, 'I'm not going to insult you by refusing to accept it!'

'Good, because it certainly isn't going back to the store, and it really isn't my size or colour.'

'Very funny.' Thia picked up the blouse carefully, not sure when she would ever find the opportunity to wear something so beautiful—and expensive!—but loving it anyway. 'I—there appears to be something else in the box…' she breathed softly as she realised the blouse had been hiding the fact that there was another article wrapped in tissue beneath it. 'Lucien?' She looked up at him uncertainly.

'Ah. Yes.' He looked less than his usual confident self as he gave a self-conscious grimace. 'That's for you to wear this evening—unless you already have something you would prefer. You looked lovely in the gown you were wearing the evening we met, for example, although you might feel happier wearing something new.'

Thia eyed him warily. 'And where am I going this evening that I would need to wear something new?'

'To a charity ball.' He stood up restlessly, instantly dwarfing the room—and Thia—with the sheer power of his personality. 'With me. It's the reason I'm dressed like this.' He indicated his formal evening clothes.

'A charity ball...?' Thia echoed softly.

He nodded. 'I thought we could spend a couple of hours at the ball and then leave when you've had enough.'

She looked at him sharply. 'Is this because of what I said to you last night?'

He grimaced. 'You said a lot of things to me last night, Cyn.'

Yes, she had—and quite a lot of them had been insulting. Most especially the part where she had suggested Lucien was hiding her away because he didn't want to be seen in public with a waitress student from London... 'There's really no need for you to do this, Lucien. I was out of line, saying what I did, and I apologise for misjudging you—'

'You apologised for that last night,' he dismissed briskly. 'Tonight we're going out to a charity ball. Most, if not all of New York society will be there too.' Lucien met her gaze unblinkingly.

'Exactly how much per ticket is this charity ball?' Thia

had seen several of these glittering affairs televised, and knew that they cost thousands of dollars to attend.

'What the hell does that have to do with—?'

'Please, Lucien.'

His mouth thinned. 'Ten thousand dollars.'

'For *both?*' she squeaked.

'Per ticket.'

'Ten thous…?' Thia couldn't even finish the sentence—could only gape at him.

He shrugged. 'The proceeds from the evening go towards the care of abused children.'

Even so… Ten thousand dollars a ticket! It was—'I can't allow you to spend that sort of money on me.' She gave a determined shake of her head.

'It isn't for you. It's for abused children. And I've already bought the tickets, whether we attend or not, so why not use them?'

'Because—because I—' She gave a pained wince. 'Why don't you just take whoever you were originally going to take?'

'I bought the extra ticket today, Cyn. You *are* the person I was originally going to take.' His gaze was compelling in its intensity.

Maybe so, but that didn't mean Thia had to go to the charity ball with him.

Did it…?

CHAPTER TWELVE

'THAT WASN'T SO bad, was it…?' Lucien turned to look at Cyn as the two of them sat in the back of the limousine, driven by Paul, with Dex seated beside him, and they left the charity ball shortly before midnight.

'It wasn't bad at all. Everyone was so…nice.' She looked at him from beneath silky dark lashes.

'They can be.' Lucien nodded.

'It probably helped that I was being escorted by the richest and most powerful man in New York!'

'I didn't notice any pitying glances being directed my way,' he teased huskily.

'If there were, they were kept well hidden!'

Lucien reached across the distance between them to lift up one of her hands before intertwining his fingers with hers—ivory and bronze. 'Will you come up to my apartment for a nightcap when we get back to the hotel?' he invited gruffly.

Thia gave him a shy glance in the dimly lit confines of the back of the limousine. The privacy partition was up between them and the front of the car. To her surprise, she had enjoyed the evening much more than she had thought she would, meeting so many more people than just the celebrity side of New York society. Such was the force of

Lucien's personality that all of them had accepted her place at his side without so much as a raised eyebrow.

The only moment of awkwardness for Thia had been when they had spoken briefly to Felix and Simone Carew. The older woman had avoided meeting Thia's gaze—that fact alone telling Thia that Jonathan must have spoken to the actress today, and that Simone knew Thia now knew about the two of them.

Lucien's manner had been extremely cool towards the other woman, and his arm had stayed possessively about Thia's waist as he spoke exclusively to Felix, before making their excuses so that he could introduce Thia to some friends of his across the room. That arm had remained firmly about her waist for the rest of the evening.

She had even worn the gown Lucien had selected and bought for her. A bright red figure-hugging, ankle-length dress that left her shoulders and the swell of her breasts bare. And she had secured the darkness of her hair at her crown. The appreciation in Lucien's eyes when she'd rejoined him in the sitting room of her suite had been enough to tell her that he approved of her appearance.

She moistened her lips with the tip of her tongue now. 'Is that a good idea?'

His fingers tightened about hers. 'We can go to your suite if you would prefer it?'

'I've had a lovely time this evening, Lucien, but—'

'This sounds suspiciously like a brush-off to me.' He had tensed beside her.

Thia gave a shake of her head. 'I'm leaving in the morning, Lucien. Let's not make things complicated.'

His eyes glowed in the dim light. 'What if I want to complicate the hell out of things?'

She smiled sadly. 'We both know that isn't a good idea. I'm…what I am, and you're…what you are.'

'And didn't tonight prove to you that I don't give a damn about the waitress/student/billionaire/businessman thing?'

Thia chuckled huskily. 'The difference between us I was referring to was actually the virgin and the man of experience thing!'

'Ah.'

'Yes—*ah*. A difference that horrified you last night,' she reminded him huskily.

'It didn't horrify me. I was just surprised,' he amended impatiently. 'But I'm over the surprise now, and—'

'And you want to continue where we left off last night?' Thia arched her brows.

'You know, Cyn, when—if—I've ever thought of proposing marriage to a woman, I certainly didn't envisage it would be in the back of a car. Even if that car *is* a limousine! But if that's how it has to be, then I guess—'

'Did you say you're proposing marriage…?' Thia turned fully on the leather seat to look at him with wide disbelieving eyes. Lucien couldn't really mean he was proposing marriage to *her*!

'Well, no,' he answered predictably. 'Because I haven't actually got around to asking you yet,' he added dryly. 'I believe I need to get down on one knee for that, and although the back of this car is plenty big enough I think you would prefer that Paul and Dex didn't make their own assumptions as to exactly what I'm doing when I drop down onto my knees in front of you!'

Thia felt the warm rush of colour that heated her cheeks just at the thought of what the other two men might think about seeing their employer falling to his knees in the back of the car.

She snatched her hand out of his. 'Stop teasing me, Lucien— What are you doing?' she gasped as he moved down onto his knees in front of her after all, before taking both of her hands in his. 'Lucien!'

What *was* he doing?

How the hell did Lucien know? He was still travelling that untrodden path with no signs or indications to guide him.

Thia had obviously enjoyed herself this evening, and he could only hope part of that enjoyment had been his own company.

She looked so beautiful tonight Lucien hadn't been able to take his eyes off her. The fact that other men had also looked at her covetously had been enough for Lucien to keep his arm possessively about her waist all evening, rather than just accepting the glances of admiration his dates usually merited. He didn't want any other man admiring Thia but him.

He knew it was probably too soon for Cyn. That the two of them had only known each other a couple of days. But what a couple of days they had been!

That first evening, when he had literally looked across a crowded room and seen her for the first time, she'd been so beautiful she had taken his breath away. And he had felt as if she had punched him in the chest later on, when she'd preferred to walk away from him, in the middle of a crowded New York street, rather than accompany him to Steele Heights Hotel. The following morning, when he had seen the disreputable hotel where she had spent the night, he'd actually had palpitations! And when she had arrived at his office later that afternoon, wearing that cropped pink T-shirt and those figure-hugging low-rider denims, his physical reaction had been so wonderfully different...!

Cooking dinner last night with Cyn had been fun, and their conversation stimulating, while at the same time Lucien had felt more comfortable, more at ease in her company than he had ever been before. And she had looked so cute in his over-sized T-shirt. He had even enjoyed shopping for the blouse and gown for her earlier today. As for making love with her last night... How Cyn had responded, the way she had given herself to him totally, only for him to learn later that she was inexperienced, an innocent, had literally brought him to his knees.

And he had been on his knees ever since.

He was on his knees again now...

'I'm really not insane, Cyn.' His hands tightened about hers as he looked up intently into her beautiful pale face. 'I am, however, currently shaking in those handmade Italian leather shoes you mentioned at our first meeting,' he admitted ruefully.

She blinked. 'Why?'

'I've never proposed to a woman before, and the thought of having you refuse is enough to make any man shake.'

Cyn gave a pained frown. 'I don't—this is just—'

'Too soon? Too sudden? I know all that, Cyn.' He grimaced. 'I've been telling myself the same thing all day. But none of it changes the fact that I've fallen in love with you—that the thought of you going back to London tomorrow, of never seeing you again, is unacceptable to me. I don't just love you, Cyn, I adore you. I love your spirit, your teasing, your intelligence, your kindness, your loyalty, the way you give the whole of yourself, no matter what the situation. I had no idea how empty my life and heart were until I met you, but you've filled both of them in a way I could never have imagined. In a way I never want to live without,' he added huskily.

Thia stared at him incredulously. Had Lucien just said—? Had he really just told her that he loved her? He adored her?

Maybe she was the one who was insane—because he really couldn't have said those things. Not to *her*. Not Lucien Steele, American zillionaire, the richest and most powerful man in New York.

And yet there he was, on his knees in front of her, her hands held tightly in his as he gazed up at her with such a look of love Thia thought her heart had actually stuttered and then stilled in her chest.

'Hey, look…you don't have to answer me now.' He'd obviously mistaken her look of disbelief for one of panic. 'There's no rush. I realise that it's too much for me to expect you to know if you'll ever feel the same way about me, but we can spend as long as you like getting to know each other better. You'll want to go back to London anyway, to finish your degree. I'll buy an apartment there, or maybe a house, so that we can spend as much time together as you have free, and then, after a few months, if you—'

'Yes.'

'If you still don't think you could ever love me the way I love you, then I'll—'

'Yes.'

'I'll somehow have to learn to accept it, to live with that. I won't like it, but—'

'I said *yes,* Lucien.' Thia squeezed his hands to pull him up so that she could look directly into his face. 'I said yes, Lucien…' she repeated softly as he returned her gaze questioningly.

'Yes, what...?'

Her breath caught in her throat, tears stinging the backs of her eyes. But they were tears of happiness. Lucien loved her. He really loved her. He knew that she had struggled to finance her degree and understood she was determined to finish it. He was going to buy a home in London so that he could be close to her while she did so. He had asked her to *marry* him!

Yes, it was too soon.

For other people.

Not for Lucien and Thia.

Because they were a result of their past—people who had both lost the security of their parents in different ways, at a vulnerable time in their lives. As a result they were two people who didn't love or trust easily—and the fact that they had fallen in love with each other surely had to be fate's reward for all those previous years of loneliness.

Thia slid forward on the leather seat and then down onto her knees in the carpeted footwell beside him. 'I said yes, Lucien.' She raised her hands to cup each side of his beloved and handsome face. 'Yes, I love you, too. Yes, I'll marry you. Tomorrow, if you like.'

'I— But—'

'Or maybe we can wait a while, if that's too soon for you. Lucien!' She gasped as he pulled her tightly against him before his mouth claimed hers hungrily.

'I'll take that as a yes to us getting married, then,' Lucien murmured a long time later, when the two of them were cuddled up together on one of the sofas in the sitting room of his penthouse apartment at Steele Heights, with only a side lamp to illuminate the room.

Cyn stirred beside him. 'I still think you're mean to make me wait for you until our wedding night.'

'Shouldn't that be my line?' he came back indulgently, more relaxed, happier than he had ever been in his life before. How could he feel any other way when he had the woman he loved beside him?

'It should, yes.' She pouted up at him. 'But you're the one who's gone all "not until we're married" on me.'

Lucien chuckled softly, trailing her loosened hair like midnight silk over his fingers. 'That doesn't mean we can't...*be* together before then. I would just prefer that we left things the way they are for now. I can't wait to see you walk down the aisle to me, all dressed in white and all the time knowing that I'm going to undress you later that night and make love to you for the first time.'

When he put it like that...

Cyn moved up on her elbow to look down at him, loving how relaxed Lucien looked, how *loved* he looked. 'What do you mean, we can *be* together before then...?'

His mouth quirked seductively. 'You enjoyed what we did last night, didn't you?'

'Oh, yes.' Her cheeks grew hot at the memory of their lovemaking.

'Would you like to repeat it tonight?'

'That depends...'

His smile faded to a frown. 'On what?'

Thia gave a rueful smile. 'On whether or not you'll allow me to...reciprocate. You'll have to show me how, of course, but I'm sure I'll quickly get the hang of it—'

'Dear God...!' Lucien gave a pained groan and closed his eyes briefly, before opening them again, those same eyes narrowing as he saw how mischievously she returned his gaze. 'You're teasing me again!' he realised self-derisively.

'Only partly.' She wrinkled her nose at him. 'I know the mechanics, of course, but I'm guessing that doesn't mean a whole lot when it comes to the real thing?'

'Let's go and see for ourselves, shall we...?' Lucien stood up, bending down to lift her up into his arms and cradling her tenderly against his chest.

Thia wrapped her arms about his shoulders and gazed up at him adoringly. 'I could get used to this.'

'I very much hope that you do—because I intend spoiling and petting you for the rest of your life.' That same love glowed in Lucien's eyes as he looked down at her. 'I love you very much, Cynthia Hammond. Thank you for coming into my life.'

Her lips trembled with emotion. 'I love *you* very much, Lucien Steele. Thank *you* for coming into my life.'

It was everything.

Now.

Tomorrow.

Always.

* * * * *

CLAIMED BY THE WEALTHY MAGNATE

NINA MILNE

CHAPTER ONE

LADY KAITLIN DERWENT, poster girl for the aristocracy, daughter of the Duke and Duchess of Fairfax, stared at her nigh on unrecognisable reflection and wondered if she'd run mad... No, she *knew* she must have run mad.

There could be no other explanation for the fact that she was standing in this glitzy Barcelona hotel room, her Titian-red hair obscured under a bottleful of cheap blonde dye, her green eyes masked by baby-blue contact lenses, on a 'Blonde Hair and Blue Eyes in Barcelona' themed hen weekend for a woman she hadn't seen for years.

'You OK?' Lynette Cooper, her childhood playmate and the bride-to-be, leant forward to peer more closely into the dressing table mirror and layered on another sheen of letterbox-red lipstick. 'Are you sure you won't come out tonight? We're making cocktails and then we're drinking cocktails.'

Kaitlin summoned a smile. 'No, thank you. I appreciate it, but I'd be gatecrashing.'

She didn't know any of the other guests; it had been a crazy impulse of the type she never, *ever* demonstrated to ask Lynette if she could join the hen group so that she could escape for a weekend. Travel as part of a group with a degree of anonymity and gain some time out, some space to think.

'I will truly be happy chilling out here. I'll order room service, watch a film and go to sleep.'

Lynette tipped her blonde head to one side. 'You sure?'

'I'm sure.'

'OK.' Lynette's smile was genuine, and so reminiscent of her ten-year-old self that Kaitlin couldn't help but smile back.

'And, Lynette... Thank you.'

'You're welcome, Kaitlin. I know we've lost touch, but I'm glad I could help. Really.'

Lynette looked as though she wanted to say more, and Kaitlin knew she needed to forestall her. She wouldn't explain the reasons for the breakdown of their friendship all those years ago—*couldn't* revisit the memories of a trauma she had relegated to the surreal.

'And I am really grateful, Lynette. Now, go and have fun. Don't worry about me.'

Lynette stood, undecided, and then nodded. 'OK. Be good. Call me if you change your mind and want to meet up with us.'

With that she swirled from the room in a gust of perfume.

Be good. No problem there. Lady Kaitlin Derwent was always good—never a breath of scandal to her name and that was the way it would stay. This was as mad as she was ever likely to be—disguised as a blonde, holed up in a hotel room in Barcelona, so that she could contemplate her future.

The recent conversation with her parents pounded her temples.

Her mother's voice, warm with honey. Yet it was a warmth all the Derwent children knew to be false. 'Kaitlin. We have good news. Prince Frederick of Lycander is looking for a bride. We think you fit the bill.'

The Duke of Fairfax had snorted. 'We know you do, and we expect you to do everything in your power to en-

sure it is you who joins him at the altar. Royal blood and Derwent blood joined in alliance.'

The Duchess had looked at her with something as near to approval as she ever showed, eyed her up and down and nodded her ash-blonde head. 'So it shall be.'

Her parents had spoken and Kaitlin had smiled her cool, poised, serene smile—one of many practised in front of the mirror until her cheek muscles ached. 'I'll do my best.'

Now, sitting on the single bed of the Barcelona hotel room, Kaitlin closed her eyes and wondered what on earth she was doing here. What was the point of contemplation? There was nothing to muse over. After all, her future had been mapped out, her destiny already determined. Granted, it was a future most women would kill for—a guarantee of wealth and a young handsome sovereign prince to go with it.

A glance out of the window showed the dusky Barcelona evening. The breeze carried in staccato bursts of chatter, the smell of heat-hazed streets and a hint of sangria. Another glance at the mirror reassured her that her own siblings wouldn't recognise her.

Well, Cora might, with her twin's intuition, but Gabriel certainly wouldn't. A familiar pang of guilt touched her at the thought of Cora—at the knowledge that her relationship with her sister had lost any semblance of closeness. As for Gabriel—right now she didn't even know where her brother was. The future Duke of Fairfax had disappeared on a prolonged sojourn abroad, leaving behind a supposedly jilted girlfriend and no indication of when he would return.

The Derwent siblings—on the surface they had it all, but in reality...

The impetus of emotion made her decision for her—

pent-up energy roiled inside her, making the room's confines too restrictive, and instinct propelled her to the door, out of the room and down the carpeted stairs towards the lobby.

But as she looked around at the bustle in the marble foyer, the people all strangers, a tsunami of panic welled inside her without warning. Alarm and anxiety crashed in as they hadn't for—oh, so many years.

Fool that she was.

This had been a mistake. She should never have come here—never have set foot out of her carefully planned life trajectory. At best she should at least have remained in the safety of her room. She needed to retrace her steps. If only her legs would co-operate. Dots danced in front of her eyes and her lungs refused to work.

A last vestige of common sense had her leaning against a marble pillar in the hope of obscurity…

Daniel Harrington stepped out of the elevator into the hotel lobby. Feelings of futile anger mixed with equally pointless hurt banded his chest.

Stupidity incarnate.

Who knew what had possessed him to attempt a reunion with his family? Ten years ago they had turned their backs on him, refused to countenance his decision to go legitimate, to no longer turn a blind eye.

'If you walk out of that door, Danny, you don't get to come back. Ever. You will be dead to us.'

That walk had been the hardest choice he'd ever made. But he'd done it, and he'd been a fool to think there would be any softening now. So he had only himself to blame for this wasted journey. But he had hoped that his mother, at least, would relent, would want to see her eldest son.

Instead his stepfather had sent his deputy in her stead—

a man who had delivered his message with a cruelty that had exercised Daniel's self-restraint to the utmost.

As he strode towards the revolving doors, the message echoed in his ears.

'Ghosts get no visitors. Dead is dead, Danny boy. Dead is for ever, and you are dead to the Rosso family.'

He nearly missed the movement that had caught at the edge of his vision.

Dyed blonde hair caught back in a messy ponytail, blue eyes filled with anguish... The woman leant against a marble pillar that mostly concealed her from the guests that dotted the foyer. Her breath rasped in heaving gasps that indicated a full-scale panic attack.

With an abrupt turn Daniel veered off and halted in front of her. 'Are you OK?'

Stupid question, but the words seemed at least to steady her slightly, and she blinked her eyes in rapid succession.

'I'm fi...' she began, then gasped out a half-laugh. 'No, I'm not.'

Daniel gestured to a concierge. 'Water, please.' Turning, he held an arm out to the woman. 'Let me help you. You need to sit down.'

'Thank you.'

He watched as she visibly pulled herself together, almost as if through sheer will power. Her breathing was still ragged, but no longer desperate as she pushed away from the fluted column and stood with one hand resting on it.

'I'll be fine.' She nodded her thanks to the hotel staff member who came over with a bottle of water. 'Really.'

'Is there someone I can call or get for you? Or...?'

'No!' The syllable was a touch too sharp. 'Really, I'm fine now. Thank you for your help.'

'I've hardly helped.'

He studied her for a long moment, saw the vulnerability still in her eyes, along with an anxiety she was clearly doing her best to mask.

'But I'd like to. How about I buy you a drink? Stay with you until I'm sure you're OK?'

Surprise touched with an understandable wariness etched a frown on her face.

'No, thank you.' The words were polite but final. 'I don't drink with strangers.'

'And *I* don't leave damsels in distress on their own in hotel lobbies. We can have a drink here. In the public bar, full of plenty of people. If you're in trouble maybe I can help you.'

'What makes you think I'm in trouble?'

Daniel shrugged. 'Instinct. I'm a lawyer. Lots of my clients are in trouble. You get to know the signs.'

'Well, in this case you've misread the signals. I appreciate your concern, but I'm not in trouble and I don't need any more help than you've already given me.'

The words, though softly spoken, were uttered with determination, and Daniel knew he should go on his currently less than merry way. But his instincts were usually bang on the button, and the idea that this woman was in dire straits of some sort persisted.

Not his business. Though there was more to it than that. Dammit, she was beautiful. Wide blue eyes were fringed with thick dark lashes and unenhanced by make-up. A few tendrils of blonde hair had escaped the ponytail and framed a classically oval face. Slender and long-legged, she held herself with a poise and grace that added distinction to her beauty.

As if made uncomfortable by his scrutiny, she shifted from foot to foot and turned her head slightly to one side.

'If you don't need my help then perhaps we could just

enjoy each other's company? You wouldn't think it to look at me, but I am a scintillating conversationalist.'

He accompanied the words with a wriggle of his eyebrows and to his surprise, and perhaps hers, her lips curved up into a smile. Though she still her shook her head.

'Humour me. One drink. So I can be sure you are OK. You can ask the staff to keep an eye on us, if you're worried. In fact I think they already are.'

The smile vanished and her eyes shaded with a hint of anxiety as she glanced round to where the concierge still watched them.

'OK. One drink.'

He held out a hand. 'I'm Daniel.'

The woman hesitated a moment before reaching her hand out to his. 'Lynette.'

Half an hour later, seated across from Daniel in the cool anonymity of the elegant yet highly functional hotel bar, Kaitlin sipped the last of her pomegranate cooler. The non-alcoholic blend of sweet and sour was exactly what she'd needed to revive her.

Come on, Kaitlin.

It wasn't the beverage, nor the comfort of the cream-cushioned round-backed seats, nor even the vivid splash of bright yellow flower arrangements—it was the man.

Daniel lacked her brother's classic handsomeness—the slight crook to his nose indicated that it might well have been broken once, and his features were craggy rather than aquiline—but in sheer presence he could rival Gabriel, even if the latter *was* the Earl of Wycliffe.

He projected a raw energy—a force that showed in the intense blue of his eyes, the jut of his jaw, the sheer focus he bestowed on her. It was a focus underlain with a pull of attraction that caused a warning bell to toll in the dim recesses of her brain that knew the sheer scale of the stupidity of all this.

Attraction was a tug she couldn't afford to feel—an emotion that in truth she had never felt. The blight, she assumed, was a result of her childhood trauma.

Stop, Kaitlin. Don't go there.

The kidnap was an experience she had done her best to suppress, and she had every intention of keeping it buried in the deepest, darkest depths of her psyche, never to surface. After all she had created her safe, controlled Lady Kaitlin persona to achieve that exact obliteration of her memory banks.

'Another drink?' he asked, and his deep voice caressed her skin like velvet and decadent chocolate. 'Or how about dinner?'

'Thank you.'

But no—they were the words she knew she should say. Each minute she spent with Daniel increased the risk of recognition, the possibility that she would slip up and reveal her true identity. That would be a disaster—her parents would be incoherent with anger if Lady Kaitlin Derwent was revealed to have been picked up by a stranger in a Barcelona bar. Because—and she might as well face it—if she agreed to dinner this would no longer be a 'medical' interlude. It would move into different territory altogether. An unfamiliar minefield of a terrain. So...

'But I don't want to disrupt your plans. I'm fine now. Thank you for coming to my rescue.'

'I have no plans.' There was a bleak note in his voice under the casual disclaimer.

'You must have had *some* plans,' she countered. 'You were on your way somewhere when you ran into me.'

'Nowhere specific. Wherever the night took me.'

His shoulders lifted and her gaze snagged on their

breadth. Once again awareness struck—an undercurrent that swirled between them across the square glass-topped table.

'So what do you say?'

'I… I shouldn't.'

'Why not?' Ice-blue eyes met hers. 'Is anyone else expecting you?'

'No.'

'So you're here alone?'

Kaitlin hesitated…couldn't face the complications involved in a full explanation. And, anyway, to all intents and purposes she was alone. 'Yes.'

'You're sure?'

'Yes.'

'Then how about dinner? No strings. We're two people alone in a vibrant city and I could do with some company.'

The words held a ring of truth, and for a moment she wondered what demons he wanted to hold at bay.

Temptation warred with the final grains of common sense, which pointed out that after all she had to eat.

His shoulders lifted in a shrug. 'I had a reservation at one of Barcelona's best restaurants—I could try and resurrect it.'

Kaitlin frowned. 'So you *did* have plans?'

'Let's say my plans didn't materialise.'

An underlying harshness coated the words and pain flashed across those blue eyes.

Kaitlin hesitated, sensing that the man opposite her was hurting. Clearly he'd been stood up. Doubt unfurled—somehow that didn't seem a possibility. It wasn't a scenario that played true.

*Ridiculou*s. Yes, he was good-looking and magnetic and…and… But she hardly knew him or his relationship background.

Yet more reasons to make her exit now.

But she didn't want to. Never again would she have a chance like this. To be free, to shed the 'Lady Kaitlin' persona. Because soon there would be the meeting with Prince Frederick of Lycander—a meeting at which she needed to demonstrate her suitability to be a Lycander bride and then...

Enough. She wouldn't—couldn't think of that now.

'Dinner sounds wonderful. A night of freedom before I step into a gilded cage.'

Oh, hell. She'd said the words out loud. and now this stranger looked at her with a sharpness, an intensity she couldn't fathom. Almost as if it were someone else he saw, not her.

'Never voluntarily step into a cage you don't have a key to unlock.'

The words had an edge—a meaning she needed to deflect. Tonight she didn't want to think about the marriage that awaited her—a marriage that she had believed she wanted. An alliance...a safe future and a role she would excel in.

'I'll bear it in mind.' She turned her lips up into her Lady Kaitlin smile—friendly yet deflecting. 'Now, I'd prefer to think about dinner. But there's no need for Barcelona's best restaurant.' That was Lady Kaitlin's milieu. 'Let's just walk and see where the night takes us.'

Innate caution pointed out that this man was a stranger—instinct told her she could trust him, but she knew all too well the follies of trust and a tendril of panic unfurled.

Think.

'In the meantime, before we go, I'm going to call a friend and tell her I'll be checking in every hour.'

No need to tell Lynette that she was having dinner with

a stranger; instead she'd say she was walking alone and would feel better if she could check in.

'Works for me.'

'I'll be back in a minute.'

To Kaitlin's relief Lynette didn't make a big deal of the situation—she seemed to accept that Kaitlin never travelled alone and that the aristocracy were ultra-security-conscious.

And so ten minutes later she and Daniel stepped out of the hotel's revolving doors into the hustle and bustle of the Barcelona street.

Instinctively Kaitlin halted, almost overwhelmed by the sheer buzz that emanated from the throngs of chattering people. Her gaze darted to the street performers who plied their expertise for the amusement of passers-by. The scents of garlic and chilli and spices wafted from the numerous tapas bars that dotted the early medieval streets and overflowed with evening revellers.

'You OK?'

Kaitlin pushed her shoulders back and nodded. Panic would *not* ruin this evening. The old dormant fear that coloured her every move, that made her live her life bound by rules and regulations and routine, would be suspended tonight. No one knew her identity; no one had any interest in snatching her now.

'I'm fine. It's just so vibrant it stopped me in my tracks.'

Yet instinct had her walking close to his reassuring warmth—logical or not, she sensed that Daniel would keep her safe. Perhaps it was the confident, swagger-free, don't-mess-with-me aura he projected, or the sheer lithe muscular strength in each step. Whatever it was, it worked, and as they walked Kaitlin relaxed, absorbed the sights, the awe-inspiring grand patchwork of architectural styles that graced the skyline, where dark Gothic façades neighboured the harlequin buildings of the Modernistas.

But it wasn't only the Barcelona experience that she absorbed—as they walked her whole body hummed with an awareness of Daniel… Something shimmered and sizzled in the air between them, exacerbated by the occasional brush of their hands or the press of their bodies against each other in the crowds. Each touch sent heat through her, caused her tummy to loop the loop.

Even more head-spinning was the knowledge that he felt the same way; she could sense it—see it in the hunger of his blue gaze when it rested on her.

Some space, time out, seemed a good idea, so she could make an attempt to process the enormity of her reactions. 'Shall we eat?' she suggested pointing to a tapas bar. 'That one looks as good as any.'

'Sure.'

She followed him into the dimly lit packed interior and watched as he managed to snag one of the few small square tables covered in plastic red and white checked tablecloths.

As they looked around she realised where they were. 'It's a *pintxo* bar. I've never been in one—but I think they originate from the Basque region of Spain.'

He nodded. 'Basically *pintxos* are mouth-sized tapas—always skewered with toothpicks. We just go up to the bar, help ourselves and tuck in. We keep the toothpicks and at the end we pay by the number of toothpicks.'

Kaitlin eyed the throng of people at the bar, most of them standing and eating, chatting and drinking with abandon. She knew that even with the new-found freedom of being 'Lynette' she couldn't risk it. Not the possibility of another panic attack brought on by the crowd or that of being recognised.

Daniel looked at her with a glint of amusement. 'I can go and get a selection for us both.'

'Thank you. That would be kind.' Perhaps a touch too much aristocratic hauteur in her voice there, and she eased it with a smile. 'I'll order the drinks.'

Ten minutes later he returned to the table. 'Here we go.'

'Delicious. Ham *empanadillas*, *sobrassada* sausage with honey, apple and crispy Idiazabal cheese *pintxos* made of chicken, tempura with saffron mayonnaise, melted *provolone* with mango and ham, and a mini-*brochette* of pork.'

'That's an impressive Spanish accent. I take it you speak the language?'

'A little.' The Duchess had ensured Kaitlin was fluent in a number of languages.

'You must be prepared, Kaitlin, should you marry into European aristocracy.'

'As part of your job?'

'No. I work in an art gallery.' No harm in sharing *that* fact; lots of people worked in art galleries, after all.

He speared a *pinxto* and surveyed her thoughtfully. 'So, are you here on business? Barcelona has plenty of art.'

Kaitlin shook her head. 'This trip is personal.'

'Are you in trouble?'

The unexpectedness of the question caused her to tense, and a drop of sangria slopped over the edge of her glass and hit the wooden table. Placing her glass down carefully, Kaitlin mopped up the red liquid with a napkin, watching the cloth absorb the ruby stain.

'We had this conversation earlier and I said no.'

'I know you did. I'm not sure I believe you.'

'I'm not in trouble. I came to Barcelona because I needed some space. Tonight I want to forget the past and the future and live in the present.'

An arrested expression flickered across his face in the

candlelit alcove. 'A night of freedom?' he said, quoting her words from earlier.

'Yes.'

Daniel raised his glass. 'To your night of freedom.'

His blue eyes met hers and what she saw shot a funny little thrill through her and she stilled. The sheer unfamiliarity of the sensation made her light-headed, made her dizzy with its intensity, and her body felt energised as every nerve-end tingled in anticipation.

The hours danced by, and the air was tinged with motes of awareness as they talked of everything and nothing. By mutual unspoken consent the conversation veered away from the personal, so they discussed music, films and philosophy. But every word was punctuated by a growing expectancy—a heady underlying responsiveness and a growing realisation of where the evening might end up.

Eventually they shared a dessert, a decadent dark chocolate concoction, and as she spooned up the last sumptuous bite she met his gaze, saw desire ignite in his eyes. Then gently he took the spoon from her suddenly nerveless fingers and placed it on the plate. The chink of metal on china rang loud in her ear.

Oh, so gently he reached out and ran his thumb across her lower lip. She gasped—a small, involuntary sound—at the potency of her own reaction. Sensation uncoiled in her tummy...a need she'd never felt before. Without thought she cupped his jaw, wondered at the feel of his six o'clock shadow. Then his lips descended to hers and the world seemed to stop.

There was the taste of coffee and chocolate, the whirling rush of need, and the intense, sweet pleasure that streamed through her veins and sent a tingling rush to every bit of her body. Never before had she felt like this.

He pulled back, his breathing ragged, and he looked at her with such intensity as he said her name. 'Lynette...'

It was a reminder that she had this night and this night only. Ideas swirled round her head. A touch of fear as to whether she *could* do this, however much she wanted to—and, dammit, she *wanted* to.

For one grim instant the image of her dark, bearded kidnapper splayed through her vision, and then she looked at Daniel and the picture faded, dissipated by the white-hot burn of desire.

'I think we should move this somewhere else.'

'Are you sure?'

She was so sure—because she knew that these feelings could never happen to Lady Kaitlin. Perhaps because of the horror of what had happened during the kidnap... Whatever the reason, it didn't matter. The fact remained that the odds were she would never feel like this again, and right now, caught in the sheer, dizzying sensual mesh of desire, Kaitlin knew she wanted this man. Against all reason it felt right. It could only be for one night, but so be it.

'Yes. I'm sure.'

CHAPTER TWO

Nine months later...

DANIEL HARRINGTON PAUSED on the threshold of the immense marquee, his ice-blue eyes scanning the wedding guests with ruthless disregard. One part of his brain registered the glorious elegance that graced the wedding reception of Gabriel Derwent, Earl of Wycliffe, heir to the Duke of Fairfax. The sumptuous drapes of organza, the glittering twinkle of the fairy lights and the splash of colour provided by the overhanging Chinese lanterns. The delicate scent of flowers pervaded the air—gloriosa and hyacinth, decked the canvas in lavish arrangements.

But in truth Daniel had no interest in the décor, and limited interest in the bride and groom. He was here for one reason and one reason only, and his eyes continued their systematic search, skipping over the rich, the famous and the ordinary on a quest to find Lady Kaitlin Derwent— sister to the groom, and the bride's maid of honour.

Earlier in the proceedings he'd watched her walk down the aisle amidst a bevy of bridesmaids, all dressed in different jewel shades, a medley of beauty. But the only woman he'd been interested in was her, Lady Kaitlin, and as he'd studied her poised, graceful movements suspicion had begun the conversion process to confirmation.

Yet it was still nigh on impossible to believe that the poised Titian-haired beauty, clad in expensive designer teal-green, was the same woman he'd met nine months before in a Barcelona hotel. But as the hymns and the vows had resonated from the rafters of the picturesque medieval church his gaze had never once ceased its lingering on her beautiful features, and certainty had dawned.

Daniel had no doubt whatsoever that 'Lynette' and Katlin Derwent were one and the same.

Now, in the vast marquee that housed the reception party, he located her. Stood in a corner, deep in conversation with a tall blond man he knew to be Prince Frederick, ruler of the Principality of Lycander. Raw emotion slammed into his gut. Anger alongside the unwanted sting of desire and a primal instinct that yelled *mine*.

Instinctively he bunched his hands into fists.

Cool it, Dan. Violence no longer featured in his life as a solution, and initiating a brawl was not an option. After all, Prince Frederick was blameless in this whole sorry mess, and it shouldn't matter to Daniel that Kaitlin's hand rested on the Prince's forearm as she looked up at him.

Yet anger at her deception still pulsed in his veins. Along with the memory of his sense of loss and chagrin when he'd woken up in the swish Barcelona hotel to find no sign of the woman he'd shared such an amazing night with. Not so much as a blonde hair curled on the pillow had spoken of her presence. No strand or fibre of clothing. Just an elusive trace of her rose scent, and the ache in his body that had awoken him in the expectation of her still being beside him.

Then had come worry—heightened by the fact that it had been her first time...a fact she had refused to elaborate on or discuss. Had he mistaken the wonder of the night? Did she have regrets that her first experience had been with a stranger?

Then had come the conviction that she *was* in trouble.

Hell, he'd even wondered if she'd been forced to leave. More fool him.

Anger burned cold under his control.

He allowed only the civilised approach—Daniel got what he wanted through law, order and fair negotiation. That had been his vow a decade ago, and he'd lived by those rules ever since.

Frustration tautened his sinews with the desire to lash out. He would not revert to type—would not embrace the ethos of his family. That was why he'd walked away ten years before, though the cost had been high.

A memory snaked into his brain: his mother's beautiful face, twisted in entreaty as she'd stretched out a pleading hand. *'Don't go, Danny. Please don't walk out through that door.'*

'Daniel.'

He swivelled in recognition of the well-modulated tones of Gabriel Derwent, groom and brother of the Lady Kaitlin.

'Glad you could make it.'

Gabriel smiled and Daniel blinked—the Earl radiated palpable happiness.

'Etta. This is Daniel Harrington—CEO of Harrington Legal, a new associate of my father's, and also a new patron of the Caversham Foundation.'

Daniel recognised the slight edge to Gabriel's voice and couldn't blame him. He'd negotiated an invitation to this wedding with the Duke of Fairfax, Gabriel's father, by dint of making a sizeable donation to the Derwent Manor restoration fund. When Gabriel had found out he'd called Daniel and explained that he wanted an additional price—a 'donation with a difference' to the Caversham Foundation, a charitable trust that helped troubled teenagers.

'Daniel, this is my wife—Etta.'

Pride and awe touched the syllables, and Etta positively beamed, her tawny eyes sparkling with joy.

Daniel searched his repertoire of happy wedding talk. 'Congratulations,' he mustered.

Though who knew for what? Marriage shackled you, created ties that would bind and link and imprison you. His own mother's marriage was proof of that.

'Thank you.' Gabriel studied his expression and his smile widened. 'Though I get the feeling you aren't a fan of marriage.'

'It's just not for me.'

Etta shook her head. 'Perhaps you haven't met the right woman.'

His gaze must have flicked across to Kaitlin for a fraction of a second, because Gabriel followed his line of sight and his forehead creased in a small frown.

Daniel thought rapidly. 'Though from what I've read it sounds as though your sister will follow in your footsteps shortly?'

Keep it casual.

'Perhaps,' Gabriel said, his frown deepening, almost as if he didn't like the idea.

'Why don't we introduce you?' Etta suggested.

Bingo. Not exactly the way he'd planned it—but Daniel was nothing if not versatile. 'Great.'

Gabriel strode towards where Kaitlin and the Prince were engrossed in conversation. Satisfaction brought a small, cold smile to Daniel's lips as he followed.

Kaitlin looked up at Prince Frederick and tried to suppress the all too familiar feelings of panic. *Chill out. Or chillax.* Or whatever the current phrase was. But she couldn't—despite the size of the marquee she felt hemmed in, and fear knotted her tummy into a tangle of panic. Which was nuts. She was standing next to royalty—how much safer could she be? The Prince would have strategically placed bodyguards everywhere.

Though you *could* argue that those bodyguards were only interested in the protection of the Prince—she'd no doubt be seen as collateral damage.

No, that wasn't fair. Frederick would care. Not because he loved her—he'd been upfront about that—but because he was a dutiful man. Or at least she thought he was—the Prince was even better than she was at keeping his true self under wraps.

Yet over the past months she'd learnt he had a moral code that meant he would protect her out of duty.

So she was safe. But, however many times her brain told her that, her nerves still fluttered with an anxiety that increased daily—a throwback to all those years ago when it had been her constant companion. If she was honest, the panic had been on the up ever since her disastrous trip to Barcelona nine months before.

Barcelona. Don't go there.

As for the panic—she'd tamed it once, and she'd tame it again. All she had to do was *be* Lady Kaitlin—be the calm, in control woman she'd taught herself to be. The woman who could produce suitable emotion on tap without feeling a thing.

'We need to talk, Kaitlin. In private.'

Oh, hell. She knew exactly what Prince Frederick wanted to talk about—he wanted to propose and she just didn't want him to. Not yet. *Not ever,* said a small, defiant voice that she tuned out without compunction. This was what she wanted—what most women would rip their own arm off for. Marriage to a wealthy, handsome prince who also possessed the bonus of a moral code. So *of course* she wanted him to propose—but just not *now*.

'Yes, we do. But not here. This is Gabe and Etta's day. I don't want us to overshadow it in any way.'

She'd been there and done that at her sister's wedding, and the guilt still pinged within her.

He raised an eyebrow. 'I don't think us having a conversation will overshadow Gabe's wedding. In truth, I don't think *anything* could overshadow this day for him. Gabe is a man in love.'

Frederick was right—though who would have thought it? Her big brother, nearly as big an emotional disaster zone as Kaitlin herself, had succumbed to the biggest emotion of all and fallen hook, line and sinker for Etta Mason.

'Even so...it is still their day. If we disappear to have a "private" conversation every reporter in the room will clock it.'

To say nothing of her parents. The Duke and Duchess of Fairfax were watching their eldest daughter like a pair of hawk-eagle hybrids.

The Prince frowned, and it was a relief to hear the deep sound of her brother's voice from behind her.

'Kait.'

She turned gracefully, smile in place to greet the euphoric bridegroom, and then she froze. Her brain scrambled for purchase and her stomach nosedived as her eyes absorbed the identity of the man standing next to her brother. Surely she was in the throes of a hallucination? *Please let that be the case.* She'd take the prospect of insanity over reality in a heartbeat.

Pulling up every ounce of learned poise and ability to rise to any social occasion, she forced her jaw to remain clenched and prayed that no one could hear the accelerated pounding of her heart as she let her gaze rest on the man next to Gabe.

No doubt about it—it was Daniel.

Same dark brown hair, same raw energy that couldn't be concealed by the expensively tailored suit. Those oh-so-familiar ice-blue eyes met hers full-on and she could read the anger in their depths. An anger she didn't—couldn't—blame him for. After the most magical night imaginable she'd sneaked away into the chilly Barcelona dawn without so much as a by your leave. Worse, she had lied shamelessly about her identity.

What to do? What to do *now*?

There was zilch she could do—except hope that he wouldn't expose her. Yet even as her head reeled with the sheer horror of the situation, and its potential for disaster, her body betrayed her with a frisson of memory that prickled her skin.

'Sorry to interrupt,' Gabe said, though Kaitlin noted there was not so much as a hint of apology in his tone. 'But I wanted to introduce you to someone. Kaitlin, this is Daniel Harrington. He has made a generous contribution to the manor and is also linked with the Caversham Foundation.'

Mind racing, Kaitlin forced her lips to turn up in a polite smile with a touch of appreciation. Her years of careful practice in front of a mirror to perfect a smile for any occasion was coming in handy. Even as her brain seethed with tumult it tried to come to terms with the scale of the disaster.

'Pleased to meet you,' she said, her voice even as she held out one perfectly manicured hand, impressed to see that her fingers didn't so much as tremble. It was a shame the same couldn't be said of her insides. Then he clasped her hand in his, in the briefest of handshakes, and a funny little thrill raced through her bloodstream.

No! No! No! There could be no thrills of any sort—that was a complete non-starter. It was imperative to focus, to work out a way to end this whole scenario before her life imploded. In public.

'Likewise,' Daniel said, his voice silk-smooth and deadly as nightshade. 'I must admit I hoped to meet you today.' A smile utterly devoid of mirth turned up his lips. 'I'd like to discuss a project with you—I realise this is a big day for you, and you have lots of duties as maid of honour, but it will only take a few minutes.'

Kaitlin quelled the urge to cover her ears, close her eyes and hope that would equate to sudden invisibility. But that wasn't an option. Somehow Daniel had worked out her identity and he now had the ammunition to embroil her in a scandal. Worse it would impact not just herself, but Frederick as well—and that wasn't fair. True enough, technically Kaitlin had done nothing wrong—but her association with Frederick had begun near enough to that disastrous Barcelona night as would make no difference. To the press, at least.

This scenario was a nightmare. She had hoped—believed—that she would never see Daniel again, and here he was, requesting a few minutes of her time.

Who was she kidding? His words had been posed as a request, but his eyes were glacial, his jaw was set, and she knew if she didn't acquiesce he'd have no hesitation in forcing the issue.

'Of course,' she murmured. 'I'd be interested to hear what you have to say.'

The words fell from her lips automatically—she didn't want anyone to suspect how rattled she was. Lady Kaitlin Derwent didn't *do* rattled, and now was not the time to start.

'Well, there's no time like the present. Would anyone mind if I whisk Kaitlin off?'

Kaitlin blinked. That was not what she had in mind—she'd wanted time to think, regroup.

Prince Frederick glanced at her. 'It is entirely up to Kaitlin whether it is convenient for her to speak with you now.'

Etta glanced from Daniel to Kaitlin and back again. 'I don't need you to do anything but enjoy yourself. That's what I'm hoping *everyone* will do.'

Daniel smiled. 'I promise I'll keep the business talk to a minimum.'

'Make sure you do,' Etta said with a light laugh. 'Now, we had better mingle.'

Gabe twined an arm round his bride's waist and they smiled at each other—smiles that could only be described as goofy—and Kaitlin experienced a small pang of envy, felt the sudden ache of emptiness. Exacerbated as she glanced from Frederick's closed expression to Daniel's glacial one. Not so much as a hint of goofiness in the vicinity.

Frederick nodded. 'Make sure you're back in time for the waltz.'

With that he moved away, through the throng of guests, and within moments had been absorbed into a group.

For a second Kaitlin stood, her high-heeled sandals rooted to the marquee floor, frozen by the surreal impossibility of Daniel's presence. Fear dried her mouth. How had he found her? What was he going to do? Questions crowded and jostled in her brain, even as she kept her expression neutral. Yet alongside the anxiety that stretched her nerves there was…*awareness*.

Try as she might, she couldn't stop the memories from tumbling back. Sensations, taste, passion, laughter…the feel of his touch skimming her skin… The very thought made her shiver across the nine-month gap.

Rein it in, Kaitlin.

Because clearly Daniel was not walking that path of

memory—his expression displayed a cold anger that was *not* a happy omen for the forthcoming discussion.

Come on, Kaitlin.

It might still be all right—if he'd wanted to create a scene he surely would have done so by now.

'How about we take this outside?' he suggested, his voice hard.

Kaitlin shook her head. 'No. I don't want anyone to get the wrong idea about us.'

Lord knew she didn't want anyone to get *any* idea about them at all—even a glimmer of the truth had the potential to destroy her future.

He raised an eyebrow. 'Bit late to worry about that now, isn't it?'

'Shh! For goodness' sake, could you please keep your voice down? We need to be discreet.'

Her head spun, though she took pride in the knowledge that not a single observer would notice her inner turmoil. All that was on show was the poised, collected Lady Kaitlin Derwent, chatting politely to a wedding guest. Unless, of course, anyone actually overheard the content of the conversation...

He shook his head. 'Wrong. *You* need to be discreet. I couldn't care less. So, if you want discretion I suggest we take this outside. There's less chance we'll be overheard or interrupted out there.'

Daniel had a point, and surely there would be some guests outside. The afternoon sun shone down, and what could be more natural than she should show a guest the famed Derwent Manor gardens?

'OK. Fine.'

They walked towards the entrance of the marquee and somehow, from somewhere, Kaitlin summoned up con-

versation. 'So you're linked with the Caversham Foundation? That's interesting.'

Daniel's stride slowed as he stared at her, genuine incredulity etched on the craggy contours of his face. 'Are
you for real? You want to make chit-chat?'

'For the benefit of the people watching us—yes, I do.'

'So your image matters that much to you?'

'Yes.' Her voice was flat. 'Haven't you heard? Image
is everything.'

To her it truly was. The creation of Lady Kaitlin Derwent's
image had been her own personal version of therapy—the
way she'd coped after the kidnap fourteen years before. It
had been her way to block out the memories, the fear that
lived with her day and night, the coil of panic that lashed
round her without warning. Being Lady Kaitlin allowed her
to live her life.

'So, yes, seeing as we are supposed to be engaging in
polite conversation, let's do that.'

He gave one last head-shake of disbelief. 'Sure. My association with the Caversham Foundation is actually the
price your brother requested in return for a wedding invitation. On top of my donation to Derwent Manor—which
was your father's stipulation.'

Keep walking.

'And you agreed to this just so you could talk to me?'

'Yes. It's a good cause, and an association with the Duke
and Duchess of Fairfax and their son will be good publicity for my firm. Clients like things like that.'

'Which firm do you work for?'

'I'm CEO of Harrington Legal Services.'

Now her footsteps *did* falter. HLS was huge—a global
law firm with offices in every major city in the world.

'In Barcelona you told me you were a lawyer.'

'I *am* a lawyer. And you aren't in any position to accuse *me* of messing with the truth.'

Touché.

Kaitlin quickened her pace slightly as they exited the marquee and stepped into the late-afternoon sunshine that bathed the lush green landscaped lawns with dappled light. Other guests stood in small groups as Kaitlin led the way along the gravelled path, lined with lush green manicured hedges, towards a bench she judged to be secluded, but not so isolated as to give anyone reason to gossip.

Once seated, she turned towards him, keeping her smile in place for the benefit of onlookers. 'So, why are you here, Daniel?'

CHAPTER THREE

It was a good question. Why *was* he here? Sitting in the splendour of Derwent Manor's famed landscaped gardens. Nearby camellias provided vivid splashes of pink, and their bench overlooked the breathtaking glory of the rhododendron garden for which the Manor was famed.

But in truth the surroundings didn't matter; right now all that mattered was the woman next to him on the wooden bench in the sunshine. The woman he'd known as 'Lynette'. The woman whose true identity had turned out to be Lady Kaitlin Derwent.

Anger battled an unwanted stab of desire as he absorbed her sheer beauty.

Titian hair of a near-indescribable shade—tints of auburn interwoven with shades of reddish-gold—cascaded in loose waves to meet creamy bare shoulders that had his fingers tingling. Her dark green eyes met his gaze in a mixture of defiance, vulnerability and hope.

'Well?' she repeated. 'Why are you here?'

'Because I wanted to check for myself whether Lady Kaitlin Derwent and "Lynette" were one and the same.'

'How did you find out?'

'I saw a recent picture of you and Prince Frederick.'

Glaring up at him from the glossy cover of a celebrity magazine, the image had caught his eye at an airport lounge just weeks ago. About to look away something elusive had nagged at him: the set of Lady Kaitlin's head, the angle of her cheekbones…a willow-the-wisp of recognition.

'And you recognised me from that?'

'Not at first.'

At first he'd thought nothing of it. But some instinct had made him purchase his very first gossip rag and study the photograph further. One business flight later he'd known he must be losing the plot—big-time—but the conviction that Lady Kaitlin Derwent and his 'Lynette' were one and the same wouldn't quit. The more he'd researched Lady Kaitlin the more sure he'd become, preposterous though the idea was, that he'd found 'Lynette'.

'Until today I wasn't a hundred per cent sure.'

Her hands twisted together on her lap. Then, as if aware of the gesture, she loosed the grip. 'You could just have called me. This is a disaster—now you've made contact with my family…we have an association.' Horror etched her classical features. 'What if we end up meeting again?'

'Then so be it. I wanted to see you face to face—make sure beyond a shadow of a doubt that you are "Lynette". Without calling first and giving you a chance to lie. Again.'

Forcing himself to lean back, Daniel kept his anger in check.

'Plus, it's hard to call someone who didn't leave a number, didn't even give their real name, and who vanished without so much as a goodbye.'

'You knew it was one night only.'

A night of freedom.

'Yes, but I didn't know your "one night of freedom" was an aristocrat slumming it with the hoi-polloi.' Anger at her deception, wrath at his own stupidity in falling for her show, fuelled his words. 'Is that the new trend—to lose your vir—?'

Her poise broke and a laser of ire flashed in her eyes.

'Stop right there. How dare you? That is *not* what it was. That night was—'

Breaking off, she pressed her lips together and for a moment vulnerability lit those emerald-green eyes and momentarily sideswiped his anger.

'Was what?'

'It doesn't matter. I know it was shabby to leave like that, but I had no choice. In case you woke up and realised who I really was. Or someone might have recognised me... seen us together.'

Sheesh.

'Would that have been so bad?' Good thing his ego was in good shape.

'Yes.' The word was delivered with simplicity. 'The scandal would have been too much. Especially....'

'Especially because you were planning to marry a prince.'

'No! I mean... I hadn't decided what to do.' She twisted her hands into the teal-green folds of her skirt and then, as if realising what she was doing, she smoothed the material and pulled her shoulders back. 'I wasn't dating Frederick at the time, but I knew there was a possibility that I would in the future. I was a free agent that night, Daniel, and I didn't offer more than I could give. One night.'

'But you *lied*. And you took what I gave under false pretences. I wouldn't have spent the night with you in Barcelona if I'd known who you were and exactly what your gilded cage was.'

'Why not?' The question tumbled out and she pressed her lips together as if in regret.

'Because you were as good as promised to another man and I don't poach.' The idea was anathema—he'd watched his mother's repeated humiliation at his stepfather's numerous infidelities.

Kaitlin leant forward, shook her head, her red-gold hair swinging as if in emphasis. 'I was *not* promised to anyone. Frederick and I had no understanding at that point. It was simply an idea that my parents had put to me. He hadn't approached me—there had been no discussions.'

'But you *knew*.' His voice was implacable. 'All the time you were with me you knew that you would soon be dating someone else. You as good as said it.'

'One night of freedom before I step into a gilded cage.'

Her words in Barcelona had been poignant. Because he knew all too well the iron bars of a gilded cage.

He'd grown up in one—benefited from the gilding, the luxuries, the power, the money, the lifestyle. At what point had he suspected that all those advantages had been bought with money raised from illegal sources? When had he realised what his mother had done?

Guilt coated his insides. She'd done it for him—to give him all those advantages. His father had been dead, she had been destitute, and so his mother had stepped into a gilded cage, married into the mob, and taken two-year-old Daniel in with her.

Enough. That part of his life was over. Here and now he focused on Kaitlin, studied her cool, aloof expression, and felt curiosity as to her motivations surface. 'I don't get why you took such an enormous risk.'

Because every scrap of research he had done on Kaitlin Derwent had shown that risk wasn't in her personality. Never a hair out of place…always ready with a witty quip or the correct comment. Always serene, poised, calm and in control—not the type of person to risk a scandal for a one-night stand. Yet that was exactly what she had done.

'It doesn't matter.' Her tone had lost all colour, and a sudden image of 'Lynette' filled his mind—her vivacity, the way she'd laughed, spoken, enthused. It seemed almost impossible that Lynette and Kaitlin were one and the same.

Not his business. Kaitlin was right. It didn't matter—he'd come here to satisfy his curiosity, confirm his near conviction. No more.

Kaitlin glanced around. 'We've been out here too long; people will start to talk soon. I need to go. This is Gabe's wedding—I don't want to ruin it in any way.' She closed her eyes for a second. 'But we need to finish this conversation.'

They did? As far as he was concerned it was over bar the farewell. But Kaitlin clearly disagreed.

'I'd appreciate a few more minutes of your time. Maybe tomorrow?'

'Sure.' Curiosity prompted his acquiescence. Along with the knowledge that it was never wise to refuse information. All good lawyers knew that information was power. The last thing he wanted was for this farce to come back and bite him in the future. If Lady Kaitlin Derwent believed there was an issue to discuss then he'd go along for the ride.

'Breakfast. Tomorrow. Faircliffe Hotel. I'll book a private room.'

'Thank you.' She gave a fatalistic lift of her shoulders. 'I'll be there.'

The morning spring sunshine slanted through the windows of the hotel bedroom, reflecting off the mirror where Kaitlin surveyed her reflection. She put the final touches to her discreet layer of make-up—the mask that ensured Lady Kaitlin retained her image of cool perfection.

'I wish you'd tell me what is going on,' her sister said from where she sat on the bed.

Not surprisingly, given it was the closest hotel in the

neighbourhood, Cora and her husband, Rafael, had stayed in the same hotel as Daniel the previous night. Kaitlin had figured it was better to tell Cora about the meeting rather than have her twin waylay her en route to breakfast. Now she was beginning to think she should just have kept quiet. Cora had insisted on seeing Kaitlin before the meeting, and her dark blue eyes reflected her usual intuitive discern.

Kaitlin met her sister's gaze in the mirror. 'Nothing is going on.'

'Rubbish. I'm your twin, Kait. There are times when I just *know*, and this is one of them.'

It was true—there was a bond, despite how different she and Cora were. Years before, when the kidnap had occurred, her twin had been distraught, refusing to believe her parents assertion that Kaitlin was staying with friends.

There were times when Kaitlin wished she had rebelled against her parents' dictate and confided in Cora. But she hadn't—she'd convinced herself that if she supressed the memories, locked them away, they would become a dream, lose the sharp edges of reality. So she'd done what her parents had instructed her to do—and never told a soul what had happened.

'What's done is done, Kaitlin. The important thing now is to forget it ever happened. And never, ever disobey us again.' The Duchess's stern voice had hardened further. *'You understand that no one must ever know. It shows us as weak and, worse, those kidnappers have photos of you that cannot be made public. You will not disgrace the Derwent name.'*

'Kait?' Cora's voice was edged with concern, and Kaitlin focused on her twin. 'Is it something to do with the Prince? Because I've wanted to talk to you about Frederick for a long time and...'

Kaitlin had used guile and every conversational trick

in the library to avoid the subject. 'I don't need to discuss Fredrick.'

'Well, I do. All I want to say is that before I met Rafael I would have done anything to win Mum and Dad's approval. Because I thought that was the way to win their love.'

'I—'

Cora raised a hand. 'Let me finish. I *need* to say this. Don't marry him if you don't love him. Love has transformed my life and I'd like you to have an opportunity to feel the way I feel.'

And there was the crux of the matter. Lady Kaitlin didn't do feelings—*couldn't* feel, didn't want to experience the tsunami of emotions that might be unleashed if she allowed feelings in.

'Cora, I am truly happy for you, and your happiness, but everyone experiences happiness in a different way. My road is different from yours.' Ignoring the small sigh from her sister, she glanced at her watch. 'Now, I've got to go.'

Suspicion narrowed Cora's blue eyes. 'That's another thing. I'm getting a vibe about Daniel Harrington as well. Remind me why you're meeting him.'

'I told you. He wants to discuss a project—and, given the amount he donated to the Derwent Manor restoration fund, I think it's polite to at least see what he has to say. *And* he's linked to the Caversham Foundation.'

That should reassure Cora, bearing in mind her friendship with Ethan and Ruby Caversham.

Kaitlin rose from the dressing table in one graceful move and cast a last look in the mirror, taking comfort in the fact that outwardly no one except her pesky twin would be able to tell her inner self was in turmoil. The dove-grey light wool coat dress was perfect for the occasion. It spoke of an aloof elegance with businesslike overtones that would assure any nosey reporter that this breakfast had no innuendo attached. The intricate hand-stitched ribbon embroidered around the neck and falling across the front gave it the Kaitlin Derwent 'edge', and she gave a small satisfied nod.

'I'll see you later, Cora. And quit worrying.'

As Kaitlin exited the room and made her way down the carpeted grand staircase of the country hotel her heart pounded her ribcage. It was only the years of practice that kept her upright. Her gaze darted around the lobby in an automatic check for danger even as she focused on keeping her gait unhurried.

She managed a smile for Sophia, the member of staff who manned the small desk that led to the breakfast room. 'I have a meeting with Daniel Harrington.'

The girl nodded with enthusiasm. 'Mr Harrington has booked for a private room. Come through here.'

'Thank you.' She followed the girl into a small room and braced herself as Daniel rose from the table to greet her.

'Lady Kaitlin.'

To her relief his voice was formal, but as she met his gaze she saw something flash in his eyes and her own body instinctively responded. Knowing her voice would suffer from lack of breath, she nodded in acknowledgement.

'Can I get you anything?' Sophia asked,

'We're good, thanks.'

There was silence when the young woman had left.

Get it together, Kaitlin.

If only this man didn't affect her so much. Her expert eye recognised the quality of the understated light blue silk cotton shirt and suit trousers. But it wasn't the expensive clothes—it was the raw energy they contained, the solid, muscular bulk of his body, the strength of his craggy features, the square determination of his jaw and the set of his lips.

Lips that had given her such aching pleasure she nearly shivered with the memory.

Get it together now, *Kaitlin.*

He gestured to the side table pushed against the wall of the room. 'Help yourself to food.'

Kaitlin contemplated refusing, unsure whether she could physically eat, given the fact her tummy was busy tying itself up in a lanyard of knots. But this was supposedly a business breakfast, and therefore she'd do better to play along. The last thing she wanted was for the hotel staff to notice anything amiss.

Two minutes later she seated herself at the circular table, with a plate holding a croissant, a dab of butter and a small pot of strawberry jam in front of her. Somehow she had to focus—she was here to negotiate herself out of this mess. Channelling every single iota of her inner poise, she managed a cool smile. Whatever it cost her she would not show Daniel even a particle of her discomfort.

'So, Kaitlin. You requested this meeting. Why?'

'I need to know what you plan to do.'

For a fleeting second confusion flashed across his face, and then a small mirthless smile tipped his lips up. 'You're worried I'll go public with the whole Barcelona story?'

'Yes.'

In truth, the idea of the press getting hold of this made her quake. Her parents would... Her imagination couldn't even begin to conjure up the Duke's and Duchess's reactions. But it was more than that...

'I realise you have no obligation not to,' she continued quietly, 'but it wouldn't just impact me. The scandal would affect Prince Frederick as well.'

The House of Lycander had been besmirched by more

than its fair share of disgrace and rocked by tragedy, and the idea that she might add to Frederick's troubles filled her with horror.

'I don't want my stupidity to discredit Frederick or make him look a fool in the eyes of the media.'

'Because you love him?'

The question was posed as though the answer mattered and it caused her vocal chords to tighten.

'Or because it would make your relationship and marriage to him problematical?'

Perhaps she should lie—claim that she *did* love Frederick, throw herself on Daniel's mercy. *Ha!* Instinct informed her that that wouldn't work, because she sensed he didn't have any. But, more than that, she didn't want to lie—she'd lied enough.

'That's none of your business. I will not discuss Prince Frederick with you. That's not fair to him.'

'You didn't worry about fairness in Barcelona.'

'I told you—I hadn't met him then. Or at least I hadn't started to date him.'

'But you knew you were going to.'

Daniel's voice was soft, but the edge could have cut a diamond. Easy to imagine him in a courtroom now.

'All the time you were with me you knew that you would soon be dating someone else.'

The contempt in his voice made her feel exposed and she leant forward, needing him to understand even as she knew she shouldn't care about his opinion.

'Yes.' There could be no denial there, but she'd be damned if she apologised either. 'But I didn't plan that night. I didn't go to Barcelona to have a one-night stand.'

'Why *did* you go?'

'I had a moment of panic.'

'No. A moment of panic is when you have a few drinks,

breathe into a paper bag or eat your bodyweight in choc-olate. It's not when you assume a fake identity and sleep with a stranger.'

'OK. So I had a *spectacular* moment of panic.'

'Because of Prince Frederick? That seems extreme. No one was going to march you to the altar on the spot.'

'I know that.'

How to explain panic to this man? A man who clearly knew who he was and what he wanted from life. To Kait-lin, panic was a mortal enemy—kept on a leash, tamed by her determination not to let it conquer her. Time had taught her the best way to achieve dominance was control—if she micromanaged every second of her life, created a secure zone, a persona that was in command, that way she won.

'I just wanted some space to process the future...some time out. The plan was to stay in my hotel room and order room service. Instead...' She tipped a palm up and let out a sigh.

Instead she'd deviated from the script for the first time in a decade, stepped out of her comfort zone and into di-saster.

'Instead you ended up with me. It doesn't make sense. As far as I can tell, from the publicity that surrounds you, you are the personification of discretion. You've never so much as been caught tipsy, and any relationships you have had haven't caused even a breath of scandal. As for you and Prince Frederick—you haven't even been seen hold-ing hands in public...'

Impossible to explain that there was no spark between her and Prince Frederick—had never been a spark with any man until Daniel. Dating Frederick was calm, correct and dutiful. In truth that had surprised her as much as it had relieved her. Prince Frederick of Lycander had once been a noted playboy—had 'dated', for want of a better euphemism, plenty of women, and been photographed on yachts and in night clubs. But clearly that wasn't the way he treated a possible wife. Formal duty characterised their relationship, and that suited her fine.

'I agree it didn't make sense. I acted out of character and it was a mistake.' Of enormous proportions.

The sparks between her and Daniel had set off an inferno that could affect the rest of her life.

'So now you've decided to enter the gilded cage? That's the gilded cage you were talking about in Barcelona, isn't it?'

The words slammed into her—seemed to echo across the months.

'The Lycander marriage.'

Kaitlin summoned as much aristocratic hauteur as was possible. 'My marriage is my business and I know what I'm doing.'

Amazing she could say that with a straight face. No! She *did* know what she was doing; it was just this man, this horrible scenario, that was messing with her head.

'There is nothing wrong with a gilded cage.'

'Dammit. There is *everything* wrong with a gilded cage.'

The force in his voice made her jump, caused her heart to pound.

'It's a prison of the worst kind.'

Bleakness flashed across his blue eyes and for a mad second she wanted to reach out and offer comfort. *Ridiculous.* She had to focus on what was important here.

'You are entitled to your opinion, but I disagree.'

His fingers drummed the snowy white linen of the tablecloth and his gaze seemed to bore into her soul. 'That's not what you thought nine months ago.''

'Yes, it is. I had a moment of insanity that night, but however mad I was I always knew what my future held.'

Daniel shook his head and she wondered why this mattered so much to him. She felt an urge to ask—a wish that this conversation didn't have to be so antagonistic. A sudden memory of the conversations they'd shared that Barcelona night clouded her mind: the ease, the banter, the sharing of opinions. Compared with the sophisticated, carefully constructed exchange of her talk with Frederick. *Enough.* Bad enough that her body was on alert—heaven help her if her mind joined the party.

'And I should never have jeopardised it with a meaningless one-night stand.'

His eyebrows rose. 'Meaningless?' he repeated softly.

'Meaningless on any real level.' It was impossible to infuse her words with more than a mocking semblance of truth—not when she knew that their night together had been little short of a miracle for her.

'You sure about that?'

His voice deepened and Kaitlin caught her breath on the smallest of gasps. She dropped her gaze from the look in his eye. The ice-blue had darkened to cobalt and she knew what she would see in their depths—the memory of the levels, the sheer *heights* of the passion they had scaled. Heat crept up her cheekbones and her gaze lingered on his hands, on their strength, their capability, and an image flashed into her brain. The touch of his fingers as they'd caressed her skin...her own fingers trailing down the skin of his bare back...the ripple of muscle, the taste of...

Momentarily she closed her eyes, made dizzy by a mix of horror and sheer sensuous memory. *Enough.* That had been a night of madness, and if anything it had shown her that spontaneity led to disaster. Reinforced her need to be Lady Kaitlin Derwent—poised, calm, serene and safe.

That was who she needed to be now; being 'Lynette' had landed her in a mess of horrific proportions, and right now she needed to stay focused on getting herself out.

She could only hope that the effort it took to keep her voice steady wasn't beading her brow with perspiration.

Kaitlin looked down at the croissant on her plate…realised that at some point in this quagmire of a conversation she had crumbled the flaky pastry into a pile of crumbs. It was not her usual behaviour, and impatience rippled through her along with a touch of panic. She could not afford to unravel now.

'Meaningless,' she repeated, and this time she succeeded in imbuing her voice with aloofness. 'Surely you aren't claiming it meant anything to *you*?'

If she'd hoped to gain his agreement she was disappointed.

'Of course it did. Not because I wanted more, but because I liked and respected "Lynette" and I hoped that the night was meaningful to us both.'

Ouch.

The words hurt, but she knew she deserved them. It had been poor form to deceive him and it had been disingenuous of her to say that the night had been meaningless. But she wouldn't—*couldn't*—back down now. Daniel Harrington had the power to bring her name and, more importantly, the name of Lycander into disrepute.

'None of this is relevant, Mr Harrington. I need to know whether you plan to go public.'

Her breath caught in her lungs as she waited for his answer.

There was a silence as he looked at her, and then he shook his head. 'Is that all you care about?'

'Right now, yes. And I won't apologise for that. This isn't only my name at stake—it's Frederick's as well.'

His lips twisted in a grimace. 'To say nothing of mine. So you have no need to fret, Kaitlin. I won't go public. Believe it or not, I have no wish to be embroiled in some sordid media scandal.'

The intensity of his voice alerted her, and she couldn't help but wonder at the nuance of revulsion. As if he sensed her interest he shrugged. 'I'm a lawyer—a serious one—it wouldn't be good for my business.'

That made sense, and yet she had an instinct that there was more to it than that. Not that it mattered—the point was that he would keep their time in Barcelona to himself. But even as relief washed over her, her doubts grew. Could Daniel *really* not want anything? Could she trust him?

Even though an irrational gut feeling told her she could, she *knew* the world didn't turn like that. A woman she'd trusted completely had been the one to collude with her kidnappers. Since then she'd made a point of not listening to her instincts—after all, she was living proof of how foolish trust could be.

'So, you'll walk away?'

There was a second's hesitation as he studied her, and she swore she could see a flicker of concern in his ice-blue eyes.

'Yes. But I'll give you the same advice that I gave "Lynette" nine months ago. Don't enter a gilded cage unless you have the means to leave.'

'OK.' Once again she wondered why it mattered so much to him. 'And, thank you, Daniel.'

He rose to his feet and held out a hand. 'Good luck, Kaitlin.'

Rising to her feet, she looked at his hand for a fraction too long, absurdly worried about so much as a touch. *Truly absurd.* She pulled on a smile that hopefully combined farewell with gratitude and placed her hand in his.

Not so absurd after all. His touch made her feel… It didn't matter what it made her feel. Because it shouldn't make her feel *anything*.

'Goodbye, Daniel.'

As she turned to exit the room she waited for relief to wash over her. But instead her tummy felt weighted with a ridiculous sense of loss. An echo of nine months before, when she had walked away from that hotel room in Barcelona.

CHAPTER FOUR

Two weeks later

KAITLIN STARED IN the mirror, marvelled at the serenity of her reflection that thankfully showed no indication of the inner hysterics gallivanting inside her. But she shouldn't be surprised. After all this was her forte—looking the part.

Her outfit was the perfect choice for a woman about to receive a marriage proposal from a prince. The flared cream trouser suit was cool and casual, and saved from blandness by the sparkly shimmer of a silver-grey camisole-style blouse. Her freshly washed hair fell in simple loose waves to her shoulders, and her make-up epitomised the art of discretion.

Time to go—even though her nerves quivered as she exited her old bedroom in Derwent Manor, taking comfort from the familiar smooth sheen of the oak under her fingertips as she descended the stairs and walked past the line of portraits of her ancestors. It was easy to imagine them all applauding with approval at the prospective alliance.

As she entered the lounge Prince Frederick turned from where he stood at the ornate fireplace.

'Kaitlin.'

'Frederick.'

He stepped towards her, his face expressionless, a picture of formal decorum, dressed in a tailor-made suit, his hazel eyes unreadable, but without a hint of warmth.

This is not how it is supposed to be, pointed out a small, insistent voice at the back of her brain.

And as if he too realised that, Frederick smiled.

But the smile didn't reach his eyes and Kaitlin, a connoisseur of smiles, recognised its stoic element. He took another step forward, so he was near enough to take her hand, though of course he didn't.

'Thank you for seeing me. I assume you know why we are here?'

'Yes.'

Don't enter a gilded cage unless you have the means to leave.

Daniel's words rang in her brain. *Stupid.* A man she barely knew. Yet a man she had trusted with not only her own name but that of the House of Lycander. A house that had been plagued with scandal enough to rock the throne with sufficient force to require the Prince to seek a marriage that would prove to his people that their sovereign cared. For that Prince Frederick needed a bride untainted by even the smallest germ of scandal.

Realisation weighted her tummy—she'd had no right to place her blind trust in a veritable stranger...to gamble with Prince Frederick's name without his knowledge.

'Wait.' Kaitlin raised a hand. 'There is something I need to tell you.'

Dread tightened her chest as she braced herself for the storm about to break.

'What the...?' Daniel stared down at the headline that confronted him from the top of his newly cleared desk.

'I thought you might be interested,' his PA explained, her voice carefully devoid of emotion. 'As you attended the Earl's wedding and...'

Daniel wrenched his gaze away from the laptop screen

that displayed a website devoted to celebrity gossip and eyed Caroline, who returned his gaze expressionlessly.

Caroline Winterbourne looked as cool, collected and indifferent as ever, but Daniel knew differently. He'd given her a chance, despite her prison record, and in return she offered unassailable loyalty.

'I'll leave you to it.'

Daniel returned his attention to the article and an expletive dropped from his lips as the words slammed into his retinas.

Lycander Split: It's All Off!
Lady Kaitlin Derwent and Prince Frederick of Lycander have announced the end of their relationship after 'mutual agreement'. Neither side is willing to elaborate, but friends and acquaintances have declared shock and surprise.

The couple have been seen together for months and the world had awaited the announcement of an engagement—not a break-up. However, the ex-couple insist they will remain friends.

Watch this space as we try to discover the real reason behind the surprise split...

His intercom buzzed. 'Daniel, I have an April Fotherington on the line. She's a celebrity reporter. Shall I get rid of her?'

Caroline's tone suggested she'd be happy to bury the body as well.

'No. I'll talk to her.' There was a click and then he said, 'Daniel Harrington speaking.'

'Mr Harrington. Thank you for speaking with me. I wanted to get your reaction to the break-up between Lady Kaitlin Derwent and Prince Frederick.'

'I don't *have* a reaction. Am I supposed to?'

'My sources inform me that you and Lady Kaitlin were spotted deep in private conversation at the Earl of Wycliffe's wedding recently.'

'That is hardly a basis for me to have formed any opinion on Lady Kaitlin's relationship with Prince Frederick.'

'Hmm…' The reporter's tone was heavy with scepticism. 'Thank you for your time. Maybe we'll speak again soon.'

Daniel put down the phone and cursed under his breath. He drummed his fingers on the desk and then picked up the phone. 'Caroline, please can you get me Lady Kaitlin Derwent's number?'

'Leave it with me.'

Twenty minutes later he was en route across London. Forty minutes later he had parked in the vicinity of Lady Kaitlin's Chelsea flat and alighted from the car. He eyed the group of reporters that crowded the pavement outside.

Walk as if you have the right and then you do have the right.

Advice given to him by his stepbrother—the man he'd once revered more than any other being.

Moving through the baying throng of press, he ignored all the shouted questions, reached the door and banged on its navy blue surface in the pre-agreed code. Kaitlin pulled the door open a crack and he squeezed through.

Even now, when circumstance dictated frustration and anger, her beauty socked him. Her stance, her poise, the strength of her features, the vividness of her eyes—all endowed her with looks that wouldn't fade with the ravages of time.

He followed her into a lounge that exuded elegance and good taste, where she turned to face him. 'You said on the phone that we may have a problem.'

'April Fotherington rang me an hour ago for my reaction to your split with Prince Frederick. She suspects I am involved and I believe she will dig until she uncovers a link between us.'

The clenching of her hands was an indication that the news was less than welcome.

'That woman has got some sort of super-sense about me. Probably because she has made it her business to be the Derwent family media expert.'

'Well, she will not become an expert on *me* because I have no intention of being pulled into some media gossip frenzy.'

'You may have no choice.' Emerald eyes lasered bitterness at him. 'Why, Daniel? Why did you have to come to the wedding? Why did you track me down? Come to that, why did I ever agree to have a drink with you?' She gave a shake of her head and took a deep breath. 'Doesn't matter. You can't turn the clock back.'

Her voice echoed motes of sadness across the air and he knew with gut deep certainty that she wasn't just referring to her present predicament.

Not his business.

'No you can't. Time cannot be dialled back. That is why it's always best to face forward.' That was the vow he'd made when he'd walked away from his family, from his life of wealth and privilege.

Kaitlin sank down onto the sofa. 'Unfortunately what I am facing is a tabloid tsunami that you have only made worse. Once April discovers you hot-footed it over here I am doomed—she'll have all the "evidence" she needs to know there is a juicy story to unearth.'

'So that still bothers you?'

'Of course it does. If April digs up Barcelona I am the

one who'll bear the brunt of the damage. My image would be in tatters. I'd be painted as the woman who cheated on the Prince of Lycander and I have no wish to embroil myself in that kind of mire. In addition, this isn't Prince Frederick's fault—it is mine, and I feel I owe it to him to avert the scandal if I can.'

Her words rang true, yet for a second her gaze fluttered away and the slightest rose tint flushed the high angle of her cheekbone.

Irrelevant—his only concern here was to scotch the scandal. For his own sake.

'OK. Then we are on the same page. I came here because I have a plan.'

Wary surprise touched her expression. 'The only possible plan is to deny any connection between us.'

Daniel shook his head. 'Too late for that. April will find out we met for breakfast and she'll keep on digging. I propose to head her off at the pass. But to do that I need information—the real reason you and the Prince split.'

Her gaze dropped, but not before he saw a glint of hurt in her eyes—a glimmer she erased before she raised her head.

'That is not your concern.'

'Yes, it is. If we want to avoid a scandal then we need to put all our cards on the table.'

A half-laugh totally devoid of mirth fell from her lips. 'By that you mean *I* need to put my cards on the table, when I don't even understand why this matters so much to *you*.'

'I told you. I have an international reputation to maintain as well, and I have no wish to see my name splashed across the tabloids. It would hardly make me look good in court.'

Though that would be the least of his worries if his connection to the mob was revealed. The adverse effect of that would reverberate through his company and impact on his employees, and he would not let that happen.

Her slim shoulders lifted in a shrug. 'I'm not an idiot either, and I'm pretty sure that's not your full hand of cards.'

'That is irrelevant. What matters now is that we prevent April Fotherington from unearthing what happened in Barcelona.'

A memory of that night, the sheer magic of their connection, sneaked up from nowhere and blindsided him with a bombardment of images. He rubbed a hand over his face, swiped them away. Their physical connection had been based on illusion, and as such its worth was *zero*. In any currency.

'To do that I need to know why you and the Prince broke up.'

'Give me a minute.'

For the first time since he'd entered Daniel looked round the room. It was impeccably furnished, and good taste abounded—neutral cream walls a backdrop for a fourth wall of elegant patterned wallpaper with a splash of colour in the bird-themed print. Pictures dotted the walls in a mix of modern and retro, and the simply striped upholstered furniture looked both comfortable and stylish.

Yet something grated on his nerves; it was the knowledge that the lounge looked exactly as Lady Kaitlin's lounge *should* look—ready for a photographer to descend at any moment. The fact that there wasn't so much as a hint of 'Lynette' to be seen.

Kaitlin gestured to the armchair opposite. 'OK. I'll bite. The Prince and I split up because I told him about Barcelona.'

Daniel stared at her, wondered if perhaps his ears had

ceased to function, whether his brain had somehow rewritten the signals and garbled her words. 'You *told* Prince Frederick about Barcelona. Why?'

'It wasn't fair to put his good name at stake without his knowledge. I couldn't place trust in your discretion on Frederick's behalf—he needed to make that decision for himself.'

A mix of emotion hit him—chagrin at her lack of faith, and admiration and surprise at a level of principle he hadn't expected from the woman who had duped him...a woman set on a marriage made of glitter and lined with gold.

'So he decided to break up with you because of the potential scandal or because he felt angry at the thought of you with another man?'

Weariness made her shoulders slump for a fraction of a heartbeat and then she straightened, dropped her hands to her lap from their mid-rise to a defensive fold.

'The former. Frederick needs a scandal-free bride and I no longer qualify.'

'In which case I could talk to him and convince him I won't go public.'

'It wouldn't work; his view is that it happened, therefore there is always a risk of discovery. However small the risk, he doesn't feel it's worth it.'

Didn't feel *Kaitlin* was worth it. That had to hurt. Whatever the ins and outs of their relationship, however political or convenient it had been, they had spent nine months together.

'And they say chivalry is dead.'

'I don't want chivalry—I messed up and there are consequences.' A shadow flitted across the emerald-green eyes—one that spoke of weariness and a bitter knowledge of how cause and effect worked. 'Anyway, I've given you the information you requested, so now it's your turn. Tell me your plan to deal with April Fotherington.'

The idea that had spun into his mind as he'd travelled across London coalesced into a tangible reality. 'OK. Listen up.'

CHAPTER FIVE

A PLAN—A POTENTIAL solution to their predicament was a good thing, right? Kaitlin tried to focus, to think… But right now it was hard to think at all through the confusion brought on by Daniel's unexpected arrival on the scene. A veritable knight in shining armour. *Not.*

Daniel's involvement suited his own purposes—her rescue was a mere by-product, and she'd do well to install that fact in her memory banks. But no matter—the past twenty-four hours had been abysmal, as she'd watched her future spiral out of her control, so if she could ride his coattails out of this mess then she would.

'Go ahead.'

He rose to his feet in a lithe ripple of muscle. Clad in blue jeans and a dark blue T-shirt, he exuded energy as he paced the beige coir carpet.

'At the wedding I said I had a project to discuss with you. We'll run with that story. As I told you, in return for an invitation to your brother's wedding I agreed to make a donation to the Caversham Foundation. Gabriel insisted that the donation not be monetary—instead he demanded I pledge a week of my time. I spoke with Ethan Caversham and I agreed.'

'Why?' The question was not germane to the situation, but curiosity propelled the question from her lips.

'I wanted the invitation—your brother and Ethan are valuable contacts—and Ethan is a very persuasive man.

Enough that I agreed to take this week off work. I'm to travel to the Highlands, where I will spend three days participating in outdoor activities with a group of troubled teenagers. Then I fly to Venice to host a fundraising ball.' He halted and turned to face her. 'I propose that *you* come with me. What do you think?'

Say what?

He stood there as if he had come up with the equivalent of a winning lottery ticket instead of the nuttiest scheme ever.

'I don't think anything. I *know* you've run mad.'

'That is because you haven't thought it through.'

'Nope. It's because it doesn't make any sense—we would need to spend a whole week together.' The idea fuzzed her brain with cotton wool even as her insides twisted in panic. 'That will only fuel speculation about us—not prevent it.'

'Not if we play it right. The story provides a perfectly logical explanation for the time we've spent together, both at the wedding and at breakfast the next day. I tried to persuade you to get involved—you couldn't because of your commitments with Prince Frederick. So when I heard about the split I hot-footed it over here to see if I could convince you to join me now.'

There was a certain plausibility about it, but... 'That might work as a cover, but I could have still refused to join you. There is no need for me to actually *come* to Scotland or Venice.' The idea shortened her breath, pierced her chest with the stab of anxiety that preceded panic.

Chill, Kaitlin.

'But it would be better if you did come.'

'Better for whom?'

'Better for the project. Right now the press is focused on you—you could make a real difference...raise awareness of the Caversham Foundation by a substantial amount.' His eyebrows rose with more than a hint of derision. 'Think of your image as well. A refusal to participate wouldn't look good.'

Whereas an agreement would be an opportunity to re-model Lady Kaitlin—transition her from prospective royal bride to a woman who had moved on from her break-up in a positive manner, the champion of a good cause that she genuinely believed in.

Yet caution still raised its head. 'The press will try to find a romantic angle.'

'Let them try. They won't be able to locate it, because it doesn't exist.' His mouth twisted in a wry upturn that held more than a hint of challenge. 'Unless, of course, you're worried you'll succumb to my deadly charm?'

Kaitlin narrowed her eyes. 'In your dreams, Daniel.' Been there, got the T-shirt and never again.

'Then what are you so worried about? Worst-case sce-nario is that they speculate—you're a free agent now.' He eyed her for a moment, fingers drumming on his thigh, and then he snapped his fingers. 'Unless you are hoping for a reconciliation with Prince Frederick?' Disdain dripped from his voice. 'Is that the plan—did he agree that if you weather the storm you will requalify as a Lycander bride?'

'No!' His contempt stung. 'There is no plan. But it's… complicated.'

With an effort she kept the crack of emotion from her voice as scenes from the previous day filled her mind.

The Duke and Duchess had taken disappointment to new heights—their frustration had filled the living room at Derwent Manor with palpable waves of fury.

You have let us down, Kaitlin. Not just us, but the Der-went name. The only way to redeem yourself is to get him back. Your destiny is with the House of Lycander—we want at least one grandchild with royal blood in his veins. Is that understood?'

The message had been loud and clear, and had been followed by the outline of a 'Win Frederick Back' action plan that had made her burn with humiliation. Yet she had listened in silence—had neither agreed to obey nor expressed refusal to comply. It had seemed the easiest option until she figured out for herself what she wanted to do. For months she'd been on a path and now...now she felt as though the proverbial rug had been pulled from under her designer wedge shoes.

'So, explain.'

The blue of his eyes held not so much as a glint of compassion, but at least his censure had been put on hold.

'This marriage is important to my parents and they believe I should keep my options open. I don't want to rock the boat.'

'You can't marry Prince Frederick for your parents' sake. They have no right to ask that of you.'

The sheer intensity of his voice rocked her backwards. 'They have every right to ask. My father is recovering from a heart attack and my brother and sister have both made marriages my parents' disapprove of. I have it within my power to make them happy by marrying a wealthy, handsome prince. It seemed like a no brainer.'

'Seemed,' he repeated. 'Past tense. What about now?' He tipped his palms up in patent disbelief. 'The wealthy, handsome Prince has ruthlessly discarded you for fear of scandal. You can't possibly still want to marry him.'

Kaitlin resisted the urge to cover her ears and tune out his questions. She had erected a block against Prince Frederick's judgement. But now his words buzzed through the barrier like pellets of venom.

'I am sorry, Kaitlin—you would have made a good Ly-

cander princess, but I can't take the risk of scandal or ridicule. Not now. My bride needs to be untainted by even a breath of scandal. You no longer qualify.'

For a moment the meaning of his words hadn't dawned on her—and then the realisation that nine months could be dismissed so summarily had had her reeling, caused a wire of irrational hurt and anger to tighten her chest. Clearly once again she wasn't worth fighting for; the threat of scandal outweighed her value as a person.

All those years ago her parents had made it plain that they wouldn't expose her kidnappers—wouldn't bring them to justice because of the potential smearing of the Derwent name. Now history had repeated itself with a vengeance.

It didn't matter—she wouldn't let it matter. Lady Kaitlin Derwent did *not* succumb to feelings. She had learnt to lock them down. Thus she had rid herself of pain, anxiety and the slither of horrific memories. So no way would she be goaded into emotion now.

Rising from the sofa, she faced him. 'My association with Prince Frederick was an alliance, not a relationship, and as such he had the right to break it if expedient. End of.'

'But you want to keep your options open to renew that alliance?'

His expression had dialled right back to disdain, but this time she steeled herself to suck it up. This conversation had gone far enough—exceeded the parameters of her comfort zone by a long way.

'It's always wise to keep your options open. Let's go back to your plan.'

'Your call. You're the one with the concerns about the possibility of a romantic angle.'

Instinct warned her that a week with Daniel Harrington might lead to disaster, but logic reiterated the benefits.

'I'm in.'

'Good. Let's face the press on your doorstep now. After that, I'm flying out to Scotland early tomorrow—we might as well travel together.'

'No! Wait!' Seeing the surprise in his eyes, she dialled down the volume of her response. 'I mean, yes, but I need more information before we leave.'

New places had the ability to overwhelm her and trigger a panic attack, so she needed information so that she could prepare, research, lay the groundwork to minimise the chance. Plus she had to ensure she had knowledge of the correct image Lady Kaitlin should project, which facet of her persona would be on show.

'So would it be possible to brief me more thoroughly after we do the press interview?'

'No problem—we can combine it with dinner.'

'Great.' Her tummy was as hollow as the adjective— after all the last time she'd had dinner with Daniel Harrington...

Stop. Don't go there.

Daniel glanced sideways at Kaitlin as they traversed the busy London streets en route to a restaurant of her choosing. Her elusive rose scent tantalised him, brought back unwanted reminders of another city, another time.

Another woman.

Once again he marvelled at the difference between 'Lynette' and Kaitlin, squashed the urge to see if he could delve beneath the layers of Kaitlin to free 'Lynette'.

Get a grip.

That perfume had clearly sent him towards delirium. No one needed freeing. From anywhere.

'It's here.' Kaitlin slowed down and gestured to a small restaurant. 'Cora and I eat here sometimes. It's private, but it won't give the wrong idea.'

As they entered Daniel saw what she meant. The effect was both quirky and fun; the mezzanine deck of the restaurant, where a number of booths were located, was approached by ladders, and the clientele was a mix of parents out with their kids, groups of friends and the occasional couple.

'Lady Kaitlin.' A stocky dark-haired man came forward. 'Welcome. Will there be reporters who need to be quietly ejected?'

'Hi, Carlos. We should be safe today.'

Daniel hoped so—the press had decamped from her door, having seemed to swallow their story, delivered with admirable aplomb by Kaitlin. It was a dexterity he had only been able to admire: the way she had sidestepped personal questions, explained her enthusiasm for the opportunity to support a cause her siblings already espoused. Though whether April Fotherington would fall for it or not was yet to be seen.

'Then follow me.'

They climbed to the upper level, where Carlos ushered them into a wooden booth hung with low lighting that gave a homely impression of warmth, enhanced by the warm polish of the rustic pine table between high-backed benches, padded with lengths of cheerful red cushion.

'I recommend the special.'

'I'm good with that,' Kaitlin said.

'That's fine with me too,' Daniel concurred.

'Then leave it all to me.' With a beaming smile Carlos departed.

'I hope that's all right? The food is good, it's not pretentious, and whilst Carlos isn't averse to a little publicity he draws the line if it becomes too intrusive.'

'Did you bring Prince Frederick here?' Lord knew where *that* had come from—it hardly mattered.

'No.' Her hand rose to tuck a tendril of hair behind her ear, and then she reached down into her bag and pulled out a notebook and pen. 'Give me five minutes, please, to list some questions, and then we can start.'

He watched as she bent over the notebook and started to write, took in the classical slant of her features, the glory of her hair, tinted with flecks of red and gold by the light, her small intent frown, the graceful line of her neck. Once again desire tugged at his gut, and it was a relief when a waiter appeared with sparkling wine and a bowl of glistening green and black olives.

And still she continued to write—until his limited store of patience ran out and he cleared his throat with theatrical emphasis.

Kaitlin looked up and her lips twisted in a small guilty moue. 'Sorry. I got a bit absorbed. Let's get started.'

Daniel pushed the olives towards her. 'Shoot.'

'First I need some background to this project. And an overview of our itinerary and what you want me to do.'

'The idea is to help teens who come from abusive backgrounds, or who have been in prison, failed at school, and feel they have no future. The Cavershams aim to show them that they can stop the cycle, that they don't have to repeat their parents' mistakes and that their background does not have to define them. They can choose to walk away from the past, choose to leave the cycle of crime and move forward.'

'Breaking a cycle is tough—especially when that cycle involves your family. Sometimes it doesn't feel like there is a choice.'

'There is *always* a choice. However tough. However hefty the price tag.' He'd lost his family and it had nearly broken him, but it had been the choice he had made.

Give it a rest, Daniel.

Her green eyes were way too discerning.

'Anyway, it's an admirable cause. This trip is about giving them new experiences and a chance to have fun. Using the wilderness to illustrate the power of nature, give them a different environment to the one they are used to. So that's an overview of what's happening in the Highlands. Venice is a whole different scenario.'

'What's our remit there?'

'The whole event is already organised—we will just need to double-check the details, sort out any last-minute glitches, host the ball and run the auction. Ethan and Ruby had planned to go, but they have had to change their plans.'

The Cavershams were adopting two children, a brother and a sister, and they were due to move in with them as soon as all the red tape and processes were completed.

Kaitlin nodded. 'Cora told me—they must be over the moon.'

'Yes.'

Try as he might he couldn't inject his voice with any enthusiasm, and she frowned.

'You don't believe in adoption?' Her perfect brows rose in a gesture that marked disapproval.

'I *do* believe in adoption—and I wish the Cavershams well. But, speaking for myself, I don't believe in parenthood.'

'You don't want children?' The surprise in her voice was genuine.

'No, I don't.'

The idea of being a father caused him to break out in a cold sweat that had nothing to do with the late-evening sunshine that slanted through the restaurant's open sash windows.

'Too much responsibility.'

He'd seen what it had done to his own parents. His father had been so desperate to do his parental duty that he'd died before Daniel had even been born. Giovanni Romano had worked all hours in a bid to provide for his family, and exhaustion had caused him to fall asleep behind the wheel of a lorry—with fatal consequences.

Kaitlin watched him with eyes that combined judgement with question. 'Children are a huge responsibility, but I believe a worthwhile one.'

Daniel wondered if his father, killed in his prime, would have agreed. If it hadn't been for his unborn son he might well be alive today. It was a question he could never know the answer to, and guilt tinged the sadness that tightened his chest with a familiar ache.

Enough. Face forward.

'That is your prerogative. I'm happy to keep my life childfree.'

'Yet you don't strike me as someone who shirks responsibility. You certainly haven't skimped on hard work.' She looked down at her notebook. 'According to my research, ten years ago you established a small firm in the North of England. You are now CEO of a global law firm.'

'That's a different type of responsibility, and I've loved every minute of it. I grew the company regionally at first, then nationally, and recently it has become global through a process of partnerships, mergers and acquisitions. A key to my success has been successful branding, but also an ability to create and maintain true corporate spirit and a shared ethos.'

Pride warmed him—success was what drove him. That and a need to prove he could make it without the backing of the mob, a desire to show his mother *he* could provide for her.

He glanced across at Kaitlin, who scribbled industriously in her book. 'Why the research?'

'Because having some information about you enables me to know the right thing to say to different people. So, for example, if I know you love archery and I am speaking to a guest in Venice who also loves archery I can put you together.'

Daniel studied her expression—the small frown of concentration that crinkled her brow, the serious set of her lips. Clearly the conversational prowess she was known for came at a price, and he wondered if she did this before *any* conversation, public or private, if she always vetted each and every word.

'For the record, I've never done archery. I used to be a dab hand at basketball, and I've done some boxing, but nowadays I mostly work. I will admit to a love of food, though, and I like to cook. Does that help?'

'Yes. Thank you. Now, can you tell me the exact itinerary for the days in Scotland? What activities are we participating in? How many teenagers will be there?'

'Fifteen kids, aged from fifteen to nineteen. Nine boys, six girls. The first day we'll be kayaking, the next day hiking, the third day there will be a choice—' He broke off. 'Is there a problem?'

'No.'

'Then why have you gone pale?'

'It must be a trick of the light.'

Bending over the notebook, she appeared to be writing ferociously, but her fingers held the pen in a death grip and the pallor of her skin had nothing to do with the lighting.

She released the pen and looked over his shoulder. 'Here comes the main course.'

CHAPTER SIX

DESPITE THE INCREDIBLY appetising scent that wafted up from their plates—garlic interlaced with a touch of parsley and a tang of lemon—foreboding touched Kaitlin. *Kayaking...* As if everything wasn't bad enough already, she would have to face a water-based activity. Water had always inspired her with unease, and it was a fear her kidnappers had played upon—revealed to them by the Derwent Manor staff member who had help lure her to her capture.

After the kidnap that unease had matured into a full-scale phobia, alongside a multitude of anxieties that had had her seeing danger lurking at each and every corner. But water had been the worst... The idea of it dragging her down, of not being able to breathe, had been too reminiscent of what her captors had inflicted upon her. Black terror as she'd been blindfolded, held under the water and pulled out only when her lungs had teetered on the verge of collapse.

Anxiety unfurled tendril after tendril of fear that twisted her tummy into knots of apprehension.

'Earth to Kaitlin?'

The deep timbre of Daniel's voice pulled her back to reality.

Focus.

A glance down at her plate. The swirl of linguine. Rings of calamari. The vibrant red of tomato sauce patterned by tiny green capers. Next she looked at the pale gold of the white wine. Up to Daniel's face. Craggy, strong, intensity in his ice-blue eyes as they watched her, the formation of a frown on his forehead.

'Is everything OK?' he asked.

'Everything is fine.' The panic began to recede and she knew she had it under control. 'Why wouldn't it be?'

The attempt at lightness not quite pulled off.

'You've gone pale, and you zoned out for a couple of minutes there.'

Pride stiffened her spine—she would *not* admit her fear to Mr Fearless over there. She would work this out. 'I have no idea what you mean.'

Daniel's blue eyes watched her with a scrutiny way too deep, whilst his lawyer instincts were no doubt limbering up.

'Something I've said has bothered you big-time and I want to know what it is. I am responsible for this project and I want it to work. So—spill.'

'It's not a problem, as such, but I've never kayaked before and I don't want to make an absolute fool of myself.' Or expose her panic attacks to the eyes of the world. 'The thought of the press catching a candid camera shot of me tumbling into the water fills me with horror.'

'That hardly warrants your reaction.'

Think.

'Actually. it does. I told you. Image is everything.'

The Lady Kaitlin Derwent persona she'd built for herself relied on poise—she projected self-possession and people believed she was filled with an abundance of self-confidence. She couldn't afford a chink in that façade.

'I'd like to maintain mine.'

Because it was all she had. And if that made her look shallow so be it.

Twirling a forkful of linguine, she glanced down at her notebook. 'Next question—which hotel are we staying in?'

'We're not. One of the directors of the Caversham Foundation owns a cottage in Inverness—it happens to be empty now, so we'll stay there. It saves on costs and in actual fact will give us more privacy than a hotel.'

Just freaking fabulous. As if she wasn't sufficiently all over the place.

'That's a problem.' She'd been idiot enough to utter the words aloud. Clearly a breakdown was underway, because Lady Kaitlin did *not* blurt out foolish statements. 'I mean…from the perspective of the press, the less privacy the better. The whole point of this exercise is to scotch any hint of a rumour.'

'Exactly. In which case staying in a property offered to us for free makes sense. Declining it to stay in a hotel would look as if we *did* have something to hide. It's all arranged—to change it now would arouse way more suspicion.'

Kaitlin picked up her wine glass and took a healthy slug—this whole scenario got worse and worse as each course progressed.

'OK. Fine. But, for the record, I believe it is a mistake.'

'Noted. Next question…'

And the next and the next…

By the end of dinner her hand threatened to cramp but hopefully she had enough information to stave off panic.

'Thank you for this. It has really helped.'

She scraped up the last bit of tiramisu from her bowl, savoured the gossamer lightness of the lady's fingers kissed with the tang of espresso.

'You're welcome. I'll walk you home and then pick you up tomorrow to take you to the airport.'

* * *

Fifteen hours later Daniel observed Kaitlin's study of the private jet. 'I didn't realise we would be travelling by private jet.'

'A company perk. I can't tell if you disapprove or if you are relieved.'

'A bit of both. It does seem morally wrong that we'll be taking these teenagers into the wilds and yet we're imposing this massive carbon footprint on the environment. On the other hand we will avoid the crowds and the publicity, and today that suits me.'

Presumably because she was tired, Daniel thought. Despite her trademark elegance, showcased in a patterned dress that combined turquoise and red and was worn, he suspected, to divert attention from the smudges under her eyes—eyes that had dulled to a flat, almost lacklustre green.

Yet he sensed that if they had been on a chartered flight she would have sparkled, chatting with ease to anyone who recognised her, flight attendants and squalling children alike.

'The way I see it is that this brings us privacy and convenience. I like it.'

'So is this how you *always* travel?'

'A fair amount. I travel a lot, and it's useful to be able to utilise the time to work. It's what a lot of corporate clients expect as well—and, as someone once told me, image is everything.'

This pulled a smile from her. 'If the image you're trying to project is one of success, you've nailed it. My bet is that you have a sports car in your garage and the clothes you are wearing set you back a hefty sum. Though you've gone for discreet quality over brash designer label.'

'Was the car a guess or research?' He nodded at the

ubiquitous notebook that rested on the table in front of her, close to hand, almost like a talisman.

'It was a guess. Though there *is* some more research I'd like to do.'

His eyebrows rose of their own volition as he eyed the notebook with more than a hint of fascination 'There can't possibly be any more questions to ask.'

'There is always more information to collect. I assume you research before you go to court? This is the same idea. It's my job. If you want this project to get good publicity then I have to work out the best way to do that—my strategy, how I will project Lady Kaitlin to maximise benefit. So it's important I wear the right outfit, say the right thing at the right time.'

'Fair enough.' Yet a good few of the questions the previous night had been about their destination, the exact location of the kayaking school, the website for the cottage in Inverness and the hotel in Venice... Surely irrelevant for publicity purposes. 'So what else do you want to know?'

'How to handle the kids.' Her gaze met his, fair and square. 'I want to figure out how to relate to the teenagers—find a frame of reference.' Her slender fingers tapped the notebook. 'I come from a wealthy, privileged background, so these teenagers may well resent me. I'm looking for a way round that. If you come from a similar background you may have some ideas how to combat that.'

Discomfort scratched his skin at the knowledge that his privileged upbringing, the wealth that had cushioned his childhood, the expensive education, had all come from the proceeds of crime. True, he'd funded his own way through law school, through sheer hard graft, but that didn't cancel out the sting of guilt.

Kaitlin huffed out a sigh. 'Actually, scrub that. However you started out, you've clearly worked damned hard to get where you are. The kids will respect that. But they will see that I was born to wealth and position and have done nothing to earn it. I'm worried my presence may goad them, make them feel patronised, especially because I'm not sure what I can offer them.'

Despite her matter-of-fact tone, he could sense the tremor of vulnerability and it touched him. 'You earn a living. You have a job. Tell me about it.'

'I work in an art gallery. I liaise with customers and artists. I help decide who we represent. I organise promotional events and I am the "face" of the gallery.'

'So you have a knowledge of art, an ability to sell and to interact with people—not to mention organisational skills. There is plenty there to earn respect. You can discuss art and painting. Hell, you may spark an interest that means some teenager goes on to become the next Picasso.'

For a second her green eyes were luminous with wist. 'Perhaps. But it's a job that was given to me because the owner knows my mother and likes the kudos of having a "Lady" working for her.'

'Is it a job you wanted?'

'It was a job that was presented to me and that fits in with my duties to Derwent Manor, and I'm good at it.'

'That doesn't answer my question.'

Daniel frowned. With Kaitlin's intelligence, connections, looks and personality she could surely have pursued any career she wanted?

'I didn't know what I wanted to do, so this seemed as suitable as anything else. Did you always know you wanted to be a lawyer?'

'Yes.'

Perhaps because once he'd understood what had happened to his father he'd been able to see the burning injustice of it all.

Giovanni Romano's family had disowned him for marrying Daniel's mother. Part of that rejection had entailed sacking him from his job in the family business. The young Daniel had wondered what would have happened if his parents had consulted a lawyer, found grounds for unfair dismissal. Then there had been his father's subsequent contract to drive a lorry. The young Daniel had been sure there must be some flaw in it—perhaps too many hours, some kind of exploitation, something that the law would have found. That way his father's death when he'd crashed the lorry through sheer exhaustion would have been prevented.

Daniel wiped a hand down his face, swiped the memory away. History could not be rewritten, and in the here and now it was Kaitlin who intrigued him. 'I did. But don't change the subject. We were talking about *you*. You must have had some idea of what you wanted to do.'

'Nope. I didn't. I did well at school, but nothing inspired me.' Her green eyes widened, as if she was looking back to a past that held less than stellar memories. She shrugged. 'I guess I have no ambition.'

'Except to marry well?'

'That's my parents' ambition—not mine,' she flashed back, and then pressed her lips together in clear self-irritation. 'The point is that I do not have any burning career drive.'

'You must have had a childhood dream. Everyone does.'

'Of course.' Her hand waved in a dismissive gesture. 'As a child I believed I could do anything. Thought I could pick between doctor, singer, dancer, scientist…you name it, I'd imagined it.'

Daniel's frown deepened. It didn't make sense that she'd gone from being a motivated, ambitious kid to someone who had drifted into a job that clearly did not set her world on fire.

'Then look around. You're twenty-seven years old—the world is your oyster. You can still be a dancer, a singer, a doctor or a scientist. That's the message we want to give those teenagers—that no matter what your background you need to strive to be what you want to be. It doesn't matter if it's a lawyer or a shop assistant—it needs to give you satisfaction.'

Kaitlin's expression shuttered and she glanced away, out of the window, just as the pilot announced their descent. 'I'll do my best to get that message across.'

The other message she had best get across to herself was to stop talking—*cease conversation* with Daniel. Perhaps it was the lawyer in him, but the man had an uncanny knack of extracting information from her she had no wish to share. Somehow her lips opened and out came the words; she pitied any witness who came up against him.

Which was exactly why she had feigned sleep for the entire car journey from the airport to their destination. A location she had spent a considerable time researching—enough so that she knew she'd need to filter out the background noise of the Caledonian Canal that ran along the edge of the spacious garden that graced the property.

Instead, as she alighted from the car with a theatrical stretch that Daniel surveyed with a scepticism that suggested he had seen straight through the fake nap, she focused on the cottage itself.

Lush vegetation nestled around white walls that gleamed bright through the mizzle of rain that hazed the air and contrasted with the dark orange of the roof, whilst large glass windows indicated that the inside would prove spacious and light.

'It's even prettier than the photographs on the website.' Pictures Kaitlin had studied until her eyeballs ached in the knowledge that the more prepared she was the more likely it was she could stave off panic. It was a strategy that worked—as they entered she felt in control, with not so much as a twinge of nerves daring to show.

'I asked for food to be left for us, so there won't be a need to go out unless you want to,' Daniel said as they entered the well-equipped kitchen.

'Nope. Sounds great. I'm happy to stay in.'

At least in theory. In reality the idea of staying in with Daniel made her feel…jittery, and awareness slid over her skin.

Both stood frozen to the linoleum floor, eyes locked, until Daniel spun on his heel in an abrupt movement and headed to the fridge, yanked it open with a jerk.

'Yup, plenty of provisions. I could make us a three-cheese omelette with ham, or spaghetti carbonara? Your choice. Unless you want to cook?'

'Cooking isn't one of my talents—so an omelette sounds great, if you don't mind.'

'No problem. It'll be ready in half an hour.'

'Great.' Which was apparently her new word for the evening.

Goodness knew she needed that thirty minutes to think, to work out how to get through a cosy, domestic dinner without disgrace.

A shower and a change of clothes undoubtedly helped. Ruffle edged shirt tucked into smart casual black trousers cinched at the waist with a simple buckled brown belt. The ensemble would hopefully ditch any semblance of 'cosy' and the near severity of her chignon, softened by the release of only a few stray tendrils of hair, conveyed business.

One final deep breath and she entered the kitchen,

from where a truly tantalising scent wafted, along with the strains of a classical music radio station.

'That smells glorious.'

'Thank you. Help yourself to wine.'

'Great.'

Really, Kaitlin? Get yourself a thesaurus.

Opening the fridge, she located an open bottle of white wine and poured herself a glass. 'Can I help?'

'You can set the table.'

'No problem.'

A surreal feeling hit her as she carefully arranged place-mats and cutlery, carried the blue glass salad bowl heaped with spinach, its dark green leaves sprinkled with shavings of parmesan, to the square wooden table. She was trying to convince her brain that this was no different from a business dinner—it was only the setting that gave it this false sense of domesticity.

Yet once she was seated her brain scrambled for *any* conversational topic, and for once in her life came up short. It seemed as if Daniel was suffering from a similar affliction, and she could only be thankful for the music, which was at least filling the void of silence.

This was ridiculous—the entire concept of social awkwardness was an impossibility to Kaitlin. She had not spent years of her life perfecting her conversational skills to be beaten by this. Whatever *this* was.

Pressing her lips together, she considered the options. Clearly she needed to re-arm herself, pull her Lady Kaitlin persona together and keep it together. Somehow Daniel Harrington had messed with her head—and that had to be because of this unwanted physical attraction, this stupid hum that she had never felt before and needed to eradicate or at the very least neutralise.

'Penny for them?'

Daniel's deep voice broke her reverie and she glanced up. 'They aren't worth it. I'm sure *your* thoughts would be far more interesting.'

That was better.

'I'm not sure that is the adjective I'd use.'

Uh-oh. There was an amused tone to his voice—a glint in his eye that sent a skitter of heat along her veins.

'What adjective *would* you use?'

'Inappropriate probably best covers it.'

'Oh.' There was no textbook answer to that.

'Don't worry—I am not about to act on my thoughts, but perhaps we need to clear the air? So that we can get on with what we are here to do—focus on the teenagers.'

'OK. You first.'

He pushed his empty plate away and picked up his wine. 'I'm still attracted to you. A lot. But it doesn't have to be a big deal.'

'But it *is* a big deal to me.' Kaitlin closed her eyes in silent despair; disbelief rippling through her at her blurted words even as her mind raced to think how to explain them. 'Because…because it feels awkward.'

'"Awkward" as in you feel embarrassed or uncomfortable? Or "awkward" as in the attraction still exists?'

With a supreme effort she forced her brain into gear, shut down the idiotic thrill that surged through her bloodstream at the knowledge that he felt the same attraction. *Big-time.*

Thrill or not, it made life too complicated. One-sided attraction was bad—mutual attraction was disastrous. So she'd opt for a strategy that had served her well. Good old denial.

'For me, the attraction no longer exists—Barcelona was an aberration that makes me feel both embarrassed and uncomfortable.'

The sheer scale of the lie was immense, but she kept her gaze on his, channelled every fibre of Lady Kaitlin and hoped her body language was on point.

'I just want to get through this week and move on.'

Daniel was silent. Then he lifted his shoulders in another shrug. 'I acknowledge that I misread the situation and I apologise if I have caused you embarrassment.'

'Thank you.' Guilt touched her, along with a sense of profound regret. 'I'll help clear up and then I'll head to my room.'

Kaitlin opened her eyes, stared up at the off-white Artex ceiling. Where *was* she? A feeling of panic invaded but she headed it off at the pass, studied the swirls and whorls of the plaster and allowed knowledge to seep in. Fort William. Scotland. She was safe.

The belated beep of her alarm was a reminder that she had set up a kayaking lesson, in the hope that it would prevent any unseemly panic the following day.

She swung her legs out of bed and picked her phone up from the pine chest of drawers that doubled as a bedside cabinet. Taxi called, bathroom utilised, she donned the outfit she'd set out the previous night on the square-backed cream armchair tucked in the room's corner. Jeans, T-shirt, a plain white shirt and a dark blue lightweight knit jumper provided the layers recommended.

Half an hour later she exited the house, relieved that there was no sight nor sound of Daniel, and twenty minutes after that she stood at the meeting point.

Her head told her to feast her eyes on the scenery—the vibrant green foliage, the backdrop of dense rolling woodland—to breathe deeply of the scent of heather and gorse that sprinkled the air.

But her gaze kept being pulled inexorably back to the

water, and the sight of it caused her heart to make a spirited attempt to leap from her chest. Her lungs constricted and little black dots danced the tango on her retinas.

Breathe.

She could do this—she *would* do this. And after tomorrow she need never ever go anywhere near water again unless it was in the safety of a bathroom.

'Kaitlin?'

The deep voice from behind her lasered her body into immobility. It couldn't be...

Forcing her feet to uproot themselves, she spun round and blinked at Daniel. 'Daniel? What are you doing here?'

There was a frown on his face and his mouth was set to grim. 'Why didn't you tell me about this lesson?'

'As far as I know I don't have to account for every minute of my day with you. Where's Matt?'

'I told him I'd take the lesson.'

Oh, great! She really wasn't sure she could deal with this overload of sensation. Panic at the proximity of the water battled with panic at the proximity of Daniel. The idea of the two combining made implosion viable.

One thing at a time, Kaitlin.

'Why?'

'I don't want it to be awkward just because I misread the signals.'

His blue eyes met hers with an unreadable expression and in that instant she wondered if he believed her.

'I thought if I took you out in the kayak it might ease things. But of course if you would prefer Matt I'll call him.'

Now what?

Digging deep, she turned back to face the water—and realised that, like it or not, his presence made her feel safe.

'If you're sure you don't mind, then let's start this lesson.'

With a brief nod he retreated, returning with two brightly coloured kayaks that he took down to the water's edge.

'OK. So here's what you need to know before we start...'

His words were concise and easy to understand as he explained safety procedures and helped her into a life jacket. But as they edged nearer to the moment where she would actually have to go into the boat on the water it became harder and harder to concentrate as she fought back fear and kept it at bay.

'Are you ready?'

'Sure.' If she didn't count clammy skin and leaden limbs. 'Just a bit nervous about actually getting into the kayak.'

The bright red-trimmed boat looked ridiculously small and outrageously fragile as it bobbed up and down.

'That can be one of the trickiest things. Don't forget what I said about bending your knees deeply, so you can get into a good low squat. That way your centre of gravity is low and you achieve stability. I'll go first and you watch.'

As he squatted down her gaze couldn't help but be snagged on the sheer strength of his torso, the power of his thighs, and for a welcome instant appreciation cut clean through her anxiety for enough precious seconds that she could manage to follow suit once he was in.

There. She was in the kayak and it would keep her afloat as long as she could focus on Daniel's instructions.

The best way to do that was to imagine the water away, fantasise that she was in the gym and focus on Daniel's tuition about how to grasp the paddle, the angle of manoeuvre, the different techniques of bracing, rolling, turning... All verbs that her tummy took as instruction even as she exerted every bit of Lady Kaitlin to demonstrate not an iota of her inner chaos.

'Brilliant! There you go. You're a natural.'

The reassurance of his voice allowed her to focus on getting through. If she didn't look at the water…if she continued the pretence that she was on a rowing machine and concentrated on the movement of the paddle…

Twenty minutes later a sudden cautious thrill of pride shot through her, and the unfamiliar feeling caught her by surprise. When was the last time she'd felt proud of herself or stepped out of her comfort zone?

For one treacherous second she revelled in the feeling and forgot the whole pretence that she was safely ensconced in a gym in Chelsea. The scenery flashed into view: the shoreline in the distance, the expanse of the canal around her, the tug of the current that rocked the boat as she lost the paddle's rhythm…

Debilitating panic struck. All pride, all her joy in her accomplishment shattered into shards of terror. The metallic taste of fear coated her tongue as she stared mesmerised into the looming menace of the water.

Common sense made an attempt to cleave through the fear—told her she had a life jacket on, that she was not in a storm-tossed sea.

But it made no headway against the inner hurricane of irrational panic that swept through her body and her mind. The pounding in her ears, the throbbing of her heart and an all too familiar clamminess swamped the voice of reason and refused to allow the tips and strategies garnered from her internet searches and research over the years to permeate.

The paddle fell from her hand and she tried to grip the side of the kayak, tried to remember how to breathe through the haze that clogged her lungs. The craft rocked and toppled and over she went, the ice cold shock of the water intensifying the nightmare.

'Kaitlin!'

The deep, authoritative sound of Daniel's voice reverberated faintly and she dimly registered a splash. Then his arms were around her. For an instant blind fear kicked her into fight or flight mode—images of her thirteen-year-old self filled her mind. Being picked up and bundled into the boot of the car, the struggle, the sickly scent of something clamped to her mouth, the wrench of pain... Being held over the water, submerged...

Then... 'Kaitlin. It's Daniel. I've got you. Trust me.'

Trust.

No, she couldn't.

'Just stop fighting and I'll let you go. The life jacket will buoy you up. You're safe.'

Slowly his voice had an effect, and she concentrated on the cold, the sensation of his arms around her.

Daniel. Daniel.

This was the here and now—not years ago. No one was trying to take her, force her... Slowly her brain kicked back into gear, pulled her into the present.

Do your breathing exercises—in and out, count to five. *Open your eyes and focus on your surroundings.* On the craggy contours of Daniel's features, the water-drenched dark hair, one curl sculpted to his brow, the intense blue of his eyes, the outline of his mouth...

Muzzy warning bells rang but she ignored them, too caught in the moment as anxiety morphed into heightened sensations of an entirely different kind. Awareness soared inside her, oblivious to the layers of clothing that separated them, to the ice-cold of the water. On some level it occurred to her that it was the surroundings she should focus on—the towering height of the pines, the bulk of the mountains in the distance, the call of a kestrel as it swooped in the sky, the kayaks bobbing gently away from them—but it all faded against his aura that projected sheer strength and safety. Made her want to remain in his hold.

Think.

But thought was nigh on impossible when an answering awareness dawned in his eyes…when he was so close… when all she wanted to do was reach up and cup the jut of his jaw…

Stop!

Any minute reporters might converge on the shore— and, more than that, Daniel represented danger. He made it harder to be the person she wanted to be—Lady Kaitlin Derwent.

So from somewhere deep inside she summoned reserves of strength. 'We need to get the kayaks. I'm all right now.'

Not entirely true, the icy fingers of water still made unease flare, but she could control it. *Would* control it.

'They aren't too far away.'

'Are you sure you're OK?' he asked.

'Yes.' But her teeth had started to chatter now, and a wave of tiredness descended as he released her.

Telling herself she'd be fine, she watched as he retrieved the kayaks and returned.

'Let's get you back in.'

The soothing tone of his voice, the confidence that he would be able to do just that, gave her the impetus to follow his instructions, and relief hit as soon as she was in the relative safety of the kayak.

'I'll be right beside you.'

Kaitlin nodded, gritted her teeth and focused on the paddle, on their movement to the shoreline and what it represented. Finally they arrived, and she scrambled out onto dry land.

'Let's get you home and out of—' He broke off and his lips turned up in a rueful smile. 'You need to warm up.'

Kaitlin managed a nod, and could only be thankful Daniel wasn't a mind-reader as her treacherous brain took the idea of being taken out of her clothes and warmed up and ran with it.

Stop it.

This was nothing more than a reaction to the panic attack. 'Let's go.'

CHAPTER SEVEN

TWO HOURS LATER Daniel rose as Kaitlin entered the tastefully furnished comfortable lounge, where a medley of cream and red sofas and overstuffed armchairs were arranged against a backdrop of Scottish landscapes and a vista of the real live Caledonian Canal seen through the enormous wall-wide windows.

Kaitlin walked across the room with her customary grace, all trace of panic eradicated. Her slightly damp hair fell in a sleek Titian curtain to touch her shoulders, and she wore a simply cut white blouse edged with lace over a pair of jeans. She looked gorgeous and exuded a clean, flowery smell he couldn't identify but which teased his nostrils.

Desire made him almost groan out loud, and it took every ounce of his will to keep him standing still. Kaitlin had made it clear she wasn't interested, and whilst his experience told him her body wasn't fully on board with that decision it wasn't in his psyche to force an admission of attraction.

Anyway, getting involved with Kaitlin was a bad, bad idea. Stupid on all levels. It would embroil him in a media hype he truly didn't want. But also Kaitlin was too complicated—he still couldn't fathom the reasons for her deception in Barcelona, and he sensed the existence of baggage that he should have no desire to open.

Yet for some reason he wanted to know what made her tick, and that was a mistake—the first footfall on a slippery path. Curiosity would lead to entanglement and the formation of bonds, however tenuous—ties that would have the potential to bind or, perhaps worse, to be broken. Either way, pain was the result.

There it was again—the grief etched on his mother's face when he'd left. Grief *he* had caused.

So any form of involvement with Kaitlin was a no-go zone. His cardinal relationship rule—keep it clean, simple and short-term—needed to remain inviolate.

'Feeling better?'

'Yes. Thank you.'

'You should have told me you were scared of water.'

Kaitlin lifted her shoulders and the sudden weariness on her face touched him with compassion.

'I hoped it would be OK...that the phobia would have gone.'

'How long have you had it?'

Her reluctance to answer was palpable in the way she smoothed her hands down her jeans, but then she turned to face him, held his gaze with an aloofness that he believed to be her best defence method.

'A few years.' A shadow darkened the green of her eyes to jade.

'Have you seen anyone about it?'

'No need. It's not like I have a yen to swim the Channel. I can manage it. I *will* manage it.'

Her voice was cool and determined, and if he hadn't witnessed her panic attack earlier he would have believed her without question,

'Uh-uh.' Daniel shook his head. 'Not on my watch. No way are you kayaking tomorrow.'

'Yes, I am. The whole point of today was to prepare me for tomorrow.'

Admiration touched him that she was willing to put

herself through the ordeal again, but he shook his head. 'Not necessary.'

'Yes, it is. I will *not* let this phobia win—I can't.'

The grit in her voice, the starkness of her tone indicated a depth to Lady Kaitlin he hadn't realised existed.

'I made a commitment to this exercise and I will honour it. The whole point of my presence is to bring publicity to the campaign. I can't do that if I'm not there.'

'It's not the publicity I'm concerned about. It's you.'

'Oh.'

Her forehead scrunched in surprise—almost as if it hadn't occurred to her that anyone could be concerned for her on a personal level.

'That's...that's very kind of you.' The words were stilted, and as if she realised it she paused to regroup. 'But truly there's no need. I will be fine. I *want* to do this, Daniel. Please.'

The low entreaty tugged at his chest and he thought quickly. 'OK. But we'll go in a tandem kayak. You and I.'

You and I.

For some reason the words held a strange sonorous significance. Ridiculous—this was no more than a practical solution.

'And if there is any sign of panic you'll tell me. Promise?'

'I promise.' Her green eyes met his with a hint of shyness. 'Thank you.'

'No problem.'

The silence stretched and twanged as awareness hovered in the air. Daniel forced his feet to remain rooted to the cream-carpeted floor, curbed the impulse that had him wanting to close the gap between them, pull her into his arms and kiss her.

Bad idea, Dan.

Though right here and now he was having a hard time remembering why.

Kaitlin seemed equally lost for conversation, but then she gave a small shake of her head and clenched her fingers into her palms. 'So, what are your plans for the rest of the day?'

'To hike over the walk we're taking the kids on. It's a beautiful trek, and I want the chance to scope it out first.' Before his brain could cut in, his mouth ran away with him. 'Would you like to come?'

Yet another bad idea. Instinct told him that the less time he spent alone with Kaitlin the better. But after her ordeal he didn't want to leave her alone, so common politeness had dictated the invitation—nothing more. Common sense would ensure non-involvement.

There was a second of hesitation and then Kaitlin nodded. 'I'd like that.' A small frown creased her forehead. 'I prefer to be prepared, so I appreciate this. Plus I'll get to break in my new hiking boots and check that I can actually manage the hike.'

Deep breath.

'I'll go and get ready.'

Kaitlin gazed at her reflection in the mirror, then leant her forehead against the cool glass in the hope it would bring her back to her senses. She should never have agreed to the walk—her second favourite strategy after denial was avoidance. Ergo, she should duck, sidestep, positively *dodge* any time with Daniel.

But it would help to check out the hike, and she *was* Lady Kaitlin Derwent, and she was in control.

Twenty minutes later, having pulled on hiking socks and what she hoped would prove to be state-of-the-art walking boots, she went in search of Daniel and found him in the kitchen, loading up a rucksack.

'I've packed us a picnic,' he explained. 'We'll drive to Fort William, park in town and walk from there.'

As Kaitlin climbed into the gleaming black four-wheel drive she glanced across at Daniel. His concentration on the road allowed her to watch the deft confidence with which he drove, the economical movements, the shape of his hands, the... *Enough.* She should be feasting her eyes on the landscape outside, not Daniel's fingers, for heaven's sake.

And so for the rest of the short car journey Kaitlin watched the many shades of green and brown morph together into rolling meadows and plains, backed by mountainous peaks and tors, until they arrived at the bustling town of Fort William, one of the largest in the Highlands.

Kaitlin inhaled deeply, reminded herself that it was no different from London—less familiar, but in many essentials the same—and the sight of familiar High Street brands grounded her as they drove through the town and parked.

They alighted from the car and left the car park behind them, and soon they were following the zig-zag path uphill, leaving the noise of traffic and the hustle behind until it was nigh on impossible to believe the proximity of a town that housed thousands of people.

The air was fresh and the crisp breeze carried the scent of the Highlands...gorse, heather with an evocative nuance of peat and whisky... After they'd scaled a small summit they paused, and Kaitlin stared out over the view and felt a sense of peace descend on her. The travails of the day, the terror the water had invoked, were paradoxically soothed by the enormity of nature.

'I can see why you want to bring the kids here,' she

said. 'All of this is timeless—makes you feel that no matter what is happening in the cities, in our lives…all the progress, all the fears…when you set it against this it gives you a certain peace.'

Whoa—the plan had been to focus on small talk, to push Daniel into the realms of acquaintance. Instead she was waxing lyrical with philosophy.

Before he could answer she turned away. 'Where next?'

The curved path led into a woodland area, where alder, willow and birch lined their ascent, and emerged to a view of a bulky hill—a foothill of Ben Nevis. Kaitlin paused and eyed the windy, steep peat path with trepidation.

Daniel raised his eyebrows. 'Worried you won't make it?'

In actual fact she'd been worried that her panic might make yet another show. But the challenge in his voice, delivered with a note of teasing and accompanied by a half-smile that notched up her heartbeat, helped shut down the fear before it could take hold.

'Not in the slightest. I may not be an outdoorsy girl, but I keep fit.'

'Then let's go. And I promise the views will be worth it.'

Lord knew he wasn't wrong—but she'd be a liar if she didn't admit, at least to herself, that the view she focused on most was the contours of his muscular body, the lithe strength of his frame, the length of his leg, the breadth of his thigh… Until they reached the top, where the panoramic stretch of moorland took her breath away.

Daniel halted. 'I don't know about you, but I am famished. Shall we stop for lunch?'

'Sure.'

He shrugged off the rucksack, unstrapped it, tugged out a tartan picnic blanket and spread it on the ground. Kaitlin sat, her eyes widening as he pulled out item after item. Long baguettes, a selection of cheese, pâté, small pies lidded with smooth pastry edges...

'It's like a magic rucksack.'

'I hope you're hungry?'

'Actually, I am. It must be the fresh air and the exercise. There is obviously a big difference between walking on a treadmill and out in the real world!'

Silence fell as they busied themselves, and it was only once their plates were laden that Kaitlin applied her mind to conversation. There would be no more awkward silences bridged by growing awareness.

'Is this the type of holiday you usually have? Or are you more the party-on-a-yacht type of guy?'

'I'm not big on holidays. I travel plenty with work, so I usually combine a weekend away with business.'

'So Ethan must have been very persuasive to get you to do this?'

'He was.' He stretched his legs out and balanced his plate. 'What about you? Where do you holiday?'

Kaitlin shrugged. 'Like you, I'm not a holiday person. The last time I tried to go with friends it turned into a publicity fest and it was ruined for them.'

But in reality that was an excuse—she didn't enjoy holidays. New places overwhelmed her, and the effort it took to research and find a new routine mostly wasn't worth it.

'Is must be hard to be on show all the time.'

'It's part of what I do and I'm good at it.'

'But surely any publicity intrusive enough to stop you going on holiday is too much?'

'It doesn't bother me. We never holidayed as children, so holidays have never been part of my life.' Her parents wouldn't have known where to begin—Derwent Manor had always been their priority. 'My parents thought it a waste of money.'

Daniel raised his eyebrows as he spread a wedge of pâté onto a cracker. 'I didn't think money was an issue for the Derwents.'

'That's what most people think. In reality Derwent Manor absorbs huge amounts of money every year in maintenance alone, Then we had a flood a few years back, and that caused extensive damage, and so it goes on. Most of my school holidays were spent fundraising.'

'Did you mind?'

'No.'

The idea of a Derwent family holiday was impossible even to imagine—any attempt and the illusion shimmered and wisped away. The Duke and Duchess had always parented from a distance, and with Kaitlin that distance had been touched with their distaste after the kidnap—as if she were soiled goods. Though they had still shown her way more attention and approval than they had ever given Cora, but on the flipside that had meant their expectations of Lady Kaitlin were correspondingly higher.

Shaking the thoughts off, Kaitlin bit into a piece of quiche and savoured the tart cheddar taste. 'What about you? What sort of holidays did you go on as a child?'

For a moment she thought he wouldn't answer; his blue eyes were looking past her towards the line of the horizon, as if he could see into the past. Then...

'Big, noisy, fun ones. We'd take off to the beach for weeks. My stepdad and brother would barbecue up a storm and the rest of us kids would run riot.'

'How many of you were there?'

'Me, my brother and sister, and a whole bunch of cousins.'

'That sounds amazing.'

'It was a long time ago.'

His voice heavy with bleakness, and what she instinctively knew was a mix of nostalgia and regret, and without even thinking she reached out and touched his arm.

'But you have the memories. We don't have any cousins—it's just the three of us, and Cora, Gabe and I weren't that close as children—we aren't a close family. It sounds like you were.' She hesitated. 'Maybe you still could be?'

Daniel shook his head. 'It didn't work out like that.' The words were uttered with a finality that indicated the subject was closed. 'Sounds like you've done better—you seem close to Gabe and Cora now.'

'We're closer than we used to be.'

He reached for a bottle of water, his gaze curious but without condemnation. 'You aren't close to your parents and yet you were happy to marry a man they chose for you?'

Kaitlin knew she should close the conversation down, but sitting out there, with the spring breeze wafting the scent of heather, surrounded by peace, she wanted him to understand. Perhaps she needed to explain it to herself.

'It's more complicated than that. I was born to the job of being Lady Kaitlin Derwent and the responsibilities that come with that. When I was little that meant posing for photo shoots in cute outfits or behaving at boring dinner parties.'

'And now those obligations include marriage to a man of your parents' choosing? That's the high jump and the pole vault combined.'

'Not if I loathed him—I wouldn't let them force me into marriage then...of course I wouldn't. But...'

But her parents had always made clear to her that it was her destiny to make a great alliance, to bring glory to the Derwent name. Once she had had other ideas, Deep inside herself she had been sure she was destined for other things, had vowed she would show her parents that she could bring glory to the Derwent name in a different way. Her options had seemed endless—she'd become a famous dancer, a Nobel prize-winning scientist, a brilliant pop singer…

With the kidnap all those aspirations had withered away.

'But…?' he prompted.

'But the idea of a husband like Frederick didn't seem like such a bad prospect. I would have done my best to be a good princess.' Placing her plate on the tartan rug, she enumerated the points on her fingers. 'I know how to garner positive publicity, I would be loyal, always look the part, always say the right thing.' A surge of confidence bolstered her against the incredulity on Daniel's face. 'I would be in a position to do good—I could make significant contributions to causes I believe in.'

'Stop.' Daniel raised a hand, the frown on his face now deeper. 'Everything you have said is about your role as Princess. What about your *actual* marriage? The nitty-gritty of real life?'

Of course she had considered that. 'I would do my best to be a good wife. I'd—'

'You'd pose nicely for the photographs? Look the part and always say the right thing?'

The sarcastic inflexion was harsh enough to make her flinch.

'Yes. There's nothing wrong with that.'

'*Everything* is wrong with that. You propose to play a part for your whole life. What about the parts that aren't acted out for the camera?'

Heat burned her cheeks and she focused on the baguette she held, crumbled it into a small mountain. 'I would do my best in private as well. But I don't think physical attraction matters.'

Daniel stared at her. 'Doesn't matter?' he echoed, his expression dumbfounded.

'There is a lot more to marriage than physical attraction.'

'Granted—but I think it is a fairly vital component.'

'Physical attraction can be a short-term illusion—marriage is for the long haul.'

'Exactly. That means the rest of your life.' His voice was slow now, imbued with urgency. 'If you are doing this for your parents you shouldn't. This is *your* life and you only get one shot. Don't waste it by living it any other way than the way you want to.'

'Marriage *is* what I want. I want security, companionship, and most of all I want children.'

For the first time in this conversation she felt solid ground beneath her—she knew that, however impossible romantic love was for her, her love for her children would be absolute.

'You don't have to marry a prince to have children. You could marry someone you love.'

'I don't want love. It's too unpredictable—too unreliable, too intangible.' Kaitlin wanted to put her trust in the tangible. 'That's why the idea of an alliance appeals to me. There would be a mutual contract to fulfil...agreed expectations.'

'What would *you* expect from *him*?'

'Liking, respect, that he's a good father to our children. Kindness. It works for me.'

Enough said—time to move this conversation away from her, before she revealed even more than she already had.

'What would work for *you*?'

Daniel blinked in surprise.

Kaitlin's eyes narrowed. 'We've discussed *my* attitude to long-term relationships—now it's your turn.'

'That's simple. Avoid them like the plague and avian flu rolled together. I'm not a "long-term" sort of guy.'

'Maybe you haven't met the right woman yet?'

'I have no intention of ever staying with a woman long enough to discover her eligibility as Ms Right. That's why I only date women on the lookout for a quick physical fling. A night here, a weekend there...'

A flush touched her face. 'Like in Barcelona?'

'Yes. Although I don't usually pick up strangers in hotel lobbies.'

Though that wasn't the reason that Barcelona had been different—'Lynette' had been a diversion from the stark realisation that his family would not accept his extended olive branch, that there would be no reunion or forgiveness or understanding.

'My usual dates are women I meet through work, on business trips or through colleagues. All are women I like and respect. But, unlike you, I don't think that's enough to warrant marriage. I have no wish to swap my bachelor lifestyle for the proverbial ball and chain. Too claustrophobic.'

A few years back he had tried a relationship, dated without a cut-off point, and it hadn't worked out. The minute the relationship had veered even slightly towards serious it had felt like the equivalent of a noose round his neck, and every day the rope had got that little bit tighter...the walls had closed in a little bit more...another barrier had gone up. Pick the analogy, but he'd learnt the lesson.

'There's always divorce.'

'Not straightforward. The desire to split might not be mutual, there could be children to consider, alongside a tangle of assets and emotions and mess, and someone will always get hurt.'

No matter what.

His mother had loved his father with all her heart and

had been devastated by his death. Her subsequent marriage to his stepdad had been a supposed 'alliance', and that had been charged with misery. Lesson learnt. Love, marriage, kids, closeness were all to be avoided—too messy, too painful, too fraught.

'Better to avoid the whole shebang.'

'But my way avoids hurt and achieves a partnership that will run on an even keel.'

No doubt that was what his mother had believed.

'You can't control emotion. There is a possibility that one or both of you may fall for someone else.'

'I wouldn't.' There was certainty in her voice. 'I'm not coded that way.'

'Maybe your husband would.'

'He wouldn't. I'd do everything in my power to be the wife he wanted.'

'It doesn't always work like that.'

'I'll cross that bridge if I get to it.'

'And tolerate infidelity?'

Kaitlin pressed her lips together. 'I don't know. Maybe if it made him happy...maybe if it didn't hurt me...'

'You cannot possibly believe that. Infidelity humiliates you in your own right *and* in the eyes of your children. Regardless of whether you love your partner or not.'

There was a pause and he knew he'd screwed up—Kaitlin made a pastime of reading people—watching their every nuance and inflexion.

'You know that as fact, don't you?' she said.

What the hell? If it showed her the stupidity of her beliefs... 'Yes, I do. My stepfather cheated on my mother on numerous occasions and she turned a blind eye. But it destroyed her inside.'

It was the price she'd paid to remain inside her gilded cage, to keep her children by her. Her defence had been the fact that as long as she accepted infidelity Antonio Russo would never divorce her. But, oh, how Daniel had loathed it. The taste of bitterness still flavoured his memories. He still felt the twist of frustrated anger at his own helplessness.

Even now his fists clenched involuntarily at the memory. Never would he risk that kind of humiliation—one that would be even worse if you actually loved the other person.

'I'm sorry. I…'

'Don't be. But don't delude yourself either.'

With a savage gesture he pulled the rucksack towards him.

'We should move on.'

CHAPTER EIGHT

KAITLIN STARED AT her reflection the following morning and tried to push the memory of that foolish conversation from her mind. Disbelief lingered and mingled with irritation that she had shared way too much.

But now was not the time to reflect on indiscretions she could not change—today she needed to battle panic and sit herself in a kayak, to ensure the teens had a brilliant day and to maximise exposure for the foundation.

She took one last look at her reflection. Walking boots, suitable kayaking clothes, minimal waterproof make-up, hair carefully pulled back in a seemingly causal ponytail. She was good to go.

A knock on the door heralded Daniel, and she forced a smile to her lips.

A smile he paid no heed to. 'It's not too late to back out.'

'No.'

Focusing on keeping her expression neutral, all signs of nerves carefully locked away, she walked alongside him to the car, climbed in and concentrated on deep breathing and meditative thoughts until they arrived at their destination.

Before the ordeal of the water she had to face—and charm—the barrage of press cameramen.

'Hi, guys. Good to see you all here.'

Friendly smile in place. *Tick*. Stance relaxed. *Tick*. Showing no untoward awareness of Daniel. *God, she hoped so.*

'I hope my team made it clear that today is about the Caversham Foundation. More than that, it is about the kids who are here to learn a new skill in this beautiful place.'

'Aw, come on, Kaitlin. Can't we ask a few questions about you?'

Kaitlin tipped her head to one side as if in consideration, as if she hadn't anticipated the request. 'Two personal questions—as long as I have your promise that your coverage will focus on what is most important here. And that's *not* me.'

'Deal.'

'Then go ahead.'

'Have you heard from Prince Frederick?'

'That one is nice and easy. No, I haven't.' For a moment disquiet touched her; they had agreed to keep in touch, to co-ordinate publicity. She'd kept her side—had emailed him a schedule of her plans—but there had been no word from the Prince.

'Are you feeling any regrets?' came the next question.

'No. Of course it's sad when a relationship doesn't work out, but I feel confident that we made the right decision for us right now.' Irritation touched her—those words left the whole thing open, and she knew it—it seemed as though she was following her parents' dictum on automatic. 'And I am focused on moving on with my life.'

'Right.' Daniel stepped in. 'The two questions are over and now Lady Kaitlin will demonstrate her kayaking skills.'

It would be fine.

As long as she didn't think about the water. Better to focus on the existence of the tandem kayak—on Daniel's aura, his reassurance and his strength. Those images crushed the slithering doubt, propelled her forward to the group of teenagers who stood in a suspicious huddle by the waterside.

A couple looked enthused, but the majority looked sullen, despite the efforts of the woman who accompanied them to chivvy them along.

Empathy stirred—memories of being told to pose, to smile, to act like a Lady when inside she had felt shrivelled and unclean after the kidnap.

Maybe these kids didn't feel like smiling—maybe being a recipient of charity didn't always inspire gratitude. Maybe they felt out of their depth, thrust into doing an activity they didn't want to do with Lady Kaitlin Derwent—a woman they probably despised as being a stuck-up, upper-class snob.

'Hey, guys. I'm Kaitlin, and this is only the second time I have kayaked in my life. I have never been an outdoor person—I'm a city girl through and through—and I sympathise if you don't actually want to be here. I had some serious doubts too, and as Daniel will attest when I kayaked for the first time yesterday I capsized. If you're lucky it may happen again.'

A few tentative smiles, and even though she was well aware they were more laughing *at* her than *with* her it was still a step in the right direction.

'The *good* thing, though, was that I was wearing a life-jacket—and whilst I am aware it won't be winning any fashion awards, I was glad of it. So everyone please buckle up.'

Cue a few groans.

Then one boy who had been glaring at her said, 'So you don't kayak and you don't like the outdoors. Whatcha doing here, then? Come to lord it over us poor little delinquents so you can feel good about yourself?'

'No.' Kaitlin stepped forward so she was near enough for him to sense her sincerity but not so close that his space was invaded. 'I was born into the family I was born into, just like you were born into the family *you* were born into. That's the lottery of life. But it doesn't give me the right to "lord it" over anyone, delinquent or not. Just like *your* family background, whatever that may be, doesn't give you the right to *be* a delinquent. I'm here because, rightly or wrongly, my presence here does get publicity—and I think you deserve a share of that publicity. At the end of the day if you wish to talk directly to the reporters you can. And feel free to give your honest opinion on the day and me.'

Even as she said the words she knew the offer was nuts—a publicity gamble of the most stupid kind. But she didn't care. It had felt….right. Even if her parents would condemn it as foolish beyond belief.

With one last smile she turned and walked back to Daniel, who was eying her with curiosity and more than a hint of admiration, as well a touch of surprise.

'Lady Kaitlin in action. They all look a lot more enthused than they did a few minutes ago, and that boy is definitely less hostile.'

'I told you: I do the research, I do the groundwork—I agreed to do this and I'll do it to the best of my ability.'

'It's more than that. You didn't need research to achieve what you just did—that was *you*, Kaitlin, not your preparation, faultless thought that was.'

'Thank you.' Absurdly, warmth encased her at his approval, sufficient to embolden her as she stared into the depths of the canal. 'Let's kayak.'

Two days later

Kaitlin ached, but it was a good ache—the kind of ache that spoke of outdoor exercise, clean air, mountains and glens.

A twinge of nerves was accompanied by more than a hint of anticipation as she hesitated outside the lounge door. The past two nights she had scurried to her room with a take-out sandwich, needing time alone to erase the Daniel effect. It was ridiculous, given her genuine absorption in the activities and the teens, and yet the whole time her body had hummed with a constant awareness—one she knew mirrored his own. She'd sensed it in the way his eyes rested on her, felt the tension vibrate from him when they were close together.

So the obvious answer was not to get close.

But right now she had no choice—there was no way round the need to actually speak with him face to face.

Get on with it, Kaitlin.

She pushed the door open and entered, swallowed the catch of breath that afflicted her whenever she saw him. Sitting on the sofa, intent on his laptop, he looked so... *yummy.* Dark hair shower-damp, dressed in a white T-shirt that showed the honey tone of his skin, the muscular forearms with a smattering of hair.

He turned to look at her, and heat lit his blue eyes for a scant second.

'Hi. Sorry—I didn't mean to disturb you.'

'It's fine.' He pushed the screen away from him and rubbed a hand over his face. 'What can I do for you?'

'I... I wondered if I could talk to you about something?'

'Sure. Would you like a drink? You definitely deserve one—you've done a brilliant job the past two days.'

The words were warm, yet the tone didn't match—there was a near cynicism that confused her. 'You sound surprised. Or upset?'

A frown creased his forehead as he rose and walked to the sideboard, where he opened a bottle of red wine. Turning, he shrugged. 'Not at all. As you said, you had a job to do and you have executed it perfectly. The press have loved this aspect of Lady Kaitlin. So have the teenagers.'

Again, despite the positive words she sensed an undercurrent.

'I sense a reservation.'

He hesitated, and then tipped his palms in the air. 'I don't get it. Is it real or a gigantic PR exercise to you? You seem so natural with the teenagers, and I can't tell if you mean it or if you are simply furthering your image.' He poured the wine into two glasses. 'Not that it matters.'

Anger and hurt swirled together in her stomach. 'Excuse me? You think I'm *faking* this?'

'That's it. I don't know. *You* are the one who told me image is everything.'

The words halted her—she *had* said that, and when she had agreed to do this her motivation had been to introduce a new facet of Lady Kaitlin Derwent. Accepting the glass he handed her, she looked down into the ruby liquid and thought back over the past days. Looked back up at him.

'These past days haven't been about my image. It's been about *them*.' Tom and Celia and Liz and Darren and…and all the youngsters she'd spoken with. 'Some of what they have been through makes my blood run cold. I like every one of them and I want to help them. For real—not as part of a PR exercise for me.'

She broke off at the sudden smile that turned up his lips and made her tummy flip. 'What?'

'That's the first time you've sounded so passionate about something.'

'I *do* feel passionate about it. Until now most of my charitable efforts have been attending events or fundraising for Derwent Manor. This is different. I've never felt so *involved*. I care about these kids.' She glanced at him and the knowledge of a shared belief made warmth bubble inside her. 'I think you do too.'

Because she'd seen him—the way he spoke with them, the discussions he'd had with them—she'd seen how serious some of them had been. Had also seen his patience as he explained how to do something, the way he'd genuinely listened to them, bantered, joked…as if he felt a connection.

'I do.'

'Why?' Kaitlin hadn't meant to ask the question but she wanted to know.

'Why do *you*?' he countered.

'Because they have made me realise how lucky I am—made me see how petty my own concerns are.' Even the horror of her kidnap faded into insignificance against what some of the children had had to face in their short lifespans. 'They've made me…*feel*.' The admission was almost too much, though it was true—these kids had got under her skin. 'Feel as if I want to help,' she completed hurriedly. 'Now your turn.'

'It's as you said. For years I have spent every minute of the day focused on success. *My* success. These past days I've wanted to help *them*.'

They stared at each other—the shared revelation buzzed between them, created a connection that shimmered in the air.

Kaitlin took a gulp of wine, felt the spice and berry notes tingle on her tongue as she tried to pull her shattered senses into order. 'Which brings me to my idea.'

'Go ahead. But sit down first.'

She sank down onto the cream armchair and tucked her feet under her. 'I know the outdoors is important, and how much benefit the kids have reaped from the kayaking and the hiking. But I want to do something a bit different tomorrow.'

'You don't have to do anything tomorrow. You've done your bit.'

'I know, but I want to—and I believe I've come up with something useful. Most of those children don't want charity—they want to make it on their own. The problem is the odds are stacked against them from the get-go. They will be judged because of their backgrounds and if they get knocked back time and again they will give up. I want to increase the odds of their success. I want to teach them how to project confidence even when they don't feel it inside, to wear the right clothes, walk the right walk.' All the things *she* had painstakingly done to construct Lady Kaitlin Derwent. 'That will give them an edge.'

'Is that how you feel? No confidence on the inside?'

His voice was low, genuine, and the edges of her façade crumbled.

'Of course not.' The words sounded brittle, even to her own ears. She uncurled her feet, placed the wine glass down with a *thunk* and rose to her feet. 'Anyway, this isn't about me. The point is I'd like to do this. I'll take them shopping—you don't need designer outfits or lots of money, it's getting the colours right, a suitable cut, finding a style. I can help them—I know I can. So what do you think?'

'I think it's a fantastic idea.'

'You do?'

'I do.'

Kaitlin felt her lips curve up in a completely spontaneous smile. 'Fabulous.' She took a step forward, towards him. 'Thank you, Daniel.' Reaching out, she put a hand on his arm.

Big mistake, Kaitlin.

She'd swear she'd heard a fizz as her fingers contacted with his skin. Worse, she might well have given the smallest of moans.

Move your hand.

But her brain refused to send the requisite signal. Instead her gaze remained riveted to her hand on his arm.

'Kaitlin...'

His voice was ever so slightly strained and she looked up, saw the unmistakeable heat in his eyes and felt an answering thrill.

'I...'

'Dammit.'

With that he put his hand on her waist and gently tugged her forward into his embrace.

Desire knocked common sense down and trampled it; her arms reached up and looped round his neck. And then his lips touched hers and she was lost.

The taste of wine, the clean, just-out-of-the-shower scent of him, the intensity as he deepened the kiss all spiralled inside her. Thought was impossible. Ripples of desire tugged her nerve-endings and the intensity of sensation hollowed her tummy, caused a deep yearning for more. Pressing herself against him, she revelled in the strength of his body, in his small groan as she parted her lips.

She never wanted the moment to end—but finally common sense picked itself off the floor and shrieked a message, jolted her back to reality.

Pulling back, she stared at him—then away. Caught an image of herself in the ornate gilt mirror above the mantel. *Hell.* She barely recognised herself. Flushed, lips swollen, hair dishevelled, eyes glazed. What was she *doing*?

Focus—she had to pull this together. Had to locate her true self, pull the Lady Kaitlin Derwent mantle round her.

'I'm sorry. That was obviously not a good move for either of us.'

Amazing how she could keep her voice so light. A quick smooth of her hair, a step backwards and an aloof, self-deprecating smile.

'I think the wine must have gone to my head on top of all that unaccustomed exercise. The best thing is to forget all about it and put it behind us.'

His blue eyes bored into her. 'If that's what you want.'

Her heart pounded her ribcage. 'There isn't any alternative.'

'Sure there is. There is always a choice, Kaitlin. We could take this further. Instead of fighting this attraction we could enjoy it. Enjoy Venice together.'

Temptation crooked a finger and Kaitlin dug her nails into her palms. *At least think about it*, wailed her inner voice, but this time Kaitlin was prepared, and common sense was ready and waiting.

'The risk is too great. All it takes is for one reporter to suspect. Hell, we could have been photographed through the window just now. And I won't risk the scandal for the sake of a few hours in bed.'

Her parents would be livid, the press would have a field-day and she would have regrets—because it wasn't Lady Kaitlin Derwent's style.

'So from now on it is business all the way. I'll see you in the morning.'

CHAPTER NINE

DANIEL LOOKED ACROSS the private jet to where Kaitlin sat, back ramrod-straight, not so much as a crease in her white and blue floral dress, her focus apparently completely on the book in her hand. No sign now of the Kaitlin of two days before, curled up on the sofa, relaxed and animated, as she talked about her plans for the teens.

That Kaitlin had gone for good after the kiss they had shared—a kiss that still haunted his body and his mind. Despite the common sense that told him he had been a fool one hundred times over to suggest a fling with Kaitlin. Kaitlin was too complex, too different from the women he usually slept with.

Plus, the idea was fraught with risks of disastrous consequences for either or both of them. Three days with Kaitlin wasn't worth the risk of having his family unearthed. Three days with him wasn't worth Kaitlin scuppering her chances of a reunion with Prince Frederick or an alliance with some other member of royalty.

That was what she wanted—the path she had chosen or had had chosen for her—a life of wealth and security and pomp and ceremony and children. He could offer her only the first, on a temporary basis—hardly an offer worth consideration. And an offer he should never had considered.

He must have been mad to so much as kiss her.

Since then she had been coolly polite, kept herself distant both physically and mentally, and they hadn't exchanged a word in private, hadn't spent more than a minute alone. But, hell, he had a captive audience now, at forty thousand feet in the air—there was nowhere for her to go and his inner devil prompted him to speak.

'Good book?' he enquired.

'Very, thank you.'

'Hmm... Because I can't help but notice you haven't turned a page in the past twenty minutes.'

Her lips pressed together in clear annoyance. 'You must be mistaken.'

'I don't think so. You do realise that even though we have decided not to pursue our attraction further that doesn't mean we have to give up on actual conversation?'

'Conversation is overrated.' Kaitlin shook her head. 'Sorry—that was rude. But it was conversation that led us to being so stupid, so it seems to me that we should keep all contact to a minimum.'

'I don't think that will work.'

'Why?'

'Because I figure we need to talk about what happened and this seems like a good opportunity.'

'There is nothing to say.'

'So you still want to try and pretend it didn't happen?'

'Yup.'

'Make like that kiss was imaginary?'

'Yup.'

'Not going to work. You don't want the press or anyone to suspect a connection between us—but ignoring our attraction will make our body language awkward and we'll pitch a vibe someone like April Fotherington will pick up. We have a press conference scheduled before the ball. And after.'

'So what's your solution?'

'We spend as much time together as possible and eradicate the awkwardness.'

He could almost see another negative trembling on her lips, and then she closed her eyes and muttered something under her breath. Something that sounded like, 'Lady Kaitlin, do your stuff.'

Opening her eyes, she looked at him coolly. 'Fair enough. We'll give that a try. Let's start now and discuss the plan for Venice.' Leaning down, she pulled out the ubiquitous notebook. 'I've already looked at all the auction items and done some research. I've also studied the guest list and identified any people I know—art gallery owners or family friends—so I'll make sure I network with them, raise awareness so that people will dig deep at the auction. I'll also see if I can persuade a few more donations out of people as surprise items for the auction.'

'Sounds like you have it covered. Just like you had it covered with the kids. You've been so busy hiding out in your room I haven't had a chance to tell you how impressed I was. Your workshop was amazing.'

Kaitlin had taken the youngsters shopping, given each one of them a one-on-one tutorial on style and budget, followed by a workshop on image projection. There had been gales of laughter, and at the end of it they had all looked like new people. He'd been left in no doubt that any preconceptions about aristocracy had been knocked to flinders.

'Enough so that I want to talk to Ethan and Ruby about you running those workshops regularly, if you would be up for it.'

'Really?'

For a moment her face lit up and he blinked at the sheer beauty of her.

'Really. What do you think?'

Suddenly, like the Christmas tree lights being extinguished on Twelfth Night, her expression was closed off. 'It may be too big a commitment. I guess the workshops would be all over the country, and it would be hard for me to juggle them. Maybe I could train someone else to do them?'

Daniel frowned 'Or maybe you could throw in the art gallery job and build up a whole new business? People would pay to learn how to project confidence. You have the organisational skills needed, and the business acumen, and...'

A firm shake of her head greeted this suggestion. Firm enough that her gorgeous hair rippled. 'I'm happy where I am now. I don't want to stray out of my comfort zone. I know where I am with the art gallery and I like that.'

Daniel frowned, wondered why Kaitlin had set her comfort zone at such a low threshold. Something didn't add up, but the rigidity of her expression indicated that she wouldn't be offering him the solution to the sum.

Her head bent over the notebook. 'Ethan seems to have been a bit vague about exactly what he needs us to do prior to the ball.'

'Make sure all the arrangements are in place—check the catering, ensure all the auction items have been collected and stored. With luck we'll have some time to explore Venice. Have you been before?'

'No.' Her expression was neutral, with no hint of anticipation at visiting one of the most historic, beautiful cities in the world. 'Have you?'

'Yes. Once.'

His mother had always wanted to go to Venice—had told him how his father and she had dreamed of one day settling in the city where his father's people had originated. Daniel had promised her that one day he would take her. Instead he had gone on his own, in celebration when he'd graduated from law school. He had wandered the narrow streets and determination had pulsed in his veins that he *would* succeed and one day he *would* bring his mother to the city.

Now, eight years later, he was no longer so sure and loss touched him.

Seeing her eyes rest on his face with question and concern, he smiled. 'It's an incredible place.'

'I am quite happy to field the organisational side of the ball to give you time to see Venice,' she offered.

'Absolutely not. We've agreed that the more time we spend together the better.' An arrangement that suddenly seemed foolhardy. 'So we'll organise together and explore together.'

A definite wince greeted his suggestion, but before he could comment the pilot announced their descent to Marco Polo airport and he figured it was better to leave well enough alone.

As Kaitlin emerged from the jet onto the Tarmac she could feel the onset of panic start to unfurl in her tummy, despite her efforts to prepare. Airports always had the ability to overwhelm her—too dangerous, insecure, too busy.

Instinct had her stepping her towards Daniel.

Bad idea.

The memory of their kiss seared her with a burn that increased the closer he was. Which, perversely, was the reason for her agreement to spend time with him. For the first time in over a decade Kaitlin was not in control of an emotion and, dammit, she *loathed* that sensation. So she *would* learn to subdue this unwanted attraction. Just as she had subdued panic, anger, anxiety…*insert emotion here.*

Once they'd negotiated Customs a man bustled towards them, a beaming smile on his face. 'Signor Harrington

and Signora Derwent. I am Roberto, and I am delighted
to welcome you on behalf of the hotel. But first—the press
have contacted us, requesting to see you on your arrival.
Of course if you do not wish it we will ensure your arrival
is kept private...'

Kaitlin kept her expression neutral, though her brain
whirred furiously. There had been no scheduled press
meeting, yet they couldn't forego a chance of extra publicity for the ball.

Daniel had clearly come to the same conclusion. 'We'll
do a brief meet-and-greet.'

'Very well. Now, come with me, for I have arranged for
you to travel to the hotel by water taxi. We have our own
private jetty at the *palazzo*.'

Just what she needed. But no way could she disappoint
Roberto's expectant smile. 'That sounds wonderful, *signor*—you have my utmost thanks.'

Within minutes Roberto had driven them to a boat-
house, where they boarded a polished wood-panelled boat.
Averting her eyes from the water, Kaitlin climbed in, aware
of Daniel's watchful gaze.

'Have a wonderful journey. I will meet you at the hotel.'

Once Roberto had gone, Daniel questioned her. 'Is this
a problem? There *are* other ways of getting to the hotel.'

'I know that.' Ferry, bus, train... She'd researched them
all. 'But it would have been rude and provoked questions to
refuse this. Anyway, I'll be fine—it's not as if I can fall in.'

Kaitlin perched on the cream leather seat and watched
as Daniel settled opposite her. Those blue eyes held a hint
of scepticism and she forced herself to lean back, though
nothing could have compelled her to actually look out of
the window as the boat set off.

To her relief Daniel maintained a flow of conversation, including a potted history of Venice, so all she had to do was listen.

As she focused on his voice and concentrated on memorising the facts she felt better. Perhaps more than anything his sheer presence helped—the solid, reassuring strength of him. Which didn't make sense. The Prince had never made her feel like this. Even Gabe, her big brother, didn't have this effect on her.

Ugh. Gritting her teeth, Kaitlin shifted ever so slightly away from him. Her treacherous body could not be so foolish as to trust in Daniel Harrington—a man she would never see again after this trip to Venice. Though perhaps in that case she might as well make use of him whilst she could—after all, the most important imperative was to get through this ride.

Eventually they neared their destination and she began to prepare for the press conference. The water taxi glided between the bright mooring poles that demarcated the hotel's boat deck and she braced herself for the bevy of reporters standing on the wooden slats.

As she alighted her relief at feeling dry land underfoot was matched by trepidation as her finely honed publicity antennae tuned into an undercurrent. These reporters had an anticipatory air about them—which could only mean one thing.

'They've got something,' she murmured to Daniel as foreboding tickled her nerves.

Surely no one could have glimpsed that kiss?

'So, Kaitlin, can you shed any light on why Prince Frederick has made an unannounced trip to India?'

Careful.

Her brain clicked and whirred, joined the dots and anticipated the next volley even as her lips turned up in the trademark Kaitlin smile.

'No, that's news to me as well.'

'Do you think there could be a link to Sunita?'

The model and Bollywood actress known only as Sunita *had* been linked to Frederick, but as far as Kaitlin knew she had been one of Frederick's many short-term liaisons with beautiful women, with nothing in particular to distinguish her from any other.

'I really couldn't comment on that.'

'So there is no connection to your break-up?'

'No.'

'Perhaps the best person to ask that question of would be Sunita. Or even the Prince himself.'

Daniel's interruption turned the attention to him and April Fotherington stepped forward, her eyes darting from Daniel to Kaitlin with curiosity.

'Perhaps you're right. So let's discuss the past few days. How was your stay in that lovely cottage on the Caledonian Canal? I heard it was quite cosy.'

It was a shot in the dark—Kaitlin *knew* that—yet she also knew she had given the smallest of tell-tale flinches. Dammit—Daniel had been right. They needed to eradicate whatever signals of awkwardness they exuded.

'I'd hardly describe a three-bedroom property, however picturesque, as "cosy".' Daniel's voice held exactly the right mix of amusement and derision. 'I know you all want to sell copy, and I get it that that means you want to believe there is an angle here, but there isn't. Kaitlin and I want this week to be about the Caversham Foundation—so if you want a different type of story then I repeat: go and find Prince Frederick and Sunita and try your luck there.'

Outrage swirled inside Kaitlin at the realisation that he'd thrown Frederick to the wolves even as she acknowledged that it appeared to have worked. The reporters had turned their questions to the upcoming ball. So, smile in place, she answered questions about the guest list, her outfit and her shoes, all the time aware that April in particular was watching her with speculation.

Once the press had dispersed they made their way into the sanctuary of the hotel—where Kaitlin stopped short at the sight of the lobby's sheer elegant magnificence. The pink and white chequered floor, the marble busts that lined the walls and the enormous lantern that dominated the ceiling all combined to create an opulence that inspired awe.

Two hotel staff glided towards them, one bearing a tray with two flutes of sparkling amber liquid. 'To refresh you after the journey,' one murmured.

Within seconds, almost without knowing how it had happened, she and Daniel were seated on chairs of extraordinary comfort and Roberto had materialised in front of them.

'Welcome. Your suite is of course ready—two en-suite double bedrooms, with a sitting room in between for you to work. I hope that is acceptable—we accommodated Signora Derwent at late notice.'

'That sounds wonderful,' Kaitlin lied as she stemmed a panic of a different type. A suite sounded too...*close*.

For heaven's sake.

They would be separated by a lounge, and she knew that the rooms in this hotel were positively palatial. Yet a quick sideways glance at Daniel showed a definite tension to his jaw—hard to figure whether that should make her feel better or worse.

'I will take you up, and on the way I will give you a brief tour,' Roberto continued, pride clear in his voice. 'The hotel is truly worthy of a grand tour. It was built in the sixteenth century as a *palazzo* and we have changed as little as possible of its splendour—whilst of course incorporating maximum twenty-first-century comfort and amenities.'

As they followed Roberto to the grand sweeping curve of the staircase and through a maze of passageways and public rooms it seemed clear that he hadn't exaggerated. The restoration was a timeless fusion of old and new, the colour schemes a tribute to taste. Historic murals and frescoes were subtly showcased, the library felt heavy with knowledge, and yet the overall impression was one of elegant, gorgeous comfort.

Then they came to their suite, and Roberto stopped at the door and handed them two ornate iron keys. 'One last item—we have arranged complimentary tickets for a private tour of the Doge's Palace today. Tomorrow we will meet to show you all the arrangements for the ball.' A small bow and he turned and headed back to the staircase.

For a moment they both stood in the panelled passageway and eyed the door, before Daniel swiped a hand down his face and stepped forward. 'Shall we?'

She followed him through and her eyes widened as she looked around the lounge. 'Wow!'

But Daniel didn't seem inclined to view the authentic silk wall coverings, or to *ooh* and *ah* over the sixteenth-century architecture, or even the intricate splendour of the chandelier.

Instead he leant back against the wall and surveyed her. 'Is it likely that Prince Frederick is with Sunita?'

'I don't know.'

'Don't you care?'

The thought caused a mix of emotions. The sensation of a weight lifted from her shoulders, alongside a ripple of fear of the unknown... 'If you mean am I hurt or jealous? Then, no, I'm not.'

A lightning-fast thought shot through her head—an

image of Daniel with a woman—and to her surprise her hands clenched involuntarily. Of *course* that wasn't what Daniel meant—he wouldn't be interested in her emotional state.

Time to retrieve the gaffe.

'In terms of how the publicity will affect the ball—I don't know. I don't think the press will lose interest in me, but you're right. It depends on whether the story is true. Either way I think it's win-win for us. If he is with Sunita they will still want my reaction. If he isn't we haven't lost anything. Right now I'm more concerned about April Fotherington. So let's hope you're right—the more time we spend together the less awkward our body language will become.'

Though now she came to think about it that didn't make a vast amount of sense. But no matter—there was no choice.

She glanced at her watch. 'Anyway, I'm going to unpack and settle in before the Doge's Palace tour.'

Once in her room Kaitlin sat on the edge of her sumptuous king-sized bed and took a moment to appreciate the room's baroque splendour. Gold and gilt and intricate plasterwork was offset by the minimalist functional furniture, the heavy curtains that would guarantee a good night's sleep.

For a moment she was tempted to lie back and simply study the ceiling, adorned with the beauty of a painting by one of Venice's best-known artists centuries before. To shut herself in this sanctuary of a room—away from the tumultuous feelings Daniel evoked, away from the panic it was becoming harder to keep at bay—and admit it was all too much. That she'd bitten off more than she could fit in her mouth, let alone chew.

No! That was *not* her way. So instead, with resolution,

she walked to the window and looked out—perhaps if she looked around from the safety of her room she could at least acclimatise herself?

But seconds later she propelled herself backwards, her senses reeling as panic slammed her. Unfamiliarity surrounded her—but, worse, everywhere she looked there was *water*.

Tendrils of memory unfurled and clamped her in a stranglehold of panic. The rough, grating tone of the kidnappers, the heart wrenching terror, the conviction that they would drown her. The blindfold…their chilling description of exactly what would happen to her as she drowned… The humiliation of her own voice begging, promising to do as they said.

Not now. These memories could not resurface now.

She backed further away from the window, hauled in a breath and perched on the end of the bed. She closed her eyes and tried to call up peaceful, safe thoughts.

'Kaitlin?'

Daniel's deep voice pervaded her meditation and she opened her eyes.

'I knocked three times. I was worried. Are you ready to go?'

Realisation hit her that she couldn't do it; she'd shot her bolt, thrown in the towel—you name it, she'd done it.

'Actually, I'm exhausted. I think I'll give it a miss.' Rising to her feet she tried to project cool assurance.

'*"Give it a miss"*? A private tour round the Doge's Palace your first time in Venice?' His voice registered utter disbelief. 'Are you nuts?'

'No. It's been a tiring few days, and I want to conserve my energy for the ball and the preparations.' Turning, she shook her hair slightly forward. 'But you go.'

A frown, and then he shrugged. 'OK. But I think you're

making a mistake. The Doge's Palace epitomises Venice at the height of its power—every single one of Venice's greatest painters and sculptors is represented somewhere. That palace is where history was made.'

A solitary tear prickled at her eyelid—damn it, she *wanted* to go. Wanted to experience Venice, see the splendour of what he described with such fervour. But how could she risk being overtaken by panic in the cobbled streets? Or even in the immensity of the palace itself? And panic was imminent—she sensed it.

'You go,' she repeated.

CHAPTER TEN

DANIEL REACHED THE door of the suite, opened it and exited into the corridor. If Kaitlin truly wanted to pass up this opportunity then that was her choice. That was what he believed in—the power of choice. Yet her decision stung more than it should.

Don't make this personal.

Because his lawyer's instinct told him that Kaitlin had withheld information. Impossible that the woman who had embraced the Highlands, who worked in an art gallery, wouldn't want to go to the Doge's Palace.

Not his business.

Yes, it was.

He turned round and retraced his steps, re-entered the suite and banged a perfunctory knock on her bedroom door.

A few seconds later Kaitlin peered out and surprise widened her green eyes. 'Did you forget something?'

'Yes, I did. I forgot you.'

'Huh?'

'You need to come to the palace. Think how it will look to Roberto, to the guests at the ball, when they hear you passed up this chance. If it's because you don't want my company I'd rather you went and I stayed here—I've seen the palace before.'

'It's fine, Daniel. I told you to go.'

'Nope.' Daniel sat down in an armchair and stretched his legs out.

'What are you doing now?'

'Sitting.'

'Why?'

'Because I'm not going to the Doge's Palace unless you come with me or explain why you won't.'

Her mouth formed a small circle of outrage. 'That is ridiculous. It's daft for us both to miss out.'

A frown creased her forehead as she realised the impact of her words.

'So you admit you're missing out?'

'Stop it!'

'Not till you explain.'

Indecision etched her face and her hands smoothed the skirt of her dress, her fingers outlining first one printed blue flower then another, and then she shook her head. 'It doesn't matter.'

'Yes, it does.'

And it did. As he looked at her he could see hurt in the strain that lined the green of her eyes and the uncharacteristic slump to her posture.

'Tell me.'

'Leave it, Daniel. It's not important.'

'It is to me.'

'Why?' The syllable was tart, almost a challenge. 'If you're worried that it will impact the ball, it won't. I'll come up with a plausible reason.'

'I don't care about the ball. I care about—'

You? No.

'I care about the fact that a colleague of mine will miss out on an opportunity to experience something wonderful. Plus, I believe that you *want* to go. So what's stopping you?'

'It's personal, and you and I don't do personal.'

Of course he knew he should leave it, but he couldn't—the knowledge that he was near to an important truth was something he couldn't ignore or impede.

'Maybe we should change that.'

She shook her head, and a short, mirthless laugh dropped from her lips. 'By which you mean *I* should share something personal with *you*, not vice versa.'

The truth caused heat to warm the back of his neck. *Touché*. Now he really needed to back off. But the glint in her eye, the challenge, brought out the advocate in him.

'I can do personal. I just choose not to. You don't do personal because you don't trust anyone. You think if you confide in me I may use the information—go public, tell the reporters... I won't. You have already trusted me with Barcelona—why not go a step further?'

'Why does it matter to you?'

'Because I want you to see the Doge's Palace.'

Keep it casual.

'And you think that if I confide in you the issue will go away?'

'It's worth a shot.'

A long silence and then, 'It won't, but you're right. You already have so much power over me, one more item is neither here nor there.' Hands in her lap, she took in an audible breath before saying, 'I suffer from panic attacks.'

The words took a couple of seconds to register—given the serenity and calm for which Kaitlin was famed, they seemed incredible. But then he remembered Barcelona—his first glimpse of 'Lynette'—remembered Kaitlin's frenzy when she'd fallen into the water, her over-the-top preparations for Scotland and Venice. Admiration touched him at her courage in taking on both places.

'I'm so sorry, Kaitlin. I wish I could say more, but it

makes everything you have achieved even more impressive.' He rose to his feet, squashed the urge to go and sit next to her, put an arm around her and tell her he'd make it all OK, and started to pace instead. 'I'm guessing water and new places trigger the attacks?'

'*Anything* can trigger the attacks.' There was bitterness and resignation in her tone. 'But, yes, I find unfamiliar places overwhelming—and as for water... I do my best to avoid it.'

'Is that what you've been advised to do? Avoid anything that might trigger the panic?' He was no expert, but that tactic would surely impose nigh on impossible limitations.

'It's what I've worked out for myself.'

There was defiance in the jut of her chin and defence in the folding of her arms as she glared at him in a clear dare to challenge her.

It was a dare he was more than happy to take up. 'How long have you had these attacks?'

'Since childhood.'

'Then surely you must have seen a doctor or a counsellor? Someone must have noticed you panic—your parents, a teacher, Gabe, Cora...'

'I didn't need to see anyone.'

'Did your parents know?'

Easy, Daniel. This isn't a witness in the stand.

'Yes. But they decided it was better to deal with it ourselves.'

By that, Daniel was pretty sure Kaitlin meant they had left her to deal with it by herself. His mind whirred, put together the hints and conversational snippets of the past few days.

'Something happened to incite the panic and they didn't want the publicity.'

'Leave it.'

Her face had blanched and Daniel knew that whatever had happened to her had been catastrophic.

'I'm not under oath and I will not discuss the cause of the attacks.'

There was strength and dignity in her stance and in her voice, underlain with such vulnerability that his chest ached. Whatever burden she bore she clearly carried it alone. Anger with her parents caused his stride to increase even as he determined not to spook her further.

'I understand. I won't ask any more. But I strongly believe that you need to talk to an expert.'

'I have it under control.'

'I totally admire that you have managed this for so long, but there may be a better way. A way to overcome the panic rather than control it—a way to make it go away. The best way to find out is to talk to someone—an expert, a therapist.'

'I can't do that.'

'Yes, you can. If the story leaks out so be it.' Halting in front of her, he reached out a hand and pulled her up, kept her hand in his. 'Kaitlin, this is your *life* we're talking about.'

'Stop it. You're messing with my head. My life is fine as it is.'

'Yes, it is. I would never belittle what you have achieved. But the panic imposes limits on you. Without it your life could take a different trajectory.'

'That is akin to the assertion that a blind person's life would be different if they could see. It is as it is.'

'Maybe it doesn't have to be. You owe it to yourself to find out.'

She huffed out a sigh that signalled exasperation, pulled her hand from his. 'Until you came along my life was on the exact trajectory I wanted it to be on, and I have every intention of returning it there after Venice. End of discussion.'

Frustrated, he opened his mouth to continue the argument—until he saw the stubborn set to her jaw. Perhaps a softly-softly approach would make more sense, but he wouldn't let this go for long. Just for now.

'Fair enough. No more discussion. But I have an idea about the Doge's Palace. Think back to Barcelona.'

'I really don't want to remember Barcelona.'

'Yes, you do.' He took her hands back, ignored the shiver of sensation that rippled up his arm in response. 'You walked the streets, you went into the hustle and bustle of a tapas bar and you were fine.'

'That's because—'

She broke off, pressed her lips together, and he wondered what she had been about to say.

'Because you were 'Lynette'?'

'Something like that. But that won't work here.'

'No. But you have something else here that you had in Barcelona.'

Her eyes narrowed.

'Me,' he completed.

'You?' Disbelief tinged the very air. 'So you reckon *you* are the magical solution to my panic attacks?'

'No. Of course not. But maybe I can be a temporary sticking plaster. I promise that I will keep you safe. If you can bring yourself to believe that, maybe it will help keep the panic at bay enough to allow you to appreciate Venice. I promise you that if it all gets too much I will get you back here quickly and discreetly, and although I understand there is nothing tangible you are worried about I am more than equipped to keep you safe from pickpockets. What do you think?'

Kaitlin moved away from his presence and walked over

to the window, almost as if to brave the view of the scenery again.

'Why does this matter to you? Why not just leave me here and go and enjoy Venice?'

'Because that would make me a complete heel. And I could use the company.'

Seeing the disbelief in her face, he dug deep. Kaitlin had shared something huge with him. Surely he could choose to reciprocate a little.

'It's the truth. My father died before I was born. But my mother told me that they had planned to move to Venice some day. So the city always makes me feel a little melancholy.'

Kaitlin's eyes darted to his face. 'That must be hard—never having known your dad.'

'I had my mother, and she was amazing.'

'She must have felt so blessed to have had you.'

Blessed. Daniel didn't think so. Oh, his mother had loved him—so much that she had sacrificed her very soul for him. It was a shame it had proved such a poor investment. The bitter taste of guilt flooded him and he swiped a hand down his face. *Enough.* This was about Kaitlin.

She looked at him, her green eyes serious.

'OK. Let's do this. Doge's Palace, here I come.'

As they approached the splendour of the palace Kaitlin caught her breath in sheer awe. Here she was, standing in front of this incredible building, and a wave of emotion swathed her—a lightness, an unfamiliar joy that made her want to laugh out loud.

Without thought she reached out, took Daniel's hand and smiled up at him. 'This is fabulous—thank you for your persistence.'

'No trouble.'

But it had been—Daniel had cared enough to return for her, to convince her to accompany him, and the idea sent further warmth to her insides.

Careful, Kaitlin.

But she didn't want to be careful; for once she wanted to go with the flow, with the thoroughly unfamiliar sense of trust.

Bad idea.

But it wasn't. It wasn't as if she proposed to trust in Daniel long-term. This was purely a three-day fix. If he could help her enjoy Venice then it made sense to let him. And his presence did seem to have a positive effect on her panic—sure, the swirl of unease was present, but it hadn't escalated.

Now they stood in the slanting Venetian spring sunshine and gazed at the Gothic structure of the enormous building—an epicentre of history where political decisions had been made, where justice had been meted out over the centuries by each elected Doge.

'It is such an influential place, and yet it has a fairytale element.'

Enhanced by the candy cane effect of huge walls of white limestone and pink marble and the series of balconies.

Daniel nodded. 'Apparently experts say that the sense of lightness is because of the way it was built, with the loggias below and the solid walls above. That gives it an openness that was meant to indicate how powerful Venice was. Most cities back then would build more fortified castles.'

Suddenly aware that she was still holding Daniel's hand, she looked down at their clasped fingers and wondered what to do. Placing temporary trust in him was one thing—venturing into any realm of physical contact was another.

Yet letting go required an effort of will that had her alarm bells ringing again.

'Shall we go in?'

Daniel nodded and they made their way into the courtyard.

'It's impossible to know what to look at first,' Kaitlin marvelled.

'Yes.'

She glanced at him, observed the light in his blue eyes as they rested on her, and felt heat climb her cheekbones. Suddenly their surroundings, despite the magnificence of the giant ceremonial staircase, the enormous statues of Neptune and Mars, even the imposing yet ethereal beauty of the Foscari arch, faded into the background.

All she could see—all she was aware of—was Daniel. The strength of his features, the dark curl of his hair, the absurd length of his eyelashes and the growing heat in his eyes. A step closer to him and she was enmeshed by his aura, focused on the breadth of his chest, the toned masculinity of the sinews of his arms...

The sound of a man's throat being cleared, followed by the uttering of their names, broke the spell and she turned, pinning a smile in place.

'I am your guide for the tour. My name is Marco.'

'Pleased to meet you.'

'Follow me. As you know, this part of the palace is a separate tour—I will be showing you the nitty-gritty, the less salubrious side, as well as the places where the real work was done over the centuries.'

As the guide moved forward Daniel looked down at her. 'You're sure about this?'

'Yes.' She'd done some research before they left, and although there was a definite risk that some of the rooms might trigger panic, she wanted to give it a try. 'I want to see the behind-the-scenes reality as well as all the treasures and art-work.'

Plus the tickets had been gifted to them, and she had no wish to explain why she hadn't done the tour now they had got this far.

Kaitlin followed the guide through the narrow door and into the *'pozzi'*, and gave a shudder as she looked round in horror at the tiny stone-walled cells; their only ventilation small round holes. She saw the drawings on the wall—depictions of the prisoners' despair. Moisture sheened her neck and for a horrible moment the walls seemed to close in, the dank atmosphere blanketed her and terror rippled her body with memories.

The turn of a lock...the cloying feeling of powerlessness...the remembered pain as she'd repeatedly thumped the door until she'd realised no one would come. No one would rescue her.

She shook her head and focused on Marco's words, tried to remember that prisoners in times gone by had had it way worse than she had during her ten-day incarceration.

Then Daniel enclosed her hand in his and his deep voice offered reprieve.

'Would it be possible to move on, Marco? I suffer from a touch of claustrophobia and these walls are enough to cause me discomfort.'

'Of course, of course. Let us move on.'

For the next half an hour Kaitlin was transported back in time as they walked the chambers where the Council of Ten—a group of elected men with immense power—would have convened, rooms where they would have made life-and-death decisions, plotted and schemed. Then they toured the spacious Chamber of the Secret Chancellery, with its magnificent mirrored upper doors and cabinet-lined walls.

And the whole time the knowledge that Daniel still held her hand firmly in his grasp burned in her with a small white light of awareness. The sane Lady Kaitlin part of her told her that this was a public place and they were courting disaster. Yet his grasp made her feel safe, secure, protected, and therefore it behoved her to hang on. After all, there was no meaning to it—it was simply a tactic to keep panic at bay, the equivalent of a stress ball, nothing more.

You're kidding yourself, warned the voice of reason. Because if his grasp was warding off panic it was also ushering in other sensations: a warmth, a thrill, a delicious ripple of sensation reminiscent of their time walking through Barcelona hand in hand. And look where *that* had ended up.

Yet as they explored the horror of the torture chamber, known as the Chamber of Torment, and listened to the chilling stories from the guide, she shifted closer to Daniel's bulk, remained there as they viewed the wood-panelled prison cell that had once housed Casanova himself, before his daring escape.

Only once the tour was over and they'd returned to the majesty of the main rooms of the palace did she drop his hand, forcing herself to do so without so much as tremor. Simply a cool smile.

'Thank you Daniel. Having something to hold did help.'

'Glad to be of service.'

It was a service she must not allow herself the luxury of using too often, or her stupid body would get the wrong idea. Distance—she *had* to keep her distance.

CHAPTER ELEVEN

FOR HOURS KAITLIN did manage to do exactly that—to maintain distance. As they toured the rest of the palace she submerged herself in the spectacular splendour of the Doge's apartments, in the ornate gold interior of the rooms, the impossible to describe detail of the frescoes, the sheer splendour of the art.

'Glad you came?' Daniel asked as they emerged onto the Bridge of Sighs.

'Yes. Truly. Thank you.'

'You're welcome.'

They paused on the bridge. 'Why is it called the Bridge of Sighs?' Kaitlin asked, testing herself as she looked into the chill green of the water. If she wanted to enjoy Venice she had to get her head round the fact it was a water-based city.

'Prisoners crossing the bridge knew it would be their last taste of freedom and open air, so they are said to have sighed as they crossed it. Other people say it is the sigh lovers make. Legend has it that if you take a gondola ride under the Bridge of Sighs as the sun sets with your significant other and you kiss then your love will be eternal.'

'Lucky I don't believe in love, then, because there is no way on this earth I'm getting in a gondola. Or even a *vaporetto*. My enjoyment of Venice is going to be on land!'

'But your plan *is* to enjoy Venice?'

Kaitlin pulled in a breath. 'If you still want my company?'

There was a pause, and for a moment she wondered if she had just made a complete idiot of herself.

'Though if you would rather spend time alone here because of your dad and everything I understand.'

'Shh.'

Lifting a hand, he brushed a finger softly against her lips, and she froze at the exquisite sensation that ran through her, then backed a step away, looking around to make sure no one had seen. But the throngs of tourists had no interest in them—were too busy gazing at the Palace.

'I do still want your company.'

'Then why the hesitation? I don't want your pity because of what I told you.'

'You don't have my pity.' His lips turned up in a rueful twist. 'My hesitation was due to a momentary worry that I might succumb to the temptation to kiss you. The problem is, I want more than that.'

'Oh.'

Please kiss me.

Get a grip.

There could be no kissing. Though right now Kaitlin wanted him to kiss her with a yearning so great she could taste it. But that wasn't possible—she and Daniel weren't a normal couple on holiday in Venice, like so many of the men and women around them, who could stop and kiss whenever they liked.

Come to that they weren't a couple of any description. She was Lady Kaitlin Derwent—a woman who wanted an alliance that would bring glory to the Derwent name, who wanted a family, children, marriage. Daniel was a man who wanted success and all its trappings—a man who could offer no more than a few days of pleasure to any woman.

For Lady Kaitlin Derwent that pleasure would come at way too high a price. The gossip, the scandal, her parents' fury... And more than that there was the risk of losing herself—the risk that her whole being would unravel. Daniel represented danger and disorder. Any involvement with him would be too scary. It sent a skitter of anxiety through her whole body.

'You can't kiss me.' Her voice was breathless, a squeak of pure panic.

The rueful look on his face intensified. 'Don't look so troubled, Kaitlin. I understand that. Forget I said anything and let's focus on enjoying Venice. Agreed?'

'Agreed.' Pushing her doubts away, Kaitlin nodded.

How hard could it be not to kiss someone for two days?

Daniel glanced out of the latticed semi-circular window at the late-morning sunshine that glinted off the canal and rooftops of St Mark's Square before turning to where Kaitlin sat at the round marble-topped table, pen tucked behind her ear.

'What would you like to do today?' He gestured at their now closed laptops and neat pile of papers. 'Now that we know the ball is completely under control.'

They had spent the morning checking and double-checking that the arrangements were in place and watertight.

'The rest of today is ours to do with as we choose.'

Kaitlin rose from the table and headed to the window, oh, so careful not to so much as brush past him. 'There is a part of me that's tempted to stay right here in safety, but most of me feels cautiously optimistic that I can deal with outside. I would like to go to the Scuola Grande di

San Rocco, if that's OK with you? It's a little off the beaten track, but I'd love to see so many of Tintoretto's works under one incredible roof. '

'Sounds like a plan. I'll get directions, and we can always use our phones to navigate.'

He sat down and pulled his computer towards him to source exact directions—sure that for Kaitlin the idea of getting lost would hold little appeal and might indeed trigger panic.

'Thank you.'

As he glanced at her he felt a funny little tug pull at his chest. Dressed in a blue lace dress that combined simple elegance and comfort, Kaitlin looked...relaxed—more relaxed than he could have imagined. Her glorious hair hung in loose waves to her shoulders, her green eyes held a glint of emerald and her body held minimal tension.

He glanced at the map of Venice and made some quick calculations. 'OK. Route mastered. Let's go.'

As they exited the hotel from the back entrance, walked through the peaceful courtyard and through the wrought-iron gates that led out onto a bustling Venetian street, Daniel glanced down at her. Her body held more tension now, as they joined the crowds, and he couldn't help but wonder how hard it must be for her to contain her panic—the amount of energy and strain she expended in simple day-to-day life.

'I know what you need. You need pizza.'

'I do?'

'Yup. We'll get takeaway pizza and eat it whilst we watch the world go by.'

Twenty minutes later he had made good on his promise and they were seated in a small courtyard—a pocket-sized garden of tranquillity. The scents of oleander and laurel mingled with the pungent tomato sauce of the pizza, and the background sounds of the fountains merged with the noise of St Mark's square just metres away.

Kaitlin sat on a bench and took a bite of pizza. 'This is fabulous.' For a while they ate in companionable and appreciative silence. Until she wiped her mouth with a napkin and turned to face him. 'You keep asking how I am. Now it's my turn. How are *you*?'

'Fine.'

A shake of her head indicated disbelief. 'You told me that last time you came to Venice it made you feel melancholy. What about this time? I'm not trying to pry.' Her expression was soft, pensive. 'But you have helped me—you *are* helping me, so much—and I want you to know that if I can reciprocate I want to.' She sighed. 'Not in a tit-for-tat way—more in a… I'd like to.' A shake of her head. 'I can't believe how garbled I'm being.'

'It's OK. I get it.'

Ironically, he did—way more than he got her carefully thought out sentences, however clever or apposite they might be. *This* Kaitlin was real, genuine, and he didn't want to close the conversation down. Because to do so would be to send the real Kaitlin away.

'Last time I came here was eight years ago—I was much younger and more emotional and it felt like a pilgrimage. This time I'm older and wiser.'

This time he also had Kaitlin, but that was neither here nor there.

'I wish my parents had had this chance—a chance to make a go of it, enjoy the beauty of the city—but I can't change the past.'

'No. You can only face forward,' she said, quoting his words back at him. 'But the past is still important, because it shapes your future.'

'Your own choices shape your future.'

'Of course. But you can't deny the past has an effect. Even if you wish it didn't. You are a different person than the one you would have been if your father had lived.'

'So you don't believe our fate is ordained from birth?'

'Perhaps some of it is. Or maybe not "ordained" but made probable. It is more likely that I will mix in aristocratic circles because I am from an aristocratic family. But it's not set in stone. My sister Cora was never very interested in that side of things.' She tucked a stray strand of hair behind her ear. 'So it's not only our birth but also our family who influences us. After your father died I'm sure your grandparents must have had an impact on your life.'

'Unfortunately not.' The age-old anger flared in his gut. 'My mother had run away from her own family as a teenager—she would never speak of the reasons, but I assume her childhood was pretty horrific. My dad's family wanted nothing to do with us.'

'Why?'

'They thought my mother was beneath my father. When she got pregnant and they decided to get married my dad's parents were furious. They asked him to choose between them and my mother.'

The irony of the situation caused bitterness to rise in his throat.

'He chose my mother, so they disowned him—fired him from his job in the family restaurant business and blackened his name. My dad took any job he could find, because he was determined to provide for us—for his baby, his family. He worked all hours because he was determined to succeed on his own. One of the jobs he took on was as a lorry driver—he was so exhausted he fell asleep at the wheel, the lorry crashed and he died. Luckily at least no one else was hurt.'

As he told the story he had almost forgotten he had an

audience. His desire for the tale to have a different ending burned as deep as it had in childhood. Accompanied by the same sear of guilt.

A feeling of warmth permeated his senses, the scent of rose, the sense of comfort, as Kaitlin shifted closer to him on the bench, leant forward and touched his arm. 'Your poor, poor mum. The shock must have been awful—your dad sounds so vital, so strong. And poor you as well. To never have known him.'

'My mother told me about him. He was the love of her life—according to her, love at first sight *is* possible. She was a waitress in one of his family's restaurants—they met and *kaboom*.' The sound of his mother's voice echoed across the years. The click of her fingers as she'd said the word. 'They had so many hopes and dreams and plans—if it hadn't been for me their story would have played out differently.'

'It's not *your* fault.' Her voice was urgent; fervour brightened the green of her eye to emerald.

'It's not about fault. It is about fact. My grandparents cast him off because of the pregnancy. He was working all those jobs to provide for me.'

Kaitlin shook her head, studying his expression with way too much understanding, and discomfort caused him to shift on the wooden slats of the bench.

'It sounds to me as though your dad loved you, and it is a tragedy he didn't live to see the man you have become. But the fact is that it is *not* your fault.' As if sensing his unease, with her usual unerring social poise she changed tack. 'So, what were their plans and dreams? Did your mother tell you?'

'They wanted to set up a restaurant—here in Venice, where his family originated. Travel...have a brood of children.'

'So your dad was Italian?'

'Yes.'

'But you took your stepfather's surname?'

Easy does it.

This was why he should have never have embarked on this conversation. Perhaps the ambience of Venice, the flavour of might-have-beens, the sudden urge to keep his father's memory alive had all combined to loosen his tongue. The suspicion that in actual fact it was Kaitlin—her understanding, her sheer presence—that had caused the hitherto unheard of confidence-sharing unnerved him.

It was an unacceptable possibility—letting people close caused potential hurt to all concerned and it was time to bring this to a halt.

'I kept my mother's name.' In fact he had changed it when he'd left the States—had needed a clean start with no connection at all to his past. A past he had left behind.

Daniel screwed up his napkin with a savage scrunch and rose to his feet, saw Kaitlin's troubled look and pulled a smile to his face. This was not her fault—it was his. And he wouldn't let it happen again. From now on in this was about enjoyment of Venice—no more than that.

'If you're ready, I know the perfect place for dessert.'

As they walked back towards the hustle and bustle of St Mark's Square Kaitlin couldn't help but dwell on what Daniel had shared.

Next to her, she could sense the strength of his body and the vibration of frustrated anger, and she wondered about his current family situation. The way he had spoken of his mother suggested distance—she had no immediate sense of the woman whose life had been touched by such tragedy.

Walking closer to him, she wanted to soothe him, remembered how much comfort she had derived from human contact. So she slipped her hand into his. For a second his stride faltered, and then he returned the pressure and they kept walking until they arrived at a café.

Though 'café' seemed way too commonplace a word— this was a real, proper European coffee house.

'If I narrow my eyes to filter out the modern-day clothing I can imagine that we've stepped back in time.'

'This was once the haunt of the likes of Casanova, Proust and Charles Dickens. Lord Byron used to brood and breakfast here as well.'

'Where would you like to sit?'

Outside, tables and chairs were scattered under the colonnades, and an orchestra played classical music that further added to the sense of history.

'Wherever you prefer,' Daniel said.

'Let's go inside,' she decided. 'If the outside is so magnificent I can't imagine the inside.'

And indeed it did defy description. As they sat in the gilded interior, where vast mirrors, stuccos and paintings ranging from the Oriental to portraits vied for attention, listening to the strains of beautiful notes that wafted in from outside and mingled with the smells of cakes and pastries, Kaitlin felt joy touch her.

'This is incredible.'

She looked down at the sheer decadence of her *gianduia* and pistachio *parfait* and dug her spoon into the concoction. Savoured the smallest bite, the cool, smooth texture, the tang of hazelnut complemented by the rich dark chocolate.

'I almost can't bear to actually eat it—it is so beautiful. And as for this hot chocolate…that is too mundane a translation. I think I prefer the Italian—*cioccolata calda con panna.*'

Daniel's face lit up in a grin and she felt the effect right down to her perfectly painted toes. 'Take as long as you like. You look like a little girl at her first birthday party.'

'That's how I feel.'

In fact she felt suddenly lightheaded, and she knew it was nothing to do with the sugar rush. It was to do with her sense of accomplishment and it was to do with Daniel. Danger tolled a bell in the deep recesses of her brain but Kaitlin ignored it, suddenly determined that nothing would spoil this day.

'That's awesome.' He lifted his espresso. 'Long may it last.'

For a moment she thought he might expound on his views on her getting help, but he didn't. Instead his gaze rested on her and something sparked in his eyes—something that warmed her from the inside out, made her want to hurl caution to the spring breeze. All that mattered was this moment in time, the glide of the tuxedoed waiters, their platters expertly balanced, the strum of the orchestra, the smell of cake and sugar mingled with the tang of rosemary, and the dark, bittersweet melting of chocolate on her tongue.

But most of all there was Daniel—his aura, his potency, his sheer being as his lips turned up into a smile that stole the breath from her lungs.

'You look happy.' The depth of his voice caressed her skin. 'And relaxed, and…' A chuckle accompanied the words. 'You have a smudge of sugar on the tip of your nose…'

Kaitlin reached into her bag for a pocket mirror and looked at her reflection. 'And a chocolate moustache,' she completed for him. 'I really *do* look as if I'm at a kid's birthday party.'

To her surprise a small laugh bubbled up, and then she couldn't quite help herself—scooping up a bit of whipped cream, she leant over and dabbed it on the end of Daniel's nose.

Surprise daubed his expression with a comical grimace as he wiped it off and her laughter bubbled over, erupting in a stream of giggles that she couldn't stem. A second later and he had joined in, with a deep belly laugh that caused the neighbouring customers to turn and look.

Then, as their laughter subsided, he grinned at her and Kaitlin could feel an answering smile tilt her lips as he reached out and gently swiped his finger down the bridge of her nose.

A tingle shot through her, and for a long moment their gazes intermingled before she hauled in breath. 'Thank you. I haven't laughed like that in a long time.'

'Neither have I.'

Those alarm bells clanged again.

Get it together.

This was *not* how Lady Kaitlin Derwent behaved.

'Right. Um…well, I guess I'd better get eating and we'd better get a move on. After all, we only have today.'

Regret twinged and she gave her head a small shake. They might only have today, but perhaps that meant she should enjoy every second, silence the alarm bells and live in the moment. After all there could be no danger in wandering the streets of Venice chaperoned by throngs of fellow tourists.

Scooping up another exquisite bite, she smiled at him. 'Onward.'

CHAPTER TWELVE

ONWARD. DANIEL GLANCED down at Kaitlin as they left the café and for a scant second wondered exactly where 'onward' was taking them. Disquiet prickled his skin as he quenched the urge to clasp her hand in his again.

Ridiculous.

Kaitlin did not need to hold his hand—it seemed clear that her panic had at least temporarily been held at bay, granting her a reprieve.

So it was best that he held his distance and continued to ignore the attraction that hazed the air between them. Instead he focused on their environment—the washing hanging to dry from windows, the aromas of cooking, a woman in her doorway shelling peas, the scent of the canal and the snatches of conversation as they wandered the narrow streets lined with brightly painted houses.

But at increasingly regular intervals his attention strayed back to Kaitlin, to the vibrant splash of her hair, the grace with which she walked, effortlessly cool and elegant in the lace dress. A vibe radiated from her of relaxed, confident enthusiasm, and her green eyes sparkled as she looked around, absorbing the sights and sounds of the city, and an unwanted warmth spread through his veins and brought a scowl to his face.

'Is something wrong?'

Daniel glanced down and forced his expression to neutral as he saw the question in her eyes. 'Not at all. For a moment there I thought I'd got us lost, but I haven't. If I'm right we should arrive in the next few minutes.'

Her forehead creased into a small frown, as if she didn't believe his answer, but then she gave a small lift of her shoulders, indicative of a decision to leave well enough alone.

A few more twists and turns and... '*Voilà.*'

The stone and marble building of the Scuola Grande di San Rocco was a truly impressive example of Renaissance architecture—a fitting home for its incredible interior.

Kaitlin's green eyes widened, her movements slow and deliberate as she stood in front of each painting. 'It's almost as if I am being pulled in by the depth of emotion, the fervour. It makes me feel...*humbled.*'

'This one defines the meaning of awesome,' Daniel said. 'In that it fills me with awe and incredulity at its sheer....vastness.'

Tintoretto's attention to detail combined with the overall message each image portrayed showed him to be master of artistry and allegory.

'It stuns me that one man could create all of this in one lifetime. The detail, the anguish, the dedication....' Her voice was soft with reverence. 'But also the intelligence and the thought he must have put into it—the way each individual picture is part of the overall panorama.'

She turned away from the paintings and looked up at him, her face alight with curiosity.

'Is that how you feel about your company? That it's like a work of art, or a sculpture that you've built up piece by piece?'

It was an interesting concept. 'I've never thought of it like that.' The burn of ambition had motivated him to focus on growth and money, but in a way Harrington Legal Services *was* a work of art—a tapestry of success. 'But, yes, HLS is my creation.'

And he was proud of it for reasons other than its success—he was proud of what it represented, of the fact all his employees shared its ethos and principles.

'One that you were driven to create. Just like a lot of artists paint because they have no choice.'

'I have a choice.' *Didn't he?*

'Do you? Your life is all about work. You don't holiday, you don't want a family...'

Her words were matter-of-fact, yet he fought an absurd urge to fold his arms in defensiveness.

'I'm not a holiday type of person. I get edgy. Bored.'

The thought flitted in his brain that he hadn't been bored in Scotland or here in Venice. Obviously because this was a *working* holiday, even if the work wasn't associated with the law.

'I prefer to work—it's a choice. As for family—that is also my choice. It's not for me.'

Kaitlin shook her head. 'How often do you drive your sports car? Or cars?'

'Often enough.'

But quite possibly not often enough to warrant their price tag. In truth his cars were simply tokens that marked his climb up the ladder of success—an indication that he was as successful as his step-family, proof that he had enough lucre to support his mother and his half-sister in the lifestyle they had become accustomed to.

'I don't think you do. You told me that my panic imposes limitations on my life—maybe your drive to succeed imposes limitations on *yours*.'

As she walked over to placard headed 'The Life of Tintoretto' she gestured for him to follow.

'Look. Tintoretto had it all. He lived a long, prosperous

life, married and had eight children, and even trained three of them to follow in his footsteps. Yet he managed to paint all this and way more. He had *balance*. I—'

Her words came to an abrupt cessation, her animation replaced by a frozen mask of terror, her body preternaturally still. He turned to follow her line of glazed vision, saw that a group of English tourists had entered—a man and two women, the man dark-haired and bearded with his sunglasses still on. His voice was loud and argumentative, and clearly he had been dragged here by his companions against his will. But he was paying no heed to Kaitlin, and he couldn't see what there was to trigger her panic.

No matter—Kaitlin swayed slightly and he could almost see her fight-or-flight instinct come to the fore.

'We're out of here,' he said, keeping his voice calm and even as he approached her. 'Come on, Kaitlin, start walking.'

She flinched away from him, backed up a step.

'I'll get you out of here. No problem. I'll keep you safe. No need to panic.'

The words came automatically and he was careful to keep his hands by his sides, sensing she had to come of her own choice. In the meantime he stepped in front of her, blocked her view of the man and hoped the group wouldn't approach.

'Let's walk. Easy does it.'

Kaitlin hesitated and he saw her eyes refocus, gaze up at the ceiling and then around her, before ending up riveted to his face. She puffed out a small sigh and started to walk.

The pace she set was a half-march, her usual poise ragged, hands clenching and unclenching as they stepped out into the early dusk. Casting a glance over her shoulder, another into the shadows, she increased speed.

After five minutes Daniel decided they had put enough

distance between themselves and whatever or whoever had spooked her with such radical effect.

'Kaitlin—stop. Or at least tell me where you want to go.'

'Home.' A half-laugh. 'The hotel, I suppose. I need to be somewhere safe.'

'You *are*.' Without thought he turned and halted in front of her, and took her hands in his. 'Whilst you are with me you are safe. I will not let any harm come to you.'

A tug of her hands as she shook her head. 'Those are *words*, Daniel. Anyone can use words to manipulate, to lie…'

'Or to tell the truth. And that is what I am doing. You are safe. Right here, right now. If you want to go back to the hotel then that's where we will go, but we don't need to run there. If you want to stay out we can, and you will be safe. Trust me.'

Her breathing slowed as she met his gaze and he could almost see the cogs and wheels whirring in her brain.

Trust him. Kaitlin tried to think past the glut of emotions that clogged her brain. Logic told her to return pronto to the hotel, shut herself in her room and calm down. A deeper instinct wanted to stay with Daniel—to recapture the confidence and the freedom of earlier, to have a night in Venice. Shades of the past, of Barcelona…

No. This was different—she wasn't faking her identity and Daniel was no longer a stranger.

Her heart-rate thudded back to as near to normal as possible when he was this close and she made her decision. Maybe she'd regret it—most likely she would—but… 'I'd like to stay out.'

A squeeze of her hands and then he released one and retained the other in a clasp of reassurance. 'How does a night at a jazz club sound?'

'Perfect.' Once again warmth touched her at the way he seemed able to read her needs—a jazz club was far less likely to trigger panic than a standing-room-only bar packed with people, and the music would help.

For the journey there she simply followed Daniel, didn't so much as give any protest a thought when he clasped her hand in his because it felt *right*. The fear triggered in the *scuola* had abated, but her nerves were still frayed and memories danced in grotesque shadows at the back of her mind.

But the memories were held at bay by Daniel's presence, by both the reassurance and the thrill his touch bestowed.

The club itself was everything she could have wished for—both quirky and eclectic enough to push the past further away. Vibrantly painted walls were offset by dim illumination, the club's love of jazz clear in its themed memorabilia, a homage to artists past and present.

The proprietor showed them to a candlelit bistro-type table, secluded by the width of a Gothic column, and the tension drained from her body as she watched the band tune up, ate a selection of cold meat and cheese and bread, and listened to the notes jump and dance on the air, rebounding into her brain with a cleansing beat.

Then Daniel leant forward. 'Better?' he asked.

'Yes.'

'So what happened back there? Did you know that man?'

Reluctance to answer pressed her lips together, and then common sense prevailed. Daniel had made her a promise to keep her safe—he couldn't do that without facts.

'No. He reminded me of someone from my past and I went into panic freefall.'

With an effort she kept her tone light, tucked a tendril

of hair behind her ear, focused on the tang of wine on her tongue.

'You can talk about it if you want. Maybe I'm a good choice, because after tomorrow our paths won't cross again.'

The words caused her an unexpected wince of hurt, a fluttery sensation in her chest, and for a second she would swear there was sadness in the twist of his lips.

Daft.

Daniel Harrington was no good for her—time spent with him seemed to have somehow frayed her entire Lady Kaitlin persona around the edges. Worse, she wasn't sure she cared. Because he was a good man—good enough that she was sorely tempted to take him at his word. To tell him about the incident that had changed her whole life's path, intrinsically altered her from the inside out.

But to do that she would have to take trust a whole sky-scraper further.

He picked his drink up and lifted his broad shoulders. 'I understand if you can't trust me enough. That is a decision only you can make.'

As she picked up an olive and took a small bite she remembered what he had told her of his family—information she knew was personal to him. She remembered that he hadn't gone public with Barcelona, remembered how he had helped her these past days, allowed her a chance to experience Venice in a way that would have been impossible otherwise. She recalled how he had been in Scotland, with the teenagers. If she couldn't trust this man, who had such a sense of integrity, then all her remaining belief in human nature would shatter.

'I do trust you enough,' she said quietly. 'And I appreciate your offer to listen—maybe it *will* help.'

She swirled her drink round the glass, gazed down into it, unable to face him, to see his expression when she told him.

'Hey. Look at me. Whatever you tell me I will respect your confidence. And I won't judge you and I won't pity you.' Leaning over the table, he placed a gentle finger under her chin. 'I promise.'

Drawing in a shaky breath, she closed her eyes. Then opened them and forced herself to look into the deep blue depths of his.

'When I was thirteen I was kidnapped. I wanted to go to a concert and my parents said no. One of the staff, Natalie, offered to help me—I trusted her, and she helped sneak me out of the manor. Turned out it was all a plan to kidnap me.'

Daniel sat very still, but she could sense the anger that emanated from him, saw his hands clench into purposeful fists. 'You must have been terrified.'

'It took me a while to truly comprehend what was happening. To this day I don't know where they held me—but I was there for ten days whilst they negotiated with my parents. The longer it went on, the more frustrated they got and the worse it was for me. Especially after I tried and nearly managed to escape.'

Kaitlin couldn't contain the shudder.

'Did they hurt you?'

Now there was no mistaking his anger, and that fury made her feel protected in a way she never had before. Her parents' anger had been directed at *her*, not at the kidnappers. The blame had been handed to her and she'd borne it for the past fourteen years.

'They threatened me. Natalie told them about my fear of water and they exploited that. Held me under in the bath. They also—'

Her voice broke as memories crowded in. The taste of

sheer humiliation, the clammy sheen of bone-deep terror at the realisation of her powerlessness and her kidnappers' strength.

'They made me pose for photographs—threatened my parents that they would release them.'

'Oh, hell, Kaitlin. If I could get my hands on them I swear to you I'd make them pay.'

He rose and moved round the secluded table, sat next to her so he shielded her from anyone's view.

'I'm OK. It happened in the past. I was shaken today because that bearded man reminded me of one of the men who held me. Mostly I face forward.'

'You can't face forward if the demons are constantly at your back. First you have to deal with them.'

As she saw the determination on his face she wondered if he had dealt with whatever demons lay behind him. 'I have dealt with them. For the most part.'

'By yourself. I still don't understand why your parents didn't get you some help?'

'They couldn't risk the publicity—they were terrified of what the kidnappers would do with those photographs, and they were furious with me. If I hadn't sneaked out to go to that concert the whole situation wouldn't have arisen. It cost them a lot of money to get me back.'

Hearing the bitterness in her own words, she shook her head.

'No. That makes them sound terrible. Of course they were glad to have me back in one piece. But as far as they were concerned I'd messed up, there had been terrible consequences, but they had sorted it out and we all needed to put it behind us and move on.'

'But they must have realised the experience had traumatised you—would traumatise *anyone*.'

'No, they didn't. They didn't want to talk about it, forbade me to tell anyone, ever, and that was that. So I figured out how to deal with it myself. As I got older I did some research into panic attacks and I have worked out various strategies for how to deal with it.'

Strategies that had worked just fine until Daniel had entered her orbit.

'So here I am.'

'Here you are and here's to you, Kaitlin.' He held up his glass. 'To your strength and determination.'

Shyness mingled with appreciation of his words and brought heat to her cheeks. 'Thank you. And thank you for listening.'

Sharing the experience that had clouded her life for so long had drained her, and yet it had also brought her a strange feeling of peace.

'Now, I'm ready to go back to the hotel—if that's OK with you?'

'Of course it is.'

CHAPTER THIRTEEN

THEY WALKED BACK to the hotel in a silence that held comfort and an inevitable closeness. Daniel walked close to her, felt a surge of protectiveness towards this woman who was so much more than he could have imagined. The idea of what she had gone through fuelled anger inside him—at the staff member who had betrayed a young girl's trust, at the kidnappers themselves, and at the Duke and Duchess for their reactions. For allowing their daughter to take the blame for an atrocity perpetrated by others, for not giving her any help or sympathy or understanding.

'It's all right.' Kaitlin looked up at him, her face illuminated in the moonlight. 'I'm OK. I didn't tell you what I told you because I want you to be angry on my behalf. It's done.'

'Hey... You aren't meant to be comforting *me*!'

'I'm not. If I'm honest, I like it that you're angry on my behalf, because no one else ever has been. But I don't want your blood pressure to skyrocket whilst you brood on it.'

'It just makes me mad that they got away with it—that they are out there somewhere.'

'I have to believe that what goes around comes around—that karma will take care of them.' She moved a little closer to him. 'But now I think we should be enjoying Venice by moonlight.'

As they walked the magic of Venice seemed to swirl around them—the majesty of the darkened streets swathed in moonlight, the occasional sound of oars on the canal breaking the stillness alongside the laughter of a late-night reveller. And subtly the atmosphere changed. Daniel's anger faded away and the balm of the evening breeze, the rose scent she emanated, seemed to cast a spell he knew he should try and dispel.

But he couldn't. As they approached St Mark's Square—now nigh on deserted, vast and truly breathtaking in its illuminated splendour—it wasn't possible not to turn and pull her into his arms.

And as if Kaitlin felt exactly the same way—as if she too had been imbued by the same magical allure—she stood on tiptoe, her green eyes wide with wonder as she touched her lips to his.

That was all he had meant it to be—a brush of the lips—but her closeness, the warmth of her body, the taste of her lips, spun him into a vortex of desire and he deepened the kiss.

Kaitlin gave a small moan as her lips parted and he was lost. He tightened his arms around her, gathered her body flush against his. Need jolted his body as she twined her arms around his neck and whispered his name. Time lost all meaning as passion captivated them in an embrace that rocked his body and consumed his mind.

Until finally some small fragment of sense pervaded the enchantment, reminded him of who she was and gently he pulled away.

They stared at each other for a long moment, their ragged breaths mingling in the air.

Eventually she looked around and let out a sigh. 'We must have been mad, but right now I don't care.'

Her lips turned up in a smile so beautiful his breath caught.

'So what now?'

'That's up to you.' However much he wanted her, the decision had to be hers.

Her step was sure as she moved towards him. 'We have one more night—I want to make the most of it. Of this.'

'Are you sure?'

'I'm sure. It's a risk worth taking. If the reporters find out, so be it. I want this night. With you. If that's what you want too.'

'It is exactly what I want.'

A small, breathless laugh dropped from her lips. 'Then let's go.'

The short walk back to their hotel was achieved at a half-run, his urge to hold her hand restrained only by the knowledge that there was a chance that reporters and guests for the ball the following night might already have arrived.

As they approached Kaitlin slowed, and he could almost see her morph into the persona of Lady Kaitlin Derwent. He wondered whether that had been another defence mechanism against the after-effects of the kidnap.

They entered the hotel, where Roberto awaited them, discussed the ball and their plans for the following day without even a hint of impatience, and then finally made their way across the lobby to an elevator that began an excruciatingly slow ascent.

Finally—*finally*—they reached the suite, entered and closed the door behind them.

'Now, where were we...?' he asked.

Stepping forward into his arms, she gave a slow smile. 'I think we left off about *here*. But we can make it even better if we move to the bedroom.'

'Your wish is my command.'

With that he scooped her into his arms and headed for the bed.

* * *

Kaitlin opened her eyes and for a second a tendril of panic coiled in her tummy. Then she remembered exactly where she was. The weight of Daniel's arm cocooned her and she shifted gently on the sumptuous smooth silk of the sheet. In repose he looked younger, one lock of dark hair curled on his forehead, the craggy strength of his features slightly softened by sleep.

She waited for regret to consume her but realised that in truth she repented nothing; she couldn't feel *any* remorse over the beauty of the past few hours. The passion and the laughter and the sheer pleasure—it had been a night that she would treasure the memories of for ever.

As for sharing her past with him... There was no regret over that either—no shadow of doubt that she could trust him to keep her confidence. She trusted him.

The realisation was shocking in its simplicity, terrifying in its complexity. Because she had broken a cardinal Lady Kaitlin rule.

Unfamiliar emotion crept up her veins, coursed through her body with unidentifiable sensations as she gazed at Daniel. Joy mingled with a yearning to lie down again in the safety of his arms, to wake him up and make love. To make him breakfast, to spend the day walking the streets of Venice hand in hand...

A new type of panic sparked and morphed into dread and disbelief.

What was she *doing*? Weaving a fantasy out of an illusion? The reality was that the night was over and so was her time with Daniel. It was time to assume Lady Kaitlin Derwent's mantle and get back to her routine—the life she had so carefully and painstakingly built up. She could not, *would* not let that crumble, and she would not, *could* not fall in love with Daniel Harrington.

Daniel opened his eyes and met her gaze sleepily. 'Morning.'

'Good morning.'

Surprise banished sleep and a small frown creased his forehead. 'What's wrong?'

'Nothing is wrong.'

Everything was wrong, and her brain threatened to short-circuit as emotions overloaded it. The primary emotion was horror at her body's treachery. She had never meant to fall in love—this was meant to have been an interlude, time outside time, the opportunity to experience physical attraction. Not this crazy freefall. She had to get out of here before it took hold. Before she did something super-crazy.

Before he figured it out.

From somewhere she summoned reserves of pride—the idea of discovery was a humiliation impossible to contemplate. So she had to dig deep and locate Lady Kaitlin—who disdained love as a messy, unpleasant, unnecessary component to life and relationships.

Play the part. Image is everything.

Holding the sheet to her, she leant over in a desperate bid to find at least her bra and knickers.

'I've woken up with my head buzzing with all the things we need to get done for the ball. Plus I need to get back to my room and make sure it looks like I slept there.'

Finally her fingers found her bra, and somehow she wriggled into it whilst shielding herself as best she could with the sheet.

'Kaitlin.'

Don't look at him.

If she could just make it to the sanctuary of her room she would be able to get herself together.

He swung himself out of bed and she resisted the temptation to close her eyes, to block out the masculinity, the clean muscular lines of his body. A body that had given her so much joy.

'Let me help.' He picked the rest of her clothes up from the floor and placed them on the bed.

Scooping up the clothes and tucking the sheet around her, Kaitlin sought refuge in the sumptuous bathroom. She avoided her reflection in the ornate gilded mirror as she scrambled into her dress. It would all be fine once she'd had a chance to shower and put on fresh clothes and focus.

On her return to the bedroom she found Daniel standing by the door, clad now in jeans, leaning back on the wall.

'What's the rush? This doesn't have to be awkward.'

'It's not awkward. It's realistic. We have to make sure no one suspects what happened last night.'

Not that she cared—all that mattered now was the imperative to curtail the rot of unwanted emotion. Filter her heart of even the tiniest propensity towards love. To do that she needed to be Lady Kaitlin Derwent with all the fibre of her body and soul.

Confusion flickered in his blue eyes and then it was gone. He pushed himself away from the wall and nodded. 'Of course. I suggest we go downstairs in half an hour— I'll see if Roberto can chaperone us over breakfast.'

'Perfect.'

The irony was not lost on her—*perfection* did not encompass the prickle of incipient tears or add weight to her heart. More stupid pointless feelings that she had to stop, crush, destroy. No matter what it cost her she would find her even keel once more—all she had to do was get through the next hours and it would be over. Daniel would be banished from her life and her mind.

There was no alternative.

* * *

Yet as she surveyed her reflection that evening, prior to
the meet-and-greet, tears still threatened to seep.

Why had she chosen lace for her ball gown? The floor-
length, deep V-necked dress was beautiful, it was true—
French lace with a floral motif over a nude silk lining. The
top half hugged her figure, a slim black band emphasised
her slender waist and the skirt flared to the floor. The back
view was equally demure, with a bit of sass provided by
the keyhole opening.

But the lace reminded her too much of the night before—
the short blue dress, sun-kissed by Venice, being slipped off
her shoulders in an urgent sweep of Daniel's strong hands,
the sensation against her skin as it fell to the floor...

Stop.

Different dress. Different night. Different woman.

Tonight Lady Kaitlin Derwent would prevail.

The night took on an *Alice in Wonderland* quality, and
she really wouldn't have been surprised to see a white
rabbit materialise amongst the bejewelled, designer-clad
guests. The ballroom seethed with glamour, amid the pop
of champagne corks and under the brilliant glitter of the
glorious neo-baroque chandeliers.

Through it all Kaitlin conversed and smiled, made witty
and scintillating conversation, and felt the balm of being
Lady Kaitlin heal her. From somewhere she found the dignity not to let her gaze follow Daniel's powerful form as
he too played his part—the host with the most.

Yet some inner radar gave her an unerring insight into
his exact location at any point...some hyper-awareness
of him.

'Good-looking devil, isn't he?'

Kaitlin found the correct smile for the three-times Os-
car-nominated actor, gorgeous in a dress that shimmered

silver. 'There are a number of men here who could be described as such.'

'Daniel Harrington... He doesn't usually grace events like this—in fact he's a bit of a dark horse. Is he yours, darling, or can I see if I can win his favour?'

The demon of jealousy tore its claws across her heart, but Lady Kaitlin didn't waver. A slight rise of the eyebrows, exactly the right touch of aristocratic hauteur offset by a smile that indicated understanding. 'He's as free as the proverbial bird, as far as I'm aware.'

Surely that must be the worst of this evening? But no... Next up was the auction where she stood next to Daniel, her cheeks aching under the weight of her smile, her vocal cords straining to deliver. But she did it. She managed to get over the impact of him, the smell of him, the memory of him.

Because as they bantered and delivered just the right sales pitch she remembered the teens she had met and bonded with, and all those other children out there who would benefit from this auction, and she threw herself into it heart and soul.

All she wanted at the end was to be allowed to leave and seek the sanctuary of her room, but that wasn't possible.

'And now let the dancing begin! And I'd like to invite our gracious hosts to open the proceedings with the waltz which I understand from Daniel you danced so beautifully at your brother's wedding, Lady Kaitlin.'

Please, no. This had to be some sort of joke. But, no— Roberto beamed at her and Kaitlin realised that the nightmare scenario had, against all the odds, got worse.

Daniel turned to her. 'I would, of course, be honoured.'

He held out his hand and his blue eyes glinted with challenge and more than a hint of anger. It enabled her to move towards him, hand outstretched.

'Likewise.'

As they walked to the dance floor she couldn't help but ask.

'Was this your idea?'

'No. Roberto asked me if I could waltz. If I'd known what he proposed I wouldn't have said yes. The only reason I can dance is that my PA dragged me along to classes when her husband somewhat conveniently broke his leg just before they were about to embark on a course. I won't disgrace you—don't worry.'

In truth Kaitlin was more worried about disgracing herself as the strains of Strauss's waltz began and they took to the floor. Poignancy pierced her as she placed her hand in his, the gap between their bodies so small and yet so full of significance. Because it was a gap that they would never close again.

For an instant she wasn't sure she could do it; she wanted to drop his hand and run but that wasn't possible. Dammit, she had too much pride. She could picture the headlines, taste the humiliation. Reporters would no doubt attribute it to her feelings for Prince Frederick, but Daniel wouldn't. He would guess the truth and she wouldn't let that happen. All this emotion had to be stopped, controlled, bottled up—starting now.

But as she stepped forward in one graceful, fluid movement she could swear she heard the crack of her heart.

Finally the night was over. The music, the chatter, the thud of the auctioneer's gavel and the sound of shoes on the dance floor were just faint memories that lingered like wraiths.

Daniel looked across at Kaitlin, standing in the shadows of the balcony that overlooked the ballroom, leaning against the ornate railings with the backdrop of silk hangings behind her.

'There's nothing left to do,' he said.

No one else remained. The last tasks had been completed, the last guest had departed, the staff had gone to recapture their strength for breakfast in a few scant hours. The silence was almost eerie, broken only by the thud of his heart as he surveyed her—so very beautiful in the lace concoction that showcased her poise and emphasised the vividness of her hair.

Confusion churned in his gut as he tried to work out what the hell had happened that morning to make Kaitlin so unapproachable, to make her withdraw and remain behind that mask of aristocracy.

'We need to talk.'

She turned in one graceful movement, her expression unreadable. 'No we don't. The ball is over and now we'll go our separate ways.'

Separate ways. The words filled him with a sudden bleakness.

'Then before we do that I'd like to talk.'

'There is nothing to talk about.'

'I disagree.'

She hesitated and then shrugged—a fatalistic lift of her shoulders. 'OK. Talk.'

'I want to know what happened this morning.'

A roll of her green eyes. 'Nothing happened except the fact that the night was over. It's time to face forward and that means saying goodbye. It's time for us both to get back to real life. *Normal* life.'

Something was wrong; his senses were on edge. And it wasn't only something wrong with Kaitlin—frustration built inside him at the idea of the vibrant woman he had come to know these past days morphing back into Lady Kaitlin Derwent.

'Is that really what you want—to go back to your "normal" life?'

'Yes, it is.'

'Then it shouldn't be.'

The frustration, the knowledge that he didn't want to say goodbye, the fact that he felt befuddled by emotions he didn't understand all made his voice sound harsh. But he didn't care.

'You are more than that, Kaitlin—you have the potential to soar. This past week you've been out of your comfort zone and in your element. You can be whatever you want to be.'

'I already am who I want to be.'

'Rubbish. I don't believe that you want to go back to that art gallery and wait until your parents identify your next eligible husband.'

Her wince was as palpable as her anger, and he almost regretted the starkness of his words. Almost, but not quite. Because the idea of Kaitlin entering that gilded cage made anger roil in his gut and caused his fists to clench.

An answering fury flashed back at him as her hands slammed on the curve of her hips. 'And what is so wrong with that, if it gives me what I want? A family. Children to love and cherish.'

Suddenly all his anger drained away, replaced by a sudden wish that *he* could give her what she wanted alongside the bleak knowledge that he couldn't. For one fleeting moment he tried to imagine it—but even the thought sent a cartwheel of panic through him. He was a man who had brought sorrow to the family he had—family was not for him. It was too messy, too complicated....too demanding.

But perhaps there was *something* he could do for Kaitlin. 'It doesn't always work out like that.'

'What do you mean?'

'My mother entered a gilded cage, made a deal—an alliance with my stepfather. After my father died she had no one to turn to and a baby on the way. She kept working as a waitress until the last possible moment but it wasn't easy. And it didn't become easier after I was born. She met my stepfather—he was older than her, he was rich and he was powerful and he wanted her. So she made a deal with him and married him. She did it for me—so that I could have everything in life.'

Guilt twisted its ever-present dagger once more—a reminder that love led to pain.

Kaitlin stepped towards him, the light of the ornate chandelier glinted off her Titian hair, bathed her skin in a golden glow, as she placed a hand on his arm. 'Maybe she did it for herself as well. I can't imagine how desperate and lonely she must have felt.'

'She didn't do it for herself. My stepfather is in the mob.'

Kaitlin's mouth formed a circle of surprise. 'The *mafia*?'

'Yes.' The fact brought an extra burn of shame. 'A bona fide criminal and my mother knew it. He wanted more children and she wanted a big family and he promised that he would give me the benefits of wealth—a luxurious lifestyle and an excellent education with all the extras.'

Impossible to blame his mother for her acceptance when it had been done for love of *him*.

'But every penny of his money came from the proceeds of crime. My mother isn't a bad person—she did it for me because she could see the way her life was headed and she couldn't see a better way out.'

'But…what happened? You aren't still connected to the mob, are you?'

'No. I walked away when I was eighteen—when I realised the deal was that I would go to law school and then work for the family, to protect the criminals. Until then I had turned a blind eye, but I couldn't play an active part.'

His skin prickled in recognition of the hypocrisy of his own culpability. He'd reaped the benefits of his stepfather's crimes and then refused to help him in return.

'I told my stepfather I would pay him back but that I wanted to go legit—make my own way. He went ballistic.'

It was then that he'd seen the man his stepfather could be—the side of him he kept away from his family, the part of him that had allowed him to rise in the ranks of the mafia. Even now he could feel the ripple of fear and shock as he'd faced the man he had believed cared for him.

'I'm not sure what would have happened if my stepbrother hadn't stepped in.'

'What did you do?'

'They told me I had a choice. I either had to comply or they would turn their backs on me. By which they meant I would no longer be part of the family—I would be as good as dead to them. I left.'

'But your mother...'

'I haven't seen my mother or my half-siblings since. I send a birthday card every year, and this year I asked her to come to Barcelona. It's ten years ago, and now I have the means to support her and my siblings, to match my stepfather's wealth. But she didn't come. Instead one of the family goons came—with a message. No one wants to meet a ghost. I am still dead to them and that is the way it will remain.' He shrugged. 'They're right. I made my choice to walk away. I was a fool to expect her to come running when I asked her after what I did.'

'No. You weren't a fool. I cannot imagine the pain it caused you to walk away. And you were right to try for a reunion—everything you told me about your mother makes me *know* that she must still love you. Life isn't black and white—it is not as simple as you walking away so she can never forgive you. But maybe first you need to forgive *yourself*.'

The near anguish in her voice as she tightened her clasp on his arm, moved closer, recalled him to the here and now. He saw the compassion in her eyes and for a heartbeat he wanted to step forward and hold her, let her hold him, accept her warmth and offer her...

Offer her what?

Ironically enough, he had nothing to offer her—just as he had nothing to offer his mother. What Kaitlin deserved was love—the type of love that had existed between his parents. All he could give her was the benefit of experience and hope that he could prevent her from making the same errors his mother had made.

Stepping back, he pulled away from her clasp, forced his expression into neutral. 'I didn't tell you any of this for sympathy or analysis.'

Hurt flickered across her eyes but he forced his arms to remain by his side.

'I told you because I want you to understand that the type of alliance you are thinking about can backfire. My mother gained security and a family, but at a price—she's had a loveless marriage, endured humiliation as part of the fabric of her very being and lived off the proceeds of crime. She did it for me, and I repaid her by walking away. It is that black and white. So sometimes choices, however good they sound on paper, turn out to have far-reaching consequences. You deserve better than an alliance, Kaitlin—you deserve love. You deserve what my parents had.'

Her fingers twined in the dramatic sweep of her gown and her mouth opened in preparation for speech. Then came that small characteristic shake of the head and she pressed her lips together in a gesture he had come to know and love—

His feet froze to the plush carpet and his limbs grew heavy with shock. *Love?* The word wasn't in his lexicon and he didn't want it to be. *Did* he? His hand rose almost of its own volition and he forced it down. Words hovered on his tongue in a tangle and he swallowed them. He didn't have time for love—didn't understand the concept or what went with it. Couldn't offer something he didn't have the ability to give.

She raised her eyes to his, brilliant with a glitter he didn't understand. 'What about you, Daniel? Don't *you* deserve love as well?'

'No.' The syllable reverberated in the confines of the balcony with a harsh echo. 'I don't want love—neither to give or receive it.'

'You see, neither do I. But I *do* want children. So, I truly appreciate everything you have said, and I won't enter into any alliance unless I have a watertight exit route that enables me to take my children with me.'

He felt frustration mixed with the bitter tang of failure as she backed away.

'I also appreciate the past days and I truly wish you a happy life—I hope you get to see your mother and your siblings again. Goodbye.'

Words tumbled about in his brain, emotions churned in his gut and he knew they needed to be dispelled, eradicated, because they could do neither Kaitlin nor himself any good. So he would exit from her life, go back to his own—to a life ruled by his sheer will to succeed, make his company even bigger and better, grow his own personal fortune, buy a car, a yacht—whatever it took to prove he'd made it.

'Goodbye, Kaitlin. I wish you happiness.'

For a heartbeat she stood stock-still and he etched her image into his brain, and then she turned and left the balcony, her back ramrod-straight, the click of her heels echoing and fading with finality.

CHAPTER FOURTEEN

KAITLIN TOLD HERSELF to be strong. She recalled the words of
the counsellor she'd been seeing for the past three months—
a woman who had helped her in ways she couldn't possibly
have helped herself.

'Sometimes the safe option isn't the right one.'

Pushing her shoulders back, she entered the lounge
where her parents sat. For an instant guilt touched her—
the Duke and Duchess were getting older, and for all their
faults their love and pride in the Derwent name and heritage was real.

'Kaitlin.' Her mother didn't bother with preliminaries.
'We have news for you. We believe there is a possibility
that Prince Frederick may consider a renewal of his offer
to you.'

The news was not a shock—in the past three months
Prince Frederick hadn't been seen with any other eligible
women, but then again neither had he contacted Kaitlin.

'So,' continued the Duchess. 'We will arrange a dinner, ask the Prince and his two brothers—and others, of
course.'

'I'd be happy to attend a dinner but...' Kaitlin hauled
in breath. 'But I am not interested in a renewal of Prince
Frederick's offer.'

'Excuse me?'

For the first time in Kaitlin's memory the Duchess

looked shocked, her mouth agape, her usual calm and serene beauty marred by the twist of her lips.

'I don't want to marry Prince Frederick or any other prince.' More to the point, she *couldn't*. Because it wouldn't be fair to anyone—least of all herself—not when she loved Daniel.

It was a love that had endured her most persistent attempts to remodel it, purge it, suppress it. Instead his image permeated her being, her dreams. The idea of an alliance with anyone else curdled her soul.

'You will do as we say, Kaitlin.'

'No, Mother. I won't. I am sorry to let you down but I cannot marry the Prince—though I am happy to see him and explain the situation to him.'

The Duchess pursed her lips, clearly for once without words.

'Now…' Kaitlin glanced at her watch. 'I need to go. I'm meeting Cora.'

It was time to share some things with her sister, lay some ghosts to rest before she embarked on the next phase of her plan.

Daniel stared down at the two items on his desk—each one a sucker-punch to the gut.

Item one—a newspaper article that featured a picture of Lady Kaitlin Derwent and Prince Frederick in close conversation under the caption: *'On Again?'*

> *The Duke and Duchess of Derwent entertained in lavish style and their guests included the Lycander brothers—including, of course, Lycander's ruler, Prince Frederick, who was seen in deep conversation with Lady Kaitlin, prompting speculation that the couple might seek to rekindle their romance.*

Since the split Prince Frederick has kept a low profile, and not so much as one woman has been seen on the former playboy's arm.

Daniel stared down at the photo, scrutinised Kaitlin's expression for the umpteenth time and still derived nothing from it.

So on to item two—a note on delicate blue paper that he could swear bore a touch of her rose scent. Fanciful idiocy of a type that occurred with depressing regularity—wherever he went there seemed to be echoes of his time with Kaitlin.

He read the note. Again.

Dear Daniel

Forgive the short notice, but I wonder if you could meet me in Barcelona this Saturday?

Given the lack of notice, if you can't make it I will, of course, understand. I will be at the hotel where we met at six p.m.

Best wishes

Kaitlin

Best wishes—what the hell did *that* mean? *Why* did she want to meet? To tell him of her new alliance with the Prince? Why Barcelona?

The only way to find out was to go.

Lady Kaitlin Derwent, poster girl for the aristocracy, daughter of the Duke and Duchess of Fairfax, stared at her reflection and wondered if…no, *knew* that she had run mad. There could be no other explanation for the fact that she was standing here, in this glitzy Barcelona hotel room, about to act in a way so wildly out of character that she could barely believe her presence here.

Yet it felt so *right*—more than that, it felt in character, like the real Kaitlin. But that didn't prevent the rush of nerves, the pounding of her heart as she looked at the wall-mounted clock and saw that it was six o'clock. One last glance at the simple jeans and T-shirt ensemble she'd picked, after choosing and discarding countless other outfits, and then she turned, exited the room and headed down the stairs.

Entered the lobby and stopped.

There he was, and it took all her will-power not to run across the marble floor and launch herself into his arms. That wasn't how this was going to play out—Daniel wasn't that sort of a man.

'Daniel.'

'Kaitlin.'

For a timeless moment they stood and stared at each other, and a sense of imminent sadness touched her. Daniel looked wary, aloof, and not at all like a man who was happy to see her.

For a second she was tempted to abandon the plan, recalling all the reasons why it truly sucked, but then she gritted her teeth. If she didn't do this she would regret it for the rest of her life. Or so Cora had assured her, anyway.

'Shall we?' he asked as he gestured to the bar.

'Yes. Actually, no. Let's walk. So, how have you been?'

The banality of her question was almost unbearable, but she wanted some time to absorb his presence, to look at him, to revel in his nearness even if her feelings clearly weren't reciprocated.

'Fine. You? You look well.'

'I *am* well. That was part of what I wanted to tell you. I took your advice. I went and found myself a therapist—one recommended by the Cavershams, in fact. She has been fantastic—and apparently I'm not a lost cause.'

It had been balm for her soul to realise exactly how far she had come by herself, and to see how much further she could now go.

'I'm pleased, Kaitlin. That took courage. But I never doubted you had that.'

'Thank you.'

'You said that's partly why you wanted to meet me. What was the other reason?'

Hurt touched her—clearly Daniel wanted to cut to the chase and close this down as soon as possible. Yet there was a tension in him, as if he were reining himself in, exerting every ounce of his iron will. There was a rigidity to his shoulders, a tension to his jaw that she couldn't read. Doubts jostled and hustled her brain.

'Could we stop somewhere?' Glancing round, she realised they had wandered to the Magic Fountain of Montjuïc—one of Barcelona's top attractions. 'We could watch the show whilst we talk.'

Perhaps the beauty of the spectacle would give her courage or bring her luck.

Daniel nodded and led the way to the steps opposite the fountain, where they seated themselves in the anonymity of the throng of tourists.

'Go ahead.'

For a moment she inhaled the spicy scents of the food being sold by the numerous vendors who hawked their wares. She watched the acrobatics of the street entertainers, sought and found the courage of her conviction that she needed to be honest with this man.

'I wanted to tell you that Frederick and I—'

'Don't do it.'

The urgency in his voice effectively rendered her speechless for a moment, until understanding dawned.

'I know you don't think I should make an alliance, enter a gilded cage, and I wish I had told you in Venice how much I appreciated you confiding your mother's situation to me.'

He made a dismissive noise, brushed his hand over his head and clenched his fists as he leant forward. 'That's not what I meant. I meant don't marry Frederick because I love you.'

The words stunned her, and for a long moment she was sure her ears must have deceived her. 'I... I... Excuse me?'

'I love you, Kaitlin—I know you don't want love, but there you have it. I *love* you. The past three months have been hell. I've missed you and nothing cures it—I've dreamt of you, thought about you. About the way you press your lips together, the way your face lights up when you smile, the glorious intensity of your eyes, the way you walk, your strength, your stubbornness, your...your *everything*. I love you.'

'But...*how*?'

'I don't know.'

His expression was so flummoxed that it startled a small laugh from her lips.

'I thought I was incapable of love, but then you came along and you changed everything. You slipped under my guard and under my skin right from that first night in Barcelona. I fought it all the way, but now I don't want to fight it any more. Loving you is a joy.'

'But what changed your mind? Why do you want to stop fighting it?'

The first scratching of joy was beginning to unfurl inside her, but caution prompted the fear that this was an illusion—that Daniel had mistaken love for some other emotion.

'Because I realised you were right. Life isn't black and white and love isn't a tangible thing that I can conquer or deal with the way I can deal with a court case. Which is why I went to see my mother.'

'Oh, Daniel. Tell me.'

As he spoke the scene played out before Kaitlin's eyes...

Daniel parked the hire car and climbed out, wondering why he hadn't done this before. Did he truly believe his family would shoot him on sight?

Seeing the house he'd grown up in brought back a surge of memories that replayed in his mind like a cinematic reel.

Taken alone, they were happy memories, yet all tainted now with the knowledge of hindsight.

Kaitlin's words echoed in his brain. 'Life isn't black and white.'

Yet for so long to him it had been... But now here he was—he had no idea if he would be allowed entry, but at least he would have tried.

More than aware that there would be people watching his every move, he moved away from the car and walked to the door.

Walk as though you have the right to be here.

He could only hope his stepbrother could see him now. Knocking on the door with the shiny brass knocker, he could feel the accelerated thud of his heart as he heard the approach of footsteps.

The door swung open and shock glanced through him. Shock and relief and near disbelief.

'Danny...' His mother's soft voice, her lavender scent, her beauty that had worn the scourges of time. 'Come in.'

'I wasn't sure if you would see me.'

'You asked for an hour of my time, a chance to say the

goodbye we never had time to say before. What mother could refuse that? Let me look at you, Danny. You have grown into a fine man.'

'My stepfather doesn't think so.' The words of bitterness were out before he could stop them.

'Antonio knows you are here. He understands that I need to see you.'

'But just this once?'

'That is my will, Danny.'

'Why?'

'Because I look at you and see all you have achieved. We are your skeletons in the closet—the people who can bring you down. How would it look if your colleagues, your clients, discovered you were once part of the Russo family?'

'That is my look-out, Mamma. If the choice now is between my family and my career I choose my family. I don't want to walk away again.'

'You don't understand.'

'Then explain to me.'

'When I married Antonio I made a deal, knowing what I knew about him. I will not renege on the deal I made when he has kept his part. Your stepfather is not a bad man, though he has done bad things. But things have changed since you left. Your brother, your sister—they will not enter the family business. This he agreed. Because he did not want to lose them like he lost you. Antonio was born into the business and he did not have the strength to break away like you did—part of his anger was because of that. I know my marriage was not based on love, but we have a bond, your stepfather and I, and I have loyalty. I am not choosing him over you, Danny. Try to understand that. And understand something else as well. I never once regretted the deal I made—I love you, and love is a joyful,

wonderful emotion. Even when your father died I could never regret loving him, knowing him. And without that love I wouldn't have you. Is there love in your life, Danny? All you have told me in your letters is about material success—incredible achievements—but I want there to be love in your life...'

Daniel looked across at Kaitlin. 'It was as if the scales had dropped from my eyes and instead of black and white I could see the world in shades of colour.'

He gestured to the fountains, where the show had begun. Thousands of jets of water shot skyward, illuminated in various transitory hues and shades of colour.

'And I realised that to have love in my life is a glorious thing. And I could see you—an image of you by my side—loving, talking, laughing.'

'Then why didn't you come and find me?'

'Because I didn't want to complicate your life. You were so sure of your path, so sure you didn't want love, and I was...scared. But then I saw the article about you and the Prince. If you hadn't asked me here I would have come to find you, because I couldn't let you go through with it without telling you that I love you. Give me a chance, Kaitlin, and I swear I'll win your love.'

Now laughter bubbled up inside her. 'Daniel, you....you *idiot*. Why do you think I asked you back to Barcelona? To tell you that I love you! That I am *not* going to marry Prince Frederick.'

'You *love* me?'

Surprise flitted across his face and then he smiled—a smile that curled her toes and frizzed her hair.

'I do. With all my heart. You showed me how to be myself, how to stop hiding behind a façade, a persona that wasn't real. I didn't want love because I didn't feel I could handle the rollercoaster of emotions. After the kidnap all

I wanted to do was shut my feelings down—all of them: the good, the bad and the ugly. It's how I coped.'

'Oh, sweetheart. That is understandable.'

'Maybe, but until I met you I'd succeeded only in achieving lockdown. Then Barcelona happened, and the feelings started, and I panicked, suppressed them. And then you arrived at Gabe's wedding... Since then, however hard I've tried—and, believe me, I've tried—I haven't been able to stop them. It's like the hydra—I chop one down and two more sprout in their place. That's why I had to get away after Venice—to try and build Lady Kaitlin back up.'

'What happened?'

He pulled her closer and she revelled in the ability to put her head on his shoulder, to touch him, to hold him.

'It didn't work. The feelings refused to go away, refused to be squashed or shut down. I missed you so much it hurt. But I didn't know what to do. I was scared. So I decided I needed to sort myself out. Work out who I was in case I didn't love you, in case I'd just been dazzled by physical attraction. So I found a therapist, talked to the Cavershams about setting up more workshops, changed my gallery hours to part-time. But through it all I couldn't stop thinking about you. The more I achieved, the more I missed you. I wanted to tell you everything. Then, when my parents suggested a reunion with Prince Fredrick...'

His grip around her tightened and she shifted closer to him in reassurance.

'I knew that no matter what I would *never* go back to being the Kaitlin who wanted an alliance, and I knew I had to have the courage to tell you how I feel. I needed to tell you. I wanted you to know that whether you want to receive love or not you have it. I spoke to Cora as well— told her about the kidnapping.'

Her voice broke slightly—the scene with Cora had been

heart-wrenchingly emotional but it had restored the twins'
bond that had been lost so long ago.

'She told me that love is so precious it should be given
where it can. So that was what I came here to give it to
you. My love.'

But she had never expected to have it reciprocated.

'I have no idea what comes next.' For a moment a small
doubt shadowed her joy. 'I mean, what will happen to you
if we start a relationship? The press will be interested and
your family connections might come out.'

'It doesn't matter.' His voice was strong. 'I have already set the truth in motion. I won't *not* see my mother
just because she thinks that is the way to protect me and
my business. I have done nothing wrong, So over the past
weeks I have held various meetings, explained the truth to
my employees, and soon I will issue a statement explaining the truth. Of course there will be repercussions, but I
believe I'll ride the storm.'

Her heart swelled at his sheer courage, integrity and
self-belief. 'I know you will, and I will be riding it right
beside you. But I promise I won't crowd you—I don't want
you to make any deals or any rash promises. I know how
you feel about children and marriage, and I'm good with
that. I just want us to move forward together.'

'That is what I want. But I would *like* to make some
promises. I promise to cherish and love you, body and soul.
And as for children—that has changed, Kaitlin. Until now
I was too scared of the responsibility that comes with par-
enting—I felt as though I had blighted my parents' life and
in some way I felt that disqualified me from parenthood.
Or maybe I was just too selfish—maybe I didn't want to
feel so much love for another human being. But now...the
idea of creating a child with *you*, of bringing a family up
together...it feels right.'

'But not yet.' Kaitlin smiled. 'You see, now I can see that that isn't the be all and end all. I was being selfish too—I wanted children because I *did* want to give and receive love, and I couldn't think of another way. Now I have you, and that is plenty. I want to set up a new business. I want to travel. I want to learn how to be *me*. And I want to do all that with you by my side.'

'Then let's face forward and go into our future together.'

As he kissed her the fountain danced in a beautiful tapestry of colour against the night sky. And Kaitlin couldn't think of a better future than one shared with this wonderful man.

EPILOGUE

Six months later

DANIEL TIGHTENED HIS arm round Kaitlin's shoulders and felt the now familiar but still so welcome heady thrill of being able to hold her—the wondrous sense of amazed joy that they had found each other.

'You sure about this?' he asked as they both looked out over Venice's Grand Canal and then down at the gondola, manned by a smiling gondolier in a blue-striped top.

'A hundred per cent.'

'Then let's do it.'

Her beautiful face was set with concentration, and a small frown creased her brow as she climbed into the craft. But she smiled as he joined her and took her hand in his.

The gondolier set off and then stood at the front, a discreet distance away, facing forward and focused on his task.

'I can't believe I can do this now!' Kaitlin said, her voice light with happiness.

'I can. You've worked hard and you deserve this.'

Her panic attacks hardly ever surfaced now, and his pride and admiration for Kaitlin had grown every day, every minute, as she'd blossomed.

'Thank you—and thank you for all your support and understanding and love.'

'You have those for ever, Kaitlin.'

Her smile lit up her face as she gestured forward to the Bridge of Sighs. 'Then it is appropriate that we are here.'

'It's perfect timing, indeed.'

His heart thudded in anticipation as he reached into his pocket and pulled out a jewellery box. Not a doubt crossed his mind. Instead hope and love filled his heart as he flicked the lid open to reveal the ring he had designed himself—a twist of emerald, ruby and diamond that glinted in the wintry November sun.

'Lady Kaitlin Derwent—love of my life, the woman I want to wake up next to for the rest of my life—will you marry me?'

Joy tinged her expression and her green eyes sparkled with the happiness he knew to be reflected in his own.

'Daniel Harrington—love of my life, my rock, my best friend—I would be more than honoured.'

He slipped the ring on to her finger, and as they swept under the Bridge of Sighs he kissed her and knew that their love would indeed be eternal.

* * * * *

PLAYING FOR KEEPS

CATHERINE MANN

To the charter members of "The Tree House Club", karaoke singers extraordinaire: Johnny, Tom, Elena, Lori, Mike, Vicky, George, Jerry, Linda, Shawn, Chris, and Daphne.

One

Midway through the junior-high choir's rehearsal of "It's a Small World," Celia Patel found out just how small the world could shrink.

She dodged left and right as half the singers—the female half—sprinted down the stands, squealing in fangirl glee. Their footsteps rattled metal risers and squeaked on the gymnasium floor, the stampeding herd moving as one. All their energy focused on racing to the back of the gymnasium where *he* stood.

Malcolm Douglas.

Seven-time Grammy award winner.

Platinum-selling soft-rock star.

And the man who'd broken Celia's heart when they were both sixteen years old.

Celia hefted aside her music stand before the last of the middle-school girls rushed by, oblivious to her attempts to stop them. Identical twins Valentina and Valeria nearly plowed her down in their dash to the back. Already, a couple dozen students circled him. Two bodyguards shuffled their feet uncertainly while more squeals and giggles ricocheted into the rafters.

Malcolm raised a stalling hand to the ominous bodyguards while keeping his eyes locked on Celia, smiling that million-watt grin that had graced CD covers and promo shots. Tall and honed, he still had a hometown-boy-handsome appeal that hadn't dimmed. He'd merely matured—now polished with confidence and about twenty more pounds of whipcord muscle.

Success and chart-topping wealth probably didn't hurt.

She wanted him gone. For her sanity's sake, she *needed* him gone. But now that he was here, she couldn't look away.

He wore his khakis and designer loafers—sockless—with the easy confidence of a man comfortable in his skin. Sleeves rolled up on his chambray shirt exposed strong, tanned forearms and musician's hands.

Best not to think about his talented, nimble hands.

His sandy-brown hair was as thick as she remembered. It was still a little long, skimming over his forehead in a way that once called to her fingers to stroke it back. And those blue eyes—heaven help her—she recalled well how indigo-dark they went just before he kissed her with the enthusiasm and ardor of a hormone-pumped teenager.

There was no denying he was all man now.

What in the hell was he doing here? Malcolm hadn't set foot in Azalea, Mississippi, since a judge crony of her father's had offered Malcolm the choice of juvie or military reform school nearly eighteen years ago. Since he'd left her behind—scared, *pregnant* and determined to salvage her life.

Even though he showed up regularly in the tabloids,

seeing him in person after all these years was different. Not that she'd gone searching for photos of him. But given his popularity, she couldn't help but be periodically blindsided by glimpses of him. Worst of all, though, was hearing the sound of his voice crooning over the radio as she changed the station.

Now, across the room, he pressed a paper against his knee to sign an autograph for Valentina—or Valeria. No one could tell them apart, not even their mother sometimes. Totally beside the point, because watching Malcolm with the young girl twisted Celia's heart with what could have been if somehow, against the odds and all better judgment, they'd been able to keep and raise their baby.

But they weren't sixteen anymore, and she'd put aside reckless dreams the day she'd handed her newborn daughter over to a couple who could give the precious child everything Celia and Malcolm couldn't.

She threw back her shoulders and started toward the cluster across the gym, determined to get through this surprise visit with her pride in place. At least the nine boys in the choir were sitting on the risers, making the most of the chance to play with video games banned during class. She let that slide for now and zeroed in on the mini-mob collected by a rolling cart full of basketballs just under a red exit sign.

"Class, we need to give Mr. Douglas some breathing room." She closed in on the circle of girls, resisting the urge to smooth her hands down her sunshine-yellow sundress. She gently tapped Sarah Lynn Thompson's wrist. "And no pulling hair to sell online, girls."

Sarah Lynn dropped her hand to her side, a guilty flush spreading up her face.

Malcolm passed back the last of the autographs and

tucked the pen in his shirt pocket. "I'm fine, Celia, but thanks for making sure I don't go prematurely bald."

"Celia? *Celia?*" asked Valeria. Or was it Valentina? "Miss Patel, you know him? Oh, my God! How? Why didn't you tell us?"

She didn't intend to delve too deeply into those murky waters. "We went to high school together." His name was etched on the sign that proclaimed "Welcome to Azalea, Home of Malcolm Douglas" as if the town hadn't once tried to send him to jail because of her. "Now, let's get back to the risers, and I'm sure Mr. Douglas will answer your questions in an orderly fashion since he disrupted our rehearsal."

She shot him a censorious look that merely prompted an unrepentant grin in return.

Sarah Lynn stayed glued to Celia's side. "Did you two date?"

The bell rang—thank God—signaling the end of class and no time for questions after all. "Students, line up for your last class."

And wouldn't you know, both the principal and the secretary stood in the doorway as starstruck as their students in spite of the fact that both ladies were happily married and grandmothers. How had he gotten into the gym/auditorium without causing a riot?

Celia led the students to the double door, her sandals slapping the wood floor. Step by step, she realized the pair of guards inside were only a part of Malcolm's security detail. Four more muscle-bound men stood outside in the hallway while a large limo lurked beyond the glassed front entrance. Additional cars with majorly tinted windows were parked in front of and behind the stretch limo.

Malcolm shook hands with the principal and secretary, making small talk as he introduced himself, ironic as all get-out since at least half of the free world knew his face. "I'll leave autographed photos for your students."

Sarah Lynn called over her shoulder, dragging her feet on the way down the hall, "For all of us?"

"Miss Patel will let me know how many."

The last of the students stepped into the corridor, the door swooshing closed after the administrators left. How had their departure managed to suck all the air out of the massive gym along with them? She stood an arm's reach away from Malcolm, his two bodyguards looming just behind him.

So much for privacy.

"I assume you're here to see me?" Although she couldn't for the life of her fathom why.

"Yes, I am, darlin'," he drawled, his smooth baritone voice stroking over her senses like fine wine. "Is there somewhere we can talk without being interrupted?"

"Your security detail makes that rather moot, don't you think?" She smiled at the bulky duo, who stared back at her with such expressionless faces they could have been auditioning for positions as guards at Buckingham Palace.

Malcolm nodded to the stony-faced pair and without a word they both silently stepped out into the hall. "They'll stay outside the door, but they're here for your protection as much as mine."

"*My* protection?" She inched a step away to put a little distance between herself and the tempting scent of his aftershave. "I seriously doubt your fans will start worshipping me just because I knew you aeons ago."

"That's not what I meant." He scratched the back of his neck as if choosing his words carefully. "I hear via the grapevine there have been some threats made against you. A little extra security's a good thing, right?"

Perhaps some security from the temptation of hav-

ing him around disrupting her well-ordered life, not to
mention her hormones. "Thanks, but I'm good. It's just
some crank calls and some strange notes. That kind of
thing happens all too often when my dad has a high-
profile case."

Although how in the world had Malcolm heard about
it? Something uneasy shifted inside her, a stirring of
panic she quickly squashed down. She refused to let Malcolm's appearance here yank the rug out from under her
blessedly routine existence. She refused to give him the
power to send her pulse racing.

Damn it all, she was a confident adult and this was
her turf. Still, her nerves were as tight as piano strings.
Fighting back the urge to snap at him for turning her
world upside down, she folded her arms and waited. She
wasn't an indulged, impulsive only child any longer. She
wasn't a terrified, pregnant teen.

She wasn't a catatonic, broken young woman caught
in the grips of a postpartum depression so deep her life
had been at risk.

Her road back to peace had been hard-won with the
help of the best shrinks money could buy. She refused
to let anything or anyone—especially not Malcolm
Douglas—threaten the future she'd built for herself.

Loving Celia Patel had changed his life forever. The
jury was still out as to whether that had been a good or
bad thing.

Regardless, their lives were linked. For nearly eighteen years, Malcolm had been able to keep his distance
from her. But he'd never mastered the art of looking away,
even when they were a couple of continents apart. Which
was what had brought him here now, knowing too much
about her life, too much about a threat to her safety that

sent old protective urges into high gear. He just had to figure out how to persuade her to let him back into her life so he could help her. And by helping her, he could atone for how he'd wrecked their lives. Maybe then he could finally let go of a glorified puppy love that after so many years he doubted was real.

Although given his physical reaction to her at the moment, the memories of their attraction were 100 percent real. Once again, desire for Celia Patel threatened to knock him flat on his ass.

Hell, no, he hadn't been able to forget her even while across the world singing to sold-out stadiums. He certainly couldn't tear his eyes off her now when she walked only a step ahead. Her wavy dark hair hung loose halfway down her back, swaying with each step. The bright yellow sundress hugged her curves the way his hands once had.

He followed her across the gymnasium floor, the same building where they'd gone to school together. He'd performed on that stage in the junior-high choir to be with her. Taunts hadn't bothered him—until one stupid little idiot had said something off-color about Celia. Malcolm had decked him and gotten suspended for three days. Small price to pay. There was nothing he wouldn't do then for Celia.

Apparently that hadn't changed. One of his contacts had gotten wind of a case on her judge father's docket, a high-profile drug case with a kingpin who'd drawn a target on Celia's back. Malcolm had notified local authorities, but they hadn't bothered looking into the evidence he'd gifted them with. Evidence that detailed a money trail connecting a hit man to the suspected drug dealer.

Local authorities didn't like outsiders and were stubborn about their ability to handle matters on their own. Someone had to do something, and apparently that someone was Malcolm. Nothing, absolutely nothing, could derail him from his plan to protect Celia. He had to do this in order to make up for all the ways he'd let her down eighteen years ago.

She opened the door by the stage steps, her spine stiff and straight as she entered her small office lined with shelves surrounding a tiny desk. Musical scores and boxes of instruments packed the room—everything from triangles to xylophones to bongo drums. The smell of paper, ink and leather mixed with the familiar praline scent of Celia.

She spun to face him, her hair fanning gently, a strand caressing over his wrist. "It's more of a closet really, where I store my cart, instruments and paperwork. I travel from classroom to classroom, or we meet in the gym."

He adjusted the fit of his watch to cover rubbing away the sensation of her hair skimming his skin. "Just like the old days. Not much has changed here."

The police department was every bit as slack as before, swayed by the person with the most influence.

"Some things are different, Malcolm. *I* am different," she said in a cool tone he didn't recognize at all.

And he was a man who specialized in the timbre of the voice.

"Aren't you going to chew me out for disrupting your class?"

"That would be rude of me." Her fingers toyed restlessly with the ukulele on her desk, notes lightly filling the air. "Meeting you was obviously the highlight of their young lives."

"But obviously not the highlight of yours." Leaning back, he tucked his hands in his pockets to keep from stroking the strings along with her. Memories taunted him of how they'd played the guitar and piano together, their shared love of music leading to a shared love of each other's bodies. Had his mind exaggerated those memories into something more than they really were? So much time had passed since he'd seen her that he couldn't be sure.

"Why are you here?" The sight of her slim fingers moving along the strings damn near mesmerized him. "You don't have a performance scheduled in the area."

"You follow my tour schedule?" His eyes snapped up to her face.

She snorted on a laugh. "The whole freakin' town follows your every breath. What you eat for breakfast. Who you dated. I would have to be blind and deaf not to hear what the town has to say about their wonder boy. But personally? I'm no longer a charter member of the Malcolm Douglas fan club."

"Now, there's the Celia I remember." He grinned.

She didn't. "You still haven't answered my question. Why are you here?"

"I'm here for you." His libido shouted a resounding echo. Damn it all, why did she have to be even more lushly sensual now than she had been before?

"For me? I think not," she said coolly, her fingers still lightly stroking the ukulele with instinctive sensuality, as if she savored the feel of every note as much as the sound. "I have plans for tonight. You should have called ahead."

"You're much more level now than you were before."

Her expression flickered with something he couldn't quite grasp before she continued, "I was a teenager then. I'm an adult now, with adult responsibilities. So if we could speed this up, please?"

"You may not have kept track of my schedule, but I kept up with yours." He knew every detail of the threatening phone calls, the flat tire and the other threats increasing in frequency by the day. He also knew she'd only told her father half of what happened. The thought of each threat chilled Malcolm's ardor and ramped up his protectiveness. "I know you finished your music degree with honors from the University of Southern Mississippi. You've been teaching here since graduation."

"I'm proud of my life, thank you very much, far more than can be summed up in a couple of sentences. Did you come to give me a belated graduation gift? Because if not, you can go finish signing autographs."

"Let's cut to the chase, then." He shoved away from the door and stood toe-to-toe with her, just to prove to himself he could be near her and not haul her against him. "I came here to protect you."

Her fingers popped a string on the ukulele, and even though she didn't back away, her gaze skittered to the side. "Um, would you care to clarify?"

"You know full well what I'm talking about. Those crank calls you mentioned earlier." Why was she hiding the incidents from her old man? Anger nipped at his gut—at her for being reckless and at himself for having taken that tempting step closer. As if the room wasn't small enough already. "Your father's current case. Drug lord, kingpin. Ring a bell?"

"My father's a judge. He prosecutes bad guys and often they get angry, make empty threats." Her eyes met his again, any signs of unease gone, replaced with a poised distance so alien to the wild child she'd once been. "I'm not sure why this is your concern."

And there she'd hit on the truth. She wasn't his to watch over, but that didn't stop the urge to protect her any more than her dress could stop him from remembering what she looked like with only her long hair draped over her bare shoulders. His frustration snapped as surely as that nylon string. "Damn it, Celia, you're smarter than this."

Her plump lips pressed into a tight line. "Time for you to leave."

He gritted back his temper, recognizing it for what it was—frustrated desire. His attraction to her was even more powerful than he'd expected. "I apologize for being less than diplomatic. I heard about the threats on your life, and call me a nostalgic idiot, but I'm worried about you."

"How did you get the details?" Her face creased with confusion—and suspicion. "My father and I have made sure to keep everything out of the press."

"Dear old Dad may be a powerful judge, but his power doesn't reach everywhere."

"That doesn't explain how you found out."

He couldn't explain the "how" of that. There were things about him she didn't know. He kept much better secrets than her father. "But I'm right."

"One of the cases my father's prosecuting has gotten... messy. The police are investigating."

"You're really going to put your faith in the three-man shop they call a police department?" He couldn't keep the cynicism from his voice. "Security around you is awe-inspiring. I should get my men to make notes."

"No need to be sarcastic. I'm taking precautions. This isn't the first time someone has threatened our family because of my father's job."

"But this is the most serious threat." If he told her about the paper trail, he would have to explain how he got it. But that was a last resort. If he couldn't convince her to accept his help any other way, he would tell her what he could about the work he did outside the music industry.

"You seem to know a lot about what's going on in my life."

She studied him with deep brown eyes that still had the power to draw him in and lure him past reason.

"I told you, Celia. I care enough to keep tabs. I care enough to want to make sure you're okay."

"Thank you. That's…nice." Her braced shoulders eased, some of her defensiveness draining away, as well. "I appreciate your concern, even if it's a little confusing. I will be careful. Now that you've fulfilled your sense of…obligation or whatever, I truly do need to pack up and go home."

"I'll walk you to your car." He raised a hand and plastered on his best smile. "Don't bother saying no. I can carry your books, like old times."

"Except for your whole secret-service-style protective detail."

"You'll be safe with me." More than she could know.

"That's what we thought eighteen years ago." She stopped and pressed a hand to her forehead. "I'm sorry. That wasn't fair of me."

His mind exploded with images of their teenage passion, out-of-control hormones that had led them to reckless sex. A lot of sex. He cleared his throat. Too bad his brain still hitched on the past.

"Apology not needed but accepted." He knew he'd let her down then, and damned if he would repeat the mistake. "Let me take you out to dinner, and we can talk over an idea I have for making sure you're safe until the trial's over."

"Thank you, but no." She closed the laptop on her desk and tucked it in a case. "I have end-of-the-year grades to finish."

"You have to eat."

"And I will. I have half of a leftover panino waiting in my refrigerator at home."

She might be a more poised woman now, but there was no missing the old Celia stubbornness. She'd dug in her heels, and it would take serious maneuvering to budge her.

"Fine, then you leave me no choice. I'll talk now. This threat against your life is real. Very real. In my line of work—" his real line of work, which only a handful of people knew about "—I have access to security sources you can't imagine. You need protection beyond anything the local police department can provide and more than your father can buy."

"You're being overly dramatic."

"Drug lords, Celia, have unlimited funds and no scruples." He'd taken the fall for those types as a teenager to keep his mother safe. And it was his own fault for putting himself in their path by working in that club as a last-ditch effort to make enough money to support Celia and their baby on the way. "They will hurt you, badly, even kill you, in hopes of swaying your father."

"Do you think I don't already know this?" Her jaw flexed as she clenched her teeth, the only slip in her carefully controlled composure. "I've done everything I can."

He saw his opening and took it. "Not everything."

"Fine, Mr. Know-It-All," she said with a sigh, sweeping back her silky hair from her face. "What else can I do?"

Clasping her arms, he stepped closer, willing himself not to cave to the temptation to gather her soft body close against him and kiss her until she was too dizzy to disagree. Although if he had to use passion to persuade her, then so be it. Because one way or another, he would convince her. "Let my bodyguards protect you. Come with me on my European tour."

Two

Go on a European tour? With Malcolm?

Celia grabbed the edge of her desk for balance and choked back her shock at his outlandish offer. He couldn't possibly be serious. Not after eighteen years apart, with only a few short letters and a couple of phone calls exchanged in the beginning. They'd broken up, drifted away from each other, eventually cut off contact completely after the baby's adoption was complete.

Back at the start of Malcolm's music career, she'd been in her early twenties, under the care of a good therapist and going to college. She'd dreamed of what it would be like if Malcolm showed up on her doorstep. What if he swept her off her feet and they picked up where they'd left off?

But those fantasies never came to fruition. They only held her back, and she'd learned to make her own realities—concrete and reasonable plans for the future.

Even if he *had* shown up before, she wasn't sure then or now if she would have gone with him. Her mental health had been a hard-won battle. It could have been risky, in her fragile state, to trade stability for the upheaval of a life on the road with a high-profile music star.

But it sure would have been nice to have the choice, for him to have cared enough to come back and offer. His ridiculous request now was too little, too late.

Celia hitched her floral computer bag over her shoulder and eyed her office door a few short steps away. "Joke's over, Malcolm. Of course I'm not going to Europe with you. Thanks for the laugh, though. I'm heading home now rather than stick around through my planning period since, for the first day in forever, I'm not slated for bus duty. You may have time to waste playing games, but I have grades to tabulate."

His hand fell to rest on her bare arm, stopping her. "I'm completely serious."

Hair prickled. Goose bumps rose. And damn it, desire stirred in her belly.

After all this time, her body still reacted to his touch, and she resented the hell out of that fact. "You're never serious. Just ask the tabloid reporters. They fill articles with tales of your charm on and off camera."

He angled closer, his grip firm, stoking long-buried embers. "When it comes to you, I've always been one hundred percent serious."

And wasn't that an about-face for them? She used to be the wild, adventurous one while Malcolm worked hard to secure his future. Or at least, she'd thought he'd been serious about the future—until he'd ended up in handcuffs, arrested.

Her breath hitched in her throat for three heavy heartbeats before she regained her equilibrium. "Then I'll be the rational one here. There's truly no way I'm leaving for Europe with you. Thank you again for the offer to protect me, but you're off the hook."

He tipped his head to the side, his face so close a puff of her breath would rustle the stubborn lock of hair that fell over his forehead. "You used to fantasize about making love in Paris in the shadow of the Eiffel Tower." His voice went husky and seductive, those million-dollar vocal cords stroking her as effectively as any glide of his fingers.

She moved his hand slowly—and deliberately—off her arm. "Now I'm *really* not going anywhere with you."

"Fine. I'll cancel my concert tour and become your shadow until we're sure you're safe." He grinned unrepentantly, stuffing his hands in his pockets. "But my fans will be so pissed. They can get rabid sometimes, dangerous even, and above all, my goal is to keep you safe."

Was he for real?

"This is too bizarre." She clenched her fists to resist the urge to pull her hair—or his. "How did you say you found out about the Martin case?"

He hesitated for the barest instant before answering, "I have contacts."

"Money can buy anything." She couldn't help but think of how he'd once disdained her father's portfolio and now he could buy her dad out more than twice over.

"Extra cash would have bought us both some help eighteen years ago."

And just that fast, their final fight came rolling back over her, how he'd insisted on playing the gig at that seedy music joint because it paid well. He'd been determined for them to get married and be a family. She'd been equally as certain they were both too young to make that happen.

He'd gotten arrested in a drug raid on the bar, and she'd been sent to a Swiss "boarding school" to have her baby.

Even now, she saw the regret in his eyes, mixed with censure. She couldn't go down this path with him, not again. Tears of rage and pain and loss welled inside her, and while she understood how unhealthy it was to bottle her emotions, she refused to crumble in front of him.

She needed to get out of there before she lost it altogether and succumbed to the temptation to throw herself into the comfort of his arms, to bury her face in his shirt.

To inhale the scent of him until it filled her senses.

"Things would have turned out better for you with more financial options," Celia said, reminded of how he'd lost out on the promise of a scholarship to Juilliard. "But no amount of money would have changed the choices I made. What we shared is in the past." Securing her computer tote bag on her shoulder, she pushed past him. "Thank you for worrying about me, but we're done here. Goodbye, Malcolm."

She rushed by, her foot knocking and jangling a box of tambourines on her way out into the gymnasium. Malcolm could stay or go, but he wasn't her concern anymore. The custodian would lock her office after he swept up. She had to get away from Malcolm before she made a fool of herself over him.

Again.

Her sandals slapped an even but fast pace through the exit and directly into the teachers' parking lot. Thank heavens she didn't have to march through the halls with the whole school watching and whispering. Tears burning her eyes, she registered the sound of his footsteps behind her, but she kept moving out into the muggy afternoon.

The parking lot was all but empty, another hour still left in the school day. In the distance, the playground hummed with the cheers of happy children. What a double-edged sword it was working here, a job she loved but with constant reminders of what she'd given up.

Her head fell back, and she blinked hard. The sunshine blinded her, making her eyes water all the more. Damn Malcolm Douglas for coming into her life again and damn her own foolish attraction to him that hadn't dimmed one bit. She swiped away the tears and charged ahead to her little green sedan. Heat steamed up from the asphalt. Magnolia-scented wind rustled the trees and rolled across the parking lot. A flyer flapped under the windshield wiper.

She stopped in her tracks, her hand flying to her throat. Was that *another* veiled warning from her father's latest enemy?

Every day for a week, she'd found a flyer under her wiper, all relating to death. A funeral parlor. Cemetery plots. Life insurance. The police had called it a coincidence.

She pinched the paper out from under the blade, shuffling her computer bag higher up onto her shoulder. The flyer advertised...

A coupon for flowers? A sigh of relief shuddered through her.

An absolutely benign piece of paper. She laughed, crumpling the ad in her hand. She was actually getting paranoid, which meant whoever was trying to scare her had won. She fished out her keys and thumbed the unlock button on the key fob. Then she reached to slide her computer bag onto the passenger seat...

And stopped short.

A black rose rested precisely in the cup holder. There was no mistaking the ominous message. Somehow that macabre rosebud had gotten into her car. Some*one* had been in her locked vehicle.

Bile rose in her throat. Her mind raced back to the florist ad under her windshield wiper. She pulled the paper out of her computer bag and flattened the coupon on the seat.

Panic snapped through her veins, her emotions already on edge from the unexpected encounter with Malcolm. She bolted out of her sedan, stumbling as she backed away. Her body slammed into someone. A hard male chest. She stifled a scream and spun fast to find Malcolm standing behind her.

He cupped the back of her head. "What's wrong?"

With his fingers in her hair and her nerves in shambles, she couldn't even pretend to be composed. "There's a black rose in my car—completely creepy. I don't know how it got there since I locked up this morning. I know I did, because I had to use my key fob to get in."

"We call the cops, now."

She shook her head, nudging his hand aside. "The police chief will write it up and say I'm paranoid about some disgruntled students."

The old chief would make veiled references to mental instability in her past, something her father had tried to keep under wraps. Few knew. Still, for them, a stigma lingered. Unfair—not to mention dangerous since she wasn't being taken seriously.

From the thunderclouds gathering in Malcolm's eyes, he was definitely taking her seriously. He clasped her shoulders in broad, warm hands, gently urging her to the side and into the long shadows of his bodyguards. Malcolm strode past her to the sedan, looking first at the rose, then kneeling to peer under the car.

For a bomb or something?

She swallowed hard, stepping back. "Malcolm, let's just call the police after all. Please, get away from my car."

Standing, he faced her again, casting a tall and broad-shouldered shadow over her in a phantom caress. "We're in agreement on that." He charged forward and clasped her arm, the calluses on his fingers rasping against her skin. "Let's go."

"Did you see something under there?"

"No, but I haven't looked under the hood. I'm getting you out of here while my men make sure it's safe before the rest of the school comes pouring out."

The rest of the school? The sound of the children playing ball in the distance struck fear in her gut. The faces of her teacher friends and students scrolled through her head. To put an entire school in harm's way? She couldn't fathom whoever was threatening her would risk drawing this much attention—would risk this many lives. But there was definitely something more sinister about this latest threat, and that rattled her.

Malcolm tugged her farther from the vehicle.

"Where are we going?" She looked back over her shoulder at the redbrick building with the flags flapping in the wind. "I need to warn everyone."

"My bodyguards are already taking care of that," he reassured her. "We're going to my limo. It has reinforced windows and an armor-plated body. We can talk there and figure out your next move."

Reinforced windows? Armor plating? Security in front and behind? He truly did have all the money he'd once dreamed of, access to resources beyond her own local law enforcement. Enough resources to protect her from all threats, real or imagined.

She shivered in apprehension and didn't bother denying herself the comforting protection of Malcolm's presence all the way to his stretch Cadillac.

Malcolm stopped seeing red once he had Celia tucked into the safety of his armored limousine and the chauffer was headed for her home.

Two of his bodyguards had stayed with her vehicle to wait for the police—and report the details back to him without the filter of local authorities. He didn't think there was anything else wrong with her vehicle, but better to be certain and put all of his financial resources to work. He'd done all he could for now to make sure Celia and the school weren't in danger.

He scrolled through messages on his cell phone for updates from his security detail, all too aware of the warm presence of Celia in the seat beside him. Once he had her safely settled, he would work with his contacts to find substantial proof to nail that drug-dealing bastard Martin for these threats. Malcolm had taken the fall for a drug-dealing scumbag in return for them leaving his mother alone. He hadn't known who to turn to then.

He wasn't a flat-broke teenager anymore. He had the resources and power to be there for Celia now in a way he hadn't before. Maybe then he could finally forgive himself for letting her down.

As they drove down the azalea-lined Main Street, he felt the weight of her glare.

Malcolm tucked away his phone and gave her his undivided attention. "What's wrong?"

"Something that just occurred to me. Did you put that flower in my car to scare me so I would come with you?" She stared at him suspiciously.

"You can't possibly believe that."

"I don't know what I believe right now. I haven't seen

you in nearly two decades. And the day you show up, offering to protect me, *this* happens. The thought that they were here, at the school, near my students…" Gasping for air, she grabbed her knees and leaned forward. "I think I'm going to be sick."

He palmed between her shoulder blades, holding himself back from the urge to gather her close, just to touch her again. "You know me. You know how much I wanted to take care of you before. You of all people know how much it frustrated me that my dad wasn't there to take care of my mom. Now, ask me again if I put the rose in your car?"

Sweeping her hair aside with her hands, she eyed him, her breath still shallow. "Okay, I believe you, and I'm sorry. Although a part of me wishes you had done it because then I wouldn't have to be this worried."

"It's going to be all right. Anyone coming after you will have to get through me," he said, tamping down the frustration of his teenage years when there hadn't been a damn thing he could do for Celia or his mom. Times were different now. His bank balance was definitely different. "The police are going to look over your car and secure the parking lot if there's a problem."

"Ten minutes ago you said the police can't protect me."

Dark brown locks slithered over his arm, every bit as soft as he remembered. He eased his hand away while he still could. He might not believe in the power of love anymore, but he sure as hell respected the power of lust. His body still reacted to her, but this wasn't just any woman who'd caught his eye. This was Celia. The power of the attraction—as strong as ever—had caught him unawares. But he'd come here to make up for the past. What they'd shared was over. "We still need to let the police know. Where is your father? At the courthouse?"

"At his annual doctor's checkup. His heart has been giving him trouble. He's been talking about retiring after the Martin case." She sagged back into the leather seat. "I can't believe this is happening."

He opened the mini-fridge and pulled out a bottled water. "No one will get to you now." He passed her the cooled Evian. "This vehicle is steel-reinforced, with bulletproof glass."

"Paparazzi can be persistent." She took the bottle from him, taking special care to avoid brushing his fingers. "Is it worth it living in a bubble?"

"I'm doing exactly what I want with my life." He had a freedom now that went far beyond the musician lifestyle, a side to his world with power that only a handful of people knew about.

"Then I'm happy for you." She sipped the water, all signs of her fear walled away.

But he knew what he'd seen, even if she was far better at hiding her emotions now than she'd been as a teenager. "Your school year finishes tomorrow. You'll be free for the summer. Come with me to Europe. Do it for your dad or your students, but don't let pride keep you from accepting my proposal."

She rolled the bottle between her hands, watching him from under the dark sweep of her eyelashes. "Wouldn't it be selfish of me to take you up on this offer? What if I put you in danger?"

Ah. He resisted the urge to smile. She hadn't said no. Something was shifting in her; he could sense it. She was actually considering his offer.

"The Celia I knew before wouldn't have worried about that. You would have just blasted ahead while we tackled the problem together."

A bump in the road jostled her against him. His arm

clamped around her instinctively, and just as fast his senses went on overload. The praline scent of her. The feel of her soft breasts pressed against his side, her palm flattened on his chest. And God, what he wouldn't give for a taste of her as she stared up at him. Her wide brown eyes filled with the same electric awareness that snapped through his veins.

Biting her lip, she eased away, sliding to the far side of the seat. Away from him.

"We're all grown up, and a more measured approach is called for," she said primly, setting the water bottle into a holder. "I can't simply go to Europe with you. That's just…unthinkable. As for my students, you already noted the school year's over, and if the threat truly is stemming from my father's case, it should be resolved by the time summer's over. See? All logical. Thank you for the offer, though."

"Stop thanking me," he snapped, knowing too well the ways he'd come up short in taking care of her and their child. This was his chance to make up for that, damn it, and he couldn't let it pass him by.

The limo cruised down the familiar roads of Azalea with blessedly smaller potholes. Not much had changed; only a few of the mom-and-pop diners had folded into chain restaurants near a small mall.

Otherwise, this could have been a date of theirs years ago, driving around town in search of a spot to park and make out. They'd both lost their virginity in the back of the BMW she'd gotten for her sixteenth birthday. The memories… Damn… Too much to think about now while trying to keep his head clear.

When he'd come up with the plan to help her, he hadn't expected to still want her, to be so pulled in by her. He'd dated over the years and could have any woman he wanted. And still, here he was, aching to take *this* woman. Had he gotten himself in too deep with his offer of protection? The prospect of touring Europe together, staying alone in hotels, suddenly didn't sound like such a smart idea.

"Malcolm?" Her voice drew him back to the present. "Why did you look me up now? I truly don't believe you've watched my every move for nearly eighteen years."

Fair enough. He had kept track of her over the years. But this time of year, thoughts of their shared past weighed heavier on his conscience. "You've been on my mind this week. It's the time of year."

Celia's eyes shut briefly before she acknowledged, "Her birthday."

His throat closed, so he simply nodded.

Her face flooded with pain, the first deep and true emotion she'd shown since he arrived. "I am sorry."

"I signed the papers, too." He'd given up all custodial rights to his child. He'd known he had no choice, nothing to offer and no hope of offering her anything in the foreseeable future. He'd been lucky not to be in jail, but the military reform school in North Carolina had been a lockdown existence.

"But you didn't want to sign the papers." She touched his arm lightly, the careful poise in her eyes falling away to reveal a deep vulnerability. "I understand that."

His willpower stretched to the limit as he fought back the urge to kiss away the pain in her eyes.

"It would have been selfish of me to hold out when I had no future and no way to provide for either of you." He shifted in his seat and let the question roll out that had plagued him all these years. "Do you think about her?"

"Every day."

"And the two of us?" he pushed, studying her hand

still resting on his wrist. Her touch seared his skin with memories and, yes, a still-present desire to see if the flame between them burned as hot. "Do you think back and regret?"

"I regret that you were hurt."

He covered her hand with his and held tight. "Come with me to Europe. To stay safe. To ease stress for your old man. To put the past to rest. It's time. Let me help you the way I couldn't back then."

She nibbled her bottom lip and he sensed that victory was so damn close....

The limo eased to a stop in front of her home. She blinked fast and pulled her hand away. She gathered her computer bag from the floor. "I need to go home, to think. This is all too much, too fast."

She hadn't said an outright no, and that would have to do for now. He would win in the end. He always did these days. His fame and position had benefits.

He ducked out of the car and around to her side to walk her to her door. He didn't expect to come inside and stay the night, but he needed to be sure she was safe. His hand went to the small of her back by instinct as he guided her toward the little carriage house behind a columned mansion.

She glanced over her shoulder. "You already know where I live?"

"It's not a secret." In fact her life was too accessible. He'd seen too much corruption in the world. This kind of openness made him itchy.

Although he had to confess to being surprised at her choice for a home. The larger, brick mansion wasn't her father's house, as he'd half expected when he'd first learned of where she lived. She'd carved out her own space even if she'd stayed in her hometown.

Even so, the little white carriage house was a security nightmare. Dimly lit stairs on the outside led to the main entrance over her garage. He followed her up the steps, unable to keep his eyes off the gentle sway of her hips or the way the sunlight glinted on her silky dark hair.

She stopped at the small balcony outside her door, turning to face him. "Thank you for seeing me home and calling the cops. I truly do appreciate your help."

How many times had he kissed her good-night on her doorstep until her father started flicking the porch light off and on? More than he could count. A possessive urge to gather her close and test the old attraction seared his veins, but he was a more patient man these days. He had his eye on the larger goal.

Getting her to leave the country with him.

He held out his hand for her keys. "Once I've checked over your place, I'll be on my way for the night."

Just not far away.

Malcolm wasn't the same idealistic teen he'd once been. He'd spent every day at that military reform school plotting how he would show up at Celia's father's house. How he would prove he hadn't done a damn thing wrong. He was an honorable man who'd had his family stolen from him. He'd held on to that goal all through college, as well, playing music gigs at night to earn enough money to cover what scholarships didn't.

But he never could have foreseen the path to honor that would play out for him. He'd sure as hell never planned on being a music star with his face plastered on posters. He'd stuck with it for the money. Then surprisingly, his old headmaster had shown up in his dressing room after a concert with a crazy offer.

Malcolm's globe-trotting lifestyle offered him the perfect cover to work as a freelance agent for Interpol.

In that moment, Malcolm gained a strong compass for his life and he'd never veered from the plan. Until today.

Even after eighteen years, he couldn't look away from Celia. "The keys, please?"

Hesitating for an instant, she dropped the keys into his hand. He turned the lock—a lock he could have picked thanks to some skills he'd acquired along the way—and pushed open the door to an airy and light space with sheer frills, an antique upright piano and a lemony, clean scent.

He stepped inside to make sure there weren't any more roses—or worse—waiting for her. She disarmed the alarm, then walked beside him down the narrow hall leading toward the living area, clicking her fingernails along a panpipe hung on the wall. His sixth sense hummed on high alert. Something wasn't right, but his instincts were dulled around Celia, and damn it, that wasn't acceptable. He knew better. He'd been trained for better.

Drawing in his focus, he realized… Holy hell…

He angled back to Celia. "Did you leave the living room light on?"

Flinching, she gasped. "No. I never do…"

He tucked her behind him only to realize…a man sat on the sofa.

Her father.

Malcolm resisted the urge to step back in surprise. Judge Patel had gotten old. Intellectually, Malcolm understood the years had to have left a mark, but seeing that in person was…unsettling. He'd resented this man, even hated him at some points, but bottom line, he understood they both had a common goal: keeping Celia safe.

Malcolm was just better suited for the job, and this time, he refused to let Judge George Patel stop him.

Three

Celia could swear she heard Fate chiming with laughter.

She looked from her father to Malcolm, waiting for the explosion. They'd never gotten along. Malcolm encouraged her to think for herself. Her parents had pampered her while also being overprotective. They'd seen her relationship with Malcolm as dangerous. They'd been right, in a way. She had been out of control when it came to him.

However, their refusal to let her see him had only made her try all the harder to be with him. Malcolm had chafed at their disapproval, determined to prove himself. The whole thing had been an emotional train wreck in the works.

Could they all be more mature now? God, she hoped so. The thought of an ugly confrontation made her ill, especially at the tail end of a day that had already knocked her off balance in more ways than one.

Malcolm nodded to her father. "Good evening, sir."

"Douglas." Her father stood, extending his hand. "Welcome back."

They shook hands, something she wouldn't have believed possible eighteen years ago. Even if they were eyeing each other warily, they were keeping things civil. The last time they'd all been together, her father had punched Malcolm in the jaw over the pregnancy news, while her mother had sobbed on the couch. Malcolm hadn't fought back, even though he was at least six inches taller than her father.

Nervous about pushing their luck, she turned to Malcolm and rested her fingers lightly on his arm. "I'm fine now. You can go, but thanks again, truly."

She shuddered to think what it would have been like to find that macabre rose on her own and have her concerns discounted by the police again. This was not the work of some student pissed off over a failing grade. Malcolm seemed to grasp that right away. She hadn't considered until just this moment how much his unconditional belief meant to her.

He dipped his head and said softly, "We'll talk tomorrow. But don't say no just because I'm the one offering." Grasping the doorknob, he nodded to her father again. "Good night, sir."

And that was it? He actually left? No confrontation? Celia stood there stunned at how easily he'd departed. She wanted a proper goodbye, and it scared her how much that mattered. Although his final words swirled in her mind. Was she being contrary—like the old Celia— turning down a wise opportunity because Malcolm had made the offer?

She shook off the thoughts. Likely Malcolm just realized she was safely home, his duty done. After resetting the alarm, she turned back to face her dad. The familiarity of her place wrapped around her, soothing her at the end of a tumultuous day.

This little carriage house wasn't as grand as the historic mansion where she'd grown up or the posh resorts Malcolm frequented—according to the tabloids. But she was proud of it. She took pride in how she'd decorated on her own budget. She'd scoured estate sales and flea markets until she pieced together a home that reflected her love of antiques and music.

Her home had become a symbol of the way she'd pieced herself back together, reshaping herself by blending the best of her past and her future. Shedding the dregs, taking responsibility for her own messes, which also gave her the freedom to celebrate her own successes.

And in finding that freedom, being around her father had actually become easier. She wasn't as defensive, and right now, she was only worried—about him.

"What are you doing here, Dad? I thought you were at your doctor's appointment."

"News travels fast." He nudged aside throw pillows and sank back on the couch, looking weary with bags under his eyes and furrows in his brow. "When I heard about Malcolm Douglas's impromptu visit to the school, I told the doc to speed things along."

His shock of gray hair still caught her by surprise sometimes. Much like when she'd been stunned to realize her indomitable father was actually only five-six. He'd always had a larger-than-life presence. Yet the day her mother had died, her father had grown frail in an instant, looking more and more like Grandpa Patel—without the Indian accent.

Intellectually, she'd always understood that her mom and dad were older than her friends' parents. She'd been a late-in-life baby, born after her sister died. How strange to have a sibling she'd never met.

And yes, more than once, Celia had wondered if she would have been conceived had her sister lived.

She'd never doubted her parents' love or felt she was a replacement for the child they'd lost to cancer. But that loss had made them overprotective, and they'd spoiled her shamelessly. So much so that Celia winced now to think of what a brat she'd been, how many people she'd hurt.

Including Malcolm.

She glanced at her slim silver watch. "He showed up at school less than an hour ago. You must have rushed right over."

"As I said, small town."

There weren't many secrets around Azalea, Mississippi, which made it all the more miraculous that she'd managed to have a baby and give her up for adoption without the entire town knowing all the details. Malcolm had been sent off to a military reform school in North Carolina, and she'd been sent to Switzerland on an "exchange" program, actually a chalet where she'd been homeschooled until she delivered.

She swallowed the lump in her throat and sat on the arm of the sofa. "What did the doctor say about your shortness of breath lately?"

"I'm here, aren't I? Doc Graham wouldn't have let me leave unless she thought I was okay, so all's fine." He nudged his round steel glasses in place, ink stains on his fingers from making notes. Her dad didn't trust computers and backed everything up the old-fashioned way—on paper. "I'm more worried about you and your concerns that someone might be targeting you."

Her concerns? Did he doubt her, too? "How bad is the Martin case?"

"You know I can't talk about that."

"But it's an important one."

"Every judge dreams of leaving the bench with a landmark case, especially just before he retires." He patted the top of her hand. "Now, quit trying to distract me. Why did Malcolm Douglas show up here?"

"He heard about the current case on your docket, and somehow word got out about my reporting the threats to the police, which I find strange since no one here takes them seriously." Would they finally listen to her after today's incident?

"And Malcolm Douglas—international music star— came running after not seeing you for eighteen years?" Concern moved through his chocolate-brown eyes.

"Seems crazy, I know." She toed a footstool made of an old leather drum. "Honestly, though, I think it had more to do with the timing."

"Timing of what?"

That he even had to ask hurt her heart. "Dad, it's her seventeenth birthday."

"You still think about her?"

"Of course I do."

"But you don't talk about her."

She'd done nothing *but* talk about her baby in therapy—cry and talk more, until finally she'd reached a point where she could move forward with her life. "What's the point? Listen, Dad, I'm fine. Really. I have end-of-the-year grades to tabulate and submit."

Her dad thumped his knees. "You should move home."

"This is my home now," she reminded him gently. "I consented to letting you pay for a better security system. It's the same one at your house, as you clearly know since you chose the pass code. Now, please, go home and rest."

She worried about him, about the pale tinge to his

dusky complexion, the tired stoop to his shoulders. His job would be easier if she wasn't around since he wouldn't have to stress about her. Not taking Malcolm up on his offer suddenly felt very selfish. "Dad, I'm thinking about taking a vacation, just getting away once school ends."

"If you come to the house, you'll be waited on hand and foot." He continued to offer, and she continued to say no, a pact she'd made with herself the day she'd graduated from college at twenty-four. It had taken her an extra two years, but she'd gotten there, by God.

"I have something to tell you, and I don't want you to misunderstand or be upset."

"Well, you'd better spit it out, because just saying that jacked my blood pressure a few points."

She drew in a deep breath of fortifying air before saying quickly, "Malcolm thinks I should go on tour with him."

His gray eyebrows shot upward, and he pulled off his glasses and cleaned them with a handkerchief. "Did he offer because of the reports made to the police?"

She weighed whether or not to tell him about the incident with the rose, but then given how fast he'd heard about Malcolm's arrival, he would hear about the little "gift" in her car soon enough. "There was another threat today."

He stopped cleaning his glasses abruptly, then slid them slowly on again. "What happened?"

"A cheesy black rose left in my car." As well as the florist coupon in some kind of mocking salute. She tried to downplay the whole thing for her father, but her voice shook and she probably wasn't fooling him in the least. Still, she plowed ahead, trying her best to put his mind at ease. "Next thing you know, they'll be leaving a dead horse somewhere like a parody of *The Godfather*."

"This isn't funny. You *have* to move back home."

Seeing the vein at his temple throb made her realize all the more how her being around right now made things more difficult for him. "Malcolm offered the protection of his own security people. I guess crazed stalker fans rank up there with hired hit men."

"That's not funny, either."

"I know." And it wasn't. "I'm concerned he has a point. I make you vulnerable, and I placed my students at risk by waiting this long. If I go on his European tour, it will solve a lot of problems."

She didn't want her father to worry, but she had to admit there was something more to this decision than just her father. Malcolm had presented more than an offer of protection. He'd presented the chance to put their past to rest. Because he was right. The fact that she'd turned him down so promptly hinted at unresolved issues.

But could they really spend the whole tour together? A tour that lasted four weeks? She knew because, damn it, she periodically did internet searches on his life, wondering if maybe he would play at a local arena. He never did.

"That's the only reason you've made this decision?"

She hadn't decided yet. Or had she? "Are you asking me if I still have feelings for him?"

"Do you?" he asked and strangely didn't sound upset.

God, as if she wasn't already confused enough.

"I haven't spoken to him in years." Malcolm hadn't spoken to her, either, not since after the baby was born, and yes, that stung. "Aren't you going to push me again to come to your house?"

"Actually, no. Go to Europe." He studied her with those wise judge eyes. "Close that chapter on your life so you can quit living in limbo. I would like to see you settled before I die."

"I am settled," she said and then as an afterthought rushed to add, "and happy."

Sighing, her father stood, kissed her on top of the head. "You'll make the right decision."

"Dad—"

"Good night, Celia." He patted her arm as he walked past, snagging his suit jacket from the iron coatrack. "Set the alarm after I leave."

She followed him, stunned, certain she couldn't have heard what she thought she'd heard. Had her father really encouraged her to just pick up and travel around Europe with the former love of her life? A man reputed to have broken hearts around the globe?

Except, strangely, going to Europe with Malcolm was beginning to make sense. Going with him would solve her problems here, keeping her life ordered and safe. It was also her last chance to be with Malcolm, and the wild child she'd once been shouted for her go for it.

The newer, more logical side of her even answered that leaving with him would be the lesser of two evils.

Celia locked the door behind her father and keyed in the security code.

A noise from the hall made her jolt.

Her stomach gripped tight with fear and she spun around fast, grabbing a guitar propped against a chair and lifting it like a baseball bat. She reached for the alarm just as a large shape stepped out of her bedroom.

A man.

Malcolm.

He grinned. "Your security system sucks."

Malcolm watched the anger flush Celia's cheeks as her hand fell away from the alarm's keypad.

She placed the guitar on an armchair. "You scared the hell out of me."

"Sorry about that." He stepped deeper into her living room, a space decorated with antique musical instruments his fingers itched to try out. Later. First, he had business with Celia. "I thought I made it clear I'm worried about you being here alone."

"So you broke into my home?"

"Just to prove how crummy your security system is." He'd bypassed the alarm, climbed the nearby oak and made it inside her window in less than ten minutes. "Think about it. If someone like me—a plain ol' musician—could break into your place, then what about someone motivated to find you?"

"Your point has been made." She pointed to the door. "Now leave, please."

"But then you're still here, alone in the crappily secured apartment. My code of honor has trouble with that." He wandered lazily through her living room, inspecting the canvas over the fireplace, a sketch of band instruments and, below it on the mantel, an antique piccolo on a stand. "Gauging by your conversation with your dear old dad, you don't want to go to his place."

"You eavesdropped on my discussion with my father?"

"I did." He lifted the piccolo and blew into it, testing out a quick scale—not a bad sound for an instrument that appeared to be close to two hundred years old.

"You're shameless." She snatched the instrument from him and placed it back on the wall.

"I'm unrepentant, yes, and also concerned." He moved aside a brass music stand full of hand-scored songs—apparently for students, given her notes at the top—and sat on the piano bench in front of the old upright. "Since we're being honest, I heard it all, and even your father gave his consent for you to come with me."

"I don't need my dad's permission."

"Damn straight."

Watching him warily, she sat in a rocker by the piano. "You're trying to manipulate me."

"I'm trying to make sure you're safe—and yes..." He took her hand lightly in his. A benign enough touch. Right?

Wrong. The silkiness of her skin reminded him of times when he'd explored every inch of her. "Maybe we'll settle some old baggage along the way."

"This is too much."

He agreed. "Then don't decide tonight."

Her thick dark hair trailed over one shoulder. "We'll talk in the morning?"

"Over breakfast." He squeezed her hand once before letting go and standing. "Where are the sheets for the sofa?"

She gaped at him, smoothing her hands over wrinkles in her skirt. "You're inviting yourself to spend the night?"

He hadn't planned on it, but somehow the words had come out of him anyway, likely fueled by that reckless second when he'd touched her.

"Do you expect me to sleep on your porch?" He'd actually intended to sleep in the limo.

This was the man he was, the man he'd always been. He remembered what it was like for his mom living on her own. Call him old-fashioned, but he believed women should be protected. No way in hell could he just walk away. Especially not with images of the skirt of her dress hugging her soft legs.

"I would offer to get us a couple of rooms at a hotel or B and B, but we would have to drive for hours. People might see us. My manager likes it when I show up in the press. Me, though? I'm not as into the attention."

"Being seen at a hotel with you would be complicated." Her fingers twisted in the fabric she'd just smoothed seconds earlier.

"Very." He knelt in front of her, careful not to touch her just yet, not when every instinct inside him shouted to kiss her, to sweep her up into his arms and carry her to the bedroom. To make love to her until they both were too sated to argue or think about the past. He wasn't sure yet where he planned to go with those impulses. "So let me stay for dinner, and I'll bunk on your sofa. We won't talk about Europe tonight unless you bring it up."

"What does your girlfriend think of your being here?"

Girlfriend? Right now he couldn't even envision anyone except Celia. "Those damn tabloids again. I don't have a 'girlfriend.' My manager planted that story to make it look like I'm settling down."

Relationships were too messy, and more of that protective honor kept him from indulging in the groupies that flocked backstage. He "dated" women whose publicists lined up promo gigs with his publicist. As for sex, there had been women who kept things uncomplicated, women who needed anonymity and no strings as much as he did. Women as jaded about the notion of love.

"Is that why you're really here?" Her fingers kept toying nervously with the hem of her dress, inching it higher, revealing a tantalizing extra inch of leg. "You're between women and the timing fits?"

Something in her voice triggered warning bells in his mind. "Why is it so difficult to think I'm worried about you?"

"I just like my space. I enjoy the peace of being alone."

"So there's no guy in your life?" Damn it, where had that question come from?

A jealous corner of his brain.

She hesitated a second too long.

"Who?" And why the hell wasn't the man here watching out for her?

"I've just gone out with the high-school principal a couple of times."

The reports he'd gathered on her hadn't included that. His people had let him down.

"Is it serious?" he asked, her answer too damn important.

"No."

"Is it going to be?" He held up a hand. "I'm asking as an old friend." *Liar.* His eyes went back to her legs and the curve of her knees.

"Then you can ask without that jealous tone in your voice."

She always had been able to read him.

"Of course..." He winked. "And?"

She shrugged, absently smoothing the dress back in place again. "I don't know."

Exhaling hard, he rocked back on his heels. "I worked my ass off for that answer and that's all I get?"

"Pretty much." Hands on the arms of her chair, she pushed to her feet. "Okay. You win."

Standing, he asked, "Win what?"

"You can stay tonight—on the sofa."

He resisted the urge to pump his fist in victory. "I'm glad we're in agreement."

"You won't be so glad when you hear what's on the menu. I only have half a panino, barely enough for me. I was planning to shop once school finished."

"Dinner's on its way." He'd remembered about that

panino and had given his chauffeur instructions before he'd climbed the tree. He found the notion of an intimate dinner with Celia—discovering all the new secrets about her—stirring. "My very discreet driver will be delivering it."

"You already assumed I would agree? You're more arrogant than I recall."

"Thank you."

"That wasn't a compliment."

"That's all right." He soaked in the sight of her brown eyes flickering with awareness, her chest lifting faster with each breath. His hands ached to touch her, to relearn the curves, to find out if she still had the same sensitive areas and discover if she had new ones, as well. "It's for the best we don't exchange too many pleasantries."

She chewed the rest of the gloss off her bottom lip. "And why ever not?"

"Because honest to God," he growled softly, his body firing with a need that hadn't diminished one bit in nearly eighteen years apart, "I want to kiss you so damn badly it's already all I can do to keep my hands off you."

Four

Each seductive word out of Malcolm's mouth sent a thrill rippling through Celia. And not just his voice, but the strong lines of his handsome face, the breadth and power of his mature body—all *man*.

Teenage lust had ripened into a deeper, headier awareness. She still found him infinitely attractive, and the fact that she'd already been with him *many* times in the past only made that need edgier.

Dangerous.

Especially when they were only steps away from her bedroom.

She tipped her chin and steeled her will against temptation. "You used that line on me eighteen years ago. I would think your game would have improved since then. Or does being some kind of music legend make you lazy in the romance department?"

His head fell back, laughter rolling and rolling until he

scrubbed his hand over his face, grinning. "As I recall, my 'game' was just fine with you back then."

"Suffice it to say," she retorted, meeting his gaze with level strength, "my standards and expectations have changed."

"You want me to work harder." His eyes narrowed with the challenge.

"That's not what I meant." Her heart stuttered over a couple of beats before she found her balance and bravado again.

"What did you mean, then?" His hand grazed the keys of the upright piano, touching without stirring a note.

She shivered as she remembered the way he'd played so carefully over her skin long ago. "I was sixteen." She tapped out a quick tune on the other end of the keyboard, her nerves all too ready for an outlet. "Tough sell? I think not."

"My poor ego." He skimmed a scale.

"Sorry to have wounded you." She mirrored his notes. How many times had they done this?

"No, I mean it. You're good," he said without a trace of sarcasm. "It's nice to have someone who's real around me, someone I can trust."

"Am I supposed to cry for the poor little rich rock star?"

"Not at all." He slid onto the piano bench, his scale taking shape into a tune, the music relaxing and drawing her in at the same time.

Unable to resist, she sat down next to him and continued to twine her notes with his as easily as taking in air. "You know, one of the things that attracted me to you before was how you never seemed impressed by my father's wealth or influence."

"I respect your father—even if he did get me sent away

from you. Hell, if I had a daughter and—" His melody tangled. "Ah, crap. Okay, let me roll back that statement and reframe it."

"I know what you meant." Her hands fell to her lap, the piano going silent. "No parent would be happy about their sixteen-year-old having sex, much less reckless sex."

His face went dark with guilt, his hand gravitating to her face until he cupped her cheek. "I should have protected you better."

"We *both* should have been more responsible." She put her hand over his without thinking, her body going on autopilot around him as it always had, whether with touches or with music.

In less than a day, they'd fallen right back into the synchronicity they'd shared before, and God, that scared her spitless. She'd dated other men—slept with other men—but being with them never had this sense of ease. Already, she felt herself swaying toward him as his body leaned into hers.

Magnetic.

His hand still held her face, the calluses on his fingers familiar, a reminder of the countless hours he devoted to playing the guitar. Music hummed through her now, the sound of the two of them occupying the same space.

Her lips parted in anticipation—

The doorbell rang.

She jolted back as it rang again. How had she missed someone coming up outside?

Malcolm stood, his hand sliding away, then coming back to stroke her jaw once again. "That's dinner." He frowned. "And my phone."

He pulled his cell from his pocket.

"Supper?" she parroted, surprised she could even speak at all. She vaguely recalled him mentioning sending his driver/bodyguard for food. He had a whole staff at his disposal day and night, another reminder of how different their worlds were these days.

On his way to check the door, Malcolm said over his shoulder, "My chauffeur will set everything up while I take this call. All I need is a blanket and pillow for the sofa."

Before she could answer, he'd opened the door, waving his driver inside and stepping outside with his phone. Clearly, he didn't want her to hear his conversation. Which made her wonder a little about what he had to say.

And wonder a lot about *who* he said it to.

How the hell had he almost kissed her?

Malcolm gripped the wooden rails of Celia's small balcony landing just outside her front door. With ragged breaths, he drew in muggy night air as he listened to his driver setting up dinner inside. Bodyguards were stationed in the yard below and outside the brick-wall fence.

Malcolm's cell phone continued to buzz, and he knew he had to answer. And he would return the call—as soon as his heart rate settled back to normal.

He'd come here to make amends with Celia. To put his feelings of guilt to rest by helping her now like he couldn't before.

Where did sex factor into that?

It didn't. It hadn't. Until he'd seen her again.

These days he had control over his libido, enjoying healthy, safe relationships. He'd sure as hell never forgotten to put on a condom ever again. But he knew protecting Celia was about more than safe sex. That wouldn't keep either of them safe from the heartache of resurrecting something that was long done.

Plucking his phone from his pocket, he thumbed Redial and waited for Colonel John Salvatore to answer. His old headmaster from boarding school.

Now his Interpol handler. The man had traded in a uniform for a closet full of gray suits worn with a red tie.

"Salvatore here," his longtime mentor answered in clipped tones, gravelly from years of barking military orders.

"Calling you back, sir. Any word on Celia Patel's vehicle?"

"I checked the local department's report and they lifted prints, but with so many students in the school, there are dozens of different impressions."

His frustration ratcheted up. "And the security cameras?"

"Nothing concrete, but we did pinpoint the time the flyer was placed on the vehicle. We just couldn't see who did it. Kids were on lunch break, and a large group passed in front of the camera. Once they cleared, the flyer was under the wiper."

Malcolm scanned the street beyond the brick security wall, monitoring the lazy traffic for warning signs. "So whoever placed it there appears to be cognizant of the school's surveillance system."

"Apparently. One of my people is in between assignments and agreed to look into it."

"Thank you, sir."

Salvatore oversaw a group of freelance agents and field operatives, mostly comprised of former students. People who knew how to push the boundaries. Individuals with high-profile day jobs that allowed them to move in influential circles for gathering intelligence.

Except, today Malcolm needed Salvatore's help, and as much as he hated to ask anyone for anything, when it came to Celia…well, apparently he still had a weak spot. "I have a favor to ask."

"With what?" Salvatore answered without hesitation.

"I need an untraceable car and some ID delivered here tonight." A safeguard in place to escape with Celia in the morning, just in case his gut feeling played out. He'd learned to trust his gut.

"Not that I'm arguing, but just curious," Salvatore said drily. Nothing had gotten by the old guy when he'd been headmaster, either. "Why not have your personal detail take care of that? You've got a top-notch team."

In fact, some of them were former agents.

"This is too important." *Celia* was too important. "If it were just me, I could take care of myself. But with some-one drawing a target on Celia's back…"

His fist thumped the railing, words choking on the dread in the back of his throat.

"Fair enough." The questions ended there. The two of them worked that tightly together with that kind of faith. "Whatever you need, it's yours."

"Thanks. I owe you." More than he could ever repay.

Colonel John Salvatore had become his father figure. The only real father figure he'd ever known, since his biological dad cut out on his family in the middle of the night, moving on to play his next honky-tonk gig. The bastard had sent a birthday card from the Florida Keys when Malcolm turned eleven. He never heard from him again.

"Malcolm," Salvatore continued, "I can put security in place for her here in the States so you can go ahead with your tour without worries."

"She's safer with me."

Salvatore's chuckle echoed over the line. "You don't

trust her to anyone else. Are you sure you trust yourself with her?"

God, he hated how easily Salvatore could read him.

"With all due respect, sir, the word games aren't necessary. I would do anything to keep her safe. Anything." His eyes scanned the small patio garden beside her carriage house with flowers blooming in splashes of purples and pinks. He recognized the lavender she used to love. His mother would have known the names of them all. Some were planted in the ground, others in pots. A fountain had been built into the stone wall, a wrought-iron chair and small table beside it. One chair. She sat there alone.

He didn't have any right to wonder about who she saw. But he couldn't deny he was glad she hadn't added a chair for her principal buddy yet.

Salvatore pressed, "What if I decide you're needed elsewhere?"

"Don't ask me to make the choice," he snapped.

"Apparently you've already decided."

"I have." Celia's safety would come first, even if it meant alienating Salvatore. Malcolm just hoped it wouldn't come to that. "Sir, I'm curious as to why the reports on Celia were incomplete."

"I don't know what you mean," he answered evasively.

"I respectfully disagree." Malcolm held his temper in check. Barely. "You're just trying to get me to say what I found out on my own in case I didn't learn everything. Then you can continue to hold back."

"We can play *this* game for a long time, Malcolm."

"Are you for or against me? Because I thought we were supposed to be on the same side."

"There are more people on your side than you know." When Malcolm kept his silence, Salvatore continued, "Celia's father did you a favor in getting you sent to my school. Without his intervention, you would have gone to a juvenile detention center."

Whoa. Hold on. He'd always thought the judge had pulled strings to get him out of Celia's life. The thought that her father had actually had a hand in helping Malcolm avoid jail time... He wasn't sure what to feel. He didn't want special favors. An important part of his life now consisted of helping to make people pay for their crimes.

After resenting Judge Patel for so long, this felt... strange. But then, because of his own dad, his gut made him naturally suspicious of other father figures. Which brought him right back around to the fact that Salvatore hadn't told him everything.

"What about this guy Celia's been seeing? The principal at the high school?"

"It didn't appear serious, so we didn't include it in the report. Apparently it *is* important to you, and that should tell you something."

"There are any number of ways that information could be important. What if he's the jealous type?" Um, crap, he could understand that too well. "Or if someone else is upset over the relationship. Details are important. Did you think I would go after him? You should know I'm not a headstrong idiot teenager anymore."

"You never were an idiot. Just young." Salvatore sighed, and Malcolm could envision the guy scratching a hand over his close-shorn salt-and-pepper hair. "I apologize for not including the principal in my report. If I find out anything else, I'll let you know. Meanwhile, whatever you need for protection, just ask and I'll make it happen."

Malcolm's temper inched down a degree. "Thank you, sir."

"Of course. Good night and be careful." The line disconnected.

Malcolm tucked his phone away but didn't go inside. Not yet. He couldn't avoid the truth staring him in the face. He'd just vowed he wasn't a headstrong idiot—yet he had acted like one in snapping at Salvatore, the man who had power and resources Malcolm needed. He'd all but proved the old man right, and all because he'd been knocked off balance by just the simple possibility of a kiss.

Except, nothing with Celia was simple.

It never had been.

His hands braced on the railing, he hung his head, staring down at that little garden grotto. He wanted to bring Celia down there and have a moonlit dinner together. The scent of those purple and pink flowers filled the air, while the music of the fountain filled the silence.

But he couldn't run the risk of someone seeing them. Not the bastard who'd been tormenting her. And not the press that hounded him.

Rather than regrets, he needed to focus on what he had. He had Celia to himself for the rest of the night. And by morning, he would have her rock-solid promise to come with him to Europe.

And he would keep his hands to himself.

Dinner together had been surprising.

Celia tucked the last of the dishes into the dishwasher while Malcolm checked the window for the umpteenth time. She'd expected him to press the issue of how close they'd come to kissing each other. She'd expected a big scene with oysters and wine and sexy almost-touches.

Instead he'd ordered shredded barbecue sandwiches that tasted like none she'd had before, served with Parmesan French fries and Southern sweet tea. There had even been pecan pie à la mode for dessert. The differences in their lifestyles didn't seem so big at moments like this.

She closed the dishwasher and pressed the start button. No busywork left to occupy herself, she had no choice but to face Malcolm—and the simmering awareness still humming inside her at the thought of kissing him again, touching him, taking things further. When they were teenagers, they'd spent hours exploring just how to make the other melt with desire.

Her face went hot at the memories.

"Thank you for ordering in dinner. That beat the dickens out of a warmed-over panino."

He turned away from the window, his deep blue eyes tracking her every move. "I hope you don't mind that I indulged myself in some selfish requests. I travel so much that I miss the tastes of home. Next meal, you choose. Anything you want, I'll make it happen."

Anything?

Best not to talk about exactly what she wanted right now. She'd already let her out-of-control attraction to him embarrass her once this evening.

"What a crazy concept to have whatever you want at your fingertips." She curled up in an overstuffed chair to make sure they weren't seated close on the sofa—or piano bench—again. "Are you one of those stars with strange, nitpicky requests, like wanting all the green M&M's picked out of the candy dish?"

"God, I hope not." He dropped back onto the piano bench, sitting an arm's reach away. "I like to think I'm still me, just with a helluva lot more money, so I get to call the shots in my life these days. Maybe I should take a Southern chef with me on tour."

She hugged a throw pillow. "You always did like pecan pie."

"And blackberry cobbler. God, I miss that, and flaky buttermilk biscuits."

"You must have picked up some new favorites from traveling the world." Even in his jeans with a torn knee, he still had a more polished look with his Ferragamo loafers and...just something undefinable that spoke of how much he'd accomplished. "You must have changed. Eighteen years is a long time."

"Of course I'm different in some ways. We all change. You're certainly not exactly the same."

"How so?" she asked warily.

"There. Just what you said now and how you said it." He leaned back against the piano. "You're more careful. More controlled."

"Why is caution a bad thing?" Her impulsive nature, her spoiled determination to have everything—to have him—at any cost had nearly wrecked both their lives.

"Not bad. Just different. Plus, you don't smile as much, and I've missed your laugh. You sound better than any music I've heard. I've tried to capture it in songs, but..." He shook his head. His blue eyes went darker with emotion, just the way they'd done all those years ago, and in that familiar moment, she felt his presence as deeply as she ever had from his kiss.

"That's so...sad." And incredibly touching.

One corner of his mouth kicked up in a wry smile. "Or sappy. But then, I make my living off writing and singing sappy love songs."

"Off of making women fall in love with you." She rolled her eyes, trying to make light of all the times the tabloid photos of him with other women had made her ache with what-ifs.

"Women aren't falling for me. It's all an image created by my manager. Everyone knows it's promo. None of it's real."

On a certain level, she got what he was saying, but something about his blasé attitude niggled at her. "You used to say the music was a part of you." She waved toward the antique upright behind him. "You were so passionate about your playing and your songs."

"I was an idealistic teenager. But I became a realist." He scooped up a stack of sheet music off the stand beside the piano. "I left this town determined to earn enough money to buy your father twice over, and music—" he rattled the pages in his hand "—was the only marketable skill I had."

"You achieved your financial goal. I truly am happy for you. Congratulations on succeeding in showing up my old man."

"More than succeeded." His eyes twinkled like stars lighting the night sky.

"So you can more than buy him out twice over. How many times over, five?"

He shrugged, his eyes still smiling.

Her jaw dropped. "Eight?"

He tossed the sheet music—scores she'd written for private students—back onto the side table.

"More than ten?" Holy crap.

"That's fairly close."

"Wow." She whistled softly. "Love songs pay well." A lot better than the little compositions she made for her students with dreams of putting them into an instruction book one day.

"People want to believe in the message," he said drily.

"You sound cynical." That made her sad when she thought of how deeply he'd cared about his music. "Why sing about something you don't accept as true? You obviously don't need the money anymore."

"You used to like it when I sang to you." He turned on the bench and placed his hands on the keyboard, his fingers starting a simple ballad, hauntingly familiar.

"I was one of those sappy women falling for you." When she'd been in Switzerland, his baby growing inside her, she'd dreamed of how they could repair their relationship when she got back and he finished his probation. Except, his letters to her grew fewer and fewer until she realized what everyone had told her was true. Theirs was just a high-school romance.

He tapped out another couple of bars of the melody line of one of the songs he'd written for her back when they'd dated. He'd said songs were all he had to offer her. This particular tune, one he'd called "Playing for Keeps," had always been her favorite. His fingers picked up speed, layering new intricacies into the simpler song he'd composed long ago. When he finished, the last note echoed in her tiny carriage house.

In her heart.

Her breath caught in her throat, her eyes stinging with tears that blurred the image of his broad shoulders as he sat at the piano. She ached with the urge to wrap her arms around him and rest her cheek on his back. She hurt from the lost dreams of what she'd let slip away. Apparently, he'd let a whole lot slip away from him, too. She didn't want to think about how cynical he'd grown.

Swallowing hard, she let herself dare to ask, "Was it real, what we felt then?"

He stayed silent, turned away from her for so long she thought he wouldn't answer. Finally, he shifted around again to face her. The raw emotion on his face squeezed at her heart.

A long sigh shuddered through him before he spoke. "Real enough that we went through a lot of pain for each other. Real enough that sitting here together isn't some easygoing reunion."

With that heavy sigh of his, she realized he'd suffered, too, more than she'd ever realized. Somehow, that made her feel less alone. Yes, they'd hurt each other, but maybe they could help each other, too. Maybe the time had come for a coda of sorts, to bring their song to an end.

"Malcolm, what's Europe going to be like if just sitting here together is this difficult?"

"So you've decided to come with me? No more maybes?"

She shoved to her feet and walked to him at the piano. "I think I have to."

"Because of the stalker?"

She cupped his handsome, beard-stubbled face in her hands. "Because it's time we put this to rest."

Before she could talk herself out of something she wanted—needed—more than air, Celia pressed her lips to his.

Five

Malcolm might not have planned on kissing Celia, but the second her mouth touched his, there wasn't a chance in hell he could pull away. She tasted like the sweet, syrupy insides of pecan pie and more—more than he remembered. Familiar and new all at once.

The tip of her tongue touched his, sending a bolt of desire straight through him until he went so hard at the thought of having her that he ached. His body surged with the need to take her, here, now. Because based on even this one kiss, he knew it would be even better for them than when they had been inexperienced, fumbling teens learning their way around…then learning the pleasure of drawing it out.

God, she was flipping his world upside down all over again.

Then the kiss was over before it barely started.

Celia touched her lips with a trembling hand, her

chewed nails hinting at how frayed her nerves had been lately. "Not the smartest thing I've ever done. I pride myself on being wiser these days."

No offers to make up the couch for him. Definitely no offer for him to come to her room. He hadn't expected otherwise...although a man could hope.

"We don't always want what's good for us."

"True enough. I got caught up in the memories from the music. The fact that you remembered the song from before... Well, I would have to be heartless not to be moved. Except, now reason has set in. If I follow through on that kiss, Europe is going to be very awkward—"

"Celia, it's okay. You don't need to explain or say anything more." He traced his thumb along her mouth. "I won't go psycho because you don't invite me into your bed after one kiss."

Still, his mind filled with the fantasy of tearing each other's clothes off, of carrying her over to the piano and sitting her on the keyboard, where he would step between her legs and bury himself deep inside this woman who'd always moved him in a way no other could.

Which had him wondering if perhaps they could indulge in more. If it was every bit as inevitable now as it had been eighteen years ago.

Indecision shifted in her dark brown eyes. Could she really be considering it? His pulse ratcheted up to never-before-tested speeds. Except, then she shook her head and turned away.

"I can't do this," she mumbled, backing away until his hand slid from her face. From the hall closet, she pulled out a stack of sheets and a pillow, then tugged a quilt from the back of the sofa. "Good night, Malcolm."

She thrust the linens against his chest and pivoted on her heels before he could say a word. No question, she was every bit as rattled as he was. Resisting the urge to go after her, he still allowed himself to savor watching the gentle sway of her hips as she left. His body throbbed in response, and he knew the feel of her would stay imprinted on him long after she closed her bedroom door.

Silence echoed after her, the scent of lavender wafting up from the sheets she'd given him. He hadn't slept on a sofa since his early days in the music industry, going to college on scholarship in the mornings, still half-asleep from playing late-night gigs. He'd gotten a degree in music with a minor in accounting because, by God, no manager was ever going to take advantage of his finances. He refused to be one of those musicians who made billions only to file for bankruptcy later. He knew what poverty was like and how it hurt the people around him—how he'd hurt the people around him because of his own dumb decisions.

He was in control these days.

Shrugging the tension out of his shoulders, he tossed aside the sheet and shook out the blanket. He stayed at five-star penthouse suites on a regular basis, but he'd never forgotten where he came from—and he damn well never would. The day a person got complacent was the day someone robbed them blind.

He refused to be caught flat-footed ever again. The lowest day of his life had been sitting in that police cell, arrested for drug possession. Wondering what Celia thought. Hating that he'd let his mother down.

The part that still stuck in his craw? For some twisted reason, his brush with the law made him all the more alluring to fans. The press had spun it into a "bad turned good" kind of story. He didn't want fans glorifying him or the things he'd done.

His mistakes were his own. He took responsibility for

his past. Atonement wasn't something to parade around for others to applaud. Receiving praise diminished the power of anything he might have done right.

Speaking of atonement...

He tugged the leather briefcase from beside the sofa. His driver had left the essentials. He pulled out his tablet computer to check for an update from Salvatore on Celia.

Because, with memories of that kiss still heating his blood, he sure as hell wasn't going to fall asleep anytime soon.

Celia kept her eyes closed even though she'd woken up at least ten minutes ago after a restless night's sleep. Her white-noise machine filled the room with the sound of soothing waves. She snuggled deeper under the covers, groggy and still so sexually strung tight her skin was oversensitive to the Egyptian cotton sheets. Just one kiss, and she was already burning up for Malcolm Douglas again.

The thought of facing him was mortifying—and a little scary. What if she walked out there, lost control and plastered herself all over him again?

Last night's kiss had rocked her to her toes. And the way Malcolm hadn't pressed her to hop right into bed together? That rattled her even more. But then, he hadn't pressured her as a teenager, either. She'd been the aggressor. She'd known him for years. They'd shared a music teacher, even performed at recitals together. But something had changed when they both came back from summer break, entering their sophomore year.

Her friend had gotten hot.

The other high-school girls had noticed, too. But she'd been determined. He was hers. No one had ever denied her anything, and she could see now how that had made her all the more determined to win him over. Her self-ishness had played a part in how recklessly fast she'd pursued him.

She'd justified her actions by noting the interest in his eyes. Except, he'd insisted he didn't have the time or money for dating. He'd told her they couldn't be anything more than friends. She'd told him she didn't need fancy romancing. She just wanted him....

After they'd been dating for five months, she'd feared she was losing him. His mother had been filling out applications for scholarships for him to attend a special high school for the arts. Celia understood Terri Ann Douglas wanted the best for her son, but it seemed the push for him to attend school out of town had more to do with getting him away from Celia than obtaining a better music education.

Or at least that was how it had appeared in her self-centered teenage mind.

Already she'd felt as if she barely got to see him between his job and their music lessons and their eagle-eyed parents. Still, they'd stolen time alone together to make out, talk, dream—make out some more. Their make-out sessions had grown hotter, as hot as possible without going all the way.

She recalled every detail of that whole day, the day she'd lost her virginity. She remembered what she wore—pink jeans and a rock-band T-shirt. What she ate—cereal, an apple and not much else, because she wanted to keep fitting into those jeans.

Most of all, she remembered what it felt like stretched out on the backseat of her car with Malcolm, parked by the river at night. She'd already pitched her shirt and bra onto the floor, along with his shirt, too, because there was nothing like the feel of her breasts against his bare chest.

Her hand tunneled down his pants, and he was working the zipper on her pink jeans. They'd already learned how to give each other orgasms by stroking to take the edge off the gnawing need.

Except, that night she'd been selfish. Scared of losing him. And most of all, she'd been stupid.

They hadn't used a condom.

Although she'd still needed him to finish her with his hand afterward because it hadn't been anywhere near as earth-shattering as she'd expected. Not the first time.

But she hadn't gotten pregnant then, either. Which made them all the more reckless over the following weeks when Malcolm had been deliciously determined to figure out exactly how to bring her to that earth-shattering release while buried heart-deep inside her....

Celia snuggled deeper under the covers, cocooning herself in memories. The good—then the bad when everything had fallen apart. For years she'd told herself maybe he hadn't loved her as much as she'd loved him. That they'd only become a couple because she'd gone after him, and what red-blooded teenage boy said no to sex?

But last night, the way he'd played that song made her realize she'd only been trying to ease her guilt over how much she'd cost him, how much their breakup had hurt him, as well.

Now this new insight complicated the trip to Europe.

In the harsh light of the morning, leaving with him seemed like a reckless idea, and she didn't do "reckless" anymore. She'd left behind impulsiveness when she'd passed over her baby girl to parents who could give her all the things Celia couldn't. The pain of loss had pushed her over the edge.

She had to be smarter this time, to be careful for her

own sake, and for his. Just the thought of seeing him once she walked into the living room sent butterflies whirling in her stomach.

Damn it. He hadn't even been back in her life for twenty-four hours, and desire for him had flipped her world upside down. She hadn't helped matters with that impulsive kiss, brought on by nostalgia. She couldn't let sex cloud their judgment again. She wanted—she needed—her peaceful existence. To make that happen, she had to stay in control while facing her fears and guilt in order to move on with her life.

She flung aside the covers and clicked off her white-noise machine, the sound of waves ending abruptly, only to be replaced by a different buzz coming from outside. Frowning, she went to the window and parted the wood shutters.

Oh. My. God. Her breath caught in her throat. She stepped away fast.

Her lawn was absolutely packed.

Cars, media vans, even tents with clusters of people underneath filled her yard and beyond, overflowing onto the sidewalk. She slammed the shutters closed and locked them. Her home had been invaded, and she was damn certain it had nothing to do with her stalker.

Apparently, Malcolm had about a million of his own.

She snagged her cotton bathrobe from the foot of her bed. Sprinting for the door, she yanked on her robe and knotted the tie on her way to the living room.

Only to stop short again.

Malcolm was sprawled on the sofa wearing only his jeans, with the blanket twisted and draped over his waist. Her mouth dried up. The muscles she'd felt ripple beneath his shirt were all the more magnificent uncovered. Damn it all, why couldn't he have gone paunchy and bald? Or why couldn't he have at least become a totally arrogant jerk?

All right. He was a bit arrogant, but not at all a jerk. And the six-pack abs didn't show the least sign of paunch. His hair was so freakin' magnificent his fans named that signature lock of hair over the brow—calling it "The Malcolm." Men everywhere were letting their hair grow long over their foreheads because their girlfriends begged them to. Malcolm's fans.

His fans.

Damn. Not two minutes after vowing not to let the attraction derail her, she'd failed. She'd been so caught up in gawking at his naked chest that she'd forgotten about the sold-out audience on her lawn. Celia knelt by the sofa, her hand falling lightly on his shoulder.

His warm skin sent sparks shimmering through her.

She snatched back her hand. "Malcolm? Malcolm, you have to wake up now—"

He shot upright off the sofa. His arm whipped from under the blanket, a gun clasped in his hand and pointed at the ceiling.

A gun?

"Malcolm?" she squeaked. "Where did that come from?"

"It's mine, and it's registered. I keep it for protection, which seems appropriate given the threats against you. Probably a bit more daunting to an intruder than if I bash them over the head with a rolled-up music score." He placed the black weapon on the coffee table with a wry grin. "It's best you don't surprise me when I'm asleep."

"Do you get creepy fans waking you up often?" She rubbed her arms, suddenly chilled.

"When I first hit the charts, a fan managed to get past security into the house. But since then, no. That doesn't mean I'm letting down my guard, and my security detail is an impenetrable wall between me and overzealous fans."

"Then why sleep with the gun?"

"Because your life is too precious to trust to anyone else. I have to be sure."

Her heart squeezed in her chest, and it was all she could do not to caress his face, kiss him, claim that perfect mouth of his all over again.

Clearing her throat, she nodded to the living-room window covered with simple white shutters instead of curtains. "Check out the lawn."

His eyes narrowed, muscles along his chest bunching. He strode across the room and opened the shutters just a crack.

"Crap." He stepped to the side, out of the sight line. "Wish I could say I'm surprised, but I was afraid this might happen. I should have insisted we leave last night before they had time to rally."

Her misgivings churned again. "About leaving together for Europe. I'm…"

"Yeah, I agree." He snagged his button-down shirt off the back of the chair, tucking his feet back into his loafers. "We need to go right away."

She toyed with the tie of her bathrobe. "I'm not so sure about that."

He glanced up from buttoning his shirt. "We don't have a choice, thanks to the folks on the lawn with cameras."

"So you more than suspected this *might* happen?"

"I couldn't be certain." He tucked his tablet computer into a leather briefcase. "But I had to consider it and plan accordingly."

"What kind of plan?"

"A way for us to leave before it gets worse." He strapped his gun into a holster and stowed it in the briefcase, as well. "As soon as you get dressed."

"It can get worse than that? There's no more room on the lawn."

"There's always room," he said darkly. "Get dressed, and I'll pour some coffee into travel mugs. We'll have to eat on the road."

"What if I decide to stay here and let you leave on your own?" So much for her resolution to face her fears. *Chicken.*

He stood still. Waiting. Leaving her time to realize—she really didn't have a choice anymore. Once the press saw him leave, they would stay on her lawn until she walked out the door or until they somehow managed to break in. She needed to tuck her head and get out of here quickly.

"Right." She sighed. "I'm going with you. But why so soon? What about packing?"

"Arranged."

"Of course."

He could order anything now, thanks to his money and power. And at the moment, she wasn't in the position to turn that down. His guards had the crowd contained, but for how long?

"God, this is getting complicated." She scraped back her tangled hair in her hand. "I have an end-of-the-year concert tonight and grades to file."

Malcolm held a phone in his hand. "Tell me what you want, and I'll make it happen. I can have an army of guards around the entire school if that's what you need."

As much as it pained her, she knew there was only one solution. "That sounds frightening and dangerous. I'll call the high-school chorus teacher. She can conduct the concert if I send her the lineup, and I can file my grades online. Given the circus out there, I imagine the school will understand my decision to take a personal day."

He reached out a hand. "Celia, I'm so damn sorry about—"

"Uh, really, it's okay." The last thing she needed was his touch scrambling her thoughts again. "You were just trying to help."

Spinning on her heel, she raced back down the hall to her room. She yanked a sundress and sandals from her tiny closet before peeling off her pj's.

She couldn't help but wonder, if Malcolm suspected this kind of fan fallout, then why had he made such a public appearance? Had he been trying to force her to fall in line with his plan? If so, why? What did he have to gain from stepping in to protect her from the stalker?

None of this made sense.

She tugged out fresh underwear and didn't stop to think about why she bypassed simple white cotton for lemon-yellow lace. It shouldn't have mattered, and she shouldn't have noticed her choice.

But it did matter, and she had noticed. That made her angry with herself all over again. It had been tough enough tamping down her runaway attraction after a night spent dreaming about him and that dang kiss. Now she had the additional memory of chiseled abs and his formidable male chest etched in her brain.

She yanked on her clothes and jammed her feet into sandals while the scent of hazelnut drifted into the bedroom from her kitchen. She took a valuable thirty more seconds to brush her teeth and hair, before racing back into the living room, grabbing her floral tote bag along the way so she would have her wallet and computer. "I guess it's time to put your guards to work helping us run the gauntlet to your limo."

He passed her a travel mug of coffee. "We're not using the limo. We'll go down the inside stairs to the garage."

"My car is still at the school." She shrugged her bag over her shoulder, nerves singing freaking arias in her stomach at the thought of all those fans outside. "I really should give my dad a call. And damn it all, Malcolm, just because I'm going with you does not mean we will be sleeping together. You have to understand—"

"Celia, stop. It's okay. I hear you. Now hear me. I had a vehicle delivered last night in case we needed to make an escape—since the limo wouldn't fit in your garage. You can call your father and the other music teacher once we're on the road." He slipped his fingers down her arm in a shivery caress then clasped her hand. "Trust me. I will not let anyone—including myself—hurt you."

With a gentle tug, he guided her down the narrow enclosed staircase and opened the door to reveal...

A red Maserati.

Her jaw dropped and her feet grew roots. "Oh. Um, that's a, uh, nice car."

Sleek and sophisticated, not unlike the man beside her. The man she'd seen half-dressed this morning.

"Better yet, it's a *fast* car." He opened her door then sprinted around the front to the driver's side. He settled behind the wheel and reached into the glove compartment for a blue ball cap. "Are you ready?"

"Nope." Her fingers curled into the supple leather. All the better to prevent her from touching Malcolm. "I guess that doesn't matter, though."

"Sorry about that." He tugged on the cap, clicked the garage door opener and revved the finely tuned engine to life. She caught the scent of his aftershave in the close confines of the sports car.

Her stomach twittered at every growl of the engine. The garage door rumbled as it rolled up, revealing the clusters of people outside.

Somehow, her hand sought out his forearm and squeezed.

As he nosed out, fans pushed at the line of security guards, the high-pitched squeals and flashing bulbs piercing even the thick, tinted windows.

Only a slight flex of muscles along Malcolm's jaw showed any frustration on his part. This was, after all, everyday life to him now. And so totally alien to her.

The deeper they drove into the swarm of fans and paparazzi, the more and more she felt like Alice in Wonderland falling headfirst into the rabbit hole.

An hour later, Malcolm floored the Maserati on a deserted country road. The high-performance vehicle had given him the speed and maneuverability to dodge the paparazzi that had trailed him out of Celia's garage. Miles of empty farm fields rolled ahead of them, broken by the occasional sprawling oak or faded red barn.

Best of all, there was almost zero traffic. Tractors chewed up the land off to the side. So far, only two trucks had passed going the other direction. She'd made her calls to reassure her father and to detail the program requirements for the other music teacher.

Finally, he had Celia safely away and all to himself. He wasn't trusting the press not to find the distinctive car, so he had more change-ups planned. For now, he had a short window to be with Celia, alone on the open road. He needed to use this time wisely to help put her at ease around him again. If he expected to make a serious go at putting the past to rest, then she had to stop walking on eggshells all the time.

She'd showed signs of cold feet about coming to Europe with him when she'd seen the press and fans packing her lawn. Although, that paparazzi sit-in had also offered him the perfect excuse to whisk her away faster. Once he got her out of town and away from whoever was trying to scare the hell out of her, then he could…

What?

Somehow with that kiss, things had shifted between them. In spite of what she'd said about not sleeping together, the heat between them was still there, but matured. He'd spent most of the night thinking about her, wanting her. They were both adults. They both had settled into their lives and careers.

She hadn't been ready to see that attraction through to its conclusion last night. He could understand that. He meant it when he'd said he would not do anything to hurt her or abuse her trust. But he had to accept that the kiss changed everything. Though he'd meant to stay away, he now knew he couldn't leave this mission without having her one last time.

As for their past feelings for each other? Puppy love. The flowery notion of soul mates was a crock. Something created to sell music, movies and greeting cards. He was a more practical man these days. He and Celia could indulge in sex without risking their hearts.

Now he just needed to convince her.

He glanced over at Celia, his eyes drawn to the curve of her legs. Hell, he was even turned on by her cute feet with pink-painted toenails peeking out of her sandals.

Crap.

Focus on the road, idiot.

He downshifted around a curve on the two-lane highway. "I'm sorry to have made you miss out on the concert."

"I know you were just trying to help."

"Still, it sucks to lose something you've obviously worked hard on." He felt the weight of her stare and glanced over to find her forehead furrowed. "What?"

"Thank you for understanding how important this was to me—for not dismissing it. I know we're not a sold-out coliseum or a royal audience."

"Music isn't about the size or income of the audience."

She smiled for the first time since they'd left her home. "It's about touching the heart, the soul."

His grip tightened on the wheel as he thought of another time she'd said much the same thing. One night, he'd brought along his guitar to serenade her under the stars. He'd picked up fast food and a blanket and told himself someday he would give her better. Give her more. She'd quickly reassured him that money didn't matter to her, just the heart and the soul.

He should have listened to her. She hadn't wanted this kind of life then any more than now. Regardless of what she wanted, though, she did need him. At least for the moment.

Accelerating, he sped down the deserted two-lane road.

Celia smoothed the wrinkles from her gauzy dress. "That was quite an impressive getaway. I thought for sure someone would get hit or at the very least have their toes run over. But you got us out of there without anyone getting hurt. Where did you learn to drive like that?"

"Part of the job training." Except, it had more to do with his Interpol work than the music world, but he tried to stick to the truth as much as he could, as if that somehow made up for the huge lie of omission. But then it wasn't something he had leave to work into conversation. *Hey, I moonlight as a freelance agent for Interpol.*

She laughed lightly. "I must have missed the driving class in my music education."

"I have a friend who's a race-car driver." Another truth. "He gave me lessons."

"What friend is that?" She turned toward him, hitching her knee up so her whole body shifted.

For a second, his gaze drifted to the hem of her dress. The hint of skin the movement had exposed.

"Elliot Starc. We went to school together."

She gasped. "You went to school with Elliot Starc, the international race-car driver?"

"You know about Starc?" He stared at the road harder and told himself to keep his head on straight. "Most of the women I've met don't follow racing."

"Honey, this is the South, where people live and breathe NASCAR." Her soft drawl thickened a little as she laughed again. "Starc is, of course, more Formula One, but some of my father's friends take their racing interests further."

"Fair enough. So you've heard of Eric, then."

"There must have been a lot of lessons to get that good at maneuvering…the speed." She shook her head, her hair shifting over her shoulders. "I'm still dizzy."

He glanced at her sharply. "Are you okay? I didn't mean to scare you."

"You didn't. I'm all right." She laughed softly. "Goodness knows I got enough speeding tickets as a teenager. I'm a more sedate driver these days. I no longer expect Daddy to fix my tickets for me."

"A lot of time has passed."

"Yet you're here. *We're* here." The confusion in her voice reached out to him. But before he could figure out what the hell to say, she continued, "I just don't want you to get hurt protecting me."

"I'll be fine. I told you. I have this under control." Too bad he couldn't say the same about his resurrected feelings for Celia.

He was aware of her every movement beside him.

"Oh, right. Your plan." She straightened in her seat again. "Where are we going?"

To the one place he could be certain no one would find them. "To my mom's house."

Six

His mother's house?

Celia still couldn't wrap her brain around that nugget of information even a half hour after he'd spilled the beans. The press had reported in the past that he now supported his mother, declaring she deserved a life of luxury after all the sacrifices she'd made for him. But there were never any details about where Terri Ann Douglas had relocated after she'd left Azalea fourteen years ago.

Quite frankly, Celia hadn't been that interested in staying in touch with the woman who reminded her so deeply of all she'd lost. Terri Ann hadn't approved of Celia back then anyway, and with good reason. Celia was everything the woman had feared for her son—spoiled, selfish and more than willing to toss away her virginity if that tied Malcolm closer to her.

The thought of seeing Terri Ann again sent Celia's stomach into knots as they pulled up to a large scrolled gate covered by vines. Cameras moved ever so slightly, almost hidden in the foliage. Malcolm stopped by the security box and typed a code into the keypad. The gates swung wide, revealing a road that lead into…nothing but trees.

She couldn't see a house, and wouldn't be able to see people, even if they showed up. The security was… beyond crazy. As she began to grasp the depth of the protection here, she had to wonder, had he changed his mind about Europe and decided to stash her away here with his mother, where he'd obviously already lavished a good deal of effort to ensure privacy?

Disappointment gripped her, too much considering she'd been questioning the wisdom of going with him. But she couldn't deny a flickering wish deep inside her. Yes, her world had spun out of control since he'd returned, but she didn't want to step off the dizzying ride just yet. This was crazy and scary, out of character for the new, steadier path she'd chosen for herself.

Except, even if they didn't sleep together again— which they weren't going to do, she emphatically reminded herself—she finally had a chance for answers, for closure on her teenage years, a time in her life that had almost broken her. She didn't want to lose the opportunity.

"Malcolm, would you care to clue me in to what's going on?"

He drove the car deeper into the forest of towering oaks and pines, gravel crunching under the tires. "I needed to regain some control over the security. We're off the radar now, which gives us some breathing room."

Suddenly, he turned from the dusty path onto a paved road. The leafy branches parted to reveal—*oh, my God*—a compound.

A columned mansion was surrounded by every convenience from a pool to tennis courts. Even a pond sported a small dock with a gazebo picnic area by the shore.

The home was a magnificent getaway. But at the moment, it looked rather like a prison to her. "Do you plan for me to stay here instead?"

He looked at her quickly. "Not at all. We're still going to Europe. I told you my security would be taking care of you, and I meant that. We're simply leaving from here instead of from a public airport."

Too much relief zinged through her. Damn it, she was supposed to be gaining peace from this reunion, not wanting to spend more time with him. "Then I'm fuzzy on the details of how we're getting from this place to Europe. I don't see an airstrip."

He pointed in the distance.

A helicopter flew just over the treetops.

She shrank back in her seat even though she knew the tinted windows provided complete privacy. "The press found us already?"

"No, that's our ride." He put the Maserati in Park next to a large concrete pad.

A space large enough for that bird to land. Holy cow.

Her eyes stayed locked on the white helicopter flying closer, closer still, until it hovered. Roaring overhead, it landed a few feet away, blades stirring dust all around the car. "You're kidding."

"Nope. We'll fly in the chopper to another location, where we'll board a private jet and leave the country. Avoiding the press involves a lot more steps than going from point A to point B."

Wow, okay. He did have resources beyond anything she'd imagined. But…

"I thought you said we were visiting your mother."

"I said we were going to her house. She's not here." He pulled his briefcase from behind his seat. "She's at her vacation flat in London."

A vacation flat? "You're a good son. This amazing house. A place in England, too."

"What I give her is easy compared to all she did for me." His eyes went sober, pained even. "The house, the apartment, they don't even put a dent in my account. She worked two jobs just to put food on the table. She even cleaned my piano teacher's house in exchange for lessons. Mom deserves a retirement. Now, are you ready?"

She was running out of time to say what had been chewing at her gut since last night. "I don't want you to think that kiss meant more than it did."

"What did it mean?"

"That I'm still attracted to you, as well, that we share a very significant past. But that doesn't mean we have a future or that we should act on the attraction." Because honest to God, right now she wasn't sure how she would walk away from him a second time if they got even closer. They needed to use this trip together to talk through what happened when they were teenagers, to have the conversations they'd been denied because of immaturity—and the fact that he'd been locked away in a military school and she'd been sent to Switzerland. "It was more of a farewell to that past and a salute to friendship kind of kiss. Didn't you write a song once about goodbye kisses?"

"Someone else wrote that one." He smiled cynically. "My manager thought it would melt hearts."

"It melted hearts all the way to the top of the charts." She'd turned the radio station dozens of times to keep herself from crying over that damn song.

"Call me jaded—" he gripped the steering wheel so

tightly his knuckles went bloodless "—but sometimes I feel like I'm selling a flawed ideal to my fans."

"How can you deny there's love out there?" She turned toward him again, clenching her hands into fists to keep from reaching for him. "We felt it. I know we did. That song last night proved it. Even though it ended, what we had was real."

"Puppy love."

Her head snapped back, his words a splash of bitterly cold water. "Are you being a bastard on purpose?"

"Just helping you resist the urge to kiss me again." He reached across her and opened her door. "Our helicopter's waiting."

As her door swung wide, the biting wind blew grit and rocks inside the beautifully magnificent car, stinging her as tangibly as his angry words had. She grabbed her floral tote bag full of schoolwork and jumped out, slamming the door closed behind her. Helicopter blades whomp, whomp, whomped, slicing the air. Who traveled by helicopter besides the military and the country's president?

Apparently platinum-selling stars did.

He opened the door for her. "Sit up front."

Gingerly, she climbed inside the helicopter, the scent of leather and oil saturating the air as she settled in place. She eyed the empty copilot's seat, the thrill-seeking ways of her teenage years nowhere to be found. The thought of riding in a chopper—of actually going to Europe—made her chest grow tight. She forced herself to breathe in and out evenly, willing back the rising panic attack.

Damn it, she could do this—she had to do this. She would use this time to turn the page once and for all on the chapter of her life that included Malcolm Douglas.

She snapped her seat belt on and tugged it extra tight while glancing at the controls and the thin sides, the surrounding glass. Okay, so maybe she could do this in a different seat. She turned to ask the pilot if she could sit in back but he slid out before she could speak. He passed his headset to Malcolm and put Malcolm's ball cap on his head. The pilot sprinted toward the Maserati.

Malcolm slipped into the pilot's seat. He tugged on his headset and passed a second set to Celia. She pulled them on, her ears filling with chatter over the airwaves.

He leaned toward her. "If you want to speak privately, just tap this button."

And with that, he ran a check of the controls, his voice resonating in her ears as he called in to some tower for takeoff. How could the people on the other end of the radio not know they were speaking to Malcolm Douglas? His smooth baritone caressed her senses even when he just spoke, his voice utterly recognizable to her even without looking at him.

There was no denying he knew exactly what to do. "Um, Malcolm? Are you actually going to fly this—"

The helicopter lifted off. She bit down a yelp and grabbed her seat, terrified of touching something. It wasn't as if she was afraid to fly, but this was all happening so fast, with so little explanation. She looked out at the house growing smaller and smaller the higher they flew.

"I guess you really are flying the chopper. You have a license, right?"

"Yes, ma'am."

"You can't tell me Elliot Starc taught you to drive this, too."

"Not Elliot." He glanced at her and winked. "Private instructor."

She sagged back in her seat. "Of course. How could I not have known?"

Reservations about her decision were pointless now.

She was going to Europe with the man who'd stolen—and broken—her heart eighteen years ago.

Malcolm steered the helicopter through the sky.

He had to admit there were definite perks to having an unlimited bank account. He had the coolest toys. His work with Interpol had only expanded the scope.

Plowing through the sky in a helicopter, having the little bird at his disposal, beat the hell out of the days when he and his mom could barely afford to keep a rusted Chevy running. Vulnerable women were his weak spot, and he knew that. When it came to Celia and their history, his tendency to protect was all the more powerful.

He monitored the controls, his feet working in tandem with his hands—like playing the piano, it required two-handed coordination along with his feet. He played the chopper through the air, over tiny houses far below. Far above the threat to Celia, for now.

Because no matter how much he wanted her in his bed again—and he wanted that so much it gnawed at his gut—he could not lose sight of his primary goal here. He had to keep her safe. And that meant keeping his libido in check. A more restrained approach once he had her tucked far away from here seemed the better plan than pressing her on that kiss now.

Given her death grip on the seat, it appeared Celia had left her daredevil days behind. Her paling face sucker punched him, making him feel guilty as hell for being cranky with her when she talked about sappy emotions. Love hadn't pulled him out of his messed-up life. He'd put his world on track with practical determination and hard work.

Still, he couldn't stand to see her hurt...

He thumbed the private mic button. "It's going to be

all right, Celia. I swear. We're going to meet up with a
school friend of mine at his vacation home in the Florida
panhandle. He'll be able to help us slip out of the country without the fanfare, attention and danger of going
through an airport."

At least he had her away from Azalea now. One step
in the right direction.

She looked away from the windscreen and over at him.
"A school friend?"

"Yeah, a few of us have kept in touch." A few? A se-
lect few. The ones who worked for Salvatore, a group of
pals from school who'd dubbed themselves The Alpha
Brotherhood.

"Close friends?"

"Definitely," he said simply. "There were two types of
people at that boarding school. Those who wanted a life
in the military. And those of us who needed the regimen
of a military education."

"You were already incredibly regimented and motivated." Her soft voice caressed his ear, the hum of the
helicopter engine fading until he only heard her. "You
didn't need that."

"Apparently I did." He couldn't deny it. "Hanging out
at bars underage, knocking up my girlfriend. I wouldn't
call that succeeding at life."

"I played a part in that." Her voice held so much regret
it reached across to him.

"I'm damn lucky I ended up there, where they could
straighten me out."

"How bad was the school they sent you to?" Her hands
slid from the seat to twist in her lap. "I worried about
you."

"Not as bad as jail would have been. I know I was
lucky. Like I said, I got a top-notch education, music les-

sons and discipline." It wasn't what he would have chosen for himself, but he'd made the most of the opportunity, determined to prove himself to all the doubters. "And the major bonus? My mother didn't have to work double shifts anymore."

"Ahhh." Her melodic voice hummed softly. "So you really stayed at the school for your mother."

"You always did see right through me." He checked the controls again, refusing to let the tension knotting his gut affect his skills. "I was so angry back then that I wanted to tell the judge where he could stick his 'deal.' I was innocent and no one was going to label me a drug user. But one look at my mother's face, and I knew I had to accept."

"So you left town."

"I did." He'd left her. That had been the toughest part, knowing she was carrying his child and he'd failed to provide a future for them. "Chances of me walking away from that trial with a clean slate were slim."

She'd already told him she planned to give up the baby, and as wounded as he was by her decision, he had nothing to offer to change her mind. He'd left town. There'd been no reason to stay.

"Tell me about these close friends who are going to help us out?"

A safe enough subject. Most of the press knew who his friends were; they just didn't know the details of what bonded them to each other. "Troy Donavan will be meeting us when we land."

"The Robin Hood Hacker... I didn't expect that."

Troy had hacked into the Department of Defense's computer system as a teen to expose corruption. He'd done the crime and proudly served his time at the military school. If anything, Troy had griped about *not* being sent to jail.

He continued naming. "Conrad Hughes will meet us along the way."

"A casino magnate with questionable ties? And Elliot Starc, as well, playboy race-car driver?" She laughed, but she also sank deeper in her seat. "I'm not feeling all that safe here."

If only she knew…

He explained what he could. "Yes, we landed at that school for a reason and came out better men. If it makes you feel any better, our Alpha Brotherhood includes Dr. Rowan Boothe."

"The philanthropist doctor featured in *People* magazine's 100 Sexiest Men issue? He invented some kind of revolutionary computerized surgical technique…"

"With our computer-expert buddy Troy. Do you trust my friends now?" He glanced over at her and found a twinkle in her eyes.

Damn. She'd played him, getting him to share more than he'd intended. He'd always been susceptible to this woman. She might appear less impulsive, more steady.

But she was every bit as seductive.

Why did everything she learned about Malcolm have to be so blasted appealing?

Celia had worked during the whole helicopter ride to find a flaw in him, and the more he shared about how he'd spent his life since he left Azalea, the more she found to admire about him.

She pulled her eyes off his handsome profile as the helicopter began landing at his friend Troy Donavan's beach house on the Florida Gulf Coast. Apparently the

Robin Hood Hacker allowed choppers to land on his lawn, as well.

What an unexpected friendship. Malcolm had been so straitlaced as a teenager. Although the tabloids certainly painted him as a partying Romeo now.

But she couldn't stop thinking about his saying he'd chosen the reform-school option for his mom rather than fighting the charge. Without question, Celia knew he'd never touched drugs. And she also knew him to be very prideful of how hard he'd worked. To swallow his pride and accept a plea bargain had to have been horribly difficult for him.

This decision to go with Malcolm to Europe grew more complicated by the second—and more enticing. What other secrets might she discover about him? What other nuances were there to the adult man he'd become?

A man who flew a helicopter as adeptly as he played the piano.

The chopper touched down lightly on the lawn with a simple kiss to the earth. The blades rotated overhead, sea grass bending with the rotor gusts. A uniformed guard opened her door and offered a hand to help her out. She snagged her floral tote bag and stepped free, the ground buzzing beneath her feet.

Before she could blink, Malcolm was at her side. His arm looped around her waist, warm and muscular, guiding her not toward the stucco beach mansion but toward a small private airstrip with a Learjet parked and waiting.

She felt as if Alice had just slipped a little farther down the rabbit hole. Her father traveled first-class, and even periodically rented a Cessna, but nothing on as grand a scale as this.

Seconds later, Malcolm palmed her waist as she

stepped inside the luxury aircraft, where another couple waited in the cabin of white leather and polished brass.

A red-haired woman with freckles stood, her hand extended. "You must be Celia. I'm Hillary, Troy's wife."

The wife of the Robin Hood Hacker.

Hillary appeared down-to-earth, blessedly normal, wearing jeans and a T-shirt—no doubt designer given how perfectly they fit. But still, no fake boobs or platinum-bleached hair. Just genuine red hair and freckles with a natural smile.

Already, Malcolm had moved past her to shake hands with a man she recognized from newspaper articles—Troy Donavan, quirky computer mogul who'd once used those skills to breach the cyber walls of the Department of Defense.

She overheard Malcolm's familiar Southern drawl. "Sorry we're late. The drive out took us longer than we expected."

"No worries, brother." Troy led him to a row of computer screens at a corner-office console in the tricked-out jet. "I'll give you a quick update while my wife keeps our lovely guest occupied."

Her eyes lingered on the broad expanse of Malcolm's shoulders, the strong column of his neck exposed as he leaned over the computer.

Hillary touched her lightly on the arm to regain her attention and gestured to a seat. "You look shell-shocked. I'm guessing he didn't take much time to explain. But covering his trail from the press, the fans and whoever has been bothering you had to happen fast."

Celia sank onto the leather sofa and patted along the seat for the belt. They were leaving now? No packing, no passports? No telling her friends... What the hell had she agreed to?

Her gaze tracked back to Malcolm. Who was this man she'd just agreed to leave the country with?

Hillary sat beside her. "We've heard a lot about you from Malcolm."

She looked up quickly, warily. "What did he say?"

"That you're old friends and you're having trouble with a stalker. So he's helping you out."

"He is. I'm lucky," she conceded to Hillary and herself just as the Learjet engines buzzed to life.

The captain's voice piped over the intercom, welcoming them all. All four of them. Not just Malcolm's friend, but Donavan's wife, as well. She hadn't expected Hillary to come along. Did the woman's presence here—the whole "group" outing—mean the romantic signals she'd been getting from Malcolm were wrong?

No wonder he hadn't acted on the kiss.

She should be grateful. The pressure was off since he wouldn't be tempting her. She could tamp down the crazy desire to jump his bones and just chalk it up to nostalgia. She kept right on repeating that to herself as they climbed into the sky, heading for the first stop on Malcolm's European tour.

Except, no matter how many times she told herself otherwise, she couldn't deny the truth. She wanted more, more of Malcolm's kisses. More of *him*.

And there wasn't a chance in hell she could afford to act on that desire.

Seven

The trip across the Atlantic to France passed in a blur for Celia as the time change plunged them into the night. But then her flights usually consisted of delayed connections, long layovers and lost baggage, followed by finding a cab in the heat, rain or snow.

Thanks to Malcolm's influence, she'd experienced superstar posh luxury and speed. Even sending in her grades had seemed surreal as she'd sat at a decked-out business center on the plane, with a cabin steward bringing her tea and fruit.

Now the Learjet was parking at the terminal at the Paris–Charles de Gaulle Airport, the first stop on Malcolm's European tour—with his friends along.

Surprisingly, though, she'd enjoyed getting to know Hillary during the flight, and bottom line, she should be grateful for the distraction. Distraction? Okay, the *chaperone* who would help Celia hold strong in her resolve *not* to plaster herself against Malcolm again in some impulsive moment.

And there were at least a few hundred other chaperones outside waiting under the halo of halogen lights. She glided her fingers down the glass of the window, showcasing legions of fans waving signs that were both handmade and professional.

I heart Malcolm.

Marry me.

Je t'aime.

Police and airport guards formed a human wall between the fans and the carpet being rolled out to the Learjet. Screaming, crying females threw flowers and…

Panties? Ew. Gross.

The gentle hum of the plane stopped, and everyone unbuckled as the steward opened the door. Noise swelled inward, high-pitched cheers, squeals and screams. The words jumbled together, but their adoring enthusiasm for Malcolm Douglas was unmistakable. He was this generation's Harry Connick Jr. and Michael Bublé—times ten.

Chuckling, Troy scooped up a fedora and dropped it on his head. "Dude, I think there's a woman out there who wants you to autograph her breasts."

Malcolm scowled, shrugging on a blue jacket with his jeans and button-down. "We'll just have to tell her I forgot my marker."

Hillary held up her leather portfolio and said with a wicked glint in her eyes, "I'm sure I have one in here you could borrow."

"Not funny." Malcolm smiled tightly.

Celia agreed. The thought of women climbing all over him made her ill.

Troy clapped him on the back. "Where's your sense

of humor, man? You're always quick with the sarcasm when somebody else is stressed."

A joker? He hadn't been that way back in high school. He'd been intense and driven, but never sarcastic or jaded. The fact that his achieving his life's dream hadn't left him unscathed niggled at her.

"I'll be a lot less stressed after we reach the hotel. So let's get moving." Malcolm picked up Celia's floral bag and started to pass it to her.

Troy choked on a cough.

Malcolm looked at him sharply. "What now, Donavan?"

"I just never thought I'd see the day when you carried a woman's purse for her."

Celia snatched it from his hands. "It's not a purse. It's a tote bag for my computer and my wallet. My favorite bag, for that matter. I bought it from the Vera Bradley Collection—" She stopped short, wincing. "I'm not helping you, am I, Malcolm?"

"No worries," he reassured her, planting his hand between her shoulder blades with unsettling ease. "I'm confident enough in my manhood I could carry that pink flowery bag like a man purse straight into that crowd."

"Photo, please?" Troy asked. "I'd pay good money."

Celia watched them joke and laugh together as they made their way to the door, and she realized she'd never seen Malcolm with friends before. Not even eighteen years ago. He'd never had time for recreation then. Between school, work and music lessons, he'd been driven to succeed, to make his mother's hard work pay off even at the expense of any social life most teens expected as their due. What other changes were there in his life now?

They stopped in the open hatch, and the crowd roared to a fever pitch of squeals and screams. He'd earned this, fame and adulation, yet he was still a man at ease with carrying her bag. He waved to the crowd, stirring the cheers even louder.

His hand slid along her spine until his arm went around her waist, cutting her thoughts short with the shock of his solid hold.

"Malcolm?" Halting in the open hatchway, she glanced at him, confused. "What are you doing?"

"This," he warned her a second before sealing his mouth to hers.

So much for worrying about holding strong against kissing him again. He planted a lip-lock on her to end all lip-locks. The familiarity of his mouth on hers tempted Celia, and before she could think, her hand gravitated to his chest. Her fingers curled into the crisp linen of his jacket.

The crowd roared. Or was that her pulse?

Malcolm dipped her ever so slightly back, stroking her face and along her hair before guiding her upright again. Thank goodness he kept his arm around her waist, because her knees were less than steady as he ended the kiss. Her blood pounded in her ears, her fist still clenched along the lapel of his jacket.

"What the hell was that all about?" she hissed softly, trying not to look at his friends grinning behind him.

Malcolm covered her hand with his, his blue eyes holding hers with an intensity she couldn't mistake. "Making sure the world knows you're mine and anyone who touches you will have hell to pay."

He peeled her hand free then locked arms with her, starting down the metal steps onto the concrete. She held on tightly, her legs still wobbly from his kiss in front of a crowd of people and camera lenses. What about him warning her about the possibility of the press seeing them

at a B and B? Had he just said that before because he
wanted her to go with him?

Her skin chilled in spite of the warm summer breeze,
carrying the scent of flowers tossed by fans. A sleek white
limousine waited a few strides away.

Desperate to regain her balance, she angled toward
Malcolm to whisper, "I thought we were giving off the
impression of friends traveling. Casual companions. What
about how you worried the press would see us at a hotel?"

"I didn't want to claim you until you were safe."

Safe? Her feelings for him were anything but safe.
"Weren't you the one who made fun of puppy love in
the limo?"

His cerulean-blue eyes slid over her, soothing like cool
water on overheated flesh. "Darlin', this has nothing to
do with puppy love and everything to with adult passion.
With cameras in our face 24/7, it'll be impossible to carry
off a lie. Those photographers will pick up on the fact that
I want you so badly my damn teeth hurt."

Her breath hitched in her throat. "I don't know what
to say."

He stopped at the limo, waving to the crowds once
before he looked at her adoringly again. Totally an act.
Right? He waved her into the stretch limousine before
following her inside.

"Celia," he said quickly while Troy and Hillary were
still outside, "rather than lie about our attraction and
make the press all the more desperate to prove what they
already sense, it's better just to be honest about this. So
be forewarned. I'll be kissing you and touching you and
romancing you very publically and very often."

A shiver of anticipation skittered up her spine. How
would she ever withstand that kind of romantic assault?

"But I already told you. We can't do this. We can't go back. I'm not climbing into bed with you again."

She willed herself to believe it.

"It won't matter." He kissed the tip of her nose, then whispered against her skin, "Your eyes are crystal clear. The camera will pick up the truth."

She couldn't catch her breath, and her skin flushed where he touched her. Kissed her.

"Do tell, Malcolm. What truth might that be?"

"Darlin', you want me every bit as much as I want you." He stretched an arm along the back of the seat, going silent as Troy and Hillary settled in across from them.

Hillary grinned from ear to ear. "Welcome to Paris, the city of love."

Malcolm stood alone on the hotel balcony overlooking the Eiffel Tower. Celia and the Donavans had already settled into their rooms for the night, turning in now to combat jet lag.

He, however, was too restless to sleep, too caught up in the need to take Celia into his room, his bed. He used to fantasize about bringing Celia to France, taking her to concerts and proposing to her in a place with a view just like this one. Yet another dream that hadn't panned out the way he'd planned.

The whole flight, he'd found his eyes drawn to her again and again. Taking in the waves of her hair draping along her shoulder, even how she chewed her thumbnail while poring over grades, trying to decide whether or not to give a student an extra point for a better letter grade.

Everything about Celia entranced him. It always had. Even when they were kids on a playground, he'd known she was special, a dynamo with an electric personality that people wanted to be around. Other kids gravitated to her open smile, melodic laugh and her willingness to try anything. Even come to stick up for the new kid in the middle of an embarrassing-as-hell asthma attack.

Yet even then, as she'd helped him fish his inhaler out of his backpack, he'd been aware of their differences. For class parties, her mom brought a clown to set up an ice-cream bar, and his mom made cupcakes in their tiny kitchen. Such a strange thing to remember now, especially when money was no longer an issue.

He felt the weight of eyes on him and turned sharply, then relaxed.

Colonel John Salvatore stood in the open doorway, wearing his standard gray suit and red tie. The colonel worked at Interpol headquarters in Lyon, France, so it shouldn't be surprising he'd shown up here. Only surprising he'd arrived in the middle of the night.

"Good evening, sir." Malcolm didn't bother asking how Salvatore had gotten into his suite. "You could have called, you know. Anything new to report?"

"Nothing new." The retired headmaster stepped up beside him at the rail. "Just in town for your concert. Thought I would say hello, Mozart."

Mozart... Back in the day, his classmates had called him by the name of just about every composer out there since he spent so many hours playing classical music. Mostly, he played the classical stuff because it tended to chase off the other students, allowing him some peace in the crowded school.

"I appreciate the extra security, Salvatore. I mean that. I'll rest a lot easier knowing Celia's safe until the authorities can sort out the mess back home."

The colonel loosened his tie and tucked it into his pocket. "Are you sure you know what you're doing?"

With the simple discarding of his tie, Salvatore went from distant boss to caring mentor.

Malcolm shook his head, his eyes locked on the Eiffel Tower glowing in the night. "Hell, no, but I can't back away."

"Do you have some kind of vendetta against her?"

"What?" Malcolm looked back sharply, surprised the man even had to ask. "I would hope you know me better than that."

"I know how troubled you were when you showed up at the school."

"We all were." Angry. Defiant. Wanting to have a normal high-school experience but knowing damn well it was too late to go back.

"You tried to run away three times."

"I didn't want to be locked up," he said, dodging the real reason for why he'd risked everything, even jeopardizing the peace he'd brought his mother.

"You risked jail time leaving." Salvatore leaned his elbows on the railing, the ground seven floors below. Sparse traffic drove by, late-night partiers stepping into the hotel next door.

"But you never reported me." Malcolm still didn't know why, any more than he could figure out why they were discussing this now.

"Because I knew you were one of the few kids sent to that school who were actually innocent."

Malcolm straightened in surprise. He'd never once proclaimed his innocence, and everyone had assumed he was guilty. Everyone except Celia, but even she had pulled away from him in the end. Not that he could blame her. Still, hearing the colonel's unconditional confidence... It meant a lot, then and now. "How can you be so sure?"

"I'd seen enough users and dealers come through that

school to recognize one when he crossed my path. You weren't involved in drugs in any way, shape or form," he said with unmistakable certainty in his voice. "Besides, if you had a drug problem, this lifestyle would have wrecked you long ago." As if to lend weight to his words, drunken laughter drifted up from the street.

"So you believe in me because of your proof."

"The facts merely reinforced my gut. I also know that a man will do anything for his child. I understand. I would die for my kid," he said, offering a rare glimpse into himself. "I figured you took that job at the bar hoping to make enough money to support Celia and your child. You didn't want her to give up the baby, and I'm guessing you wanted to keep the child because your father abandoned you."

"Damn, Colonel." Malcolm stepped back, looking for an escape from the truth. "I thought your doctorate was in history, not psychology."

He'd relived enough of the past since seeing Celia again. He wasn't prepared for this kind of walk down memory lane, especially when the trip was a rough ride that always left him raw.

"Doesn't take a shrink to know you're protective of your mother, and you have reason to resent your biological father. So? Do you have a vendetta to fulfill? Some revenge plan in having Celia close to you?"

"No—hell, no." Malcolm denied it and meant it. The last thing he wanted was to see Celia hurt. "Celia and I are both adults now. And as for our kid, she's almost an adult, as well. So there's no going back. The notion of a redo or revenge is moot."

"Nothing's ever moot. Remember that."

He'd had enough of these pointless jabs at old wounds.

"Why don't we talk about your kid, then? Don't you have a ball game to go to or something?"

"Fine." Salvatore held up his hands. "I'll just spell it out for you. It's all well and good that you want to protect Celia. But you need to accept your feelings for that woman aren't moot if you're ever going to move forward with your life."

And with that parting shot, Salvatore disappeared as silently as he'd appeared, leaving Malcolm alone on the balcony. God, he needed to go inside and sleep, charge up for the performance, protect his voice from the night air.

Instead, he kept right on staring at the Eiffel Tower, battling a bellyful of regrets. Given what Salvatore had said, it didn't sound as if he had much chance of ever putting the past to rest. Try as he might to move on, he still carried a whole lot of guilt about what had happened. More than that, he still had feelings for Celia. Feelings that weren't going to go away just because he tried to ignore them.

In which case, maybe ignoring them was a piss-poor idea. He wasn't getting anywhere like this. So why the hell was he denying himself what he wanted most right now? There was nothing stopping him from persuading Celia to let him back into her bed.

And the concert tomorrow would be the perfect place to begin.

Toying with the twisted seed-pearl necklace, Celia stood backstage at the concert with Hillary as Malcolm gripped the mic, walking along the edge of the stage and serenading the swarms of females reaching up. Their screams combatted with the sound system pumping out his voice and the band. She'd spent a large portion of her life performing, so the lights, the parade of backup instruments and techies didn't faze her. Still, she couldn't help but be awed by the intensity of it all, the energy radiating off the thousands of people who'd come to hear Malcolm Douglas.

He'd been emphatic about her staying backstage. He didn't trust her safety out in the audience, even sitting in one of the exclusive boxes. So she watched from the sidelines, enjoying the sight of him in profile. He wore a black suit and shirt without a tie, his songs a mix of current soft-rock tunes and retro remixes of old classics.

And oh, God, his voice was stirring her every bit as much as his kiss at the airport.

At least she had Hillary to keep her company, along with another friend of theirs, Jayne Hughes. Jayne was apparently married to another reform-school buddy of Malcolm's. They'd all come out in force with their husbands to see him perform—and keep watch over her. Malcolm's friends and their wives were rock-solid loyal, no question.

While Hillary was fresh-faced, freckled and approachable in her jeans and sequined tank top, Jayne was so darn elegant and poised in her simple sheath dress that Celia resisted the urge to check her makeup. She smoothed her damp hands down the loose, silky dress she'd chosen from the racks of clothes Malcolm had ordered sent to her room. He'd been gone all day for sound checks.

The chic, blonde Jayne leaned toward her. "It's a little overwhelming."

Hillary arched up onto her toes for a better view. "And incredible."

Jayne continued, "And overwhelming."

Celia reevaluated her image of Jayne Hughes as a cool socialite as she realized the woman genuinely was worried for her. "You can go ahead and ask."

"Ask what?" Jayne answered.

"Why I'm here. Why I'm with Malcolm." She glanced at him onstage as he took his place behind a grand piano. So many times she'd sat beside him to play in tandem, or accompanied him on the guitar. Their shared appreciation of music had added layers to their relationship back then. "Or maybe you already know the story."

"Only that you and Malcolm grew up in the same town, and you've come here to get away from a stalker at home." Jayne smoothed her already perfectly immaculate hair, shoulder-length and bluntly cut. She looked every bit the casino magnate's wife, adored and pampered. Loved.

Celia shifted her attention back to the stage. Malcolm's smooth baritone washed over her, so familiar even with the richness of maturity adding more flavor to the tone. "We've known each other since we were kids, dated in high school."

Jayne tipped her head to the side. "You're different from the other women he's seen."

She wondered if they referred to the women he'd really dated or the ladies he'd been photographed with for—as he insisted—strictly publicity purposes. Still, she couldn't resist asking, "Different how?"

"You're smart," Jayne answered without hesitation.

Hillary chimed in, "Serious."

"Not clingy," Jayne continued.

Hillary added, "Literate."

They made her sound utterly boring. "Thank you for the…uh…"

"Compliment," Hillary said. "Totally. Malcolm's a lot deeper than he likes to let on."

He was. Or at least, he had been back then. And now? It was tough not to appear too hungry for these nuggets of information about Malcolm's life since they'd been apart.

Jayne tapped her foot lightly to the music, one of Malcolm's more upbeat songs. "I met Malcolm just over seven years ago. In all the time I've known him, he's never made friends beyond his school buddies. Even his manager went to the military academy with him."

Hillary held up a finger. "And he's close to his mother, of course."

Yeah, she knew that and respected him for it even though Terri Lynn had disapproved of her. Okay, more than disapproved. His mother had hated her. Celia smiled tightly, staying quiet.

Jayne's blue eyes slit with sympathy. "You must have been important to him."

"We share a lot of history." Understatement of the year.

"And we're nosy. Just ignore us both, and let's enjoy the concert."

Grateful to have the spotlight off her for now at least, she turned her attention to the stage, where the focus narrowed to a true spotlight on a lone bar stool with a guitar propped against it.

Malcolm sat, his foot on the lowest rung, and settled the guitar on his knee. "I have a new song to share with you tonight, a simple song straight from the heart...."

The heart? She resisted the urge to roll her eyes as she thought of how he'd vowed he didn't believe the love songs he sang. She watched with a new, more jaded perspective.

With the first stroke of his fingers along the strings, Celia gasped. Her stomach knotted in recognition.

Each strum of the acoustic, unplugged moment confirmed her fears, touched her soul and rattled her to her core. A completely low blow, unfair—and designed to bring her to her knees. She didn't know whether to cry or scream as he sang the first notes of the song he'd written for her years ago.

He sang "Playing for Keeps."

Eight

The strains of "Playing for Keeps" echoed in his head even after he'd finished the last encore, reminding him of a time when he'd actually believed that idea. The audience ate up the simple melody and sappy premise.

Exiting stage right, he began to doubt the wisdom of rolling out that old tune to soften up Celia. He couldn't read her face in the shadowy wings, but he damn well knew his insides were a raw mess. Thank God his Alpha Brotherhood buddies were backstage with her, a wall of protection behind her while a couple of the wives kept her company. So his pals had her back—and his—until he could get himself on level ground.

This whole trip down memory lane was a double-edged sword, but he wouldn't lose sight of the goal. He and Celia needed to see this through. To settle the past before they could move forward with the future. The applause and cheers swelling behind him meant nothing if he couldn't find some resolution with Celia.

God, she was gorgeous in a silky sapphire dress with a hint of ruffle teasing her knees. And the plunging neckline—he couldn't look away, especially as throughout the concert she'd toyed with those tiny strands of pearls twisted together. Her feminine curves had always driven him to his knees and drained him of the ability to think. But holy hell, he could feel.

Turned on and turned inside out.

He wanted to have her naked in his arms again more than he wanted air. More than he wanted another concert or even another assignment. Getting into her bed again had become his mission of the moment. She was, and always had been, the woman he wanted more than any other.

As he drew closer to her, though, he realized he'd made a big, big mistake with the song. Her lips were tight, her eyes sparking with anger and something even worse.

Pain.

Crap. The sight of her distress sucker punched him. He'd meant to tap into her emotions, not hurt her.

Stepping into the backstage shadows, he reached out to her. "Celia—"

She held up both hands, keeping an arm's distance between them. "Great concert. Fans adored that new *love* song of yours. Congratulations. Now, if you'll excuse me, I'm ready to turn in for the night. Looks like I have plenty of guards, so you're officially absolved of protective detail."

With a brittle smile, she pivoted on her heel and walked away, pushing through the crowd double-time.

Hillary Donavan studied him with perceptive eyes before nudging Jayne to join her in racing to catch up with

Celia. Bodyguards melted from the backstage melee, encircling the women in an almost-imperceptible bubble of protection.

Malcolm slumped against a pallet of backup amps. How could he win over stadiums full of people yet still be clueless when it came to this one woman?

A hand clapped him on the shoulder, and he damn near jumped out of his skin. Troy Donavan stood beside him to his left, Conrad Hughes to his right. The international casino magnate was a lot less brooding these days since he'd reconciled with his wife.

Troy thumped Malcolm between the shoulder blades again. "Woman troubles?"

"Always," Malcolm said simply.

Troy charged alongside. "My advice? Give her space—"

Conrad interrupted, "But not so long that she thinks you're avoiding her."

Troy continued, "Enough time to cool down about whatever lame-ass thing you did."

Fair enough and true enough, except, "I can't afford to give her space, not with—"

"A stalker." Troy finished his sentence. "Right. She has guards. We'll be in the room next to hers playing cards. Meanwhile, smile your way through the reporters and let's get back to the penthouse."

An offer his stressed-out brain could not resist.

The limo ride through the night streets of Paris with the Arc de Triomphe glowing in the distance was as awkward as hell. With Celia looking anywhere but at him, the others in the vehicle made small talk to fill the empty air.

Finally—thank God, finally—they reached their historic hotel. The women smiled their way past reporters as they charged up the steps between stone lions. And before Malcolm could say "What the hell?" he found himself staring at Celia's closed door in the penthouse suite.

He turned back to the spacious living room connecting all the bedrooms. While he tried not to take the wealth for granted, the carved antiques and gilded wood were wasted on him tonight. His longtime buddies were all doing a piss-poor job of covering their grins.

"Gentlemen." Malcolm scrubbed a hand over his bristled jaw. "There's no reason for the rest of you to hang out here in the doghouse with me. Granted, it's a luxurious doghouse. So enjoy your cards and order up whatever you want on my tab. But I'm done for the night."

Troy straddled a chair at the table in the suite's dining area. "Like hell. We're not letting you check out on us any more than you would let us leave. The rest of our party should be arriving right about—"

The private elevator to the penthouse dinged with the arrival of...

The rest of the party? Crap.

The brass doors slid open in the hall to reveal three men, each one an alumni of the North Carolina Prep School. Alpha Brotherhood comrades. And recruits of Salvatore for Interpol.

Malcolm's concerts gave them the perfect excuse for reunions. First out of the elevator, Elliot Starc, a Formula One driver who'd just been dumped by his fiancée for playing as hard and fast as he drove. Behind him, Dr. Rowan Boothe, the golden-boy saint of the bunch who devoted his life to saving AIDS/HIV orphans in Africa. And lastly, Malcolm's manager, Adam Logan, aka The Shark, who would do anything to keep his clients booked and in the news.

Shoving away from the window, Malcolm shrugged

off his jacket, which still bore the hint of sweat from the concert. "We're gonna need a bigger table."

His manager grinned. "Food and drinks are on the way up." He took his chair at the far side. "There are going to be a lot of brokenhearted fans out there once they realize this thing with Celia isn't just a new fling."

There was no escaping his pals, who knew him so well. Better to meet their questions head-on—and bluff. "Logan, I don't have a clue what you're talking about."

Conrad shuffled the cards smoothly. "Seriously, brother, you're going to play it that way?"

The saintly doctor dropped into a seat. "I thought you were over her."

"Clearly, I'm not," he said tightly and too damn truthfully. Everywhere he looked in the room, he already saw reminders of her—and it was just a hotel room, for God's sake.

Elliot poured himself a drink at the fully stocked bar. "Then why the hell did you stay away for eighteen years? It's all I can do to stay away from Gianna since she gave me my walking papers."

When had his brothers started ganging up on him? "That's the way Celia wanted things then. Now our lives are very different. We've moved on."

His manager tapped his temple. "Two musicians who're obviously attracted to each other. Hmm…still not tracking your logic on being wrong for each other."

"Breaking up was best for her," Malcolm answered, irritation chewing his already churning gut. "I wrecked her life once. I owe it to her not to do that again."

Logan kept right on pressing. "So even though you let her go, you've been making billions to show up her old man."

"Or maybe I enjoy nice toys."

Troy tipped back in his chair, smoothing a hand down his designer tie. "You're sure as hell not spending it on clothes."

"Who appointed you the fashion police?" Malcolm unbuttoned his cuffs and rolled up his sleeves. "Start dealing. I'll be back."

He strode over to the bulletproof window for a better signal and pulled out his phone to check for messages from Salvatore. He'd seen his old mentor in a private box at the performance, a glamorous woman at his side. But even when he socialized, the colonel was never off the clock. Malcolm's email filled with data from Salvatore's intelligence on the principal Celia had been "sort of seeing." His references, his awards and a dozen other ways he was an all-around great guy.

So why didn't he have even partial custody of his kids? Strange, especially for a principal. Malcolm typed an answer to Salvatore then shut down his phone.

He turned, finding the saintly doc lounging in the doorway.

"Damn, Rowan," Malcolm barked, "you could have spoken or something to let me know you were there."

"You sound a little hoarse there, buddy. Is the concert tour already wearing on your vocal cords? I can check you over if you're having trouble."

"I'm fine, thanks." He clipped his phone to his belt, and still Elliot didn't move. "Anything else?"

"As a matter of fact, yes, there is," the golden boy pressed, but then he never gave up trying to fix the world. "Why are you tearing yourself up this way by being with her again?"

"You're the good guy. I would think you'd understand. I let her down once." Malcolm started toward his bedroom door to ditch his sweaty coat and give himself a chance to regain his footing. "I need to make up for that. I have to see this through."

"And you'll just walk away when you figure out who's after her?" he asked, his sarcasm making it all too clear he didn't believe it for a second.

"She doesn't want the kind of life I lead, and no way do I fit into hers now." The last thing he wanted was to go back to Azalea, Mississippi. "I promised myself I wouldn't get involved. What she and I had was just puppy love."

"What happens if someone breaks into her house next month? Or a student lets the air out of her tires? Are you going to come running to her side?"

Rowan's logic set Malcolm's teeth on edge.

"Quit being an ass." He charged past, back into the living room.

His manager leaned back in his chair and called over to him, "Quit being delusional. Either claim the woman or don't. But time to commit to a course."

"Damn it, Adam," Malcolm growled, closing in on the round table. "Do you think you could speak a little softer? I don't think they heard you over in Russia."

He looked down the hallway toward Celia's room. Once he was confident the door wouldn't open with an angry Celia, he sat as Conrad dealt the cards.

"Claim her?" the casino magnate repeated. "I can almost hear my wife laughing at you if she heard that. Brother, they claim us. Body and soul."

Elliot grimaced, "You're sounding like one of those sappy songs of Malcolm's... 'Playing for Keeps'? Really, dude? Be straight with us. You wrote that one to get some action."

Malcolm bit back the urge to haul him out of the chair and punch him the way he'd done when Elliot ran off at the mouth in school. Only the image of Celia's pained face made him hold back, humbling him with how much he'd screwed up somehow. "Hope you're going to be happy growing old alone with your race cars and a cat." He gathered his cards. "Now, are we playing poker or what?"

Even as he pretended to shrug off what his friends had said, he couldn't deny their words had taken root. For tonight, he would let her cool down. But come morning, he needed to quit thinking about seducing Celia and actually get down to the business of romancing his way back into her bed. Romancing her, seducing her, was not the same as falling for her. He could make the distinction and so could Celia.

And by learning that, they could both quit glorifying what they'd shared in the past and move on.

Celia tipped her face toward the morning sun, the boat rolling gently under her feet as it chugged along the Seine River. Hillary Donavan told her they'd set up a private ride for their group to see some of the city before they flew out for the next stop on the tour. Such a large group of friends and their wives. While she understood their school connection, she wondered why Malcom's entourage included such luminaries. Usually artists traveled with lesser folk, always remaining the star of their circle. But Malcolm traveled with very high-placed friends from an array of backgrounds. His lack of ego was…appealing.

Gusts channeled down the canal, fluttering her gauzy blouse against her oversensitive skin. She needed this breather before she saw Malcolm again. He hadn't been in the limo with them this morning, and she'd pushed down the kick of disappointment. No doubt he must be sleeping in, exhausted after the performance.

Taking in the image of the Eiffel Tower set against the

backdrop of the historic city, she appreciated the thought-fulness, as well as the chance to escape the hotel suite. She needed this opportunity to air out her mind before they climbed onto the claustrophobic luxury jet again.

The restless night's sleep hadn't done much to settle her tumultuous nerves over how Malcolm had used that piece of their history—onstage, no less—to play with her emotions. He'd always been driven, but she'd never expected him to be ruthless. Her hair lifting in the breeze, she gripped the brass railing of the boat powering along the canal.

"Why are you ignoring me?" a male voice rumbled behind her.

Malcolm's voice.

Rich, intoxicating tones that sent a shiver down her spine.

Her toes curled in her sandals.

Celia turned on her heel to face him, leaning back against the rail. How much longer before his voice stopped making her knees go shaky? Plus the sight of him? Equally dreamy. The past and present blended in his look of faded jeans with designer loafers and a jacket. He wore a ball cap and sunglasses, likely to hide his identity, but she would have known him anywhere.

And just her luck, all of his buddies were making tracks to the other side of the boat, leaving her here. Alone. With Malcolm.

She blinked back the sparks of the morning sun behind his broad shoulders. "I thought you were still at the hotel asleep when I left."

"I came to the boat ahead of the rest of you, slipped on board with the boat captain to reduce the chances of the press finding me." He captured a lock of her hair trailing in the wind and tucked it behind her ear. "Back to my question. Why did you avoid me *last night,* after the concert?"

"Ignoring you?" She angled her head away from his stirring touch. "Why would I do that? We're not in junior high school."

"You haven't spoken to me since those few brief—vague—words after the concert last night." He frowned, shoving his hands into the pockets of his jeans. "Are you pissed because I kissed you on the plane?"

"Should I be upset that you kissed me without asking?" A kiss that still made the roots of her hair tingle. "Or should I be angry about the photos of us together plastered all over tabloids and magazines? Oh, and let's not forget TV gossip shows. We're—and I quote—'The Toast of Paris.'"

"So that is why you've refused to talk to me." He pressed a thumb against his temple, just below the ball cap.

"Actually, I got over that. But the way you mocked me by playing a song you wrote about us in high school—" her anger gained steam "—a song you recently called a puppy-love joke? Now, *that* made me mad."

"Damn it, Celia." He hooked a finger in a belt loop on her jeans and tugged her toward him. "That wasn't my intention."

"Then what did you intend?" she asked, unable to read his eyes behind those sunglasses. She flattened her palms on his chest to keep from landing flush against him, body to body. Still, with their faces a breath apart, her heart skipped a beat.

"Hell, I just wanted to pay tribute to what we shared as teenagers. Not to glorify it, but certainly not to mock it," he said with unmistakable sincerity. "We did share something special back then. I think we can share that again."

Air wooshed from her lungs, making it almost impossible to talk. The sound of the flowing water alongside the boat echoed the roar of blood rushing through her veins. Her fingers curled in the warmth of his jacket. "You missed the mark big-time in getting your meaning across on the stage, Malcolm."

"Let me make it up to you." Pulling off the shades, he rested his forehead against hers, the power of his deep blue gaze bathing her senses.

"You don't have to do anything. You're protecting me from a stalker. If anything, I owe you." She squeezed his jacket tighter. "But that's all I owe you."

His hand slid around her. "I don't want you feeling indebted to me."

Her face tipped to his, so close to kissing, so close to bliss. Her mouth tingled in anticipation. It was getting tougher and tougher to remember why this was a bad idea. The roaring of the water and her pulse grew louder and louder until she realized it wasn't the river or her heartbeat.

"Damn it, the press," Malcolm barked softly, stepping back and sliding his sunglasses on again.

Paparazzi ran along the shore with cameras in hand. Shouts carried on the wind, disjointed phrases.

"—Douglas."

"Kiss her—"

Celia raced alongside him toward the captain's cabin. "I thought you intended for us to kiss for the camera."

"Changed my mind," he called, pulling open the door. "Keeping you happy suddenly became a higher priority."

He tucked her inside, the boat captain glancing over in surprise. Malcolm waved for him to carry on. Apparently Elliot Starc hadn't him given boat-driving lessons, too, she thought, hysterical laughter starting to bubble inside her. Her nerves were seriously fraying.

"What now?" she asked.

Malcolm nodded to the floral bag dangling from her arm. "You could answer your phone."

She looked down fast, the chiming surprising her until she almost jumped out of her skin. "I didn't even hear it."

Fishing inside, she dug through until her hand closed around the phone. She pulled it out and saw her father's number blinking on the screen.

"Hello, Dad. What do you need?"

"Just checking on my baby girl," he said, concern coating every word, "making sure you're all right. I, uh, saw the newspapers this morning."

She grimaced, avoiding Malcolm's eyes. "I'm fine. The pictures were…staged. It's all a part of making sure everyone knows I'm very well protected here in Malcolm's entourage."

"Staged, huh?" her father answered skeptically. "I never knew you were a theater person, because that was some mighty fine acting in the photo."

Her chest tightened with every word from her father. "I don't know what more I can tell you."

"Well, I've been fielding calls all day."

"From the press?" The thought of them hounding her dad made her swallow hard—not easy to do when she was finding it tougher and tougher to breathe.

"My number's unlisted. You know that. The calls are from your friends at school, even that high-school principal you went out with a couple of times."

"I didn't go out with him." She glanced at Malcolm quickly as the enormity of this washed over her. Being with Malcolm now had changed her life in ways she could never undo. Her ordered existence was falling apart. She was losing control—but for once, that didn't seem to be such a bad thing. "We just happened to sit together at events we both attended for work."

"Who drove?"

"Stop it, Dad," she snapped, then backtracked, guilt pinching her. She started pacing restlessly in the small cabin. "I love you, and I appreciate your concern, but I'm an adult."

"Malcolm's standing there with you, isn't he?"

"Why does that matter?" And why couldn't she bring herself to just end the call? God, she hated being caught between them again.

Her father sighed through the phone lines. "Just protect yourself, Celia. You'll always be my baby girl."

His voice stirred more guilt as she thought of his pain over losing his oldest daughter. She pressed a hand to her head, dizzy from lack of breakfast and, yes, pangs of guilt. She thought of her own ache for the baby she'd given up, but at least she knew her child was alive somewhere, growing up loved. Worrying for her father heaped on top of her nerves, which were already stretched to the max by trying to sort through her feelings for Malcolm.

"Dad, I promise I'm being very careful." She measured her words carefully, trying not to let her perceptive father hear the quaver in her voice. "And you? Are you okay? Have you gotten any threatening messages?"

"I'm fine. Blood pressure is in the good zone, and there hasn't been so much as a peep of a threat."

"Thank God," she said, praying that wouldn't change. "I really do appreciate the call. Love you, Dad."

Her heartbeat sped up, new worries crowding her head and making her chest feel tight. Oh, no. She knew the old symptoms. Knew what might happen next if she didn't pull it together.

She thumbed the off button and dropped her phone back into her Vera Bradley bag with shaky hands. "Well, your plan is working. The whole world—even my father—thinks we're having an affair." She gasped for air, trying to fight down the encroaching panic and not succeeding all that well. "Do you think we could just go back to the hotel?"

"Are you okay?" Malcolm asked, just before she could have sworn the boat began listing to the side.

Ah, hell. She reached for Malcolm's hand just before she blacked out.

Nine

Disoriented, Celia pushed through the fog back to consciousness, confusion wrapping around her. Was it morning? Was she at home? No... She was in a *car*.

With each deep breath she inhaled, she drew in the essence of Malcolm. She knew he was beside her.

The past merged with the present, bringing memories of another time she'd fainted. When she was sixteen, she'd snuck out of her room at midnight to meet Malcolm when he finished at the burger joint where he worked after school. She'd been skipping meals because of nausea, and it had been all she could do to stay awake to meet him as promised. But talking to him had been so important. She'd needed to tell him before her parents saw the signs. Before she started to show. But before she could finish telling him, she'd passed out.

Malcolm had rushed her to the emergency room, where of course the doctor called her parents. She squeezed her eyes closed tighter even now over the explosion of anger that had erupted in that E.R. over her pregnancy. Malcolm had insisted they get married. Her father had lunged at Malcolm. Her mother had sobbed.

Celia had wanted to die....

Well, at least she knew for damn sure she wasn't pregnant now. She'd blacked out for an entirely different reason.

Slowly, she took in the feel of the leather seat of the limousine. She must have been carried and put inside. The sounds of the voices around her steadied and the cause of this fainting spell gelled in her mind. She'd been freaking out and gasping for air until she passed out on the boat. Her eyes snapped open. She was inside a limousine with Malcolm and his entire entourage of alumni pals.

He leaned over her, stroking back her hair. His buddy Dr. Rowan Boothe had her wrist in his hand, taking her pulse. The rest of their friends loomed behind them, her world narrowing to this stretch limo with tinted windows and a lot of curious, concerned faces.

How incredibly embarrassing.

She pushed up onto her elbow, sitting. "What time is it? How long have I been—"

"Whoa, whoa, hold on…" Malcolm touched her shoulders and glanced at Rowan. "Doc?"

"Her pulse is normal." Rowan set her hand aside and tucked himself back onto a seat. "I don't see any reason to go to the E.R. I can check her over more thoroughly once we're on the plane to Germany."

Malcolm moved closer again, looking unconvinced. "Are you sure you're okay? What happened back there?"

"I'm fine." She sat up straighter, blinking fast as she tried to regain equilibrium. "Probably just low blood sugar from skipping breakfast."

The lie tasted bad on her tongue. But admitting the truth? Explaining her lingering battle with panic attacks? She wasn't ready to share that.

Malcolm seemed to accept her explanation, though. His shoulders relaxed a little as he opened the mini-fridge. He passed her a bottle of orange juice and a protein bar. "No offense, beautiful, but you don't look okay."

She twisted off the cap and sipped, just to appease him and make her story more believable. What she really needed were some breathing exercises or her emergency meds. Or a way to distance herself from all the feelings Malcolm was stirring up.

She looked out the window as they drove along the shore of the Seine River.

He eyed her for five long heartbeats. "We used to understand each other well, from the second on the playground when you threw sand at that kid for making fun of my asthma attack. Now, though, I want the chance to fight back for you."

Without another word, he gave her the space she'd requested and took a seat at the far end of the stretch limo. Quite a long way. Especially with all of his friends, plus Hillary and Jayne, sitting between them and trying to pretend there wasn't a thick, awkward silence all the way to the airport.

Once the Learjet was airborne to fly them to Berlin, Malcolm continued to honor her request for space, which was actually the best way to get closer to her again. Did he remember that from their past? She fished in her floral bag for her eReader to pass the time and calm her nerves, still jangled from the incident on the boat. She had to steady herself before she ran the gauntlet for the next concert. She pulled the reader case out, her fingers fumbling with the zipper.

Dr. Boothe knelt in front of her, taking the case from her hand and opening it before setting the eReader beside her. "Want to tell me what's wrong?"

She glanced around the plane. Everyone else seemed occupied with the business station or talking in the next cabin. Hillary, an event planner, was in deep conversation with Jayne about a fundraiser in the works for Dr. Boothe's clinic—where apparently Jayne worked, as well. Even the steward was busy readying lunch in the galley.

Turning back to the fair-haired doctor, she said carefully, "I already told Malcolm. I forgot to eat breakfast, but I'm feeling better now," but he still didn't move away. "I'm just going to read until lunch. Thank you."

He picked up her wrist. "Your pulse is still racing and you're struggling for breath."

"You said back at the limo that my pulse rate was fine." She tugged her hand away.

"It wasn't Malcolm's business unless you chose to tell him."

"Thank you." She picked up her eReader pointedly. "I'll let you know if I have a heart attack. I promise."

He shifted to sit beside her. "I don't think that's what's going on here, medically speaking."

Of course it wasn't, but she didn't particularly want to trot out the details of how she'd screwed up and left her medicine at home. She didn't need it all the time, and it had been so long since she'd reached for an antianxiety pill, she'd hoped...

Dr. Boothe stretched out his legs, as if in the middle of some casual conversation. "We can make this a patient/doctor thing, and then I can't say a word to anyone else. The whole confidentiality issue."

She shot a quick look at him, and he seemed...nonjudgmental.

Weighing her options, she decided it was better to trust him and hope he could help her rather than risk another embarrassing incident. "I'm fighting down a panic attack. I left home so quickly I didn't have a chance to get my, uh, medicine. I don't have to take anything regularly anymore, but I do have a prescription for antianxiety medication. The bottle just happens to be sitting in my bathroom cabinet."

A big oversight given that she had a stalker on her tail. But oddly, the thought of being in danger like that wasn't half as scary as the resurrection of her old feelings for Malcolm. The memories of what they'd given up. She hadn't realized how deeply this time with him might affect her.

She hadn't *wanted* to admit it.

Rowan nodded slowly. "That's problematic. But not insurmountable. Your doctor can call in the prescription."

She had already thought of that. "Malcolm is so worried about the stalker back home that I can't make a move without him noticing. It's not that I'm ashamed or anything. I'm just not ready to tell him yet."

"Understood," he said simply, the window behind him revealing a small and distant Paris below. "If you'll give your doctor permission to speak with me, I can take care of a prescription."

"Thank you." The tightness in her chest began to ease at the notion of help on the horizon.

"If you don't mind my asking, when did these attacks begin?"

She recognized his question for what it was, an attempt to help talk her down. "After I broke up with Malcolm. I've had some trouble with depression and anxiety. It's not a constant, but under times of extreme stress..."

She blew out a slow breath, searching for level ground and some control over her racing pulse.

"This sure qualifies as a time of stress, with the threats back home and all the insanity of Malcolm's life."

As the engine hummed through the sky, she thought about the patients he saw on a regular basis in Africa, of their problems, and felt so darn small right now. "You treat people with such huge problems. I probably seem whiny to you, the poor little rich girl who can't handle her emotions."

"Hold on." He raised a hand. "This isn't a competition. And as I'm sure your own doctor has told you, depression and anxiety disorders are medical conditions like diabetes. Serotonin or insulin, all chemicals your body needs. And you're wise to keep watch over your health."

"But your patients—" She stopped short as Malcolm stepped away from the business center. She picked up her eReader. "Thanks, Dr. Boothe, for checking on me. I appreciate your help."

She powered up her book and pretended to read the most recent download from her book club. If only she could act her way through the rest of her problems.

But when it came to Malcolm, she'd never been all that adept at hiding her feelings—feelings that were escalating with him in such close proximity. No question, the man disrupted her well-ordered world, and she feared where that could lead.

Yet, she couldn't bring herself to say goodbye.

His suite in downtown Berlin looked much the same as their digs in Paris, except with less gild to the antiques. But then his tours usually became a blur of hotel rooms and concert halls. God knew his attempt at a bit of sightseeing for Celia in Paris hadn't played out that well. He needed to step back and rethink how to win her over.

Starting with clearing out his well-meaning, advice-peddling pals. They interfered with his plans to get Celia alone. He'd thanked them for gathering around him when he'd called them to help build a wall of protection around Celia as the concert tour started, and he appreciated their ready turnout. But the need for their help had passed. Once they left Germany, his friends would be peeling off, returning to their lives.

At least his concert in Berlin tonight had gone off without a hitch since he'd left "Playing for Keeps" off the playlist. He scanned the living room full of his friends until his eyes landed on Celia curled in a chair, her head resting on her arm as she listened to Troy turn storyteller about their school days, sharing a tale about Elliot Starc since the race-car driver had left earlier.

Not much longer and Malcolm would have Celia all to himself. Finally, they would be alone, aside from his manager. Logan knew how to make himself scarce, though, probably keeping busy working the next angle for his client. Malcolm felt like a jerk for wishing they would all hit the road now.

Part of his impatience could have something to do with what great buddies Celia and Rowan had become. More than once today, they'd sat in a corner, their heads tucked close in conversation. The good doc had even brought her a bag of pastries to make sure she ate enough.

Hell, yes, Malcolm was jealous. The guy had pastries, and Malcolm didn't even have a hint of a plan for what to do next as far as Celia was concerned. His other plans had backfired—kissing for the press, singing "Playing for Keeps." So he did what he did best. He lost himself in music, while staring at Celia's beautiful face. He hitched his guitar more securely on his knee and plucked strings softly while Troy continued his story.

"My senior year—" Troy twirled his fedora on one finger as he talked "—Elliot was new to the school and wanted to impress us, so he hot-wired one of the laundry trucks and smuggled us all out for the night. We snuck into a strip club."

Hillary snagged her husband's spinning hat from his finger. "Strip club? Seriously? This is the story you choose to tell?"

Jayne laughed softly, snuggling into the crook of her husband's arm. "Someone's sleeping alone tonight."

Troy spread his hands wide. "Let me finish. We quickly figured out the club wasn't anything like we'd seen in the movies. The women looked...weary. A couple of the guys wanted to stay but most of us left and went to a pancake house that stayed open all night."

Malcolm remembered the night well. He'd opted to stay in the truck, in a crummy mood because it was Celia's birthday and he resented like hell that he remembered. He'd been aching for her.

Not much had changed.

Hillary dropped her husband's hat onto her head. "I'm not sure I believe you."

Troy kissed his wife's head. "I would never lie to you, babe."

Hillary rolled her eyes. "I'm assuming Elliot went with them to the pancake house since otherwise how would you have gotten the truck started?"

Conrad raised his hand. "Me, too, for the record. I did not stay at the strip club, just so we're clear. I had pancakes with blueberry syrup, extra bacon on the side. Waitresses fully clothed."

Jayne thunked him in the stomach. "Enough already."

Their ease with each other reminded Malcolm of what he and Celia once had—and lost.

Celia hugged a throw pillow. "Why did Elliot end up at the school?" She glanced at Malcolm. "Is that okay to ask?"

"It's in his public bio, so it's no secret." Malcolm sat in the wingback chair beside her—before Rowan could claim the seat—and continued to strum the guitar idly, playing improvised riffs and breathing in the praline-sweet scent of her. "His Wikipedia page states that Elliot was sent to the school for stealing cars. In reality, he took his stepfather's caddy out for a spin and smashed it into a guardrail."

The calm seeped from Celia's face. "Seems like a rather extreme punishment for a joyride."

Malcolm slowed his song, searching for a way to steer the conversation in another direction so she would smile again.

Troy answered, "Multiple joyrides. Multiple wrecks. His stepfather was beating the crap out of him. He wanted to get caught or die. Either way, he was out of his house."

Celia leaned forward. "Why wasn't his stepfather stopped and prosecuted?"

"Connections, a family member on the police force. Lots of warnings, but nothing happened."

Her lips went tight, and she shook her head. "His mother should have protected him."

"Damn straight," Troy agreed. "But I'm sliding off my path here. Let's get back to more entertaining brotherhood tales, like the time a few of us were stuck staying at school over Christmas break. So we broke into Salvatore's office, spread dirt on the floor and tossed quick-grow grass seed. He had a lawn when he returned. He knew we did it, but the look on his face was priceless...."

Malcolm started strumming again, adding his own impromptu score to Troy's tales, but his brain was still stuck on the moment Celia asked why Elliot's mother hadn't protected him. Her reaction was so swift, so instinctive he couldn't avoid the image blaring in his brain. An image of Celia as the mother of his child, fiercely doing everything in her power to protect their baby. He'd been so frustrated—hell, angry—for so long over losing the chance to see his kid that he hadn't fully appreciated how much she'd been hurt.

And damn it all, that touched him deep in his gut in a way that had nothing to do with sex. Right now, he had less of a clue about what to do with this woman than he had eighteen years ago.

The next night, after Malcolm's concert in the Netherlands, Celia put together a late-night snack in their suite. Foraging through the mini-fridge, she found bottles of juice, water and soda, along with four kinds of cheese. She snagged the Gouda and Frisian clove to go with the crackers and grapes on the counter.

Yes, she was full of nervous energy since Malcolm's friends had all gone home. Now she was finally alone with him. How strange that she'd resented their presence at first and now she felt antsy without the buffer they'd provided. Malcolm's manager had stood backstage with her at the concert tonight in Amsterdam. But Logan had his own room here on another floor.

Not that Malcolm had pressured her since they'd checked into the posh hotel. In fact, since her panic attack during the Seine River tour, he'd backed off. On the one hand, she'd wanted him to quit tempting her, but on the other it hurt to think he was turned off by her anxiety.

They had a two-bedroom suite with a connecting sit-

ting room. He was showering, the lights having been
particularly powerful—and hot—tonight at yet another
sold-out show.

As she heard the shower in the next room stop, she
arranged the food on a glazed pottery tray to keep her
hands busy and her thoughts occupied with something
other than wondering how different the adult, naked Malcolm looked. And what he thought of the "adult" her. She
smoothed her hands down her little black dress, lacy, with
a scalloped hem that ended just above the knee. Should
she rush and change?

She shook off vanity as quickly as she kicked off her
heels and loosened her topknot. Lifting the tray with food
and a pot of tea, she angled around the bar, past the baby
grand piano and into the living area.

Overall the room was brighter, lighter than the other
places they'd stayed, the Dutch decor closer to her personal style. On her way past, she dipped her head to sniff
the blue floral pitcher full of tulips. She placed the tray
on top of the coffee table and curled up on the sofa with
her tea. She'd made a pot with lemon and honey to soothe
Malcolm's throat after three straight nights of concerts.
He had to be feeling the effects.

The door to his bedroom opened, and her eyes were
drawn directly to him. So drawn. Held. He stood bare-
foot, wearing a pair of jeans and T-shirt that clung to his
damp skin. His hair was wet and slicked back. And God,
did her hands ache to smooth over those damp strands.

What else did she want?

Silly question. She wanted to sleep with Malcolm
again, to experience how it would feel to be with him
as a woman. All the tantalizing snippets his friends had
shared of his past and present drew her in, seducing her
with both the Malcolm he'd been and the Malcolm he'd

become. She burned to sleep with him, and she couldn't come up with one good reason why she shouldn't.

Would she have the courage to throw caution to the wind and act on what she wanted? "I made us something to eat—as well as tea with lemon and honey to soothe your throat."

"Thanks, but you don't have to wait on me," he answered, his voice more gravelly than usual, punctuating her point about the need for tea. He walked deeper into the room, his hand grazing a miniature wooden windmill, tapping the blades until they spun in a lazy circle.

"Direct orders from your manager," Celia said. "You're to have something to eat and drink, protect your health for the tour."

"What about you? Any more dizzy spells today?" He sliced off a sliver of Gouda. "Here…have some cheese."

She rested her fingers on his wrist, a small move, just a test run to see how he would react. "I'm good. I promise. Your pal the doctor gave me two thumbs up."

Malcolm eyes narrowed before he tossed the cheese into his mouth and paced restlessly around the room, past the baby grand piano, a guitar propped against the side. "You two seemed to hit it off."

Wondering where he was going with the discussion of Rowan, she poured another cup of steaming-hot tea. "What exactly did he invent?"

Malcolm dropped onto the other end of the sofa and reluctantly took the tea. "He devised a new computerized diagnostic model with Troy. They patented it, and they both made a bundle. Essentially, Rowan can afford to retire if he wishes."

Interesting, but not surprising given what she'd gleaned about Malcolm and all his friends. "And he chose to work

in a West African clinic instead. That's very altruistic
of him."

"You can join the Rowan Boothe fan club. It's large."

She lifted an eyebrow in shock. "You don't like him?"

"Of course I do. He's one of my best friends. I would
do anything for him. I'm acting like a jealous idiot because you two seemed to hit it off." He tossed back the
tea, then cursed over the heat. He set the cup down fast
and charged over to the mini-fridge for bottled water.

He was jealous? Of her and Rowan? Hope fluttered.

She set her cup down carefully. "Your charitable donations have been widely reported. Every time I saw you
at an orphanage or children's hospital… I admire what
you've done with your success, Malcolm, and yes, I have
kept up with you the way you've kept up with me."

Malcolm downed the bottle of water before turning
back to her. "Rowan's the stable, settle-down sort you
keep swearing you want now. But damn it all, I still want
you. So if you want him or someone like him, you'd better speak up now, because I'm about five seconds away
from kissing you senseless."

"You silly, silly man." She pushed to her feet and
walked toward him. "You have nothing to be jealous of.
I was asking for his medical help."

"What did you say?" He pinned her with a laser stare.
"Are you ill? God, and I've been hauling you from country to country."

"Malcolm, stop. Listen. I have something I need to
tell you." She drew in a bracing breath and willed her
fluttering pulse to steady. Before they got to the kissing-
senseless part, she needed to be sure he was okay with
what had happened during the boat ride. Trusting him—
anyone—with this subject was tough. But she hoped she
could have faith in the genuine, good man she'd seen

earlier with his friends. "I was having a regular, old-fashioned panic attack."

He blinked uncomprehendingly for a few seconds before clasping her shoulders. "Damn it, Celia, why didn't you tell me, instead of—"

She rested a hip against the baby grand piano. "Because you would have acted just like this, freaking out, making a huge deal out of it, and believe me, that's the last thing I could have handled yesterday."

Comprehension slid across his leanly handsome face. "Rowan helped you. As a doctor." He plowed his fingers through his hair. "God, I'm such an idiot."

"Not an idiot. Just a man." She sighed with relief to finally have crossed this hurdle without a drawn-out ordeal. "I left my medicine at home. He helped connect with my doctor and get my prescription refilled."

"You've had panic attacks before?"

"Not as often as I used to, but yes, every now and again."

His shoulders rolled forward as he rubbed his forehead. "The concert tour was probably a bad idea. What was I thinking?"

"You had no way of knowing because I didn't tell you." She couldn't let him blame himself. She stroked his forehead for him, nudging aside his hand. Just a brief touch, but one that sent tingles down her arm. "Staying home with some criminal leaving dead roses in my car wasn't particularly pleasant, either. For all we know, I would have had more anxiety back home. You've taken on a major upheaval in your life to help me."

"Are you okay now?" He reached for her, stopping just short of touching her as if afraid she would break.

"Please don't go hypercautious with me." She eased back to sit on the piano bench. "I felt much better after a good night's sleep. The medicine isn't an everyday thing. Not anymore. The prescription is just on an as-needed basis. And while I needed help yesterday, today's been a good day."

He sat beside her, his warm, hard thigh pressing against her. "When did the panic attacks start? Is that okay to ask?"

Gathering her thoughts grew tougher with the brush of his leg against hers. "I had trouble with postpartum depression after... The doctor said it was hormonal, and while the stress didn't help, it wasn't the sole cause—" she pointed at him "—so don't start blaming yourself."

He clasped a hand around her finger, enfolding her hand in his. "Easier said than done."

"You are absolved." She squeezed gently, her heart softening the rest of the way for this man. She'd never had any luck resisting him, and she wondered why she'd ever assumed now would be different. "And I mean that."

"After what happened yesterday, I'm not so sure I can buy into that." Guilt dug deep furrows in his lean face.

"You have to." She cupped his cheek in her palm, the bristle of his late-day beard a seductive abrasion against her palm. Until, finally, she surrendered to the inevitable they'd been racing toward since the minute he'd walked back into her life again. "Because I desperately want to make love with you, and that's not going to happen if you're feeling guilty or sorry for me."

Ten

Malcolm wondered what the hell had just happened.

He'd been turning himself inside out to come up with a plan to romance Celia back into his bed, except then he'd been derailed by thoughts that Rowan was a better man for her, then by concerns for her health and how best to approach her in light of all she'd just told him.

Instead, she propositioned him when he was doing… absolutely nothing.

God, he would never understand Celia Patel. He'd also never been able to turn her down. "Are you sure this is what you want? It's been a stressful couple of days and I want you to be certain."

"I may have had a panic attack yesterday, but I am completely calm and certain of this." Her fingers curved around the back of his neck, her touch cool, steady… seductive. "You and I need to stop fighting the inevitable. I could have sworn you felt the same."

"I do." His answer came out hoarse and ragged, and that had nothing to do with hours of singing. No second thoughts, he reached for her. He gathered her against him. Finally, he had her in his arms again.

Kissing her was as natural as breathing. She sighed her pleasure and agreement, her lips parting for him. A hint of lemon and honey clung to her tongue. His body went harder, his need for her razor-sharp after so damn long without her. No matter how many years had passed, he'd never forgotten her or how perfect she felt in his arms. Better yet, how perfect she felt coming apart in his arms.

Pulling her closer, he stood, guiding her to her feet, as well. Her fingers plowed through his hair, tugging lightly, just hard enough to increase the pleasure. She took his mouth as fully as he took hers. Owning. Stamping possession of each other.

The press of her body against him, the roll of her hips against his, the soft give of her full breasts against his chest ramped up his pulse rate. The heat of her reached through their clothes, tempting him with how much hotter they would feel skin to skin.

His hands roved up her back, into her hair—this woman had the most amazing mass of hair. The curls tangled around his fingers as if every part of her held him, caressed him. He swept the tangled mass over her shoulder and found the top of her zipper. He tugged the tab down the back of her lacy black dress, stroking along her spine as he revealed inch after inch of the softest skin. The scent of her soap, her light fragrance, teased him, and he dragged in a deep breath to take it in.

Hungry to feel more of her, he tucked his hands in the open V of her dress and palmed the satin-covered globes of her bottom. He guided her hips closer as she rocked against him in response, the perfect fit sending his pulse throbbing louder in his ears. The sound of her ragged breathing stoked the heat in him higher, hotter as he kissed along her jaw, the delicate shell of her ear. She whispered her need for more, faster, and damned if he could scrounge the restraint to hold back.

Later, once they'd both taken the edge off, he would go slower. Oh, so much slower, taking his time rediscovering her all night long with his hands and his mouth.

He stroked up her back again, enjoying the goose bumps of pleasure rising on her skin. Cupping her shoulders, he slid the sleeves of her gown to the side, baring her skin and the satin straps of her bra. She was even more damn beautiful than he remembered, with pinup-girl curves that all but sent him to his knees from aching to be inside her again.

A growl of possessiveness rolled up his throat as he peeled the lacy dress down her body, revealing those curves that had threatened to drive him to his knees. He nipped and tasted along her satin bra, kneeling and taking the center clasp between his teeth for a sensual instant before releasing it again, leaving it in place. For now. He skimmed the dress farther down. Fabric hitched on her hips. Pressing his face to her stomach, he inhaled more of her floral scent.

"Cecelia Marie." He sighed her whole name against her, repeating again and again.

Her fingers tangled in his hair, a flush of desire spreading over her skin, encouraging him to continue. He swept her gown down to pool around her bare feet, and ah, she wore black thigh-highs that just begged for him to peel one, then the other, down her smooth legs. He gathered the shimmery hose in his hand, soaking in the residual heat of her before he set them reverently aside.

He rocked back on his heels and took in the sight of

her in black satin panties and a bra. His fantasies didn't look this good, and he'd fantasized about this woman many, many times.

"Malcolm?" A quaver threaded through her voice before she steadied it. "Are you going to sit there all night? Because I have urgent plans for you."

"Plans?" He laughed softly, grateful she didn't intend to roll out questions or doubts. She was keeping things light. "Tell me more."

"Plans for us on the sofa, in the shower and, eventually, in the bed. But the more I talk, the more time we waste. So come back up here and I'll start showing you instead." She tugged him to his feet again to kiss her.

Not that he needed much persuasion to claim her plump mouth. To claim her.

Her tongue met his in bold, familiar touches and strokes. She tugged at his T-shirt, easing back only long enough to yank it over his head. The gust of the air conditioner cooled his overheated flesh, and then she touched him. The feel of her hands against his stomach, along the fastening of his jeans, threatened to send him over the edge. He'd never been good at self-control with her. That thought alone offered enough of a splash of cold water for him to think rationally.

To be smart.

To protect her in the way he hadn't before.

"One second. Wait." He stepped back, his breathing ragged.

"Are you kidding me?" She sagged against the baby grand, and the sight of her in that pose gave him even more ideas about how he planned to spend this night.

Once he took care of one very important detail.

"Birth control," he called as he backed toward his

room, holding up a hand. "Stay right where you are. As you are. Don't move." He smiled. "Please.

A quick sprint to his suitcase, and he returned with a condom in hand. Only to halt in his tracks, mesmerized to his core. Celia had been beautiful and sexy as a teenager. She was a gorgeous, sensual woman now.

She still leaned against the baby grand as he'd requested, her satin underwear a bold contrast to her skin. Her long, dark wavy hair draped over her shoulder, skimming her skin the way he intended to very, very soon.

He tore off his jeans and boxers on the way over to her, but not nearly fast enough. Her mouth curved into a sultry smile as she eye-stroked the erection straining against his stomach. She stretched out an arm and stopped him from pressing flush against her.

Holding his gaze deliberately, seductively, she thumbed open the center clasp of her bra and let the straps slide the rest of the way off until the scrap of satin dropped to the floor. She swept away her panties and kicked them to the side.

"Celia," he groaned, "you're absolutely slaying me."

Her smile wavered. "I assure you, the feeling is entirely mutual. It always has been."

His mouth dried up, and he reached out to skim the back of his knuckles along the curve of her breasts. His body throbbed impossibly harder at just one touch to her naked flesh. And then both her palms flattened against his chest, her nails grazing him lightly—down, then up again to curl around his shoulders. She urged him toward her, body to body, his hard length flat against her stomach, and he almost came undone right then. He needed to regain control, and soon. That fantasy he'd envisioned when he'd seen her posed against the piano came blazing through his mind again, an image he could make a reality now.

He eased his body from her, still holding her face, kissing her until the very last second. And once more. Her hands grappled to hold on to him, and he almost gave in. But he had a mission.

Trailing a hand along her stomach, he walked around to the side of the piano, removed the prop and closed the sleek ebony lid.

Celia tipped her head to the side. "Care to clue me in on what you're doing?"

He clasped her waist and lifted her onto the piano. "I'm doing this. Any objections?"

Her eyes lit with approval. "None whatsoever."

He stepped closer, parting her legs with his body. Her ankles hooked around his back, and she drew him in with the press of her heels. Her arms looped around his neck. She kissed him fully, with a maturity and passion that made their teenage affair fade in his memory. This moment with her, now, the passion combusting between them, burned away everything else.

She was his again.

The impact of that reality thrummed through his veins. He kissed along her jaw, down the vulnerable curve of her neck. He took his time with her breasts even though he ached with the need to be inside her.

But he needed to be certain she was every bit as absolutely on fire for him as he was for her. He took one pebbled nipple in his mouth, tempting her with his tongue and his teeth until her head fell back and her hips rolled against him. He held on to control by a thread, such a thin edge he knew he needed to bring her to completion now, because once he buried himself deeply inside her, restraint would be damn difficult to scavenge.

His hands glided down her spine, lowering her back as he kissed lower and lower still until she reclined along the piano. Her beautiful naked body sprawled on top of the sleek ebony grand took his breath away. Her hair trailed over the side of the piano in silken waves. He would never forget this picture of her as long as he lived. She was burned in his memory, on his soul.

He trekked along her body until he reached the core of her, damp and needy for him. He nudged her legs farther apart and nuzzled her essence, tasted her and teased her until her head thrashed back and forth. Her breathy moans of pleasure filled the air with a music that had seduced him then and now.

Her sighs grew to a crescendo that flowed through him, her back arching with the power of her release. He pressed a final kiss to her, then another against her stomach before he stood again.

And as the final ripples of aftershocks shivered through her, he scooped the condom from the corner of the piano and sheathed himself. Clasping her knees, he leaned over her and nudged inside, fully, deeply. He groaned at the total bliss of being exactly where he belonged. The warm clamp of her body gripping, pulsing around him nearly finished him before he could move, and oh, how much he wanted to move inside her. And move again, and again, filling her with each rocking thrust.

Her arms splayed, she gripped the sides of the piano to anchor herself to meet him, locking him more firmly with her legs around his waist. Guiding him. Holding him. With him every second of the way as she came undone with him all over again, their shouts of completion twining together.

Gasping with the power of what they'd shared, he leaned over her, blanketed her. He buried his face in her hair, their naked bodies slick and sealed with perspiration. With each steadying inhale of her sweet, floral scent, he knew.

Even if those threats against her evaporated in the morning, there wasn't a chance in hell he could let her go.

Celia sat naked on the silk sheets in Malcolm's bedroom, her body flushed and languid from making love on the piano. Against the wall. In the bed. In the shower.

Now they were in bed again. Or rather, she was. He'd stepped into the living area for the tray of cheese and fruit.

They'd stayed up most of the night, and not just making love. He'd brought his guitar into the room about halfway through the night and sang her the silliest made-up songs. She'd laughed until her sides ached, then taunted him by taking the guitar and composing her own ditties in return.

They would leave for London in the morning. She could sleep on the plane. For now, she intended to make the most of this night with Malcolm, because thinking about the future felt too uncertain, and she refused—absolutely refused—to do anything that would risk triggering a panic attack.

Angling to the side, she grasped the neck of his guitar and lifted it from the chair by the bed. She tucked it in place, scooped a pick from the bedside table and plucked through a riff of her own, not as intricate as his by any stretch, but she loved music. Loved that they shared this between them.

Their night together had been too perfect. Too special. She didn't want to think about threats at home or what the future held.

Malcolm strode through the door, gloriously naked and

all man. Muscles filled out his lean lines, sandy-brown hair dusting along his bronzed skin. He set a large silver tray in the middle of the bed, having added bottles of sparkling water to go with the food.

"What are you playing? An ode to my masterful… pick?"

"Ha, you're a comedian *and* a rock star. Imagine that." Laughing, she started to set aside the guitar.

He stopped her with a touch to the wrist. "Don't let me keep you from playing. I'm enjoying the music and the view."

"We can 'play' more later." She set aside the guitar and plucked free a handful of grapes. "Right now, I'm starving."

He settled beside her, careful not to tip the tray on the thick, downy comforter. "I'm sorry you didn't get to see more of Amsterdam. After we arrive in London tomorrow, we'll have an evening to ourselves, a day's break before two nights of concerts, then on to Madrid." He twisted open one of the chilled bottles and poured water into the two crystal glasses. "I feel bad that you haven't had much sightseeing or relaxation while we were in some of the most beautiful cities in the world. Choose whatever you want to do on the day off."

"More of what we're doing right now." She pressed a grape to his lips.

"No arguments from me." He bit free the fruit, nipping her fingers lightly.

Purring, she leaned forward to kiss him quickly, the sweet taste lingering on his mouth. "We'll lock ourselves in the hotel—"

"Actually, I have personal accommodations in London." He toyed with a lock of her hair, still damp from the shower they'd shared.

"Oh, that's right. Your mother has a flat there." She rocked back, taking her water glass, avoiding his eyes. Would Terri Ann be more open to her presence in Malcolm's life this go-round? If not, it could be quite awkward staying in an apartment together.

"I have a house in London, as well. I bought it to spend time with her when she's in town. We don't step on each other's toes." He grinned reassuringly. "Don't worry. I'm not taking you to my mother's place, where I would have to sneak into your room in the middle of the night."

Might as well meet this head-on. She didn't play games anymore. She wasn't an immature, spoiled teen. "Your mom has never been my biggest fan, and I get it. She was protective of you. And honestly, I admire how hard she worked to give you the best life possible." The town had never been short on gossip about the way Malcolm's father—a musician in a band—played a gig in Azalea, then cut out on his family. "The past and present can't help but be entwined."

"Remember how in fourth grade we had music class together? You were like magic at the piano, so happy when you played. You made the music come alive." He caressed down her arm to link fingers with her.

She laughed, squeezing his hand. "You played right alongside me, faster, trying to show me up. I recall that day well."

"No, I wanted you to notice me, so I figured I'd better step up my game. I'd mastered the technical side, but I missed the boat when it came to understanding music the way you did." He leaned back against the headboard, his glass resting on his bent knee.

"I never guessed." She blinked in surprise. "I thought you needed a duet partner for the talent show."

"You accomplished what all those music teachers had

been pounding their heads against the keyboard to make happen. I appreciate what my mother sacrificed for me, but all of this, the concerts, none of it would have happened without you."

A stint in reform school wouldn't have happened without her relentless pursuit of him, either, she thought wryly. She'd worked hard to change, but that didn't alter the past. He'd been so angry with her for insisting the baby be put up for adoption. Had he let that anger go? Or was it just set aside for now while the adrenaline and hormones worked to keep them both sated, relaxed?

She wondered if she could bring herself to ask him about it when their reunion was still so fresh, when only heaven knew how long it would last.

Instead, she drew circles on Malcolm's muscular chest. "You would have gotten there on your own. I was just in the right place when you were on the brink of understanding the music."

She remembered those days when Malcolm had catapulted from a skilled player to a talent to be reckoned with. She could almost see the music coming from his heart instead of his head when he'd been at the piano.

"Tell yourself whatever you want." He set aside his glass and hers, then gathered her against his chest.

In spite of all her good intentions five seconds ago, she couldn't stop herself from asking, "Why didn't you contact me after you got out? It's not like I was tough to find, hanging around our old hometown."

He rested his chin on top of her head. "I'd already wrecked your life once." His voice rumbled in his chest against her. "I was mature enough not to do an encore."

"But you're with me now because my life's in danger." Instead of shying away from the tough questions, she decided she deserved real answers. "Would you have stayed away forever?"

"Would *you?*" he countered.

Ouch. Good point. "You're a world-famous singer. I wouldn't have been able to get past your first line of bodyguards. That security is why I'm here now, remember?"

"I wouldn't have turned you away." His arms wrapped tighter around her.

"It's not like we can even blame evil parents for keeping us apart. We did this to ourselves." She understood her reasons, if not his. "I've been punishing myself. Atoning for every mean-girl thing I ever did."

"Where the hell do you come up with this mean-girl notion?"

"I was a brat."

He tipped her chin up and stared at her with intensely blue eyes. "You were rebellious, funny, spoiled and absolutely magnificent. You still are."

"Spoiled?"

"Magnificent." He sealed the word with a kiss, nipping her bottom lip then nuzzling her ear. "I don't want this to end when the tour ends or even if all your father's enemies are locked up."

Stunned, she arched back, staring into his eyes. "You're serious."

She'd just managed to think about being with him tomorrow and now he was talking about longer.

"Absolutely serious," he answered. "Let's spend the summer together, explore what we're feeling and see where it takes us."

What about after the concert tour ended in four weeks? Where would they spend the rest of the summer? He'd avoided his hometown for nearly eighteen years. But the life she'd built there was a part of her, a part of who she was and the peace she'd found. She could enjoy this part of his life, but could he enjoy hers? Or did he only want the impulsive, bold girl she'd once been?

"What if I said I want to spend the rest of the summer in Azalea after your tour ends?" Why was she pushing when just that one question made her chest go tight? She didn't have to have the answers today.

"If that's where you want to be—" pausing, he cricked his neck from side to side "—I can stomach a few weeks there."

Stomach? Not a ringing endorsement for the safe life she embraced. "And in the fall?"

They were only delaying the inevitable crash, delaying the confrontation of the things that had made both of them choose to stay apart all these years. Her guilt over how she'd ruined their lives. His anger over her decisions. Her need for the stability of Azalea. His preference for luxury and travel.

Her feelings of betrayal because yes, damn it all, she'd expected him to come back for her a long time ago, but he'd chosen this life over her.

He moved the tray aside and took her hands. "This isn't going the way I intended. Do you need some kind of commitment from me? Some sign that you mean more to me than just a fling? I can do that."

That wasn't what she'd meant at all. Her heart fluttered in her chest, and it wasn't panic, but it was fear. What if he proposed and she said yes? Could she let go of the past and be with him? Could she live with the uncertainty and lavishness of his lifestyle after working so hard to create a stable existence? What if he was genuinely willing to live a regular, boring life with her when he wasn't on tour?

Was that even possible with his notoriety?

"Celia, I'm not just a musician."

"I know. You're also a gifted composer." She thought of the songs he'd written for her when they were younger, and even beyond that to the dozens of award-winning tunes he'd sent soaring up the charts over the years.

"That's not what I meant."

"Oh…" Disappointment and confusion swirled inside her. "What did you mean, then?"

He drew in a deep breath. "What I'm about to tell you can go no further, but I want you to know I trust you. That I'm committed."

There was that *commitment* word again.

"I work for Colonel Salvatore—" he paused "—and John Salvatore works for Interpol."

Eleven

Celia struggled to grasp what Malcolm had just told her, but what he'd shared seemed so unbelievable, so unexpected. He couldn't be serious. Except, as she looked at him, she saw he was completely sincere. He was some kind of secret agent.

"Interpol?" she asked, needing more details, needing some frame of reference for how this could be possible. "I'm really not tracking with what you're saying. You're going to need to help me understand."

"I'm trusting you with very sensitive information here. Salvatore manages a group of freelance operatives for Interpol. People he taps maybe once or twice a year for undercover help gathering evidence in an international criminal investigation. Because of my job, I move in some influential circles—some of them with shady ties. Having someone like me on the Interpol roll saves having to spend months building a cover."

As he explained, pieces shuffled in her mind. Other things began to make sense.

"That's how you knew about the threats against me. You have connections, intelligence connections." Her skin prickled with icy realization. "You've been watching me."

"Just keeping track of your life to make sure you're all right." He frowned. "That didn't sound right. Not in a stalking sort of way. More like a request to my boss that I be notified if you had a problem. The truth about my job isn't something I've told anyone other than you."

"Not even your manager? Or your friends?" All of his high-profile friends who had gone to Colonel Salvatore's school. Had they all gathered around to guard her? Or did they connect because they could discuss their common job? "Are they also freelance agents with high-profile lives—"

He kissed her silent. "Don't ask questions I'm not allowed to answer. I shared with you as much as I can to let you know I'm not taking what happened between us here lightly. This meant something to me. You mean something to me. I'm trusting you. Can you offer me some trust in exchange?"

His words so closely echoed ones they'd said to each other before, a replay of their past. He'd wanted her to trust that he could carve out a future for them. She'd needed him to trust her decision to give the baby up for adoption. In the end, they'd both gone their separate ways rather than risk being hurt.

They were older now, wiser. But they didn't seem to have a helluva lot more answers. As much as she wanted to lose herself in this time away from Azalea, it seemed her home and past just kept right on following her.

In fact, a huge part of that past waited for her in London when she saw his mother again.

* * *

After the flight to London, Malcolm drove his Aston Martin deeper in the rolling English countryside. He'd trusted Celia with a lot in Amsterdam, but that revelation hadn't gone as he'd expected. He'd hoped she would feel safer, that she would understand he was trying to welcome her into his world. Sharing the truth about his Interpol world had been a big step for him. Hell, admitting he still had feelings for her had been a giant leap.

And she'd reacted with silence and more silence. He could see the wheels turning but didn't have a clue what she was thinking. He could only hazard a guess. Was she upset over his hidden job? Worried? She didn't look as if she was having an anxiety attack.

He glanced at her sitting beside him in the silver sports car. "You've been quiet since we left Amsterdam."

She smiled over at him, her hair carrying on the breeze through the open window. "I thought men liked peace."

"Maybe I'm getting intuitive in my old age." He draped his wrist over the steering wheel, guiding the finely tuned machine along the curving two-lane road past an apple orchard.

"Or maybe you got those intuitive skills from your second job," she said as if joking, but not quite hitting the note.

"Freelancing for Interpol isn't nearly as intriguing as it sounds."

"Can you tell me anything about the cases?"

He weighed his words, wanting to give her what he could to bring her peace so they could move forward. He'd told her to make things easier between them, not more complicated. "Think of the corruption that goes on in the entertainment industry."

"Drugs?"

"I already have a built-in backstory on that one," he said darkly, thinking of his brush with the law as a teenager.

"Your partying lifestyle is a cover?"

"That's not what I meant." He took her palm in his, her dress silky against the back of his hand. "I haven't been a saint since I left home, but I do *not* touch drugs. I never would, especially not after what my father put my mother through."

"Your father was into drugs?" she asked, surprise lacing her voice.

"He was a meth addict." The admission burned, along with anger and betrayal. "He was the stereotypical stoned musician in a going-nowhere band. He blew through everything he and my mother had worked for. He would have sold his soul—or his family—for his next fix."

"Your mother's been through a lot." Celia's fingers gripped his tighter. "I'm sorry I put you in a position where you were forced to hurt her."

"Stop blaming yourself for everything that happened. I take responsibility for my own actions." He lifted her hand, kissing her knuckles. "You make me sound like I had no say in things. I wanted you. I would have done anything to have you in my life."

"Not anything…" she said softly, turning her head toward the open window as if the cottages and sheep were infinitely interesting.

"Hey." He tugged her hand until she turned back to him again. "What do you mean?"

"Nothing. Forget I said anything. So how much farther to this home of yours?"

He started to press her on the point, but then he noticed the nervous way she chewed at her thumbnail. She wasn't as calm as she pretended. He thought of her issues with anxiety and pulled back, saving the question for a better time.

"Not much farther. The gate's just beyond those trees." He crested the hill, revealing his home away from home for the past two years.

Celia gasped. "You leased a castle?"

He laughed. "Not a castle, actually—a manor house." A very large, brick manor house, restored but dating back to the seventeenth century. He wanted somewhere to escape the chaos around his L.A. home, and this small village called to him. "And, uh, it's not leased. I own it."

"And your mother has a flat in London. What would that be? Quarters in Buckingham Palace?"

"Not *in* the royal palace, but with a nice view of it." His mother had followed his father around for ten years while his dad played in bars and honky-tonks, dragging her son along, as well. When they reached Azalea, Mississippi, his mother had woken up the next morning to a note on the pillow. Apparently dragging a woman and kid around was killing the band. For a long time, Malcolm wondered if his mother would have left him behind if she'd been given the choice.

But she hadn't. And there was no denying she'd sacrificed everything for him and for his talent, even though his love of music had to be a hard pill for her to swallow given his father's proclivities. She'd made peace with it when she'd decided he would achieve the star power his father never had reached. He'd practiced to make her happy, to pay her back for costing her security.

He took his foot off the accelerator, coasting down the hill toward the gates covered with ivy. "My mother and I need our space after living in that crappy two-bedroom apartment for so many years."

"This is definitely...spacious."

"You disapprove?" He stopped outside the heavy iron gates, letting the security scan his irises.

She shook her head. "Your money is yours to spend. I'm just a bit overwhelmed by the scope of what you have."

He drove through, her reaction to the house he'd chosen far too important to him. "This is what I wanted to give you, a fairy-tale home."

"The sort of happily ever after you sing about." She grinned at him impishly.

He winced, downshifting around a curve on the winding driveway. "Not fair, turning my cynicism back on me, you know."

"Actually, I was being honest." She leaned out of the window, inhaling. "And oh, my goodness, there are flowers everywhere. It's truly a beautiful home."

Apparently she approved of the sculpted gardens he'd ordered with her in mind. He didn't know the names of most of the flowers. When he'd overseen the renovations, he'd just pointed to pictures in the landscaper's book, but he'd specifically requested climbing roses and lavender.

"I'm glad you like it." Pride kicked through him over pleasing her, having finally found the right way to romance this complex woman.

"Who wouldn't? The place is magnificent."

He wanted to press for more. Hell, when hadn't he wanted to push for more from Celia? He wasn't the most perceptive man on the planet, but something in her tone was still...off.

And opening some deep discussion right now didn't seem wise since his mother had just stepped out onto the lanai to greet them.

* * *

Celia dried her palms along her whispery red dress, sitting on the lanai beside Terri Ann Douglas and feeling the woman's eyes boring into her. Malcolm was parking the car and putting away their minimal luggage. Apparently, he'd had his mother arrange for everything else they would need here. Terri Ann had ordered the kitchen stocked, the beds fluffed. She'd given the main staff the weekend off, with only a catering service making very brief—discreet—stops by for meals.

"Um, Mrs. Douglas—"

"Terri Ann, please," his mother said nicely enough.

"Okay, Terri Ann, um…" She forgot what she was going to say.

God, this was awkward. She'd been semi-prepared to talk to the woman when she'd thought Malcolm was going to try to dump her on his mother back in the States. But she was totally unprepared for this visit now.

Perhaps because the memory of their night together was still so fresh in her mind and she was wondering how soon they could distract themselves with sex again. She trailed her fingers along the waist-high wall between her and those magnificent gardens with an angel fountain glistening in the late-afternoon sun. The scent carried on the air, and she couldn't even enjoy it because her stomach was in knots over this confrontation she should have seen coming. Malcolm's mother was here, serving up tea and sandwiches, for heaven's sake, as if the past didn't exist. As if they could erase the last time this woman had spoken to her.

Screamed, actually.

Crying and accusing her of wrecking Malcolm's life.

So long ago.

Time had been kind to Terri Ann, smoothing the

edges. Her dark blond hair may have grayed somewhat, but her blue eyes were no longer tired with dark circles. She still favored cowboy boots and jean skirts. Did she also hold on to grudges?

Celia tried to smile, waving to the table of pretty little sandwiches, cakes and tea. "Thank you for going to so much trouble for me."

"No trouble at all. After all Malcolm does for me, the least I can do is help him out whenever he asks." She sat on one side of the stone table and served up a plate. "And he doesn't ask often."

Celia nibbled the edge of a cucumber sandwich. "Uh, thank you."

Damn, she sounded like a broken record.

"Malcolm will want something heartier from the pantry, but these seemed more ladylike for you."

Terri Ann thought she needed some kind of special airs put on? She just wanted to have an adult, comfortable conversation with the woman.

"I'm sorry." Celia set aside the delicate china plate carefully. "Would you mind if we use this time to clear the air before Malcolm arrives?

"I don't know what you mean." Terri Ann folded the napkin on her lap once and over again.

"You made it very clear eighteen years ago that you didn't approve of me." Celia pleated the hem of her dress between her fingers and hated that she betrayed her nerves this way. Hated even more how this woman made her feel sixteen and awful again. "I don't expect us to be best friends now just because Malcolm brought me here."

"That's good to know," Terri Ann said, giving little away. "I don't want to upset my son."

"And I don't intend to run telling tales to stir trouble. I

know you don't have any reason to trust me, but I'm not the same self-centered girl I was in those days."

"If we're being honest, then yes, you were spoiled, but my son made his own choices," Terri Ann conceded—surprisingly generous. "In the long run, you didn't ruin his life. Getting sent to that military boarding school was the best thing that ever happened to him. He got opportunities there I could never give him, no matter how many second jobs I took cleaning a salon or waiting tables."

Celia had certainly never thought of it that way. His sentence had seemed like just that...a sentence for a crime he didn't commit. She kept her silence as Terri Ann continued.

"Your father made that chance happen. He pulled strings with one of his judge cronies for Malcolm to go to that school rather than to jail or some crime-riddled reform school."

Celia wrestled with the shifting image of her past and the secrets her father had kept from her. Why hadn't he told her what he'd done for Malcolm? "My dad never told me. But then I was dealing with some pretty serious issues in those days."

She'd sunk into a depression during her pregnancy that had only deepened after the baby was born. The postpartum blues had spun out of control into a full-out breakdown. Putting the pieces of her life—of her sanity—together again had been a long, painful process.

Had her father just not wanted to risk her revisiting that time, even in memories? She might not have been strong enough to discuss the subject in the beginning, but she was now. And wow, how strange if felt to realize that about herself. To accept it. To let that confidence settle deep inside her.

Terri Ann smiled, thumbing a smudge of bright pink

lipstick from the corner of her mouth. "I won't deny I was glad you were no longer in my son's life. I know what it's like to be a parent too young, and I wanted him to have better than I was able to give him."

"But Malcolm turned out amazing. He's built an incredible life for himself." Did his mother know about the Interpol angle and just how far her son took being a good guy? "You did a good job bringing him up on your own."

"It was tough as hell, but I owed him for bringing him into this world. Do you think I wanted him to go through those same struggles, even younger than I was when I had him? At least I was nineteen when I had him." Terri Ann stared at her pointedly. "But then you certainly understand what I mean about making the best choice you can for your child. We can only do what we can with the resources we are given."

And here Malcolm's mother had shocked her all over again with support from an unexpected corner.

Terri Ann's smile faded. "Now, that doesn't mean we have to be best friends, like you said. I don't know you, the adult you. So as far as I'm concerned, let's both just start with a clean slate." Standing, she smoothed her denim skirt, picked up two sandwiches, carefully wrapping them in her napkin. "I'm going to leave you and Malcolm alone. Please tell my son I put some of his favorite barbecue in the fridge and a pecan pie on the counter."

Giving Celia the tour of his home had been satisfying and nerve-racking as hell. But so far, she liked the place. She'd sighed in appreciation over the antiques in the dining room. Spun a circle in the sunlight streaming through the domed conservatory. Sighed in bliss over the music room.

And he still wasn't any closer to finding out what had set her on edge after talking to his mother.

Perhaps it was time for a more direct approach."What did you and my mom talk about?" he asked, leading her through the kitchen toward the steps to the cellar, where his favorite feature of the house waited.

"We talked about you, of course. She left you some of your favorite foods in the kitchen," she said, skimming her fingers along the cool stone walls of the narrowing corridor. Sconces lit the way with bulbs that resembled flickering flames. "And we discussed how you ended up at the military boarding school. How she felt like my dad did you a favor sending you there."

"Ohh-kay." That stunned him for at least two quick heartbeats before he said, "Not your average light chit-chat."

"Does she know about your Interpol work?" Her footsteps echoed behind him.

"No, I don't want to worry her." He glanced over his shoulder. "I meant it when I said telling you was a big commitment."

Her deep brown eyes stared back, still a little wary, confused even. Maybe he was moving too fast and should focus on how they communicated best. With sex. Really, really spectacular sex. Later, when she was ready, he could tell Celia that his feelings for her were about more than just the physical.

He stepped aside to reveal his latest treat for a woman he wanted to pamper with everything he'd earned over the years.

The old cellar enclosed a bubbling hot spring in the far corner. Except, it was more than a cellar. He'd renovated the space into a luxurious spa with modern conveniences while preserving the historical feel. Weathered bricks, tan and ancient, lined the walls of the sprawling space. The natural spring had a deck of slick stones with steps leading down into the inviting waters. Steam rose toward fans hidden in the ceiling, the wafting heat attesting to the muscle-soothing promise those springs held.

Lounge chairs filled a corner by a wooden bar refurbished from an old pub. The bar had been outfitted with a refrigerator. On top, candles glowed alongside vases of flowers and a silver wine bucket holding a bottle of champagne—he'd placed that there himself. Some things, a man simply could not ask his mother to do.

The space provided the ultimate escape from the world for a man who had one helluva time finding peace and solitude. Intricately carved screens shielded a corner for changing, with fluffy robes and towels hanging on hooks buried into the walls.

Celia's gasp of pleasure mingled with the sound of trickling water. "This place is incredible."

"I looked at quite a few manor houses, even a couple of castles. But the minute I walked down here and saw the hot springs, I knew. This place would be mine." He knew this was the home he'd once dreamed of buying for Celia. And even thinking he would never be with her again, he'd still bought the place to remind himself of what they'd had. To remind him of the mission he had to make up for past mistakes.

"You renovated it, though, didn't you?" She eyed the sconces flickering on the wall and casting shadowy illumination.

"I had some help from a professional, but yes, I gave substantive input on what I wanted the place to look like. How did you know?" He pulled out the magnum of champagne and uncorked the bottle.

"I didn't know for sure until you just confirmed it. You have a great eye."

He filled a crystal champagne flute, then a second. "One of my friends recommended this guy who does great work renovating historic homes, blending the old with the new while still listening to the owner. I didn't want this to be some showplace for magazines that no real person would ever enjoy. I wanted this for me...for you."

"But you didn't know we would see each other again when you bought this home."

"And still, every decision I've ever made has been somehow tied to you." He passed the crystal flute to her, tiny bubbles fizzing to the top. "While we were dating, I used to make lists of all the things I would give you someday."

"I'm sorry I made you feel like I needed more." She sipped the champagne. "That wasn't fair to you."

"You were a teenager with parents—very wealthy parents—who loved you."

"Parents who spoiled me, you mean."

"I was a defensive teenager, full of pride and resenting like hell that I couldn't even drive you to the movies in my mom's old rust bucket of a car because she worked nights and needed it."

She tapped the edge of her glass to his. "What else was on that list?"

"Jewels. Houses. A car to make out in, a car that wasn't bought by your dad. And flowers." His slid his hand around a vase of fresh-cut roses on the bar. "An endless supply of fresh flowers."

"I love the flowers, outdoors and here."

"I had plans for those flowers over there." He pulled a creamy-white rose free from the vase.

"Like what?"

"Bed of petals upstairs. Bath with petals down here."
He plucked a handful of petals from the heavy bloom,
sprinkling them into the bubbling springs. "And always
with you naked."

"You, too, of course." She set her glass down along
the edge of the pool.

"That can be arranged."

Celia couldn't remember a time she'd peeled off her
clothes so quickly. Not since she and Malcolm had gone
skinny-dipping in the river near where they liked to park
and make out. Luckily, he was pitching aside his clothing
just as speedily before refilling their champagne glasses.

And placing a row of condoms along the ledge.

Smiling over her shoulder seductively, she walked
down the steps. The water was a hint too hot, then completely perfect for melting tensed muscles. Her quick
acclimation made her wonder if perhaps she'd been over-
thinking things. Maybe they could take this romance one
day at a time. Simply enjoy each other and unlimited sex,
making up for all the lost years when no one else came
close to touching her in that very special way.

The steaming water wrapped around her waist, lapping
higher and then teasing along her breasts until her nipples
beaded. The slick stone floor under her feet was warm
and therapeutic, as well. She hadn't expected even her
toes to feel pampered by the experience. Bubbles flowed
around her and under her, caressing her between her legs
and along her breasts erotically. Deliciously.

"Oh, my God, this is…just beyond what I could have
needed. Did you dump Xanax into the water?" She
winced at her own word choice, glancing at him sharply.
"Okay, that was a weak attempt at a joke."

"Was it some kind of Freudian slip?" His handsome face creased with concern.

She waded through the steam and over to him, standing toe to toe, needing to read his eyes as she spoke. "I have to know that you're not freaked out by the fact that I've had a breakdown. I have to know you're not going to handle me with kid gloves for fear I'll have a panic attack."

His hands fell on her shoulders, curving around to her back. "The urge to protect you is strong, and it was there long before you told me anything about medications or the stress after...the baby was born. I can't promise I won't go Cro-Magnon if someone threatens you. But I can promise I would have reacted the same way regardless."

With those few words, he wiped away her concern. "Good enough for me."

He walked backward, guiding her with him until he sat on a stone seat cut into the pool and pulled her into his lap. "When we were together before, I hated that I didn't have the cash to take you on real dates. I planned all the ways I would romance you when I had money."

"I treasured our time together. You put so much thought into what we did, just like you have here." She sipped her champagne, enjoying the tickle to her nose almost as much as she enjoyed the feel of Malcolm's muscular legs under her. "Even back then I knew what you did was tougher than tossing money around. Like the way you planted a sunflower at the spot where we first kissed."

"I stole a sunflower from the side of the road."

"It was sweet." She stroked back his stubborn lock of hair, teasing the familiar texture between her fingers. "Don't wreck the memory."

His hands slid up to cup her breasts, his thumbs teasing lazy circles until she beaded even harder against his touch. "I wanted to buy you flowers and take you to the homecoming."

"I don't care for football anyway. I just wanted to be with you." Sparks of pleasure shimmered from her breasts, gathering between her thighs. Wriggling to face him, she straddled Malcolm's lap, his hot, thick erection pressed between them. "Amazing, but I want that exact same thing from you now. More specifically, I want you to be inside me."

"You won't get an argument from me."

She reached past him for a condom, then slid her breasts along him, the bristle of his chest hair a tantalizing abrasion against her nipples. She sighed her pleasure, the head of his erection nudging against her, rubbing against the tight bundle of nerves aching for release.

With deliberate attention to detail, she sheathed him underwater, stroking the length of him and cradling his weight in her hands until his head fell back with a groan. She knew his body well again after their time in Amsterdam, but he'd been the one orchestrating their experience there. She savored being in control now.

"Celia, darlin', you're killing me…" His jaw flexed with restraint, muscles bunching and twitching. "Celia…"

"How much do you want me?" She angled closer, digging her fingers into the corded biceps bulging under her touch and rubbing their bodies against each other. Rubbing his erection between her cleft and against her stomach. But still she held herself back from giving them both what they wanted.

He growled, nipping her shoulder. "You know I want you more than I've ever wanted anyone."

"Do you know how many nights I laid awake thinking of you, your memory making me ache from wanting you? The sound of your voice over the radio in the morning would catch me unawares, leaving me needing you. Needing this."

She sank down, taking him deep inside her, fully and quickly. A raw groan of pleasure burst from his mouth, and she reveled in knowing he was every bit as helpless when it came to this attraction. She rolled her hips against his, arched her back for his attentive mouth on her breasts. Each flick of his tongue, every suckle followed by a puff of air drew the tension tighter inside her. He knew just how to play her body, strum her most sensitive spots, stroke and pluck just so until the need to come apart in his arms was almost painfully intense.

Water sluiced around them as they moved together, her arms locked tightly around him. The wall scones flickered shadows over the hard planes of his face, teasing her with glimpses of his pleasure. His hands cupped her bottom, lifting and guiding her as he thrust upward. And her body answered, gripping him, holding him as pleasure built, higher until...

Fulfillment showered through her, sparkling through every fiber of her being. Gasping again and again with aftershocks rocking her, she scored Malcolm's shoulders, sinking in her nails as she held on. Her arms trembled. His grip tightened as he thrust faster and faster until, yes, he joined her.

And she held him close as his pleasure rocked through him, his breath hot on her neck, his beard a delicious abrasion against her temple as they clung to each other.

Even afterward, she stayed tangled with him, her legs wrapped around his waist now as she sat with him still inside her. Her skin cooled, even with the water steaming all around them. The lap of the bubbling tide stroking over her.

She gasped against the damp skin of his neck. She

wanted him, and God help her, she loved him, too. She always had.

But could she see this through with Malcolm, sign on for more? Could she live this out-of-control life with a man who played to sold-out arenas and royalty? Even if she could find her way around the anxiety of that lifestyle, there was the whole Interpol bombshell and his disdain for spending time in Azalea.

Desperately, she wanted to find a way through this crazy maze of a life he'd built for himself. An amazing life, without question, but it wasn't hers. It wasn't even close to what she wanted for herself... Well, maybe the spa part could stay....

God, she was a mess. She needed to find a path they could walk together.

Because if she didn't, staying with him only prolonged the inevitable, increasing the pain of losing Malcolm all over again.

Twelve

Malcolm sprawled in a chair on the lanai, brunch having been set up by a service his mother had arranged to make discreet appearances and speedy exits throughout their brief stay. He scrolled through his email while waiting for Celia to finish her shower.

Celia.

His hand slowed on the tablet, his eyes scanning the elaborate garden he'd had planted for her, not even knowing if she would ever see it. His gaze settled on a rose bush climbing along an archway over a bench. How many times over the past couple of years had he envisioned her there reading or singing? She'd been with him in his every thought over the years, every decision he made guided by what he'd wanted to give her.

Whatever it took, wherever his manager told him he needed to be to advance his career, he'd done it. He realized now that he'd done all this for her. He'd been keeping track of her because he wanted her back in his life. Protecting her had just been an excuse. He was so close to having what he'd dreamed of as a heartbroken kid. But he refused to let the surge of victory distract him from remembering his duty—making sure she stayed out of harm's way until Salvatore could get a lock on who'd left those threatening notes.

"Good morning." Celia smiled in the open French doors, the sun shining on her dusky beauty. Her hair glided over her shoulder in a side ponytail.

She strolled through the door. Her simple sundress, long and vibrantly blue, caressed her legs as she walked closer. Her hand glided over his chest as she dipped to kiss him, a hint of rose-petal perfume still clinging to her skin with reminders of how they'd made love in the spa for hours. If only they could block out the world awhile longer.

Protective urges surged through him, and he wondered why the hell it was proving so difficult to track down the person responsible for threatening Celia. He forced his fists to unclench and then stroked her ponytail. "Good morning to you, too, beautiful. Brunch? There's plenty."

He pulled out a chair for her at the table set with a full English fry-up of eggs, bacon, sausages, fried bread and mushrooms.

Celia bypassed it all, picking up a scone and a small pot of lemon curd as she took her seat. She swept the hem of her dress to the side as she settled in a move so utterly feminine it had him wanting to carry her out into the garden and make love to her all over again.

Except, then he noticed her brow was furrowed.

"What's wrong?" he asked, returning to his side of the table.

She slathered lemon curd on a corner of her scone.

"I'm still trying to piece together all the new things I'm learning about you, fill in the gaps of those years we missed."

"Such as?" he asked warily. He wanted to let her into his world, yet he wasn't a man used to talking about himself. He'd grown accustomed to keeping people at arm's length.

"I know you can't tell me about your friends and details about Interpol, but what about your time at school? Those early days when we were apart?"

He wasn't sure why she wanted to know, but he couldn't see the harm in sharing. "We weren't the typical button-up types who planned to go into the military. We banded together to get through, formed a new family since ours had been taken away. We broke rules, pushed boundaries. We called ourselves The Alpha Brotherhood, and in the confines of those prisonlike walls, we kept each other from losing our minds."

"You said you broke the rules—like when Elliot Starc hot-wired the truck?"

"Exactly." He speared food onto his plate. "One night, Troy broke into the security system, rewired the whole thing so Conrad's ankle monitor wouldn't register. We left school grounds, bought pizza and came back."

Laughing, she thumbed a crumb from the corner of her mouth, reminding him of all the ways she'd driven him crazy with those lips the night before. "Real rebels."

He cleared his throat. "It's like counting coup."

"Counting coup?" She broke off another bite of the scone, her attention to his words so intent it was as if the world hinged on what he would share.

"Mental games, war games—sneak into the enemy camp and leave a sign that you were there. Show your enemy their security is worthless." His mind filled with memories of how sweet those victories had tasted then as he'd lashed out at the world. "No need to destroy anything. Just let them know you're able to come and go as you please, that you can dismantle the whole system if you choose. Makes sticking around a lot easier."

"And your headmaster, this man who now works for Interpol, Colonel Salvatore. He was the enemy?"

"Back then he was, yes. And sneaking one past him was the ultimate victory for a group of teens who were feeling they'd been kicked in the teeth by the world." Little had they known then it was all a part of Salvatore's strategy to get them to work together as a unified team.

"What made you change your mind and join him?" Cradling a china teacup in her hands, she eyed him over the rim.

Malcolm set aside his silver fork with a clatter. "Turns out he was better at war games than we were. He found my weakness and he used it."

"I'm not sure I understand." She set her cup back on the saucer carefully and reached for her scone. "What did he do?"

His mind filled with memories of that fateful meeting when John Salvatore had approached him with the Interpol offer, when he'd revealed all the power that could be his if he just said yes, the power to keep track of Celia. The power to know…everything. A mixed blessing.

"He showed me pictures of our daughter."

Celia's scone crumbled in her hands, her fingers clenching too hard as shock sliced clean through her at Malcolm's words. At what he'd known all this time and never said a word about. He'd never offered her the consolation such information could have given her.

Her hands shaking, she dusted the crumbs from her

fingers and willed herself not to jump to conclusions, to be logical and hear him out.

"You had access to…things like that?"

He looked down at his uneaten food. "I haven't seen her in person or made contact. I honored the decision we made to leave that up to her."

The old ache inside her swelled. So painful. So empty.

She squeezed her eyes closed and blurted out, "I know you blame me for giving her up for adoption."

So much for the calm, logical approach.

"Celia? Celia," he insisted, taking her hand until she opened her eyes. "I signed the paperwork. I accept responsibility for my own decisions. I was in no position to be a parent stuck states away in a boarding school for misfits. It would have been selfish of me to put her life on hold waiting for me to get out."

"Then why haven't you forgiven me? Why can't we just be happy?"

"I have regrets. That's not the same as holding a grudge." He squeezed her hand in a reassurance that didn't quite warm the chill spreading inside her. "Do I wish things had turned out differently? Of course. I wanted to be the man who could take care of you both."

A whisper of suspicion curled through her like steam from the teapot. "Is that what all of this has been about? Coming to my rescue now to make up for what you think you should have done eighteen years ago?"

"In part, yes," he said, confirming her fear that things could never be simple for them, not after everything that came before. A fresh start for them wasn't an option. Malcolm leaned forward on his elbows. "What did she look like when she was born?"

"Didn't your Interpol connection give you photos from the nursery?" she snapped, then paused, holding

up a hand. "Sorry for being defensive. She looked...
wrinkled with her face scrunched up. She had dark hair
and the softest skin. I wanted her." Her breath caught in
her throat, every word slicing her like razor cuts on an
ache that had never fully healed.

She shoved back from the table, needing air, space. "I
really wanted her, and all my life I'd gotten everything I
wanted. But something changed inside me when I looked
in her eyes. I knew that as much as I wanted to keep her,
I couldn't give her what she needed on any level."

She shot to her feet, desperate to escape the painful
memories and the accusation she knew she would find
in Malcolm's eyes. "I can't do this. Not now."

Tears blurring her view of the two roses on the table,
she started toward the French doors.

"Her name is Melody," he said, his voice raw.

She stopped in her tracks, hardly daring to believe
what she'd heard. Bracing her hand on the open door,
her back to him, she said, "Her adoptive parents asked
me what I'd been calling her. I didn't expect they would
keep the name."

"They did. The photo I saw of her was taken when she
was seven years old—the only photo I saw—but even
then, she looked like you."

She clapped her hands over her ears. "Stop. If she
wants to find us, she will. That's her choice. We agreed."

"I can make this happen, though." He shoved to his
feet, closed the space between them in two strides and
clasped her shoulders. "We're a couple now. We can get
married and reach out to her."

"I meant it when I said that has to be her decision. I
owe her that choice." She blinked fast, her head whirling as her heart squeezed tight. She didn't want him to
ask for old times' sake or some need to make up for the

past. "And that proposal of yours was every bit as abrupt as when you asked me before when we were teenagers."

His eyes snapped with frustration. "And you're shutting me down just as fast."

"You're changing my life." She eased his hands from her shoulders. "You have to accept I'm not a reckless, impulsive teenager anymore. I have a life I'm proud of and have no interest in abandoning. I'm not cut out for this high-octane lifestyle of yours—the concert tour or the Interpol implications. God, Malcolm, think. We can't jump into this."

"Admit it. This isn't about where we live or what we do. It's about making a commitment to me." He took a step back, face stony with disillusionment, a replay of the way he'd looked at her so long ago. "You don't want to try now any more than you did then."

Why couldn't he understand she wasn't pushing him away, just looking for a compromise? "That's not true. You aren't even trying to see my side of this. And damn it, Malcolm, I am different now. I refuse to let you tear my heart out again."

Her chin high, her pride all she had left, she spun away and almost slammed into his mother in the doorway. Could this humiliating, heartrending moment get any worse? To hell with pride. She needed to get out of here.

Celia angled past with a mumbled "Excuse me," then ran. Her sandals slapped against the sleek wooden floors as she raced into the restored manor house. She ran up the curved staircase and into the bedroom full of antiques, florals and stripes. She slammed the door closed and sagged back against the panel only to realize...

She wasn't alone in the room.

A broad-backed male spun away from her suitcase, her tote bag in one hand, a piece of paper in the other.

"Adam Logan?" She walked toward Malcolm's manager. "What are you doing in my room?"

Her eyes went to the paper in his hand, a typed note with big block letters she'd seen on threatening notes over the past couple of weeks. Block letters that even from here she could read.

WATCH YOUR BACK, BITCH.

Malcolm scrubbed a hand over his face, trying to pull himself together before he spoke to his mother. God only knew how much of that train wreck of an argument she'd overheard. "Mom? What are you doing back here? Did you need something?"

"Actually, I was hoping to talk to you and Celia, but maybe this isn't the best time." His mother hovered uncertainly in the doorway.

"No, Mom, it's fine. Celia and I both could use some time to cool off." Although eighteen years of cooling off hadn't helped them. "Come sit down. Have a scone."

"If you're sure." She cleared the door, her yellow leather boots clicking across the tile lanai.

He moved Celia's plate aside as his mother sat. "What's on your mind?"

"I've been letting you support me for long enough," she said in a rush, as if she'd been holding the words inside.

What the hell? Who tipped the world upside down while he wasn't looking? "Mom, that's ridiculous. I owe you. I *want* to give you these things—anything you need."

"You're my son." She patted his arm. "It was my job to take care of you. You don't owe me anything."

"Damn it, Mother, the money doesn't even make a

dent in my portfolio. I don't miss it." He could have retired from the concert scene years ago.

"That's beside the point," she said primly, folding her
hands in her lap.

"To you maybe. But not to me. I can't watch you work
that hard ever again." Years of guilt piled on top of him,
so much he didn't know how he would ever dig out. "I
just can't."

"Well, I'm not looking to embrace abject poverty."
She laughed lightly. "I've gotten used to the softer side
of life. But maybe a little too used to it."

"What do you mean?" He tried to sort through her
words, really tried, because apparently he'd been missing the mark with both of the women in his life.

She took a deep breath, as if bracing herself, then said,
"Do you think that monstrously large bank account of
yours could handle sending your old mother to school?
I'd like to become a professional caterer, one who spe-
cializes in entertaining on a budget. When I said I've
become accustomed to the softer side of life, I meant it.
I'd like to bring those treats and delicacies to others who
never thought they could afford them."

He was stunned, to say the least. But the plan she'd
spelled out made perfect sense. The pieces fit, and he was
happy for her. "Mom, I think that's a great idea. But I'm
still curious. What brought this big turnaround?"

"Seeing you with Celia in the news, hearing all the reports about what she's been doing with her life. She could
have relied on her father's money, but she carved out a
place for herself in the world. That's admirable, son."

His mother was right. Celia had. And she was clearly
stronger for that, more confident. She'd been telling him
she wasn't the selfish, spoiled girl he'd once known, but
had he actually understood? Accepted? He forced himself

to focus on his mother's words. Apparently a man never got too old to learn something from his mom.

"Malcolm, those pictures the press has been running of her with students showed how much she loves her profession. This may sound strange, but I never considered that work could be fulfilling. The jobs I did before, I took pride in them, sure, but they were just a means to put food in your mouth. And there weren't a lot of choices. I have a choice now, thanks to you—"

A scream split the air.

Celia's voice.

What the hell?

Malcolm shot from his chair, toppling it as he sprinted for the stairs. Celia's screams continued, mixed with masculine shouts. His gut clenched with fear. Where were the guards? Why hadn't security been triggered? What the hell had he been thinking lowering his own guard with her just because he had her an ocean away from the threat?

He raced through the door and barely had time to register what he was seeing. Celia held a huge vase of flowers high and crashed it down on the head of...

Adam Logan?

His manager?

Logan's knees buckled, and he fell to the ground.

Malcolm barked, "What the hell's going on here? Celia, are you okay?"

She backed away, pointing at his manager, now kneeling in a puddle of water, shattered glass and roses on the thick Persian rug. "He was in my room, going through my things. He had a threatening note and a dead rose. He was putting it in my bag."

Malcolm turned to Logan, a man he'd called his friend,

his brother. "Adam? You were the one behind the threats on Celia? Why the hell would you do that?"

Logan sagged back on his heels, his shoulders slumping forward. "I just wanted to get the two of you together again."

It made no sense. Malcolm looked to Celia, who appeared just as confused. He wanted to drape an arm around her, tuck her close, but she stood quietly on the other side of the room.

"You'd better explain. And fast." His pulse pounded beneath his eye, anger roiling.

Logan leaned forward, his eyes gleaming with the cutthroat, ambitious light that had helped push Malcolm's career to the limit. "Your bad-boy image was starting to drag on your numbers. And you have to admit, we got a lot of good press out of the high-school-sweethearts-reunited angle. It was easy enough to pull off, then make sure Salvatore heard." He shrugged. "It's actually sort of funny when you think about it, pulling off a prank on the old colonel again."

Malcolm wasn't laughing. This bastard had terrified Celia for absolutely no good reason. Already brimming with frustration from his fight with Celia, Malcolm couldn't stem the anger for a second longer. He hauled back his fist and punched Logan square in the jaw.

His manager crumpled back onto the rug, out cold. A formality, actually, since Celia had clearly handled things on her own. She stood strong and magnificent, in control of the situation.

His thoughts synched up in that moment as the truth truly sank in. Celia could take care of herself. As his mother had said, Celia had built the life that she wanted. He was the one still chasing the past, trying to change the outcome or hide from the tougher parts. Like how he'd stayed away from Azalea and Celia rather than face up to his feelings. Rather than risk putting his heart on the line again.

She had every reason to be angry with him. He'd failed to acknowledge the strong and incredible woman she'd become, the completion of the dazzling young girl he first fell for. The woman he still loved.

If he didn't figure out how to get his priorities in order, he didn't stand a chance of winning her back. And losing wasn't an option. He loved this woman with every fiber of his being. Every note he played, every breath he took was for her. Always for Celia.

Whatever it took, he would be the man worthy of spending his life with her.

As Celia stood in the back of the concert hall that night, her mind was still reeling from the shock of finding Malcolm's manager in her room. Of learning he'd been behind those threats all along. Adam Logan had orchestrated everything as a way to get Malcolm some extra publicity. Her life had been horribly manipulated.

But the frustration and anger she experienced had to be nothing compared to the disillusionment Malcolm felt over his friend's betrayal. There hadn't been time to talk after the attack. Malcolm had been so focused on dealing with the crisis at hand that she'd been shut out as the mess in front of her was "handled." He'd made the decision to contact Salvatore and let him wade through the legal ramifications. The press from this, however, would be rough on Malcolm—betrayed by his own manager.

For that reason, she'd been unable to leave right away. In honor of all she and Malcolm had shared, in the past and in the present, she would stay for tonight's concert. If Adam Logan had been correct, that she'd been good press for Malcolm, she would at least give him this night to help smooth over the rough patch he was bound to face with the media. And after he sang that last encore?

She honestly didn't know. She just wished she had some kind of sign as to what she should do next. Marry Malcolm and change her life? Or return to what she'd had?

From the back of the auditorium, she watched him perform, her eyes riveted by his mesmerizing charisma. The audience hung on his every note, his every word. His performance was as smooth as ever, even though he couldn't play the piano or guitar tonight. He'd broken two fingers punching out his manager. Sometime during the chaotic day, a doctor had been called to splint Malcolm's fingers just before he left for the sound check.

In fact, his concert was beyond phenomenal tonight. She couldn't put her finger on the difference. Her eyes scanned the sold-out historic theater. The space resembled the Amsterdam venue. The acoustics of the old building were formidable, but not the best she'd heard. Nothing had changed with the lighting. Yet, still...tonight *was* different. Exponentially better in some undefinable way.

Perhaps the fact that this was a charity benefit added something to his performance? She smoothed her hands down her floor-length red satin gown, feeling a bit like Cinderella at the ball with midnight only seconds away. Certainly, Malcolm looked heart-stoppingly handsome in his tuxedo. As the concert rolled to a close, she realized he didn't intend to sing "Playing for Keeps." Although, how could she blame him after the grief she'd given him the last time he'd performed it? She'd chewed him out for selling fans a fake bill of goods, crooning to them with lyrics he didn't believe in.

And then, as he finished the final ballad of the night,

sitting on a bar stool and singing directly to the audience, she grasped the difference in tonight's show. The difference in Malcolm.

He *wasn't* performing.

Tonight when he sang about love won and lost, love's pain and joy, she would swear he really believed the words. That had to be it. He felt the emotion, believed in love and happily ever after. The feelings were so real they shone from his eyes. His proposal earlier hadn't sprung from some gut reaction or need to protect her. Somehow Malcolm's faith in happily ever after had been restored. He'd come to believe in it again. This was the sign she'd been waiting for. She'd thought his proposal was for old times' sake or to make up for the past.

And she'd thrown his proposal back in his face.

Her heart squeezed tight with emotion as she realized how very badly she'd messed up, and how every second that passed was filled with pain neither of them should have to endure. They'd both been through enough. They'd sacrificed and lost too much because of their mistakes. They'd made amends.

They deserved to be happy.

Hitching up the hem of her floor-length gown, she sprinted back out into the lobby, searching for the backstage entrance and regretting like hell that she'd refused the backstage pass earlier out of fear. Out of some contrary need to put up walls between them.

She ran toward the guards at the doors, and thank God, one of them remembered her and waved her through with a wink and a smile. He even pointed the way. High heels clicking along the concrete floors, she dashed past crates and music stands, endless equipment crowding her path. Finally, she made it to the wings, stopping beside the stage manager, who held up a finger to his lips.

Although with the loud applause as Malcolm bowed, it wasn't as if anyone could hear her.

Celia nodded anyway, breathless from her mad dash. Her heart pounded in her ears with anticipation and hope. Malcolm had already started to exit the stage, walking toward her. Although he hadn't seen her yet since he still waved to the audience, already on their feet clapping.

Malcolm stepped out of the lights and into the darkened wings, his hand already out for the customary bottled water the backstage assistants would pass him before he returned for an encore.

Celia thrust out her hand with a water bottle, their fingers brushing.

Sparks flying as always.

Malcolm halted in his tracks. "You're here."

"Where else would I be?" she said simply. She didn't bother weighing her words to preserve her pride. What a silly emotion anyway. "I love you, so I'm here."

The stage manager covered his grin.

Malcolm clasped her arm and guided her away—the stage manager's smile quickly shifting to panic as Malcolm tucked her in a private corner of storage containers.

"Celia, did I hear you right?" He set the water aside, his focus solely on her.

"I meant every word, and I'm sorry I didn't say it earlier instead of running."

He hauled her close and held her tightly. "Oh, God, Celia, I love you, too," he whispered in her hair. "I always have."

Although she knew that already. She'd heard it in his voice with every word he sang. Still, it was so very good to hear him say it plainly.

He angled back, cupping her face. "I'm sorry I let so many years go by without reaching out to you. I let pride get in the way of us having a chance at fixing the past, of building a future. And most of all, I apologize for not trusting you now, for not listening to what you want for your life. For not believing what's right in front of me."

"What might that be?" She skimmed the overlong lock away from his forehead.

"You fascinated the hell out of me eighteen years ago. But you absolutely mesmerize me now. You are an incredible woman, stunning, independent. And so damn giving I can't figure out what I did to deserve this second chance with you."

The pounding of the audience stomping the floor for another song was nothing compared to her heartbeat in her ears. "It's time we both believe and trust that we deserve to be happy. We deserve a future together."

"Darlin', I do like the way you think." He sealed his mouth to hers, a sure and perfect fit. He finished with a kiss on her nose before he rested his forehead against hers. "What would you say to my retiring?"

The stage manager hovered, but Malcolm waved him off.

"From Interpol? I know what Adam Logan did hurt you—"

He shook his head. "That's not what I meant. What if, after this tour, I retired from the stage."

"I'm…stunned."

He searched her eyes. "Good stunned or bad stunned?"

"I'm just surprised. I thought you lived for your music." She pointed toward the stage, the audience still on their feet applauding for their encore. "They live for your music. And tonight, the heart you put into your songs propelled you to another level."

"Celia, it's about you. It's always been about you. I've been chasing success to prove something to your father, to you—to myself—that really doesn't matter. I've learned so much from you these past several days... I want to compose music, and I have the financial luxury of never working again if I choose."

Wow, he really meant it. This wasn't some half-baked idea. He'd found his direction. And the fact that he attributed that to her meant more than she could say.

"Malcolm, your fans are going to grieve."

"There are plenty of singers more than ready to step into any void I might leave on the charts."

"You're really serious."

"Absolutely. I was approached not too long ago about writing a score for a movie, a sprawling postapocalyptic saga with an edgy vibe of modern-day meets classical— Adam advised me not to..." He hung his head briefly, then drew in a deep breath, meeting her eyes again. "I can do that anywhere, even in Azalea."

"Or there and here," she offered in compromise. "We could live in Azalea and London. I could still teach privately, work on a series of music books for students."

"That sheet music I saw in your office the first day..."

"Sounds like we're building a plan, together. And we can fine-tune the details later, because right now, you have a concert to finish."

His eyes glinted with an idea. "What do you say we give them their encore?"

Laughing, she rolled her eyes. "They're calling for you."

"Crazy, I know, but I don't want to let you go." He reached for a guitar. "Maybe you could play since I can't. We could sing together, like we used to. We can be a team, you and I."

Without hesitation, she hooked her arm in his and let him escort her out onto the stage. The crowd went wild at the sight of her. And when Malcolm took her hand as she settled on the bar stool, the crowd held their breath in anticipation. Celia looked out at the audience and saw his mother beaming from the front row. Celia smiled back before settling the guitar in her lap and turning to Malcolm.

Sharing a microphone with him, her heart in her eyes, she strummed the opening chords to "Playing for Keeps," the notes committed to memory years before. The melody was already a part of her heart.

* * * * *

LET'S TALK
Romance

For exclusive extracts, competitions
and special offers, find us online:

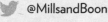 facebook.com/millsandboon

@MillsandBoon

@MillsandBoonUK

Get in touch on 01413 063232

GET YOUR ROMANCE FIX!

MILLS & BOON
— blog —

Get the latest romance news, exclusive author
interviews, story extracts and much more!

blog.millsandboon.co.uk

MILLS & BOON
MODERN
Power and Passion

Prepare to be swept off your feet by
sophisticated, sexy and seductive heroes, in
some of the world's most glamourous and
romantic locations, where power and
passion collide.